LILITH'S LOVE

Praise for Tyler R. Tichelaar's Children of Arthur Series

Arthur's Legacy: The Children of Arthur, Book One

"*Arthur's Legacy* will electrify true fans of the Arthurian legend. Tichelaar's research and his weaving of the Arthurian mythos into a cohesive story for the contemporary reader is second to none. *Arthur's Legacy* will surely take its rightful place among the canon of great Arthurian literature."

— Steven Maines, author of *The Merlin Factor* series

"If you love the mystical magic of Camelot but thrive on the excitement and tribulations of *Game of Thrones*, this book is for you. Tichelaar encompasses the familiarity of contemporary times and skillfully interweaves history and mysticism into the Arthurian legend that has withstood the test of time, and brings the characters all to life."

— Rowena Portch, award-winning author of *The Spirian Saga*

"Tichelaar's ingenious use of throwaway snippets and very obscure sources combines with a powerful imagination to make the old, old story fresh.... The finale brings the two strands of the novel together, at the same time synthesising its pagan and Christian elements into a Blakeian, poetic pantheism."

— Marcus Pitcaithly, author of *The Realm of Albion*

Melusine's Gift: The Children of Arthur, Book Two

"What if you discovered the famous legends you'd heard and believed all your life didn't happen the way they'd always been told? In *Melusine's Gift*, readers will join Adam and Anne Delaney as they hear the truth right from the mouths of the characters who lived the tales. Readers unfamiliar with Melusine's place in history will be drawn into her world, while the captivating web of multi-layered stories within stories combine and complement to obliterate the preconceived notions of those who consider themselves experts on her legend. I loved *Melusine's Gift* even more than *Arthur's Legacy* and can't wait for the twists and turns of *Ogier's Prayer*."

— Jenifer Brady, author of the *Abby's Camp Days* series

"Once again Tyler Tichelaar weaves a riveting story that mixes Arthurian lore with fact and fiction. *Melusine's Gift* is skillfully written and is reminiscent of those ancient tales from the *Arabian Nights* where one story flows into the next one and that into the next and so on. In this case, the stories reveal how the descendants of King Arthur are connected through the isle Avalon."

— Cheryl Carpinello, author of *Guinevere: On the Eve of Legend*

Ogier's Prayer: The Children of Arthur, Book Three

"A masterful blend of history, myth-tery and imagination, *Ogier's Prayer's* inspirational re-visioning of the past, and vivid, suspenseful storytelling will leave you craving the next installment of this thought-provoking, delightfully plot-twisting series!"

— Roslyn McGrath, author of *The Third Mary: 55 Messages for Empowering Truth, Peace & Grace from the Mother of Mary Magdalene*

"The world of Adam and Anne Delaney keeps getting more and more complicated. Now, in addition to finding out first hand that they are descendants of both the legendary King Arthur and the fairy Melusine, a new world is added to their curious heritage: that of Ogier the Dane. Set partially in modern-day England and partly in the past in the Eastern world of Arabia, the stakes get even higher for Adam and Anne as they search for their children's kidnapper and find out about their past."

— Jenifer Brady, author of the *Abby's Camp Days* series

LILITH'S LOVE

THE CHILDREN OF ARTHUR: BOOK FOUR

BY

TYLER R. TICHELAAR

Lilith's Love: The Children of Arthur, Book Four

copyright © 2017 by Tyler R. Tichelaar

Marquette Fiction
1202 Pine Street
Marquette, MI 49855
www.MarquetteFiction.com
www.ChildrenofArthur.com

ISBN-13: 978-0-9962400-2-4

Library of Congress Control Number: 2016916077

Printed in the United States of America
Publication managed by Superior Book Productions
www.SuperiorBookProductions.com

"The Draculas were, says Arminius, a great and noble race, though now and again were scions who were held by their coevals to have had dealings with the Evil One. They learned his secrets in the Scholomance, amongst the mountains over Lake Hermanstadt, where the devil claims the tenth scholar as his due.... There have been from the loins of this very one great men and good women, and their graves make sacred the earth where alone this foulness can dwell. For it is not the least of its terrors that this evil thing is rooted deep in all good, in soil barren of holy memories it cannot rest."

— Bram Stoker, *Dracula*

CONTENTS

PROLOGUE

CONSTANTINOPLE, MAY 29, 1453,
JUST AFTER MIDNIGHT

"The city will be both founded and lost by an emperor
Constantine whose mother was called Helen."
— Ancient Byzantine Prophecy

FOR FIFTY-THREE DAYS, the siege had held. He had never thought he would be able to hold off the Turks for as long as he had. Had Pope Nicholas V and the rest of Europe come to his aid, it might have been different; even so, his people had been remarkable in their determination not to surrender to the enemy. But any day now, even any hour, it was bound to end.

And he would be the last, he, Constantine XI, the last Emperor of the Romans. For fifteen centuries, there had been an empire, and for more than eleven centuries, the capital had been here in Constantinople, but now all that would come to an end. He had done everything he could, trying to negotiate peace with the Turks, striving to get the Orthodox

Church to concede to the Pope's demands that they become Catholic, imploring the rulers of France, England, Hungary, Venice, whoever would listen, to come to his aid, but it had all been to no avail. The Turks far outnumbered those in the city.

And the city was not even worth taking; Constantine knew that. Its wealth had diminished to almost nothing in the last two centuries, ever since the Latins had used a crusade to the Holy Land as an excuse to sack the city and then rule as its emperors for most of the thirteenth century. Although the Romans had regained the city and the throne in time, the empire had continued to shrink and weaken; continually, Constantine and his imperial predecessors had sought to keep the Turks at bay, the emperors wedding their daughters to the Ottoman sultans and doing anything necessary to ensure the empire's survival.

And as the last emperor, Constantine knew the blame would lie upon his head, without regard to how little chance he had to stop his enemy or how all of Christendom had abandoned him and his people to their fate. What would they call him? His first namesake was Constantine the Great. Would he be called Constantine the Defeated, Constantine the Failure, Constantine the Unworthy? Perhaps the best he could hope for was to be killed in battle so he would be remembered as Constantine the Martyr.

He stood alone now on the battlements, his soldiers knowing he wished to be alone with his thoughts. He looked out at the vast hordes of Turks encamped around the city. Even now they were battering at the walls, hoping to topple any one of them, not even seeking sleep as the night moved toward dawn.

How had it come to this? To some extent, Constantine could understand the reluctance and ignorance of his fellow rulers to come to his aid. Even the Pope, the supposed leader of the Christian world, he could forgive for his stubbornness when he considered that they were all men, full of weaknesses, but how could God Himself turn His back on them? How could the Holy Virgin to whom the city had been dedicated, desert them?

And there was no doubt they had been forsaken. The Holy Virgin had shown she would no longer protect them. The city had been dedicated to the Virgin since its ancient days. In desperation, the people had cried out to her ever since the siege had begun, and just three days ago, her most holy relic, the Hodegetria—an icon of her, believed to have been painted by St. Luke the Evangelist himself, which had saved the city on numerous occasions—was brought forth from Saint Sophia and carried in a procession through the streets. It had been mounted on a wooden pallet and lifted onto the shoulders of several strong men from the icon's confraternity. The people followed as the Hodegetria traveled through the city, while the priests offered up incense, and the men, women, and children walked barefoot to show their penance. Hymns were sung, prayers said, and the people repeatedly cried out to the Virgin, beseeching her protection: "Do thou save thy city, as thou knowest and willest. We put thee forward as our arms, our rampart, our shield, our general: do thou fight for thy people."

Then, before anyone realized it was happening, the Hodegetria slipped from the hands of its bearers. They struggled to grasp it, but it was too late. The people ran forward to pick it up, but it was as if it were weighted with lead, refusing to be raised. Eventually, when it was raised again, the procession had barely restarted before thunder burst through the clouds and lightning split the sky. Then the heavens poured down rain, soaking the procession and all the penitents. The downpour became torrential so that the procession had to halt; water, inches deep, filled the streets, making them slippery, and the flood soon threatened to wash away the children in the procession. Struggling, the icon's bearers eventually managed to return the Hodegetria to Saint Sophia as gloom settled over the city, less from the weather than the omens that clearly stated the Virgin had refused their prayers and penance.

Worse, the next day, God's grace had left the city. Since its construction by Emperor Justinian in the sixth century, Saint Sophia had held within it the Holy Light as its protector. But that night, a great glow was seen in the sky. First, the sentries on the walls and then people in the streets had cried out in fear that the city had caught on fire. All the sky lit up, but the flame was located only on the roof of Saint Sophia. The flame shot forth from the window and circled the entire dome several times before gathering itself into one great and indescribable flash of blinding light that shot up into the heavens. Clearly, the Holy Light had returned from whence it had come, no longer offering God's protection to the city. The sight had been so overwhelming to Constantine that now, two days later, it still made him sick to think of it. Had he himself lost favor with God? At that fatal moment, such a thought had caused him to go numb throughout his body and collapse to the ground in a faint, remaining unconscious for hours.

When Constantine finally woke, the people had begged him to flee the city before it was too late, but he had insisted he would not do so. To leave his people solely to save his own life would be to heap immortal ridicule upon his name. And even if he did leave, what life would remain for him, without a throne, marked as a coward for not standing by his supporters in their hour of greatest need? Better he stay to fight, and if need be, die with his people.

He had seen both these catastrophes with his own eyes, but

the most shocking event he alone had experienced. Early the next morning, when he had gone out walking in the palace gardens, he had come face-to-face with an old man with a flowing white beard in a tattered black robe. Constantine had never seen the man before, and he could not understand how the man had entered his private gardens. But before he could accost the man, the stranger looked him square in the eyes, his own eyes piercingly gray, and without showing fear or deference for Constantine's station, he said, "Greetings, Constantine, last of the Romans."

Constantine had frozen, feeling himself unable to speak or move. His mind went blank for what seemed the longest time as the question "Who are you?" struggled to rise to his lips. His first fear was that the man might be an assassin, sent by the Turks—who but an assassin would dare to enter his private garden at dawn? But then, slowly, the answer came to his lips in a whisper.

"The Wandering Jew."

Before the words fully escaped Constantine's mouth, the man turned and disappeared behind a clump of trees. Constantine ran after him, so stunned that he pursued him into the bushes, scratching himself on their branches but unable to see anyone. After a couple of minutes, he calmed himself and returned to the walkway, fearing his people had seen his frantic behavior. Had he dreamt it, or had he truly seen the man? But he could remember those words clearly; they yet rung in his ears: "Greetings, Constantine, last of the Romans."

He knew such a meeting forebode great ill. The Wandering Jew—he whom Christ had cursed to wander the earth until His return—had long been rumored to appear at pivotal moments in history. Stories claimed he had been seen in the city once before, back in 1204 when the Latin Crusaders had sacked Constantinople. He had also been

seen at the surrender of Jerusalem to Saladin in 1187, amid the mob during the Peasants Revolt in England in 1381, and most recently in the crowd when the Maid of Orleans had been burned at the stake in Rouen, France in 1431. Constantine had heard rumors in recent days that the Wandering Jew had been sighted in Constantinople's streets, but he had dismissed such rumors as folk tales. Now, he could not imagine who else this man could be who dared to address him as "last of the Romans"—an ominous reference, indeed.

The next day, Constantine knew his death was certain when twelve Venetian ships arrived to aid the city, bringing with them the news that no larger fleet nor other enforcements would come. Twelve ships would be of little help against the incredible Ottoman navy and the hordes of Turkish soldiers preparing for the final assault they all knew was coming. No one could accurately tell the numbers, but a city of just over fifty thousand souls—a city that in its glorious past had been home to a million residents—was being protected by an army of less than twenty thousand against some one hundred thousand Turks, plus their allies. Surely, the situation was hopeless.

Constantine had little doubt that tonight was the last time the sun would set on the city before it was taken, and pillaged, and perhaps even destroyed. The walls could well be broken through before dawn. The Turkish cannons had already damaged them beyond repair. The conquest would happen as soon as Sultan Mehmet II led the next charge.

Nothing was left to do but offer prayers, though prayers now seemed of little help. Nevertheless, Constantine had spent the last day at service in Saint Sophia, on his knees before his people and God, begging forgiveness for their transgressions. Afterwards, he had spent time here on the ramparts with his longtime friend and advisor

Sphrantzes. And then he had sought some time alone, time to prepare himself for what he did not doubt was his imminent death. He would do so nobly, as Emperor of the Romans, and in a manner to make his ancestors proud, but he would be dead nonetheless, and he had his doubts that God would have mercy upon his soul after the signs he had already seen.

"Your majesty." He turned to hear himself addressed and found the captain of the guard speaking. "The Turks are about to break through the wall. You must return to the palace. You must look to your own safety."

"You know better," Constantine replied, already in his armor. "Come; we will fight together, and may God have mercy on our souls."

The Turks were firing their cannons. It was almost half-past one in the morning. Just as the emperor joined his army before the St. Romanus Gate, a cannonball came ripping through the wall, sending stone and men flying, and by the time Constantine and his men recovered from the shock, three hundred Turks had poured through, their voices roaring as they entered the city. In panic, some of the Romans fled into the streets, desperate to see to their own and their families' safety, but most stood fighting beside their emperor and the officers.

The Romans fought violently, but they were far outnumbered, and while the battle raged at the great crumbling opening in the wall for several minutes, eventually, the Romans were cut down as the Turks began to spread and pillage throughout Constantinople.

Constantine found himself covered in blood as his sword continued to slice at the Turks before him, but within a few minutes, he was surrounded by his enemies. He had taken care not to wear anything to make the enemy suspect he was the emperor, for he knew if they discovered his identity, his life would be spared, but only because the sultan would want to hold him as a prisoner. No, he would much rather die here with his people than be forced to go down on bended knee before Mehmet II, or worse, be paraded through the streets by his captors.

Suddenly, Constantine felt a great pain in his back. He immediately became dizzy; for a moment, he felt his knees buckle and he thought he would collapse, but then he experienced a great lifting feeling, as if he were floating into the air. He could only think that his soul was leaving his body. Had he been slain? Was he now dead? Was he being taken to Heaven—could death be this quick?

Looking up, bending his head all the way back, he saw he was in the arms of a great winged man, a beautiful gorgeous man, a man a good couple of feet taller than him—no, not a man but an angel.

And then all went black.

When he opened his eyes, Constantine found himself lying on a cot inside a barren room all built of stone. He could see the sky, but nothing else from the window, making him assume he was quite high up. All he heard were birds chirping and a breeze rustling through the trees. No screams of his people. No cannons booming. And most surprisingly, he felt no fear.

Was he dead? But, surely, Heaven did not look like the barren room of a castle.

For a moment, he relished the quiet, but his curiosity overcame him. He sat up and continued to look out the window. From his sitting position, he could see what appeared to be a marsh, and beyond that a river, and then just a green row of trees and a lush countryside. He appeared to be in the middle of nowhere. Certainly, he was far from Constantinople.

"Where am I?" he muttered, about to put his feet on the floor when the door opened. In walked a man whom Constantine had only seen once before.

"You!" Constantine gasped.

PART I
ISTANBUL
OCTOBER 2013

CHAPTER 1

ADAM DELANEY WOKE to the sound of the call to prayer. Because he had left the window cracked open the night before, he could hear the recorded voice calling out in words he did not understand, although he knew the guidebook he had read said they were a call for all Muslims to come to prayer and to salvation.

It was still dark out. Adam looked at the clock and saw it was 6:20 a.m. It would be dark for another hour yet. It was late October now; the days were growing shorter, and they were even shorter here in Istanbul, which was farther south than England.

Adam wondered whether he should get up; he did not wish to disturb Anne, who lay beside him in the hotel bed. She needed her rest, and she was sleeping soundly now, although throughout their married life, that had been a rarity. Not that he had ever complained; he had been known to thrash about in bed at night, even kick her when he would wake up sweating from a nightmare, but the one time they had tried to sleep apart, she had woken screaming in terror from her own dreams, and he had run from his room across the hall to her side. After that, he did not dare leave her at night, nor did she want him to. They had been through so much together that the other's presence was often the only comfort each of them had. And whenever life seemed to be improving, the anniversary of their twin sons' birth or the anniversary of their kidnapping would come around again. Their children, whom they had not seen since they were but a few months old, were eighteen now, and that was far too long a time—nearly unbearable—to be separated from your children. The great wizard Merlin, who was himself the kidnapper, though they had not known it at first, had assured them soon after that their children were safe and being protected from the evil that had been unleashed upon the world. Nevertheless, the pain of their sons' absence and their fears for their wellbeing had been never-ending during all these years.

Eventually, Adam and Anne had learned to go about their lives, functioning normally, despite the great losses they had endured—first their children's abduction, then the tragic death of Adam's mother and the simultaneous disappearance of Anne's father, whom they could only think had also been killed, although his body had never been found. Finally, a year later, Adam's grandmother had died; it could have been from old age, but grief and exhaustion had assisted in allowing death to take its hold. Adam and Anne had once envisioned a happy life together as a married couple surrounded by family, but now, the only family they had was Adam's cousin, Devin Purcell, who had moved to England, finished his Ph.D. at Cambridge, and in time become a professor at Oxford, which kept him so busy that the couple did not see him as often as they would have liked; Adam worried about Devin being so alone, for he had chosen to focus on his research and write seven books rather than marry and have children, but Adam also knew his cousin's scholarly interests were less likely to interfere in their friendship than if Devin had his own family; they saw each other at least once a month and on holidays, and they spoke on the phone frequently, and whenever needed, Devin had come to Adam and Anne's aid.

Devin had, in fact, accompanied them on this journey to Istanbul following the summons they had recently received.

"Another of Merlin's jokes," Devin had called the summons.

"A sick joke," Adam had replied, but Anne had disagreed.

The summons had come in the form of a beautiful, official invitation on fine paper with gilded calligraphy text.

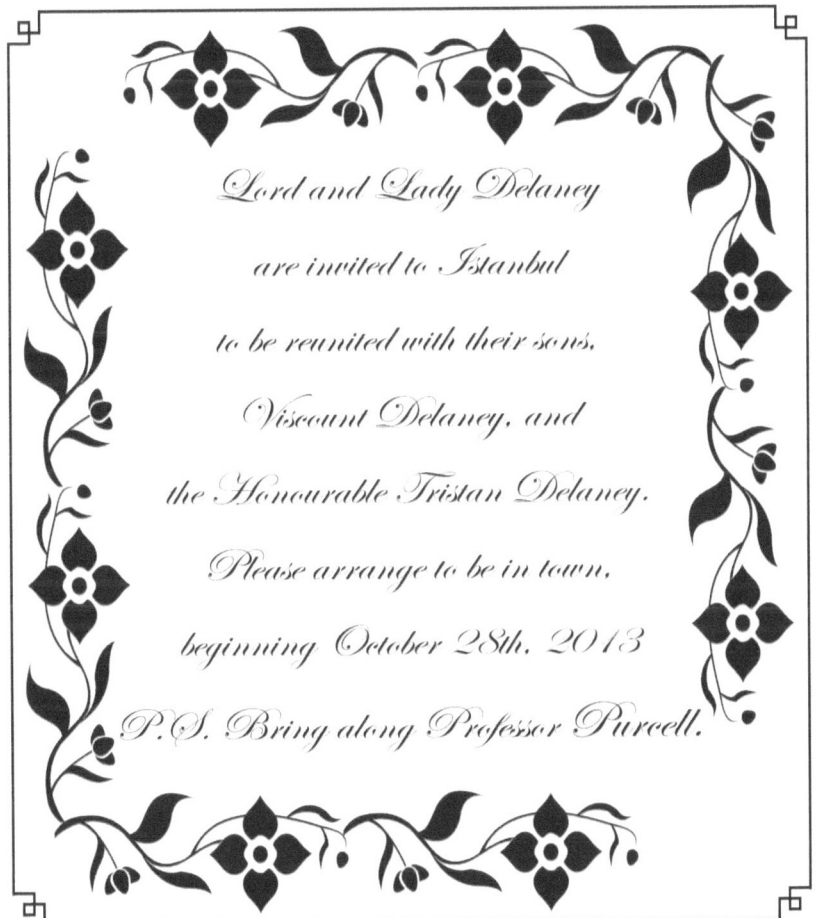

Lord and Lady Delaney

are invited to Istanbul

to be reunited with their sons,

Viscount Delaney, and

the Honourable Tristan Delaney.

Please arrange to be in town,

beginning October 28th, 2013

P.S. Bring along Professor Purcell.

Most of the invitation was not difficult to understand. Because Adam was an English earl, the Lord and Lady Delaney in the invitation clearly referred to him and his wife, Anne, while their eldest born twin son, Lancelot, was Viscount Delaney since he was heir to the earldom and their younger son was the Honorable Tristan Delaney. Obviously, Devin was Professor Purcell. But what could not be explained was why Istanbul was to be the site for this reunion, or when and how the reunion was to take place.

"It's a beautiful card," Anne had said. "Look at the flowery border and the fine paper."

"But what does it mean?" Adam asked.

"It has to be from Merlin," said Anne. "There's something about that curious phrasing "P.S. Bring along Professor Purcell" that seems like something he would add to be funny. Obviously, he wants us to meet him in Istanbul."

"But why?" Adam persisted. "Why can't he just bring our sons to us here at Delaney Castle?"

"I don't know," said Anne, "but I'm sure Merlin knows how to find us. Once we get to Istanbul, he'll give us another clue."

And so they had come to Istanbul. Devin had been ecstatic to go, not only for the children's sake, but because, as a medieval scholar, he knew all the details of Istanbul's history as the former Constantinople, capital of the Byzantine Empire, but he had never visited the great city himself. As they all prepared for their journey and learned about the former greatest European city of medieval times, they were all astounded to think that it now held 15 million souls—nearly twice as many as London itself.

"How will we ever find Merlin in such a place?" Adam had asked.

"Don't worry," Anne had insisted. "He will find us."

"It's been eighteen years since the boys disappeared," Adam had replied, "and in all that time, we've not had one word from him. Why now?"

"The boys will be eighteen soon. I imagine that's why," said Anne.

Not until the three of them were flying to Istanbul a few days later had it occurred to Adam that perhaps it had not been Merlin who sent the invitation. *What if it was sent by Gwenhwyvach?* he thought. Merlin had hidden the children away precisely because he feared that the ancient evil woman would harm them.

Gwenhwyvach was just one of this evil creature's many names. She had died and reincarnated herself many times over human history, most recently in the late twentieth century when she had been captured by the descendants of King Arthur, Adam's own mother being one of her Keepers, so she could not wreak havoc upon the human race as she had for generations past—first in her original incarnation as Lilith, wife to Adam in the Garden of Eden, but then in many new incarnations as Medusa; as Vashti; as Gwenhwyvach, or the False Guinevere, who had brought about the fall of King Arthur's Camelot; later as Gudrun, Queen of Denmark, who had sought to dishonor her stepson, Prince Ogier, and who had later married and murdered the Count of Lusignan. No doubt, she had lived other lives as well of which Adam and Anne had no knowledge. What they did know was that Merlin had told them she was the enemy of mankind. As Lilith, the first woman, she had sworn to wreak vengeance upon all the human race born of Adam and Eve's loins after her husband had spurned her and chosen Eve in her place. And century after century, she had threatened their descendants. When, in 1995, she had escaped from the underground compound where she had last been held a prisoner, she had apparently stolen both of the magical rings of Melusine—the magical rings that had first been Adam and Eve's wedding rings, and with them, she hoped finally to have the power to control and destroy the human race. At least, that was believed to be her purpose, but eighteen years had passed now, and yet she had been silent. If she had possessed the rings all this time, as Adam and Anne feared, why had she not used them?

Whenever anything tragic had happened in the world—the death of Princess Diana, the killings in Kosovo, the September 11th terrorist attacks, the great Tsunami in the Pacific, Hurricane Katrina, school shootings, or earthquakes across the globe—Adam and Anne's first thought had always been that Gwenhwyvach was behind it and now the apocalypse was about to come for mankind—and yet, in each case, it had turned out to be a human or natural cause behind the tragedy, and all these years, Gwenhwyvach had remained silent.

But could it be, Adam wondered, that Gwenhwyvach's time to act had now come, and it was she, not Merlin, who was luring them to Istanbul for reasons they could not ascertain?

All these thoughts ran through Adam's head yet again as he quietly dressed in the hotel room that morning. They were all staying at the Pera Palace, which Devin had insisted upon, saying it was the hotel in Istanbul where Europeans traditionally stayed and listing its many celebrity visitors, including Agatha Christie, Greta Garbo, and Ataturk. Adam had not even known who Ataturk was until he had come to Turkey, and he'd never seen a Garbo film or read an Agatha Christie mystery, but he didn't care what hotel they stayed at—whatever would please Devin. All he wanted was his children back. Until he knew whether Merlin or Gwenhwyvach were behind the invitation to come to Istanbul, he could only wait in the unbelievably congested and alluring city and hope for the best.

When he had finished dressing, Adam stood for a while, looking out the window, watching the sun rise over Istanbul's busy streets. Then he looked over at his beautiful wife, the streaks of gray in her hair almost invisible in the lamp's glow. He thought how those streaks of gray should not be there at her young age—she had only just turned forty and did not deserve to age so rapidly. What had either of them ever done to deserve such a fate? Yet everything in their lives had seemed to be fated, as if some god were playing a cruel trick upon them. Twenty years ago, as an American-born college student raised by his grandparents, Adam would have thought that finding out the father he had never known was an English earl would have been a great good fortune, but it had only resulted in one difficulty after another for him—even if it had led to his meeting and marrying the most beautiful woman he could possibly imagine. Was it some evil god who had caused all this, or Fate, or simply the work of Merlin, the great enchanter of King Arthur's court, and Morgana, better known as Morgan le Fay, the Lady of Avalon?

Merlin and Morgana had appeared in Adam and Anne's lives from the time of their first meeting through the events of their children's kidnapping, a period of just over a year when an insane chain of events had occurred, a time during which they had come to understand that they were descendants of King Arthur, brought together for some great purpose that Merlin and Morgana had never fully explained to them. It was apparent, however, that they were in some way destined to fight Gwenhwyvach, but even so, despite convoluted explanations and having been shown the past in curious visions that took them back to the times of King Arthur and Charlemagne, Adam and Anne had never fully understood just what their destiny was, or why they had been subjected to such a strange one. But most difficult to understand was why they could not be with their children.

"There has to be a purpose to all of this," Anne had repeatedly said over the years whenever Adam had grown frustrated and despairing.

"I just wish I knew what that purpose was," Adam had always replied. "Why don't Merlin or Morgana show up to tell us?"

That was truly the million dollar question. Those two, who had manipulated Adam and Anne's lives so that they would produce children to be King Arthur's heirs, had not been seen since just after the kidnapping, nor had they offered any form of guidance to the couple in dealing with the long investigations that had resulted and made Adam and Anne themselves suspects in their children's kidnapping until a lack of evidence had finally led to the charges being dismissed. Since then, all that had remained was the frustration Adam and Anne felt, along with the natural longing of parents to be reunited with their offspring.

Adam felt so stressed, so frustrated now to be in this foreign city without any direction. He was too restless to sit and read while Anne slept. Once he was dressed, he scribbled a note to Anne—"Went down to breakfast"—and then left the room and walked down the hall to knock on Devin's door.

His cousin answered immediately. Devin was dressed, with his glasses on and a book in his hand. Adam could see a stack of books on the dresser.

"You know, if you bought yourself an e-reader, you wouldn't have to lug all those books around with you," he told his cousin.

"I have a Kindle," said Devin. "It's fine for reading novels, but it's horrible when it comes to reading books with footnotes, and I've never figured out how to highlight things on it. You know I hate technology. I'd rather use a red pen for marking my books."

"You really are still living in the Middle Ages, aren't you?" said Adam, smiling. "Do you want to go get some coffee?"

"Sure," said Devin, setting down his copy of Roger Crowley's *1453* on the desk. "Is Anne joining us?"

"She's still asleep," Adam replied. "I'm sure she'll come down to join us when she wakes, but she needs her rest so I didn't want to wake her."

Devin followed Adam down the hall to the elevator while asking, "How did you sleep?"

"Not well," Adam admitted.

"Worried?" asked Devin.

It was a stupid question, Adam thought. Of course he was worried, but he didn't want to admit how much he feared that it might have been Gwenhwyvach and not Merlin who had invited them to Istanbul. Instead, he simply said, "I just haven't adjusted to the time change, I guess. How did you sleep?"

"Okay. I only slept maybe five hours, but I think I'm just excited finally to be in Istanbul. I've always wanted to visit here, you know."

"Yeah, so you said," said Adam as they left the elevator and crossed the hotel lobby to the dining room.

They were quickly greeted by a Turkish waiter who spoke impeccable English. In another minute, they were seated, and not long after that, they had coffee, cherry juice, scrambled eggs, sausages, and pancakes.

"I hope Anne won't mind us eating before her," said Devin.

"No, we're in no rush, so we can wait for her to eat when she comes down," said Adam. "What else do we have to do? We don't know what we're doing in Istanbul. We don't know where we're supposed to go to meet anyone or get any information. I guess we're just expected to sit around and wait, and that just pisses me off."

"I know," said Devin, seeing the strain in his cousin's face. "But I'm sure whoever summoned us here will find us."

"Yeah, and is probably spying on us. We have no privacy. We're just like marionettes in someone's play, and the director is a madman, for all we know."

"Adam," said Devin, stirring his coffee and then laying down his spoon, "I don't blame you for being upset and worried, but try to keep your spirits up for Anne's sake."

"I do that all the time, but I have to vent to someone now and then, and that's what you're for."

"Okay," sighed Devin. He was Adam's best friend, so listening to such venting was to be expected.

After a couple of silent minutes while they focused on their food, Devin dared to say, "I do hope we can see the sights since we've come all this way. After all, Istanbul is one of the world's most historic and intriguing cities."

"Is it?" said Adam, never having given Istanbul a thought until the invitation they had received.

Devin half-frowned at Adam's lack of interest. Adam finished his cup of coffee, and then seeing that his cousin looked irritated, he politely asked, "What is so important about Istanbul? I mean, historically?"

"Oh, everything," said Devin. "It was the second capital of the Roman Empire, and it became the sole capital after Rome fell in 476 A.D. It remained the capital then of what we today call the Byzantine Empire, but while the people of that empire were Greeks, they called themselves Romans and the emperor thought of himself as the Roman emperor. In fact, one of the main reasons why Charlemagne was crowned the Holy Roman Emperor in 800 A.D. was because the

Byzantine emperor was dethroned by his mother, Irene of Athens, who then became empress. The Pope frowned on the idea of a woman emperor so he crowned Charlemagne as Roman emperor, which led to east and west rivalry, of course, since the Greeks considered themselves the real Romans."

"I think I remember something about that," said Adam, groping to bring an old memory to the forefront of his mind. "Maybe it was in that dream I had about Ogier the Dane since Charlemagne was in it."

"Yes, probably," said Devin, who had not experienced the dream, although Adam had told him all about it. He envied Adam a great deal for those dreams because of his own passionate and scholarly interest in medieval history. "Not that Charlemagne being named Holy Roman Emperor made a difference. But the West continually looked down on the Byzantine empire after that; it probably helped lead to the breach that caused the Eastern Orthodox Church to break off from the Roman Catholic one. And eventually, the West grew tired of coming to Constantinople's aid during the Crusades. In the thirteenth century, the Western crusaders even invaded the city and took it over to form a Latin empire, although the Greeks regained it after many decades. They then retained the city for about two hundred years as the Turks slowly conquered more and more of their empire until 1453, when almost nothing but Constantinople was left of the empire, and then the Turks conquered the city, too. In fact, I've been reading a book about the 1453 conquest. It's fascinating history."

Adam continued to eat while his cousin launched into a long history of the Fall of Constantinople, describing the characters of Constantine XI, last of the Byzantine emperors, and Mehmet II, Sultan of the Ottoman Empire, who was later styled "The Conqueror" by his people. Devin detailed the long siege of the city and all the emperor's failed efforts to obtain aid from the West, and then the tragic signs that the city would fall to the enemy. He paused only to take a bite of food, chewing while he talked, caught up in his passion for the city's marvelous and tragic past.

"And in the great church of Hagia Sophia," Devin said, "where so many people were praying when the city was taken, the people saw—"

"Good morning," said Anne, coming up behind Adam to pat him on the shoulder and sit beside him. He gave her a kiss and was going to ask how she slept, but she quickly said, "I didn't mean to interrupt, Devin. What were you saying?"

Devin summarized what he had told Adam, ending by describing how when the city was invaded, "the priests in Hagia Sophia were seen to disappear into the wall, bearing with them many holy relics, and the legend says that they would not return until the city was Christian again."

"And that's never happened?" asked Adam.

"No," said Devin. "Istanbul has been part of Turkey and a Muslim city ever since, at least predominantly Muslim, considering that Turkey has been a secular country since the republic was declared in 1922."

"I love, though," said Anne, "that the legend says the priests will someday return."

"Sounds like King Arthur returning," Adam remarked.

"That's it!" exclaimed Devin, so excited he slammed his fist on the table, causing all the coffee in his cup to spill over.

Anne grabbed a napkin and started to clean up the table while Adam asked, "That's what?"

"There's more to the story about Constantine XI—he's like King Arthur, too. He was last seen in the thick of the battle, but no one knows how he died and his body was never found. It's likely the Greeks buried him where Mehmet II wouldn't find his body—they certainly wouldn't have wanted his body desecrated—but no records exist that he was actually found, although there's a supposed gravesite in Istanbul. But the legends say that either he was carried away by an angel, or that an angel turned him into a marble statue and placed him under one of Constantinople's gates where he waits to be brought back to life when the city is Christian again."

"That does sound like King Arthur," said Anne, setting down the napkin and drinking the last of her coffee.

"Well, it's just a legend," said Devin, "but I still find it fascinating—I mean, all of these legends about kings returning in the future."

"They must be more than legends," said Adam. "We know from experience that there is some truth behind the legends of King Arthur, also those of Melusine and Roland and Ogier the Dane and Prester John, and even behind the biblical story of Adam and Eve and Lilith, and—"

"And so that must be why we had to come to Istanbul!" exclaimed Anne. "The parallels between King Arthur and Constantine can't be just a coincidence. I bet Merlin has something to tell us, another story perhaps, or as the invitation suggests, our children are here, and—"

"Or maybe there's a clue we must find," Devin interrupted. "Adam thinks we should just wait around the hotel for Merlin to show up, but I think we should go out and tour the city, see the sights, and see whether that leads us to any clues about why we're here."

"Oh, yes," said Anne. "I could use a little sightseeing to distract my mind. I dearly want to see my children, but sitting around being glum until that happens isn't going to help. I'm sure that when he's ready, Merlin will know how to find us."

"Great," said Devin. "If you're done with breakfast, we can just go brush our teeth and then set off. Where do you want to go first?"

"I think if there's anywhere we can hope to meet Merlin, it's Hagia Sophia," said Anne. "That sounds like the place with the most legends."

CHAPTER 2

HALF AN HOUR later, Devin, Adam, and Anne found a taxi and departed the hotel to make their way to the Golden Horn's shoreline where once sultans built their palaces and chariot races had been held fifteen centuries before. Now the Hippodrome was gone, replaced by Sultan Ahmet Square. The great Blue Mosque rose up where once was the Byzantine emperor's palace, and the Ottoman sultans' Topkapi Palace had been turned into a museum, as had Hagia Sophia, but the imaginative visitor could still feel the greatness that had once been imperial Constantinople and Istanbul.

The minute they stepped out of the cab, the three of them were mobbed by men trying to sell them postcards and tourist guidebooks. Adam grabbed Anne's arm and tried to walk quickly away, but Devin pulled out his wallet, and not being able to speak Turkish, handed over more money than he probably should have; still, he ended up with a map of Istanbul and a book about the city. He then put his wallet in his front pocket to avoid pickpockets, although he knew from his research online that while the Turkish people love to get all the money out of you that they can while bartering, they are extremely honest.

Once Devin caught up with Anne and Adam, he suggested they visit the Blue Mosque first since Hagia Sophia was across the square in the other direction. Since none of them knew whether Hagia Sophia would contain the clues they sought, they all agreed and walked toward the Blue Mosque.

On the way, they came to the ruins of the Hippodrome, where once the great chariot races had been held, and Devin, referring to the guidebook, was explaining to them about the obelisks brought from Egypt and other places whose names Adam didn't catch because he wasn't terribly interested in ancient history; he was more concerned by the crowds of people, which made him uncomfortable, than matches between ancient teams named the Blues and the Greens that had once competed here against one another.

But even Adam had to admit he was overcome when he entered the Blue Mosque. He and Anne were afraid they would not be allowed into a mosque, but Anne was eager to visit it, having heard before of its great beauty. Adam wanted to get straight to Hagia Sophia to see Merlin, but Anne said, "Merlin will know where to find us, and…and well, I'm afraid of being disappointed if we don't see him there."

When she started to shed a tear, fearing they might not find their sons even though they had come all this way, Adam put his arm around her and started walking with her toward the Blue Mosque with Devin at their side.

"We'll find them," Adam said, although he had to admit he doubted just as much as she did.

Going to the mosque distracted them momentarily from their concerns. Indeed, the Sultan Ahmet Mosque, more commonly known as the Blue Mosque, was breathtaking even from the outside. Devin referred to the guidebook, learning it was open to all visitors, and then he directed them to a side entrance. There they were required to cover their feet with little plastic booties, and Anne was asked to cover her hair, and then they stepped into the grandest, most decorative and stunning room any of them had ever seen. They had dined with the Queen of England, been overnight guests at Windsor Palace, and attended services in Westminster Abbey and most of England's grandest cathedrals, but nothing could have prepared them for the simplicity, complexity, and sheer beauty of the Blue Mosque. They stood breathless, unable to take it in, noticing detail after detail of ornate design, stunned by flowers and countless colors and even stained glass, which they had not expected, and they could well believe that in this mosque, just as in any Christian church, God was present among man. "The guidebook says that even Pope Benedict XVI has visited here," Devin whispered.

"Somehow," said Anne, "such exquisite art makes me believe that despite all the evil in the world, all the fighting, there is a greater good in mankind when it can create such beauty and do it for the glory of God."

Adam said nothing other than agreeing the mosque was beautiful, but he equally felt overwhelmed by the elegance, which was far less ostentatious than many a gilded church he'd been in, but with a ceiling that seemed to reach almost to heaven. He paused and said a prayer, uncertain what to believe in a world where magic really did exist, where an evil biblical woman could continue to live for centuries, and where the only help they had to fight her supernatural powers was an eccentric old wizard who also claimed to be St. Joseph of Arimathea—and whose claim, if not true, would make him a heretic or blasphemer probably—although Adam could not doubt that Merlin did have some power, whoever or whatever he really was.

"God, whatever is meant to be, let it be," Adam found himself praying, "but if you can bring me back my children, I will be extremely grateful."

"Are you coming, Adam?" called Anne, already having moved several feet toward the exit with Devin.

"Amen," Adam said, and then he followed his wife and cousin back outside.

"Where next?" he asked once they were back in the open air.

"Hagia Sophia is right there," said Devin, pointing at a giant pink-colored stone building with a massive dome, "and behind it along the water is the Topkapi Palace."

"Let's go to the palace first," said Anne.

"But I thought," said Adam, "you felt Hagia Sophia was what we had come here to see."

"Yes," said Anne, "but I'm almost afraid to go in there if it's the place of legends, and I'm not sure I'm ready to see our sons yet—what will I say to them? I just need more time."

"We don't even know they'll be there," added Devin. "We're just guessing, and as Anne said earlier, Merlin will know where to find us."

"All right," Adam consented, feeling nervous himself. He wanted to see his sons but he also felt a dread, as if seeing them would equate with some disaster brought about by Gwenhwyvach. For all he knew, it might even have been Gwenhwyvach who had lured them to Istanbul instead of Merlin. Why did Merlin always have to play these games? Why couldn't he just show himself and put their fears at rest?

"Let's go," said Devin, leading the way around the ancient cathedral to the palace. "Then we won't feel the need to rush to the next site if we go to the palace first because we'll want to take our time at Hagia Sophia."

The Topkapi Palace was also like nothing the three of them had ever seen. Used to Western castles, they found this palace was more like an open air series of porches with individual interior rooms. They thought it beautiful, but also a tad confusing to wander through—Adam had a moment of temporary déjà vu as he remembered his dream of Roland and Ogier visiting Prester John's fabulous palace—the Topkapi Palace was the closest Adam had ever seen in real life to that fabled architecture. There were several museum rooms filled with priceless valuables, including the famous Topkapi dagger, and then there were countless rooms with porches attached and covered in beautiful mosaics. Save for the "Circumcision Room," which Adam and Devin refused to enter, they found the entire visit very pleasant and relaxing. They ended their visit by exploring the harem, finding it astounding to think that the sultans had once had as many as 150 women living here together.

"This is the most unique palace I've ever seen," said Anne. "I've been to Buckingham Palace and Versailles and plenty of others, but this one is more like a garden, and not at all gaudy."

"No, the Dolmabahce Palace that the later sultans built is far more European—and gaudy, if that's the term you want to use," said Devin, having spent half his time looking in the guidebook rather than at the palace itself.

"I'm starving," said Adam, who had seen enough. "Let's eat before we go to Hagia Sophia."

Devin and Anne agreed that they were also hungry and tired of fighting the crowds along the walkway to and from the palace. None of them said it, but they all felt they might need all their strength for their visit to Hagia Sophia and whatever might happen there, so lunch was definitely in order. They made a circle around Hagia Sophia and then turned onto a street with plenty of restaurants and even more tourists and crowds.

"Not even London is as crowded as this," said Anne.

"It's energizing, though, isn't it?" said Devin. "So many people and so much fascinating history."

"There's a Burger King," said Adam, pointing to the familiar restaurant sign up the street a ways and thinking at least the food there would be normal.

"Seriously?" said Anne. "We're in Turkey. We need to eat somewhere authentic."

"Let's eat here," said Devin, agreeing with Anne and stopping in front of a small restaurant that didn't appear to have much of a line.

Adam gave in, feeling exhausted and not even caring what he ate. He could not even pay attention to Anne and Devin chatting about everything Turkish, from carpets to Turkish Delight. He knew all their talk was largely the result of nervousness, but he still could hardly partake in it.

Once they were seated and had ordered, Adam was pleasantly surprised to find his kabobs were not overly spicy like he had feared, and the honeyed figs they had for dessert were as good as Yorkshire pudding or a hot fudge sundae. Anne was also pleased with her salad and raved about the fresh olives in it. Only Devin seemed disappointed by the rather bland Turkish pizza.

Adam felt a little better after he ate, although his stomach was rumbling, more from his nerves than his meal. But once they were walking again and had reached Hagia Sophia, Adam forgot about his stomach. He instantly felt struck with awe for the magnificent church, once the greatest cathedral in the world.

Devin read from the guidebook about the earlier churches on the site before the current Hagia Sophia, built in 537 A.D. by the Emperor Justinian, who had declared upon seeing it completed that he had surpassed King Solomon's Temple.

"It certainly looks like he did," Anne agreed, for the building was astonishingly huge, even when considering that its minarets had not been added until almost a thousand years later. The dome had been the largest ever built at the time, and even after the Ottoman conquest nine centuries after, the Turks had taken many years to determine how to fashion a dome to equal it.

"I didn't expect it to be so dark inside," said Anne, once they had entered through the doors and into the main sanctuary. And it was dark inside, yet the dome itself shown with light from the forty windows illuminating it from beneath.

"Over there is where the priests would have disappeared into the wall after the Conquest in 1453," said Devin, pointing across the massive room as he read from his guidebook, only coming up for air to pass on fascinating facts. "And those giant shield-looking pictures contain verses from the Koran because the church was made into a mosque after the Conquest. It's believed there are actually mosaics of Jesus beneath them. The church had many mosaics in its day, but the Muslims covered them because they do not approve of any icons or other depictions of God."

Adam was only half-listening, standing in awe at the giant dome, at the marble columns, at the gallery that surrounded the entire church.

"We can go upstairs," said Devin after a few minutes. "There are ramps to walk up on the sides of the church."

Adam followed along, and Anne reached back for his hand. "Isn't it incredible," she said, "to think this church is nearly fifteen hundred years old—that's five hundred years older than Westminster Abbey."

"Westminster Abbey is more ornate," said Adam.

"It's a lot more modern, too," said Devin.

"And we probably feel more connected to it because our ancestors have worshipped there for centuries," said Anne. "Even though we're descended from earls, they were constantly there paying homage to the king or joining war councils."

"But our ancestors worshipped here, too," said Devin.

"We're not Greek or Turkish," Adam replied.

"No, but we're human, and all the human race is one big family actually," said Devin. "You know when Grandma passed on, I found all kinds of family histories among her papers, including genealogy charts. When we go back far enough, we are descended from people from every country in Europe. In fact, DNA and mathematical calculations confirm that everyone of European descent living today can claim descent from any European who lived before the year 1200 A.D. who had descendants, so that would make us all descended from Alfred the Great and Charlemagne and King Arthur and also several of the Byzantine emperors. We're not descended from the Turks who conquered Turkey, but we probably have Turkish blood from earlier generations in us, and our family tree when you go back even farther includes Chinese emperors, Indian maharajahs, Egyptian pharaohs, kings of Israel, and—"

"That makes my head spin," said Anne, "just thinking of that."

"Mine too," said Adam.

Devin, seeing his genealogy lesson wasn't appreciated, quit talking until they reached the upper gallery. Once there, he followed the guidebook to lead them to where the empress and her women would have watched the services, and then they made their way to the mosaics throughout the church of Jesus, John the Baptist, and

Mary, as well as of various emperors and empresses.

"Can you imagine," said Devin, "that during Easter week, the royal family basically lived up here in the galleries because the services lasted for so long."

"Easter's my favorite holiday," said Anne, "but I don't think I could live in a church for a week."

"The church was once full of holy relics," Devin continued, "including pieces of the True Cross; the Holy Lance that pierced Christ's side; the ram's horns with which Joshua blew down the walls of Jericho; the olive branch carried by the dove to Noah's Ark after the Flood; Christ's tunic; the Crown of Thorns; and Christ's own blood."

"Wow!" said Anne.

Adam vaguely remembered hearing something about a lance that had to do with Christ, but the memory didn't quite come back to him.

"And check this out," said Devin, leading them over to a pillar. "They think this may be the oldest form of graffiti in the world—it's Old Norse—a Viking visited here and carved his name."

"Things haven't changed much, have they?" said Anne. "A bunch of schoolboys have carved their names over the centuries into the throne in Westminster Abbey."

Devin opened his mouth now to start talking about the history of Hagia Sophia as a museum since the Republic of Turkey had been established, but Adam interrupted by suddenly asking, "Where's Merlin? I thought we came here hoping he'd show up."

"Adam, honey, try to relax," said Anne. "You know he'll show up when he's ready. Maybe we just have to wait, or maybe this isn't where he wanted to meet us."

"I don't know why he has to be leading us on a wild goose chase," Adam complained.

"I'm sorry," said Devin, feeling a bit downcast. "I'm being insensitive. You're probably tired of listening to me babbling about history when you're so concerned about being reunited with your children."

"No, Devin, don't apologize," Anne replied. "All this history is fascinating and a good distraction."

"This isn't a church anymore. It's a museum," said Devin, "but maybe saying a prayer here wouldn't be such a bad idea."

"I don't think we can pray here publicly, though," said Anne.

"No, but we could say a silent prayer."

"I think I want to go off on my own for a little while," said Adam, thinking he had already prayed in the Blue Mosque. "Would you mind if we just took half an hour or so; I'll walk somewhere quiet."

"That sounds like a good idea," said Anne. "We're all getting a little irritable and could use a break from each other. Let's meet back by the main entrance in thirty minutes."

"Okay," said Devin. "I'll go check out the mosaics some more."

Adam thought his cousin would have wanted to pray as well, but he didn't bother asking. He walked off quickly, wondering what made him feel so disgruntled today. He and Anne had supported each other all these years, never becoming irritated but always being there for one another, realizing they were all they had during this stressful time, but now that Adam hoped they were close to finally seeing their sons again, he was feeling overwhelmed by the stress of anticipation.

"Where is Merlin?" he kept muttering under his breath. He walked around to the gallery on the church's other side, and he tried to pray, although the most he could do was keep repeating, "Please, God." He could not concentrate on prayer because he found himself looking at each and every tourist in Hagia Sophia and behind every column in hopes he would spot Merlin. As Adam knew from past experience, you could never predict when or how the great wizard might decide to appear.

When Adam thought about it, he found it hard to believe he was even in Istanbul. Why Istanbul of all places? Why not just London, or even Paris or Rome, or back in the U.S. somewhere? Even Jerusalem would have made more sense. Istanbul was just too strange and exotic to Adam. He didn't feel comfortable here. He wanted to go home, but he would stick it out if it meant reuniting with his sons— sons who might walk right past him and he wouldn't even recognize them because they had not seen each other in over eighteen years; he wouldn't even know how to talk to them if he did recognize them— and to think of all he'd missed—their first steps, teaching them to ride a bike, to play catch, to drive a car, explaining the birds and the bees to them, teaching them how to shave, and listening to their laughter, their games, reading them bedtime stories and—when he thought of it all, he felt like crying. What if they did not even like him, their own father, when they were reunited? He felt defeated. How could such a fate have been chosen for him? How could Merlin be so cruel? How could God permit such an evil creature as Gwenhwyvach to make such a mess of all their lives?

Whenever Adam had asked such questions in the past, Anne would remind him that Merlin had said he'd hidden away their sons for their own protection, but after all these years of seeing no evidence of Gwenhwyvach's intended destruction of humanity, Adam found it hard to believe there had been any threat at all.

But then Adam would remember that his mother had been killed. To think what it must have been like for her to fall from the top of the Space Needle! As he walked through the upper gallery, he began to feel dizzy just thinking about it, and looking down from the galleries did not help matters. He decided he had better walk back down to the main floor and reunite with Anne and Devin.

Maybe, he thought as he walked down, Merlin would still be around the next corner, or blended in with a group of Japanese tourists, or disguised as a tour guide.

But as much as Adam kept looking about him, Merlin was nowhere to be seen. Finally, Adam just stood by the main entrance, watching for Anne and Devin, who had already found each other and now approached him after just another minute.

"Let's go buy some Turkish delight," said Anne, giving him a reassuring smile.

He made a fake half-smile and consented. The three of them walked back to the area where they had eaten lunch, looking about for gift shops. Devin wanted to walk through the city a bit, following the map he had. Adam was nervous about getting lost or being unable to find a cab back to the hotel, but Devin said they could always take the subway system.

After an hour of wandering about through crowded shops and even more crowded streets, finally, Adam saw a cab, and without asking for permission from Devin or Anne, he flagged it down, and they, shrugging their shoulders, climbed in with him.

"I'm exhausted," Adam said, after telling the driver to bring them back to the Pera Palace Hotel. "Maybe I just have jet lag."

"A good cup of tea will perk us all up," said Anne, rubbing his leg soothingly in the backseat of the cab while Devin sat up front, asking the poor driver a hundred questions about the different sites while the driver, who only spoke minimal English, did his best to search for the right word to reply before Devin was on to the next question.

"Do they drink tea in Turkey?" asked Adam.

"Oh, sure," said Anne. "The Pera Palace is a European Hotel, after all. Do you think Agatha Christie would have stayed there if they didn't have tea? In fact, I think there's a tea room, and I hear also that if you tip the concierge, you can see the room that Agatha Christie stayed in."

Adam knew Anne had read all of Agatha Christie's books—and he had watched a few of the movie versions with her—but he couldn't care less about seeing the famous mystery author's room unless Hercule Poirot or Miss Marple were going to show up to help solve the mystery of where his children were.

Once they were back at the hotel, a far easier trip than Adam would have thought, considering the crowds, they paid the driver, then headed inside.

Upon entering the tea room, they saw a counter filled with pastries—enough to cheer anyone—and soon, even Adam was caught up in trying to decide which pastry he wanted, which wasn't easy considering they all had multiple layers and looked scrumptious. Finally, he settled on a Napoleon while Devin and Anne chose pastries filled with fruit.

Once Adam had tasted a couple of bites of his pastry and had a sip of tea, he started to feel better and even joined in the discussion about the sites they had seen.

"There's nothing like sweets to perk Adam up," laughed Anne, and Adam couldn't deny it.

After they finished eating, Adam kept eyeing the cabinet full of pastries until Anne finally told him to have another one. "No," he said. "I'll save room for supper."

Then Anne suggested they go see Agatha Christie's room, which Devin was willing to do, but Adam wasn't interested and said he'd go up to the room. He followed them into the lobby, but while they were busy talking to the concierge about seeing where the famous mystery writer had slept, Adam turned around and went back to the tea room, unable to resist one more sweet treat.

The tea room was now empty save for the young lady behind the counter who quickly gave him the pastry he requested and got him another cup of tea. Then feeling mischievous and the happiest he had felt in days, Adam sat down in the back of the room to eat his pastry, relishing the first bite and not wanting to rush. He knew he'd never have the figure he had during his college football days again, so what was one more pastry?

"You're going to get fat, indulging like that," said a voice.

Startled, Adam looked around, but no one else was present in the room—even the attendant had gone back into the kitchen.

"You're not a tight-end anymore; in fact, you're getting a bit of a middle-aged spread," the voice continued.

There was absolutely no one in the room; Adam had not seen anyone when he returned into it, even earlier having looked in a small alcove between two walls that jutted out about a meter and contained a domed chair on each wall, both of which had been empty then. He was facing the door, so he had seen no one enter. He could only assume that whoever had spoken was seated in the chair with its back to the wall, but how could that be when he had seen no one enter the room? For a moment, Adam hesitated, wondering whether too much sugar, added to all the stress he had been feeling today, might be causing him to imagine things. Had he really heard anyone speak? Could it be whom he hoped? He decided he would pretend casually to leave the room so he could glance toward the chair, just to make sure he wasn't hearing things.

But just as he was about to stand up from his chair, Adam saw a hand appear on the chair's arm—a wrinkled hand, but wearing a ring that Adam instantly recognized as one of Melusine's rings that he had seen in his past dreams. Was it Merlin's hand or Gwenhwyvach's—could the old witch have found him? But she had always appeared young and beautiful. It could only be—

Then a head appeared from around the side of the chair, a head with a trimmed gray beard and sunglasses, and then another hand reached around, flashing an I.D. badge toward him. "Merlin, Arch Enchanter Merlin, at your service," said the man, now looking over the top of his sunglasses.

Adam took a second to recover from being startled before he said, "Thank God it's you—I thought—"

"Haven't I told you before," Merlin interrupted him, smiling as he removed his sunglasses and returned the badge to his suit pocket, "that you think too much. It's all a game, my dear boy."

CHAPTER 3

"A GAME!" EXCLAIMED Adam, jumping to his feet. "You call sending me on a wild goose chase to a foreign country a game? You call kidnapping my sons and keeping them from Anne and me for eighteen years a game? What kind of sicko are you? You must be insane; no wonder Camelot fell—where were you when Arthur needed you, and where the hell have you been these past eighteen years?"

"That would almost hurt," said Merlin, "blaming me for Camelot's fall, if it weren't for my knowing that it wasn't a tragedy but simply the changing of the old order so new life could come forth. Now settle down, my boy, before the Turks think you a rude American for the way you're shouting."

"I'm not your boy. I'm forty-two years old and I'm sick of your crap."

Adam was tempted to pick up the pastry on his plate and throw it at Merlin, and then, unable to stop his anger, he did.

The plate went flying across the room, the pastry miraculously staying put on it; Merlin caught it like a Frisbee and said, "Thank you. I was afraid you wouldn't be asking me to tea, and those desserts do look scrumptious."

The wizard now stood up and walked over to the table that Adam was standing over.

At that moment, the tea room hostess returned to the counter. Merlin, who was wearing the latest Armani suit and did not look at all unusual in this setting, seated himself at the table across from Adam. Then he turned toward the attendant and said something in Turkish.

Adam didn't understand a word of what Merlin said, but the young lady smiled, came over with a teapot, and poured them fresh cups of tea. Then she went back to the counter and, a minute later, returned with another pastry she placed in front of Adam. Meanwhile, Merlin, after pulling a fork out of his suit sleeve, dug into the one Adam had thrown at him.

When the hostess had returned into the kitchen, Adam said, "Merlin, you have some explaining to do. Do you have any idea what it's been like for me to watch Anne worry all these years about our sons—not to mention how I've felt?"

"She didn't seem too worried today," said Merlin. "I'd say she rather enjoyed seeing Istanbul. I told the two of you not to worry. You should have gotten her out of the house more often these last eighteen years—a little fresh air can do marvels for your attitude."

"Not worry? How are we not supposed to worry when you told us the evil Gwenhwyvach was lose in the world, possessing the magical rings of Melusine, and determined to harm our children, perhaps even to destroy the entire human race?"

Merlin sipped his tea, acting like a parent who knows that if he holds out long enough, his two-year-old will cease his temper tantrum.

Adam, frustrated that he didn't receive a response, finally exclaimed, staring at Merlin's finger, "And just where did you get that ring?"

"Oh, you noticed," said Merlin, extending his hand to admire the ring with its intricate carving of a snake swallowing its tail. "I was afraid it wasn't really working as good bling to go with this suit."

"Bling?"

"Yes, bling—you know, jewelry, an accessory—you don't keep up with fashion, do you, my boy?"

"Merlin, get to the point," said Adam, resigning himself to being called "my boy" because the ring interested him more. "How did you get that ring? I thought Gwenhwyvach stole the one Cedric had, and I assumed after all these years that she also got hold of the one my mother had since she probably killed my mother."

"Yes, my boy, she did get possession of both of those rings."

"Then how did you get one away from her?" Adam repeated.

"I didn't," said Merlin, raising his eyebrow in confusion before sipping his tea.

When he lowered the teacup and found Adam staring at him, he said, "I don't know why you would think that."

"What? How...?" Adam could not understand why Merlin didn't comprehend his question. Groping for words to make his question clear, he finally said, "Merlin, how did you get one of the rings if, last I knew, Gwenhwyvach had them both?"

"Both?" said Merlin. "Oh, you think there are only two rings! Whoever told you that? Haven't you been paying attention? There are three rings."

"Three! You never told us there were three rings," Adam snapped. "I thought the whole point was that if she got possession of the two rings, she would be all powerful?"

"Oh, no, there are definitely three rings. I don't know why you would think there were only two. Sometimes, you just don't get it, do you?"

"*Get it*? How am I supposed to *get it* if you don't tell me? I can't go back into the past and figure all this stuff out by myself. You told me from the beginning that Melusine left two rings to her children."

"So she did," said Merlin, "but you didn't put two and two together, or should I say two and one. Think about it. Where did Melusine get those rings? Whose were they originally?"

"They were Adam and Eve's wedding rings. That's what you told us."

"Yes, they were, but Adam had another wife, didn't he?"

Adam was so surprised that, at first, he couldn't quite fathom the answer on his lips. "So...so Lilith had a wedding ring as well? But then, why weren't there four—Adam could have gotten rid of his first ring for his second wedding."

"There wasn't a second wedding."

"You mean...he was married to Eve and Lilith at the same time? Why, that's polygamy! Would God allow that in the Garden of Eden?"

"Jumping Jehoshaphat!" exclaimed Merlin, setting down his tea cup hard enough to make it clang loudly.

Adam looked at him, not understanding.

"Oh, goodness. You don't even know who Jehoshaphat is, so how could I expect you to know about polygamy. You never even read the Bible, did you? I just don't understand you young people today—so culturally illiterate."

Adam sighed and sat back in his chair, completely frustrated. "Okay, Merlin. I'm an idiot. You know I'm not that smart.... You should have gone after Devin if you wanted someone knowledgeable to stalk."

"Oh, well, it can't be helped now," said Merlin, brushing pastry crumbs out of his mustache. "Sometimes, I do forget what a baby you are. Not that that's any excuse for you not having read the Bible—I mean, even if taking into account that you didn't learn to read until you were six, you've had thirty-six years to do so. But I see I'll just have to keep telling you everything."

"I wish you would," said Adam.

"Polygamy," began Merlin, "well, I won't go into all the details, but it was pretty common in the Bible. Abraham had a wife, Sarah, but he also had all kinds of other women he was involved with, Hagar and numerous others—after all, he was the father of many nations. And then there was Jacob, married not only to Rachel but also to her sister Leah, and he also had children with their handmaidens, so you might as well say he had four wives. And then there was Lamech, Enoch, Elkanah, Gideon, David, Solomon...oh, too many to list in fact. The Bible doesn't condemn polygamy."

"I always thought polygamy was wrong," said Adam, wondering whether anything he thought he knew was true any longer.

"Well, now you know better. Who are we to judge what worked for another culture?"

"So," said Adam, not really caring about polygamy at all, "you have Lilith's ring?"

"Yes, when she died last time, I got hold of it, and I haven't let go of it since. I've decided, since she got hold of the other two, that it is safest that I wear it rather than leave it unprotected where she might find it. She needs all three to succeed in her evil plans. And I'm going to make sure that doesn't happen."

"Okay," said Adam. "So after eighteen years, you finally show up to clear up the polygamy/three rings issue. Why has it taken you so long to show up, and what's next?"

"You really are slow, aren't you?" said Merlin, pushing back his chair to stand up.

Adam just stared blankly at him.

"Think about it," said Merlin.

"I don't know, Merlin," said Adam, shaking his head in frustration. "You make everything into a puzzle. I don't even understand why we're in Istanbul except for the card we received saying we would be reunited with our sons. Is that going to happen?" Adam was almost afraid to ask the question, and he choked up on the last sentence.

"My boy," said Merlin, his eyes gently looking straight into Adam's, "you may think me cruel, but all I've done has been because I want what is best for you. Yes, in time, you will see your sons. Not yet, but soon. But first, there will be a final story you must be made aware of."

"Another story," muttered Adam, finding it difficult to feel angry when Merlin's eyes pierced to his very soul, yet he felt like crying to think he must still wait to see Lance and Tristan, whom he loved more than he could ever say, and the love only intensified each year with the longing.

"Yes, another story," Merlin continued. "Just as magnificently complex and important as the others. Perhaps the most important of all."

"But I still don't understand what I'm supposed to learn from these stories," said Adam, tears of frustration in his eyes as he stood up, since Merlin was now on his feet.

"You must be a lover of story, my boy. I know it's your human nature to want all the answers without the learning that goes with them, but secretly, though you express frustration with me, you want the stories more than anything because they are the stories that shaped you, the tales of your ancestors, and you are the culmination of them—you are the great conclusion to the tale."

"Then I wish it would just conclude," said Adam. "And if there's to be a happy ending, I want to know why my mother had to be killed and why my children have been kept from me."

"Your mother knew what she was doing when she risked her life; she was a martyr for the cause," said Merlin, putting back on his sunglasses, "and martyrs automatically become saints, do they not?" He lowered the glasses long enough to wink at Adam.

"I want answers, Merlin," Adam repeated, almost begging now.

Merlin simply turned and walked out of the room, shouting back, "You shall have them...soon."

Adam ran to the door of the tea room, too fast for Merlin to have passed through the lobby and out to the street before Adam reached the lobby, but already, the great wizard had vanished.

CHAPTER 4

ADAM WENT BACK up to the room, feeling more frustrated than earlier due to Merlin's inability ever to give him a straight answer, but at least he was glad to have seen the crazy wizard again after eighteen years. That must mean that some conclusion to their prolonged agony was coming—or, at least, so Adam hoped.

Exhausted, Adam removed his shoes and then collapsed upon the bed, staring up at the ceiling and wondering why Merlin had appeared only to him and not to Anne or Devin. But he only wondered for a moment before the door opened and both Anne and Devin entered.

"Were you napping?" Anne asked when he turned his head toward her.

"No," he said. "How was Agatha Christie's room?"

"It was a hotel room," said Devin.

But Anne said, "Oh, I loved it. I could just imagine her sitting there and writing *Murder on the Orient Express*. It made me want to go back and read all of her books again."

"I'm going to go back to my room and rest a while," said Devin, "but when do you think you want to go out for supper?"

"Oh, not too early," said Anne. "We just had tea and it's almost five."

"How about eight?" asked Devin, who was used to eating at six o'clock in the States but had grown accustomed to later English ways.

"Eight is fine," said Adam. "Maybe I can take a nap then. I don't think any of us got much sleep last night."

"I don't want to sit around the room for three hours while you sleep," Anne protested. "I'll go to the spa. I've been dying to try one of those Turkish baths. I bet it'll be relaxing, and if I stay here and try to sleep, I know I'll just worry."

"You definitely should try a Turkish bath," Devin told Anne. "You deserve it."

Anne smiled at Devin and then looked at Adam, who simply shrugged and said, "Well, if you want to, go ahead. You wouldn't get me in a Turkish bath, but enjoy yourself."

"Adam, you just need to be more adventurous," Anne replied. "I know you're worried about the children, but we haven't gone anywhere in so long. I want to try to enjoy Istanbul."

"And I want you to enjoy it," said Adam. "I just need a nap is all, and then we can enjoy a good meal."

"And decide what we'll do tomorrow, I hope," said Devin. "I'd love to go see some of the museums, especially the Chora Museum, which is said to have wonderful mosaics, and there's also a museum with pieces from the old Byzantine palaces."

"And I want to go see the Dolmabahce Palace," Anne added.

"Okay," said Adam. "Whatever you two want."

"We better let Grumpy sleep," Anne said to Devin.

"I know when I'm not wanted," laughed Devin. "I'll come knock on your door at eight o'clock."

"Sounds good," said Adam, feeling he'd been rude, but knowing Devin wouldn't think anything of it.

A minute after Devin left, Anne was ready to go downstairs for her Turkish bath and spa treatment. Adam had it on the tip of his tongue to tell her about his encounter with Merlin, but he did not want to worry or upset her when she was so looking forward to some "me" time. And he knew that although Merlin had said all would be well, news of his presence would just make Anne anxious, like he was already, and the wizard's appearance had not changed anything. After all, they still didn't know where their children were, or what Gwenhwyvach's movements might be.

So Adam said nothing about it, and once Anne was out the door, he rolled over and went to sleep, half-remembering how Merlin had told him he must love story and half-expecting that he would have another dream about some other medieval person he had thought only a legend.

Adam woke to the sound of Anne reentering the room, looking a bit dazed. He was only half-awake, but he could see how sleepy she looked.

Alarmed, he quickly sat up and asked, "Are you all right?"

"Oh, yes," she said, walking over to the bed and sitting down beside him. "I don't think I've ever felt this all right. I just feel so relaxed. Those masseuses are amazing."

"Better than me?" Adam could not help asking, reaching over to rub her shoulders. He realized a good long nap had been exactly what he had needed. Now he felt incredibly relaxed and very attracted to his beautiful wife.

But when he nibbled on her neck, Anne only said, "Adam, it's quarter to eight. We better get ready before Devin comes knocking."

"We have fifteen minutes," he protested.

"Not now, Adam," she said, standing up. "Later, okay?"

"Promise?" he asked. It had been several days since they had been intimate—neither being in the mood from worrying about coming to Istanbul and their sons.

"Sure," she said. "But all that relaxing has made me hungry, and I better fix my makeup before we go out for dinner."

As Anne went into the bathroom, Adam got up from the bed and tried to brush out the wrinkles from his shirt.

"Change your clothes!" Anne called, as if she could see him through the wall.

He thought the jeans and T-shirt he'd been wearing looked fine, but he knew better than to argue with her. She liked him to get dressed up in a dress shirt, pants, and suit coat when they went out; she always told him he looked "GQ sexy" when he did, and he knew if he wanted to get what he wanted later, he'd better obey now.

Prompt as always, Devin knocked on the door as Adam was buttoning up his shirt. Adam let him in and they discussed where to go for dinner while Anne finished up in the bathroom. Devin had been busy researching the best restaurants in Istanbul and had a cab already waiting to take them to one; they all agreed they wanted authentic Turkish food. Once they were in the cab, the driver told them he knew the perfect place and brought them to what they suspected must be his brother or cousin's restaurant. It was small but not overly crowded, and the patient waiter spoke English and explained everything on the menu to them. They still weren't sure exactly what they ate, but they all enjoyed it.

But no matter how good the food was, all through the meal, Adam kept thinking about his earlier meeting with Merlin. He didn't feel a public restaurant would be the place to introduce the topic, and he still feared Anne would only start worrying more if he told her he'd seen Merlin—after all, nothing more might happen for days the way Merlin operated.

On the way back to the hotel in the cab, Anne said, "Well, until Merlin tells us what to do, I guess we should just keep enjoying ourselves, so let's go sightseeing again tomorrow."

Adam did not object; his nap and a good meal had made him feel more hopeful that soon they would have answers for why they had been summoned to this bustling ancient city.

The next morning after a big breakfast at the hotel, they embarked for the Chora Museum, the Dolmabahce Palace, the Suleiman Mosque, and whatever else Anne and Devin had planned. Adam simply followed along. Everywhere they went, Devin rattled on about Byzantine history until Adam's head swam with stories of palace intrigue and crusader invasions and the names of more emperors than England ever had kings and queens. Being American, it was all Adam could do to remember most of the U.S. Presidents, so he didn't even try to keep straight all the Alexioses and Johns and Constantines and Irenes and Annas and Theodoras of Byzantine history. Anne declared that the Turks must be the most stylish people in the world, for Turkey was where East met West and she loved every piece of clothing, every carpet, every piece of art or jewelry she saw until finally she said the one thing Adam had most dreaded hearing: "I want to go to the Grand Bazaar."

Then Adam knew it was all over. Museums were bad enough, but to have to follow her on a shopping trip! How could he get out of it? Before he could even think what to say, Anne added, "Adam, don't think of going back to the hotel, either. We're strangers in a strange land, so I need my hero to protect me."

"More likely," he said, "you need me to carry the shopping bags."

"Oh, I intend to buy enough that it will have to be shipped home," she replied, laughing.

Devin was not a shopper, but he agreed to tag along, having heard that the Grand Bazaar had something for everyone...and that had to include some interesting books.

But none of them could have imagined the extensive size of the Grand Bazaar until they had reached it. Having expected some sort of open air flea market, Adam was amazed to discover the entire bazaar was covered by actual roofs with several entrances. In all, as Devin explained by summarizing the guidebook, the bazaar covered an area of sixty-one streets and more than 3,000 shops, and it was visited daily by over a quarter of a million people—which really wasn't such a surprising number considering that Istanbul boasted 15 million inhabitants, plus tourists who were continually flocking to it. The bazaar had begun about 1455 when Sultan Mehmet II, after conquering Constantinople and making it his new capital, built an edifice for the trading of textiles, and the bazaar had expanded from there. In the late seventeenth century, to prevent spreading fire, vaults were built over the streets to cover it. The result was more like an ancient shopping mall than an open-air market, but no shopping mall on the planet could compete for charm or uniqueness with Istanbul's Grand Bazaar.

For the first hour, Adam's dread of shopping actually dissipated as he felt inside himself the same "Oohs" and "Aahs" that he heard coming from Anne's mouth, and even Devin could not help saying, "This is amazing!"

Truly, the Grand Bazaar contained everything imaginable that anyone could possibly desire.

"I just want to bring it all home with me!" declared Anne. "Why don't we have an Oriental Room at Delaney Castle when they were so popular with the Victorians? You would have thought one of the earls or countesses would have designed one."

"They left it for the current Countess Delaney to do," Devin replied.

"Oh, indeed, I intend to then," said Anne. "I hope your credit card is ready for some action, your lordship."

"Buy whatever you like," said Adam, "provided it can be shipped home."

And so Anne did. She bought an ottoman—after all, what could be more suitable for an Oriental room? She bought beaded curtains. She bought wall hangings. She bought knick-knacks of all sorts, and she bought half-a-dozen beautiful, silk Turkish carpets that ran upwards of thousands of dollars each.

"I've been wanting to remodel the west wing for years," she said, "and there are several rooms we could redecorate. What fun it will be to have company over to see it."

Adam marveled that she could so easily forget about their sons in her decorating enthusiasm—or was she simply trying to distract herself from worrying? He had no interest in redecorating himself. What was the point? They never had anyone over. They barely had friends. They went to court once a year so they would not feel totally isolated, and occasionally, they went away to Scotland or to Brighton or Cornwall, or on a weekend excursion when they were invited by acquaintances, but they rarely entertained, and when they did, they only had small dinner parties with less than a dozen people, and even then, it was more because they felt they must make an effort to be sociable and reciprocate to those who had invited them in the past, rather than allowing their sons' absence to weigh them down constantly. Nothing, however, ever prepared them for the inevitable questions about their sons' disappearance once they got to know people, and that had only made them avoid guests as much as possible. As a result, they had never developed any close friendships save with Devin.

Yet Adam saw that this trip was doing Anne good. He wished years ago they had gone somewhere outside of Britain to help ease some of her pain; he knew how much she hurt over the boys' absence; she had to be just trying to compensate for her anxiety now with all her shopping enthusiasm. He wished he knew how to distract himself from the anxiety that he knew would never leave him until he was reunited with his sons—and knowing that could happen at any moment only made the anxiety worse; when he thought about it, it was sometimes all he could do not to feel that he was about to hyperventilate.

As they made their way through the bazaar, Adam and Devin never left Anne's sight from fear they would get lost or separated, although they all felt perfectly safe among the honest and friendly Turkish people, who continually spoke to them in English and tried to please them, while, of course, also wanting to sell them everything possible at "bargain prices." Anyone with less money might have felt harassed by the overzealous shopkeepers, but Anne simply handed over her credit card to each merchant and was met with many smiling faces.

She was in one shop, haggling over a pair of bookends, when Devin drew Adam's attention to several soldier figurines intended to represent the Trojan War.

"I had almost forgotten that Troy is in Turkey," said Devin. "You know, the site of the Trojan War in Homer's *Iliad*."

Adam did know because he had seen the movie *Troy*, starring Brad Pitt, when it had come out several years earlier, but he had no knowledge about Troy beyond that.

"I'm surprised I didn't think about Troy being in Turkey first thing when we came here," said Devin, "although the Middle Ages are more my area of interest than ancient Greece."

"Then why are you interested in Troy?" Adam asked, against his better judgment, because he knew Devin would give him an earful in reply.

"Adam, I'm sure I've told you before," said Devin. "Troy is largely where it all began for us."

"For us? What do you mean? Not another genealogy lesson, I hope."

Devin laughed. "I'm afraid so. After all, if we're descended from King Arthur, we're descended from the ancient Trojans. You know King Arthur was descended from Brutus, for whom Britain was reputedly named. Well, Brutus was the great-grandson of Aeneas, ancestor of the Romans, and one of the few Trojans who escaped when Troy was conquered. So you might say that we are Trojan to some degree."

"Interesting," said Adam. "I do remember something about that from one of the dreams I had—something about Brutus slaying giants, who were descendants of Avallach, when he came to Britain."

"Yes," said Devin. "King Arthur is descended from both Brutus and Avallach through different lines, if I remember correctly."

"Then do you think," asked Adam, "that Merlin wanted us to come to Turkey so we would go to Troy? Aren't there ruins of it still?"

"No," said Devin. "I mean, yes, you can visit Troy's ruins, I believe, but I don't think Troy is that significant that we should expect to meet Merlin there. I mean, the invitation said to come to Istanbul. If we were to go to Troy, wouldn't he have told us so? And the magic rings don't have a Trojan connection. They were passed along through Avallach and the line of Avalon, right?"

This question made Adam recall his surprise yesterday when he had learned from Merlin that there had been a third magical ring—one that belonged to Lilith. He was just about to tell Devin about his meeting with Merlin when he heard Anne exclaim, "Oh, that's beautiful! I must have it!"

Adam turned to see that his wife had apparently decided against the bookends since the shopkeeper was putting them back. Instead, she was now standing in front of a beautiful Oriental carpet hanging against the wall.

"You just bought half a dozen rugs," laughed Adam, going up to her.

"This one is kind of small, isn't it?" asked Devin. The carpet couldn't have been more than eight feet long or three feet wide.

"But look at the colors and the pattern in it," she exclaimed. "Look at the green and the gold. The colors are so vibrant."

"Very old rug," said the shopkeeper, struggling to find the proper English words. "It very, very special."

"Yes, I can see it's special," said Anne.

"How old is it?" Adam asked.

"Very, very old—from before Turkey; it from, how do you say the middle history time in English."

"The medieval period?" Devin corrected.

"Yes," the shopkeeper said, shaking his head. "It from the medieval time."

"It can't be that old," said Devin. "No rug would hold up that long."

"This very special rug," said the shopkeeper. "It belong to kings, and legend says it once had Holy Spear of Prophet Jesus wrapped in it. Spear was magical so made rug well-preserved, made rug stay bright colors all these years."

"The Holy Spear of the Prophet Jesus?" muttered Adam. "Could it...? No, it's not...." Then he asked the shopkeeper, "How did it get here?"

But before the shopkeeper could answer, Anne asked, "What is the pattern on it?"

"It is Garden of Paradise," said the shopkeeper. "Garden of Eden."

"The Garden of Eden," muttered Adam, wondering.

"Very popular rug theme," said the shopkeeper. "Very beautiful, yes?"

"Oh, I absolutely love it," said Anne. "I just have to have it."

"You said the Garden of Eden was a popular theme?" Adam asked.

"Yes, sir. Many rugs have Tree of Life or paradise design—very popular for Turkish rugs. Very popular with West, too, because of Bible theme, yes?"

"Yes," said Anne. "We have paradise and the Garden of Eden in our Bible. How much?"

Adam let her bargain with the salesman, not intruding, but instead, continuing to stare at the rug. It was a striking rug, though Adam wasn't quite sure why it appealed to him so much. The salesman had said the Garden of Eden pattern was very popular, so he had probably just seen it somewhere before.

After a few minutes, the shopkeeper and Anne had settled on a price and she gave him her credit card.

"Will you ship it home for us?" she asked.

"Uh, no, not this size. Too small," he replied.

"Too small?" Anne repeated, wanting to make sure she understood.

"Yes," said the shopkeeper. "Too expensive to ship when so small."

"Well, the other rugs you bought were larger," Devin told Anne.

"How will we get it home then?" asked Anne. "It won't fit in my suitcase."

"I have bag," said the shopkeeper. He went to the back of the shop and returned with what looked to be a duffel bag. He showed her how to roll the rug into it. "Very old. Very antique rug. Must be careful with it. No fold it, only roll it. I have given you very good deal," he said. "Rug priceless, but I must sell it so I eat, so what can I do?"

Anne laughed. She did not know whether or not she had really received a good deal, but it didn't matter. She and Adam were worth tens of millions of British pounds. They could never spend all their fortune—and it brought them little happiness since they had no children to leave it to. Indeed, she and Adam had decided to leave the estate and their money to charity if their children should not return, although they would rather not think about that.

The rug was soon inside the bag. The shopkeeper thanked them profusely, and then Adam, Anne, and Devin made their way out of the shop, admitting they were now exhausted and ready to go back to the hotel to rest for a little while until dinnertime.

The streets were packed with people when they emerged from the bazaar. When they could not find a cab near the bazaar exit, they decided they would walk and hail a cab when they saw one. Only, they ended up walking down a tightly-packed street so crowded with people that no vehicle could get through. Adam tried to forge ahead, his hand in Anne's as she walked behind him, clutching the bag with the carpet in the other. Devin tried his best to stay right behind them. Fortunately, he was wearing a light-colored jacket while almost everyone else in the crowd was dressed in black and other dark colors, so Anne could easily spot Devin whenever she looked back.

Despite the crowd, the three of them did not feel threatened or in danger, and while they often had to make a dash into an empty hole in the crowd to move forward, there was no real jostling, pushing, or jerking for the first several minutes of their foray through the stream of tourists and Istanbul natives.

That is, no jerking until Anne felt the bag in her hand being jerked away from her.

She screamed, letting go of Adam's arm so she could grab the bag's handle with both hands. Then she looked behind her to see who was trying to rob her, but there was no one there. People walked past her, ignoring her, none of them looking suspicious or guilty, although one old woman looked like she thought Anne might be a bit crazy for screaming.

"What's wrong?" Adam asked, turning and protectively putting his arm around her.

"Devin, did someone try to grab my bag?" Anne asked since Devin had been right behind her.

"No," said Devin. "I would have noticed if they did."

But before Devin even finished speaking, Anne felt the bag jerk again, and this time, Devin saw it move.

"What the—?" said Devin.

"What is it?" asked Adam, not having seen it move.

"My bag—it—there it goes again!" said Anne. This time all three of them saw it jerk forward.

"Something's in there," said Devin.

"Oh!" said Anne, feeling nervous as it jerked again.

"Maybe it's a bird or a mouse," said Devin. "It might have sneaked into the bag or carpet when we weren't looking.

"Maybe," said Adam. "Let's get out of the crowd and we'll open it up."

"Here, you take it," said Anne, not being fond of mice, and she handed the bag to her husband.

Adam led the way sideways through the crowd into a doorway. The moment they were free of the congested street, the bag started jerking furiously in both directions.

"I'm afraid to open it," Anne remarked, stepping back a bit to stay clear of whatever might come flying or scrambling out of the bag.

Meanwhile, Adam set it on the ground and said, "Devin, you unzip it while I hold it still."

Devin gingerly grabbed the zipper and slowly started to slide it open.

"Be careful," said Anne. "What if it's a snake?"

But when Devin had the bag unzipped, nothing popped out its head. So he carefully pulled the sides back a bit, but still nothing emerged.

"I don't want to reach in there," said Devin.

"Neither do I!" exclaimed Anne.

Adam now slowly flipped the bag upside down. Nothing happened. He shook it while making sure the carpet didn't fall out. Again nothing.

"Well, I don't know," he said. "Whatever it was is either dead or too scared to move now."

He flipped the bag right side up and zipped it again.

"That's so weird," said Anne, taking Adam's hand as he started back out into the crowd, clutching the bag with his other hand.

Devin didn't know what to think, but he didn't want to be separated from his friends so he quickly followed right behind them.

The crowd surged about them as they continued down the street. The bag's jerking seemed to have stopped, but Devin couldn't keep his eyes off the bag, and Anne felt scared of it, even though Adam was now carrying it.

Eventually, they got out of the crowded street and made their way to a square. Devin spotted the metro and wanted to take it, but Adam forged ahead, walking past the entrance. Finally, Anne spotted a taxi and pointed it out to Adam, who hailed it. In another minute, the three of them were on their way back to the hotel inside the cab. They all were nervous and kept looking at the bag, while trying to be polite to the driver, who once he heard Adam and Devin were Americans, wanted to tell them all about his sister, who lived in Washington, D.C., and his cousin, who was attending the University of Michigan.

"It's a small world," Anne told the cab driver. "We're all connected in some way."

Once they arrived at the hotel, they stepped out of the cab and Adam paid the driver. Then, they hadn't walked two steps before the carpet bag again jerked in Adam's hand, but this time, it jerked quite wildly, like a dog on a leash madly trying to get loose and run away.

"Did you see that?" Adam couldn't help shouting.

"I sure did," said Devin.

"Let's go up to the room and then empty the bag," said Adam.

"No, I don't want a rat or a snake in our room," said Anne.

"Well, then bring it up to my room," said Devin.

"No, open it here," said Anne, but Adam said, "No, there's something strange about this—some sort of mystery. Let's do it in private."

Anne didn't like the idea, but Adam was already walking into the hotel, so she quickly followed him, with Devin bringing up the rear.

They swiftly walked through the hotel lobby, hoping the bag would not continue to act up and cause the concierge to stop them because he thought they were trying to sneak in a pet. The bag actually behaved itself as they entered the elevator, rode it up to the fifth floor, and then walked down the hall to Devin's room.

Once they were inside his room, Devin closed the door and Adam set the bag on the bed.

"I'm scared," Anne confessed, but Adam showed no fear as he undid the zipper. Still cautious, however, he tipped over the bag and shook it. When nothing fell out, he grabbed its side, rather than reach into it, and then he pushed the carpet out of the bag. The carpet landed on the bed, still rolled up.

Adam now felt around the outside of the bag, then tipped it over, and finally turned it inside out.

"Nothing," he said.

"It must be a mouse," said Anne. "It must be rolled up in the carpet."

They all stepped back from the bed, staring hard at the carpet. After several seconds, Devin said, heading toward the bathroom, "I'll get something to unroll it with."

"Get something long like a broom or a stick," said Adam.

But the longest thing they could find in the room was a coat hanger, until Adam picked up the desk chair and poked the carpet with the chair leg. Then he inserted the chair leg into the carpet and tried to unfurl it.

Instantly, the carpet moved, sliding up the chair leg so fast that Adam let go of it and jumped back in fright. The chair should have fallen, but the carpet was holding it up in the air, and thrashing it about as if it were a midget up against Andre the Giant in a wrestling match. After a few seconds of this unbelievable display, the chair went crashing to the floor.

Anne screamed and ran toward the window to avoid being hit. Adam jumped in front of her to protect her from he knew not what.

In flinging the chair, the carpet had started to unfurl itself, and as it did so, it grew to more than twice the size it had been in the bazaar. Then slowly, it began to float upward until Devin exclaimed, "Why, it's a magic carpet! A flying carpet, like in *The Arabian Nights*. There's nothing in it to scare us. It's just magic."

"Of course!" Anne said, now laughing. "It's so obvious."

"But how do we control it?" asked Adam. "And is it good magic or black magic?"

Before anyone could reply, the carpet went flying across the room toward Anne, who still stood by the window.

She shrieked when the carpet came toward her, but Adam protectively pushed her to the floor, landing on top of her as the carpet went flying straight at the window, hitting the glass, and then rebounding and dropping to the floor.

"What the hell is it doing?" cried Anne as Adam helped her up. "Is it trying to kill us?"

The carpet now slowly rose and floated back toward the bed and then up against the wall. Suddenly, like a flash of lightning, as if it had only wanted to get a running start, it flew across the room and hit the window again.

"I think it's trying to escape!" shouted Devin.

"It wants to break the window," Adam agreed.

"But why?" asked Anne as the carpet kept flying into the window, backing up, and then ramming against it again.

"It's cloth; it can't break a window," said Adam.

The carpet now spun sideways, curled itself back up, and with its corner fringe, grabbed the room's reading lamp.

Before any of them knew what to expect, the carpet carried the lamp across the room and sent it hurling into the window. In a second, the glass shattered, leaving a wide opening.

"Oh, my God!" screamed Anne. "It's crazy."

They waited a second for the carpet to fly out the window and disappear, but instead, it floated back into the room, landing on the floor beside the bed.

"Is it done now?" asked Devin. "What does it want?"

At that moment, there was a knock on the door.

"Open up! Management!" someone shouted.

"Shit!" said Adam. "Now we're in trouble. No one will believe us that the carpet broke the window."

"We can afford to pay for the window," said Anne, "but we'll probably be thrown out of the hotel."

"What do I tell them?" asked Devin, hesitating to answer the door.

"It's moving again," said Anne, seeing the carpet slowly start to hover above the floor.

"Sir, open up, please! We have a report of a disturbance in your room," said the manager, still pounding on the door.

"Just a minute. I'm in the bathroom!" shouted Devin.

"Sir, if you don't open the door, I will use my key to come in."

Devin turned away from the door, which he had been facing, to look at Adam and Anne for advice. He was surprised to see they had stepped over to the carpet, which was still floating a couple of inches above the floor.

"I think it wants us to ride it," said Anne. Devin could scarcely believe it when he saw Adam and Anne, by instinct rather than reason, step onto the carpet.

"That's it, sir! I'm coming in!" shouted the hotel manager.

"Hurry, Devin! Come on," said Adam as the carpet slowly started to ascend.

The jingling of a key could be heard. Then the doorknob turned.

In desperation, Devin grabbed Adam's outstretched hand and jumped onto the carpet as the manager broke into the room. By the time the man saw them, Devin, Adam, and Anne were all seated on the carpet and floating four feet above the floor.

For a second, the manager stood staring at them, as if he were seeing a ghost—or a twelve-hundred-year-old magic carpet levitating with three people seated on it.

"Goodbye!" shouted Anne, waving, and then the carpet carried them all out the open window as the manager attempted to shout, "Stop!" but his throat was too constricted with wonder to say anything.

Several reports were made that day to the Turkish authorities about a magic carpet soaring over Istanbul. It was spotted over the Mosque of Suleiman, and in front of the Spice Bazaar; it was seen circling Ataturk's yacht along the Bosphorus, and even flying through narrow streets about three or four stories above the ground. So many calls were made to the police and so many eyewitnesses claimed to have seen it that, if the story were true, a million people must have actually witnessed it. The city authorities, however, denied that a carpet had flown through the air, and the news stations dismissed it as some sort of stunt. A few newscasters speculated it might have been a drone sent by the Russians to spy on the city, or a type of bomb manufactured by terrorists, which, fortunately, had failed to explode. Several people claimed to have taken photographs of it, but none of them had captured anything but a whirling blur, no matter how sophisticated their cameras were.

"Isn't Istanbul beautiful?" asked Anne, as the sun began to set while she, Adam, and Devin circled the Galata Tower on the magic carpet.

"It is," said Devin. "I don't imagine anyone has ever seen Istanbul like this."

"I just wish I knew how to control this thing," said Adam. "We've been riding this carpet for over an hour now, but it just keeps flying about randomly."

"I think it just wants us to enjoy the ride," said Anne. "Isn't it amazing how gentle it is, even with its speed being a bit dizzying? I haven't felt in danger at all, and heights usually make me a little nervous."

"It is cramped, though," said Adam. "There's barely room for us to sit on it. And when is it going to let us land?"

"I'm almost afraid to land," said Devin. "All those people who have been staring and pointing at us are sure to mob us if we do. And I'm sure the police will have questions if they catch us."

"Do you think the carpet is intelligent?" asked Anne. "Can it take commands? Perhaps there's a magic word that controls it."

"It's probably not intelligent," said Devin, "but it's enchanted, no doubt. It could have a magic word."

And then Adam had his realization. "I've finally remembered," he said. "It's the magic carpet that Ogier rode upon when he left the land of Prester John. Remember how the shopkeeper said it had the Holy Spear wrapped in it? Well, if you remember from what I told you of my dream about Ogier the Dane so many years ago, Ogier gave the carpet to Haroun al-Rashid, whose son later wrapped the false Holy Lance in it, which Ogier brought to Constantinople. That's how the carpet got here—it must be the same carpet."

"That makes sense," said Anne.

"But how does that help us know how to control it?" asked Devin.

"My point," said Adam, "is that when Ogier left Prester John's land, he didn't know what to do; he didn't even know he was going to leave. The carpet just knew to take him to Baghdad, so maybe this carpet now knows to take us somewhere."

"But we've flown all over Istanbul, and now we're just circling a tower," Anne objected.

Just then they heard a whirring sound. When they looked to the right, they saw a military helicopter coming straight at them. While the government might deny the flying carpet's presence to the media, it was taking no chances and investigating.

"At least it's not a fighter jet," said Devin, though his stomach began to hurt at the sight.

But the words were barely out of Devin's mouth before the carpet decided it was time to leave Istanbul's airspace. It instantly shifted into full speed ahead and flew at a frightening pace north of the city and into the gathering darkness, its passengers struggling to lie down so they wouldn't be blown over. Then they grasped its edges to keep from falling off. They all prayed their breakneck journey would soon be over.

CHAPTER 5

"GRANDFATHER, WILL IT be much longer?" asked Lance. "I'm so tired of waiting."

"I don't think so," said Cedric. "I think by morning."

"We've waited so long," said Tristan, sitting up from where he had been lying on the floor reading. When he stood up a second later to walk to the window and look out, his full height of 6'3" was displayed, just half an inch shorter than his brother, who was already looking out the castle window at the sun setting over Romania's mountains.

"We've waited eighteen years—waited even when we were too young to know we were waiting," said Lance.

"Then you can wait another twenty-four hours," said Cedric from where he sat on the other side of the small room.

"Aren't you anxious, Grandfather?" asked Tristan.

"Yes, yes," he said. "Perhaps even more anxious than you, boys, for I know what good people your parents are, and I love them dearly, more so than I realized when last I saw them."

"I wish I understood why we've had to be separated from them all these years," said Tristan, turning to cross the room and sit beside his grandfather. "Other boys grow up with parents—I've read enough books to know that—to know our lives have been unnatural."

"'I am half sick of shadows,' said the Lady of Shalott," Lance quoted, still staring out the window. "I feel like the Lady of Shalott, even if I'm named after Lancelot, who made her realize she was sick of having no real involvement in life."

"All we know of life is from reading books," Tristan said, agreeing with his brother.

"You have read all those books," said Cedric, "so you will grow wise and knowledgeable and be prepared for what is to come—you have learned math and science and music and foreign languages, and perhaps most importantly, you have read of knights and their ladies, of ogres and giants, of sorceresses and fairies, so you will know all there is to know about these beings and be prepared for what is to come."

"But we've never even seen a fairy or a giant," protested Tristan.

"You have met my father, your great-grandfather, and you know him to be a supernatural being, and you will soon know more, for the time is almost here. Nor have you only read—you have trained— you have learned sword-fighting and gymnastics and studied weight-training and rowing and had the run of all the grounds here about while you rode horses and—"

"And acted like medieval knights in training," groaned Lance, "when most boys our age go to school and drive automobiles and I don't know all what else in the modern world considering all I know of it is derived from books and the newest books I've read were *The Chronicles of Narnia* and a few Arthurian novels that are even a couple of decades old and set in medieval times so they can hardly prepare us for the modern world."

"And what's wrong with being a medieval knight?" asked Tristan. "I'd like to see one of those race car drivers of the modern world beat me in a footrace or a wrestling match." And he rolled up his shirtsleeve to flex and admire his bicep.

"Oh, Tristan," said his brother, "we live in a small world, but there must be so much more beyond it. We are locked up in a tower, but beyond us lies the world—Camelot, as the Lady of Shalott came to know to her misfortune—I hope it isn't to ours when we have the same experience."

"I know the modern world is out there," said Tristan, "but that doesn't mean there's anything wrong with who we are, or that we won't learn to adapt when the time comes."

"There is nothing wrong with who you are at all," Cedric told them. "You are beautiful, golden boys—a veritable Adonis and Apollo." He stood and walked over to muss Lance's hair, something he could not resist, for the boys were so beautiful, so intelligent, so good, and he adored them so much that it was almost impossible for him to believe they were his grandsons. "But now I must see about our supper. You boys try to be patient. It's almost dark and Merlin told me the time won't be long now."

"Merlin!" scoffed Lance. "Sometimes I wonder whether he even exists."

"Why doesn't he show himself to us?" demanded Tristan, practically sprinting across the room. "Why are you the only one he ever appears to?"

"*Why?* Why if I knew that, I would know a great many things," laughed Cedric, melancholy by nature but finding joy in his grandsons' youth. "All I can do is remind you to be patient. Go back to your books now and I'll call you down when it's time to eat."

"It's almost dark," said Lance to his brother as their grandfather departed. "We won't be able to see them approaching if they come now anyway."

"And on a magic flying carpet," said Tristan, laughing. "Grandfather must think we were born yesterday to believe they would arrive in such a way!"

Indeed, Cedric Harker thought, overhearing the boys' words as he headed downstairs, *sometimes I wonder how I can believe such things myself.* But for most of his life, he had acted on faith that all the old legends were true until that fatal day, eighteen years ago, when he had been forced to hide himself away from the world.

He had last seen his daughter and Adam when he had left for Seattle with Adam's mother, Mary Morgan, to collect one of Melusine's rings before it could fall into Gwenhwyvach's hands, but Gwenhwyvach had thwarted them, taken the ring from Mary, and hurled her over the Space Needle's observation deck. Cedric had then hid in the Space Needle in fear of Gwenhwyvach returning to destroy him, or the police finding him and charging him with Mary's murder. As Cedric later learned from Merlin, Adam and Anne had been made aware of Mary's death, but Merlin had never told Adam and Anne what had become of him; they had assumed Gwenhwyvach had killed him as well—what else could they think, though his body had never been found? But Merlin had told Cedric that it was best they keep his location a secret for his own protection and that of his grandsons.

Cedric Harker knew himself not to be a good man. He had arranged his father's death so he could have his inheritance early. He had manipulated his best friend and even committed adultery with his best friend's wife, and he had been intent upon using his daughter's husband and family to carry out his own desire for power. The only real streak of goodness in Cedric during the first forty-plus years of his life had been that he loved his daughter.

But when, in the darkness of night, Cedric had emerged from the Space Needle after witnessing Mary's murder, he had experienced the shock of his life—as if Gwenhwyvach's presence had not been shocking enough. Nothing could have prepared him for seeing his father standing before him, not having aged a day, though Cedric had thought him dead for decades.

The sight had caused Cedric to faint, believing he had completely lost his mind. But his father had caught him in his arms before his head hit the cement.

The next thing Cedric knew, he had woken inside a decrepit castle—it would be several weeks before he even understood how he had arrived there or that he was in Eastern Europe, and the reasons for his presence there. Those reasons his father had told him when he regained consciousness and his health had recovered, and now those reasons were soon to be revealed to Cedric's daughter, Anne, her husband Adam, and Adam's cousin Devin. Those reasons even Cedric's own grandchildren did not know, save one—that their grandfather had come to the castle to be their guardian.

The last thing Cedric had expected, after the horrible betrayal he had attempted against Mary Morgan and all of Adam's family, only to be thwarted in his purposes by Gwenhwyvach, was to become the guardian of his missing grandchildren—to have no one less than Merlin and his own father, Quincey Harker, entrust him—who had already proven himself a traitor to his own family—with this most delicate task in one of the most remote places in the civilized world.

And now, just a couple of days ago, Merlin had appeared to tell him the time had finally come when all would be revealed, and while

Cedric felt he should feel great relief, he also felt great fear, for he had no doubt that Gwenhwyvach would now return, again attempting to obtain complete control over, if not the destruction of, the human race. After all, the evil woman had both of Melusine's rings, so Cedric could not imagine why she had waited so long to wreak her vengeance on Adam and Eve's descendants. But what Cedric feared most was that Adam and Anne would now know how he had sought to betray them all those years ago. Caring for his grandsons all this time since could not compensate for such a crime against his loved ones. In truth, being guardian to his grandchildren had, in some ways, been the worst possible way to punish him because he knew he was unworthy of the boys' love and affection, yet they had lavished it upon him, having no one else except for their great-grandfather, Quincey, who occasionally visited.

It had been a difficult existence. With Merlin's occasional guidance, Cedric had raised his grandsons to be the most strapping, physically perfect specimens he could, and he had equally cultivated their minds, teaching them history, geography, literature, science, mathematics, and all they would need, not only to function in the outside world, but to achieve graduate level degrees at ivy league schools if they so wished. Their education and wellbeing had been his sole purpose these past eighteen years, but ironically, it had all seemed to have little purpose since they never ventured more than a few acres from the tumbling near-ruin of this castle in Romania, a castle that would send chills up Cedric's spine whenever he thought about its origins. Fortunately, its history and even the very reason why they resided here, had all been kept from Lance and Tristan.

"It won't be long now, my son," said Quincey Harker, making Cedric jump when he entered the kitchen.

"Why must you always scare me?" demanded Cedric, once he recovered from the surprise of seeing his father. "Don't I have enough gray hair already? What's left of my hair—that is."

Cedric was not much past sixty, yet his hair had turned completely white after the great shocks he had experienced at the Space Needle— he could scarcely believe how he had aged when he had first looked at himself in the mirror after that incident, and since then, much of his hair had fallen out, although the love of his grandsons had helped to rejuvenate him and prevent the aging process from growing worse. No doubt, had he kept reliving those events, they would have debilitated him into a feeble old man, decades beyond his true years, but his need to focus on his grandsons' needs had kept him active and well.

"After you tried to murder me years ago," laughed Quincey Harker, "I think I'm allowed to give you a little fright now and then."

Cedric looked uncomfortable at the reminder of the past.

"Don't worry," said Quincey, putting his hand on his son's shoulder. "We all make mistakes. God knows I've made mine. You know I long ago forgave you. You were a different person back then. You've grown a lot in the years you've been raising these boys. If I had lavished the affection on you that you've given them, things might have been a lot different for both of us."

Quincey then gave Cedric a long hug before saying, "I imagine the boys must be anxious?"

"Yes, they know their parents are finally coming."

"And you?"

"I'm terrified," said Cedric. "But I'm glad you're here. I was wondering whether you would come."

"I'm glad you still have a healthy dose of guilt," said Quincey, "but once you are forgiven by Adam and Anne, all will be well."

"I hope so," said Cedric.

"It will be," said Quincey. "If I could forgive you, certainly they can."

Forgiveness was the most Cedric could ask for, the greatest thing he hoped for since he remained doubtful that anything beyond forgiveness could be achieved—certainly not happiness for any of them, despite what Merlin or Quincey might think. Cedric had seen Gwenhwyvach's power, been in her presence, and sensed the full extent of her evil. As a result, he did not believe any power on earth—not Merlin, not his father, not anyone or anything save God Himself—if He existed—could stop her, and if God did exist and Gwenhwyvach had in her first incarnation been Lilith, Adam's wife, then why had God not stopped her at the dawn of time? Cedric was certain Gwenhwyvach would succeed in killing them all before he ever had an answer to the question of why God permitted evil. He had long ago decided it was unanswerable.

CHAPTER 6

IT HAD BEEN a long night and, at first, a frightening one, for while Adam, Anne, and Devin had flown over Istanbul on the magic carpet, they had moved at a slow and steady pace, but as the sun had dropped beyond the horizon, the carpet had picked up speed, and they had been forced to lie down on the carpet with their hands grasping the carpet's edge, their heads looking over it, just to hold on as it whizzed through the air. For a few minutes, they had been certain they would fall off, but the carpet had rolled itself up and over them to protect them and keep them warm—it seemed to have the uncanny ability to grow in length and width at will, and then shrink back so that they never knew whether or not they had a firm seat on it.

On this unreliable form of transportation, they continued to soar through the air, high above the coast of the Black Sea, then over mountains and valleys, villages and rivers. Once it had grown dark, the moonlight was not bright enough for them to know just how frighteningly high up they were or how truly dangerous their ride could be.

"Where are we going?" Anne had asked, but neither Adam nor Devin could begin to guess.

"I hope it's not Siberia," Adam had remarked, but Devin told him they were not heading in that direction. "We're definitely going north, but Siberia would be northeast, and I think we're going more northwest." A statement that was confirmed when the sun appeared to be rising on their right and slightly behind them.

Not long after, they found themselves clearly able to see the countryside below in the early morning light. They saw fields and trees below, peasants, cows, and little cottages, and then a chain of small hills or mountains.

They were so busy looking over the carpet's edge at all below them that had the carpet not come to a stop, they would likely have banged their heads into the castle's wall, but the carpet stopped in mid-air about a hundred feet from the castle. Then the travelers' exclamations of "Why are we stopping?" were followed by looking up to see they were floating in front of a great tower to a castle larger, and far older, than Delaney Castle, and clearly not built as a comfortable home, but rather, as a mountain fortification. Had it still been night, they would have felt intimidated by the imposing Gothic edifice, but in the morning light, its white walls almost sparkled and seemed like something out of a fairy tale.

"Where are we?" asked Anne.

"This place looks familiar," Devin said, trying to sit up on the carpet, "but I can't quite place it."

"I'm sure we'll soon find out," Adam replied. "The carpet must have a reason for bringing us here."

"But why did it stop?" Anne asked. "I hope to God it's not going to dump us now—we have to be fifty feet above the ground, and those cliffs don't look like a comfortable landing place."

As if the carpet had heard Anne, it now whizzed back into action. It began to circle the castle at a speed that nearly sent Devin tumbling off since he had tried to rise to a sitting position. Adam grabbed Devin just as his legs went over the carpet's side, and then Anne grabbed Devin's shirt and helped pull him back aboard the carpet. They were so involved in trying to rescue Devin that none of them paid attention to how the carpet circled around, slowly descending, until they found themselves hovering just a couple of feet over a terrace with a door that opened into the castle.

"I think the carpet wants us to get off," said Anne.

Adam hopped down onto the terrace; then he turned around to give Anne a hand as she stepped down, which prevented him from seeing the door to the terrace open, an event that surprised Anne so much that she tumbled into Adam while Devin crawled to the side of the carpet to disembark, too afraid to stand up on it since he had nearly fallen off once already.

Now, with the door fully open, Anne gasped, and as Adam turned around to see why, she said, "They—Adam—is it?"

They all felt the same astonishment. Two handsome, tall young men stepped forward. "They look just like you, Adam!" exclaimed Devin as his foot touched the terrace. And other than the young men being slightly taller than him, Adam had to agree.

"Mother? Father?" asked the slightly taller of the two boys.

"Tristan? Lance?" cried Anne, and before Adam could stop her or she even received a reply from them, she had run to her boys, somehow managing to encircle her arms around both of them while Devin and Adam stood speechless.

If his sons' presence after eighteen years was not shock enough for Adam, the next person he saw was. As for Anne, after a minute of embracing the boys in tears, she finally released them to say, "Adam, it's our sons." But before she turned toward Adam, she looked over Tristan's shoulder and let out a shriek. Quickly, Tristan grabbed her as she nearly fainted.

Adam was behind her in a moment, clutching her to him and demanding from the man standing behind his sons, "What kind of trick is this?"

And then Tristan and Lance stepped aside, realizing their grandfather was behind them.

"Anne, Adam," said Cedric, hesitating to come forward, yet longing to embrace his daughter, "it's so good to see you."

"Father?" said Anne, regaining her senses. "Is it really—you've aged, but—"

And then Adam could hold her no longer, for she was in her father's arms, asking, "How?" and exclaiming, "I'm so glad to see you!" Adam could not stop her—though he feared something was terribly wrong. But he found himself with Lance's arms wrapped around him from the front and Tristan's arms wrapped around him from the back. Both boys were overwhelmed by the reunion.

Devin stood amazed as he watched this emotional scene.

After a few seconds, Adam relaxed, sensing his sons' love for him and realizing all was well. Then he gave in to the hugs and returned them, and he even hugged his father-in-law, until his own tears flowed for the first time in years and he sobbed with utter relief.

"Where have you been?" Anne again asked Cedric at the exact same moment that Adam asked his boys the same question.

"We've always been here," said Lance.

"With grandfather," added Tristan.

Adam stepped back now to look at them in astonishment, not even knowing how to form his next question.

"Where exactly is *here*?" Devin asked for him.

"Romania—Transylvania," said Lance.

"There is much to explain," said Cedric, finally releasing his daughter from his embrace, "and I'm afraid I don't come off well in the telling of it, but I hope you will forgive me. It has all been for the good, though I did not realize it myself for a long time. Come inside. You must be starved, and we have a large breakfast ready."

They all walked to the castle door, but Devin paused, looking behind him, wondering what they were to do with the magic carpet. It had floated down to the terrace and simply lay there, content to know its mission had been accomplished. Shrugging, figuring the carpet had "parked" itself like a car, Devin followed the others inside. They all went down a hall, Anne running her fingers through Tristan's hair as they walked, and exclaiming how she couldn't believe how much the boys had grown, while Adam clung with his arm around Lance's shoulders, and Cedric was babbling with excitement about what they would all have for breakfast.

"But where have you been all these years?" Devin demanded, thinking the happy reunion was getting out of control as they entered the dining room. He was logical and methodical and more interested in answers than food.

"Oh, Devin," said Anne. "Let's eat first. We can wait to ask questions. I'm just too happy right now to care about the explanations."

Cedric quickly gestured for them all to sit around the table while he disappeared into an adjoining room. In another minute, he returned with a pushcart filled with dishes—scrambled eggs, French toast, waffles, pancakes, quiche, bacon, sausage, a pot of coffee, and a pitcher of orange juice. Once these were all set on the table, from beneath the cart he pulled out maple, blueberry, and apricot syrup; blackberry, grape, and strawberry jam; sour cream; salsa; butter; and cream and sugar.

"You must have known we were coming!" said Adam, laughing.

"We've been busy since last night getting ready because we didn't know how soon you would get here," Tristan explained.

"But how did you know we were coming?" asked Anne. "We didn't know ourselves. Did you see us arrive on that flying carpet? I never thought—"

"I've seen plenty of amazing things since parting with the two of you," said Cedric. "A flying carpet didn't surprise us much—Merlin told us you would be arriving that way."

"Merlin? You've spoken to him then?" asked Anne. "We haven't seen him since the day we found out that Adam's mother had died."

Adam now realized he had still not told Anne and Devin about his meeting with Merlin in the hotel's tea room, but it did not matter now. He was more interested in the discussion of his mother. "Cedric, were you—were you there when my mother...?"

He could not finish. Anne reached over to put her hand on his.

Cedric sat down finally, staring glumly at the table. "Yes, I was there," he said.

Adam could not speak.

"Will you tell us what happened?" Devin asked for his cousin.

"Gwenhwyvach killed her," said Cedric, a horrified look in his eyes as if he were experiencing it all again. "She threw her over the edge of the railing. She tried to make me do it, but I refused. But she got both of the—well, the rings from us."

Cedric was afraid he had just admitted that he'd still had the ring that had been in his family; he had told them Gwenhwyvach had stolen it before he went to Seattle when he had possessed it all that time, thinking he would get the other ring from Mary and then have control of both rings, but Gwenhwyvach had forced them to surrender both rings to her. Adam and Anne, however, thought nothing of Cedric's remark since they had thought Gwenhwyvach had already had the other ring anyway. And when Cedric realized they did not think him guilty, he hoped it meant that perhaps he would not have to admit that he had originally intended to betray them all before Gwenhwyvach had struck, and before his father had explained to him the error of his ways.

"I don't know why Gwenhwyvach hasn't used the rings yet," Cedric admitted, "since she has both of them now."

Adam now remembered again that there were actually three rings, but he held his tongue for a minute.

"But how did you come to be here with the children?" Anne asked her father. "How did you find them?"

"My father brought me here; Merlin had it all planned out."

"Your father!" exclaimed Anne. "But I thought he died in a car accident years ago."

"So did I," said Cedric, "but my father...you see, there are things I never told you about him—he had some strange powers, powers that scared me, and he...let's say he faked his death and survived the accident. Anyway, he told me I was to be caretaker of your sons, as a way to redeem myself."

"Redeem yourself?" Anne asked.

"Yes. Redeem myself," said Cedric, accepting now that if he were going to confess all, now was the time and he might as well get it over with quickly. Even though he thought he might keep it all secret, he knew that was not what his father or Merlin would want, and he knew his guilt would also continue to haunt him until he confessed. "You knew I was on the wrong side through all this—born of Gwenhwyvach's line—but what you didn't know is that even when I went to Seattle with Mary, I intended to steal the other ring from her. I lied to you about the ring in my possession being stolen. I had it all along. I thought if I could get the other ring from Mary, I could be all powerful, and then maybe I could somehow control Gwenhwyvach, make her do what I wanted, but...well, she was more powerful than I ever imagined. I...I don't know why I'm of an evil nature, but—"

"Grandfather!" explained the twins simultaneously. "You're not evil!"

"He's been the best grandfather," Tristan told his parents.

"We owe everything we are to him," Lance added.

"Ah, but you don't know my faults, boys," said Cedric, "because I've tried to make up for them all these years by raising you."

"It looks like you've done a good job," said Adam, feeling grateful and, as a result, also forgiving. "Cedric, whatever you did...well, Gwenhwyvach would have tried to kill my mother regardless. I can't blame you for her death. I've often wondered what part, if any, you played in her death, but it was so long ago now, and to know you've raised my sons, although I don't understand why Merlin entrusted you with the task, and to see them safe and healthy, well, I can't be angry with you."

"Thank you," said Cedric, relieved, but still embarrassed by his past guilt. "I...I have changed. I love the boys. I'd do anything for them or for any of you."

"But why did you raise them? Why did Merlin want that?" asked Anne.

"He didn't think Gwenhwyvach would come looking for me, and there were things I didn't know about my family's past, things my father had not told me—things connected to this castle. I still don't know how it all fits together or what it will have to do with trying to defeat Gwenhwyvach, but this castle is tied up in the family history. That's why we're here, I imagine. What I really don't understand is why after all these years, Gwenhwyvach has not used the rings to bring about her reign of terror."

"Because," said Adam, feeling now was the time to inform the others, "there are actually three rings!"

"Three rings?" said Anne. "No one ever told us that."

"Merlin did," said Adam. "He told me. I saw him in Istanbul; I just—you were having so much fun seeing the sights that I didn't want to upset you by mentioning it because I knew then you would start worrying about the boys, and he didn't say anything to make me feel at ease, so I decided to wait, but he did show up, and he told me there are three rings."

"But where is the third one then?" asked Devin.

"On Merlin's finger," Adam said.

"Three rings," muttered Cedric. "But I thought they were Adam and Eve's wedding rings, so why would—"

"Lilith!" exclaimed Devin. "She would have had a wedding ring, too!"

"Yes, exactly," Adam confirmed.

"But..." said Anne, trying to understand, "did Lilith keep her ring when Adam married Eve, or—?"

"Are you all going to keep talking and let the food get cold?"

They all turned at the question, uttered in a surprising foreign accent. It came from the door to the kitchen, and in another second, in walked Quincey Harker.

None of them knew him except Cedric and the boys, who said, "Great-Grandpa, come join us."

He did so, sitting down between Cedric and Tristan. Devin, Adam, and Anne all looked at the stranger curiously as he took his seat. He was about as tall as Adam, and not any older looking—he easily could have passed for Cedric's grandson, considering how much Cedric had aged.

"Anne," said Cedric, "this is my father, your grandfather, Quincey Harker."

Anne had figured out the biological connection, but she remained shocked by his appearance. "How? How can you be my grandpa?" she asked the man. "You look so young."

Quincey's piercing eyes looked at Anne in such a way that she felt the need to clutch Adam's hand. Quincey was paler than Cedric and his hair raven black. He had high cheekbones, and she noticed his long tapered fingers as he scratched his chin. His voice was deep and commanding as he replied, "How is anything possible? It just is."

Here Adam drew in a breath, for he suddenly recognized the man.

"You—you were at the motel—in France!" said Adam. "You're the one who raided our room the night the boys were kidnapped."

"I was keeping watch over you," he replied, "and I confess, I was looking to see whether you had one of the rings. You see, I didn't know Cedric had it in his possession at the time."

"But—I don't understand. Why are you so young?" Anne asked.

"He does not age like the rest of us," Cedric tried to explain.

"Is it because of the royal jelly?" asked Adam, recalling all of the secrets of life-extension he had learned in his many dreams of his ancestors. "Or the waters of...of...is it Avalon...or Prester John's land—I forget which."

"No, none of the above," said Quincey. "It is the blood in my veins that gives me my youthful appearance; it is life-giving blood, despite its tainted origin. To explain how this is so will take some time, but that is what breakfasts are for. Let us eat now while I make it all clear."

Adam sat back in his chair, remembering Merlin had said there would be another story.

"It's an amazing story," Cedric assured them all.

"It's more than that," said Quincey. "It will prepare you to understand how we may bring about the end of this great threat we have all been under."

"Then I'm all ears," said Anne.

Cedric started passing around the plate of French toast and motioned to Lance to pass around the scrambled eggs.

As they all dug into their breakfasts, Quincey Harker began his long, strange, and nearly unbelievable tale—but by now, no one in the room really found anything unbelievable anymore.

PART II
QUINCEY HARKER'S TALE

CHAPTER 1

MUCH HAS BEEN written about the famous vampire Dracula. Not just written—countless films and television shows have featured Dracula or other vampire figures derivative of him. Almost all of this material about the legendary being is complete foolishness and lies. Only Mr. Bram Stoker's book—believed by the general public to be a novel, but in actuality, a collection of historical documents— contains the truth about Dracula, or as close as Mr. Stoker dared to express the truth. I know his book to be true because my parents, Jonathan and Mina Harker, wrote many of those documents from their personal experiences with their friends and allies who participated in Dracula's final destruction. Of course, I was born after Dracula's death, so my knowledge of those events and their truth might still be questioned, were it not for another fact—that I am, in a sense, Dracula's son. His blood flows through my veins, as I will explain, so I may well be termed his heir. Much of his way of thought permeates my own thoughts, and what I have not known about him by nature or instinct, I feel I have been led by his spirit to discover—to discover secrets and his personal knowledge that lay unknown to others. Therefore, I know his story to be true.

As I said, many things have been written about Dracula, and many of them have been foolish. Often, people have created tales of how he came back to life again. He did not, save within me—and in one other, as I will make known to you shortly. Those who have read Mr. Stoker's book will recall that on the final page, my father, Jonathan Harker, wrote that he and my mother, Mina, had had a son named Quincey, named after that Quincey Morris who had died in battle against Dracula and who eventually slew him. Actually, I have a string of names honoring all of my parents' friends, but my parents called me Quincey specifically to honor the friend they had lost in the battle.

Quincey is a name I find difficult to bear because it is the name of the man who saved my parents, yet he was also the man who killed my sire, the "monster" who is perhaps more my parent than Jonathan or Mina Harker. My parentage is complex to explain, but readers of Mr. Stoker's book will recall that when Dracula began to terrorize my parents and their friends, his first victim was my mother's friend, Lucy Westenra. Several times, Dracula drained Lucy's blood, and several times, his antagonists saved her life by performing blood transfusions using their own blood. Dr. Van Helsing, Dr. Seward, and Lord Godalming all gave their blood in these transfusions in an attempt to save her life. Dracula, therefore, in drinking Lucy's blood, might be said to have drank blood from all of them. Far worse, a horrible night occurred in which Dracula transfixed my mother and forced her, in my father's presence, to suck his own blood—blood that contained within it Lucy's blood and the blood of all her would-be saviors. By being born of my mother, I had not only the blood of her and my father, but the blood of all their dear friends, save Quincey Morris. But most importantly, the blood of Dracula flowed into my newborn body.

There are those who will scoff and think this statement full of foolishness. I have scoffed over the idea myself, seeking to convince myself it is not true, but my adopted uncle, my parents' dear friend Professor Van Helsing, himself one of those whose blood was transfused into my veins by these strange events, later verified to me that it is highly possible that Dracula's blood runs through my veins, and it is the only explanation for the strange and supernatural occurrences I have endured throughout my life.

It is my purpose now to explain those strange occurrences and why they are vital to your understanding of the quest that lies before you. I hope that, in doing so, you will feel some sympathy for me and realize how I have done my best to compensate for the evils that Dracula, largely unwillingly, committed. You will also learn, if you do not already believe so, that very real evils exist in this world, and much that we would believe impossible is not only possible but actually does occur. I will have proven such general statements by the time I finish my tale, and then I will leave you to decide whether or not they be true.

Simply the fact that my years number well over a century, yet I look no older than a man of thirty, should be proof enough that I have a supernatural nature, and I can only explain it by my having Dracula's blood flowing through my veins. To tell how I came to knowledge of my mysterious background and how it has completely shaped my life, I must begin with my earliest memories.

I was born on November 6, 1893, a significant date in my parents' history. November 6th was the date that Dracula and Quincey Morris were both slain in battle together in the year 1889. Seven years later, my father wrote what became the final page of Bram Stoker's *Dracula*, and about a year after that, in 1897, Mr. Stoker published his novel, which was really little more than a collection of my parents' writings and those of their friends about their nightmarish experience with Dracula. On the novel's final page is a statement by my father: "It is an added joy to Mina and to me that our boy's birthday is the same day as that on which Quincey Morris died. His mother holds, I know, the secret belief that some of our brave friend's spirit has passed into him." My father neglected to recall that my birthday was also on the same day that Dracula died, and more than Quincey Morris' brave spirit was passed on to me—so was the Count's blood.

As a child, my parents had told me I was named for a dear friend who had died before my birth. They did not tell me how that friend had died, nor did I question them about it, being a child and never having known Mr. Morris. I knew nothing of Dracula then. I was only a few years old when my parents took me on a journey to Transylvania to revisit the scenes where they had fought Dracula, but they did not explain to me the trip's purpose, and being but a few years old, I would not have understood anyway.

My mother died soon after that journey, and my father, as I later learned, then sought out Mr. Stoker and delivered into his hand the many documents that would be compiled to create his novel. Mr. Stoker did make a few changes here and there, but almost all of the book is true, even to several of the names, for Mr. Stoker knew the story was so outlandish that people would never suspect it was true, and therefore, they would not go looking for real life people based on his "novel." Why my father chose to let Mr. Stoker, whose writing he apparently admired, have the documents I never had the chance to ask him, though I imagine he was horrified that Mr. Stoker barely altered the names, which explains why he would later attempt to keep the novel from me.

My parents apparently wished to protect me from knowledge of the horrific events they had experienced—whether forever or until they thought me old enough to understand—I will never know. When my mother died, my father continued to keep the secret, as did his friends. I was acquainted with Lord Godalming and Mr. Seward, but Lord Godalming had married close to the time of my birth and was engrossed with his own family, and Dr. Seward was always busy caring for his patients, so they seldom called upon us, and when they did, they were careful never in my presence to mention the events concerning the vampire hunt in which they had participated. Uncle Abraham, or Dr. Van Helsing as he is known to Mr. Stoker's readers, came to live permanently in Britain and near my parents' residence soon after the events described in Mr. Stoker's book. Later, I would hear that he had an insane wife in an asylum back in Amsterdam, which explained his frequent journeys during my childhood, though I know not what became of her. I know only that he became as much my parent and guardian as my own mother and father, especially following my mother's death. Uncle Abraham had always had a special fondness for my mother, and he felt it his duty to look after her husband and her child after she was gone. He became a perpetual inmate of our home and my constant playmate. Despite his advanced age, he never failed to crawl on the floor with me, help me to stack my blocks, read me bedtime stories, or engage in a dozen other childish things that endeared him to my youthful heart. Of the principal characters of Mr. Stoker's book, only my father and Dr. Van Helsing were well-known to me, and they both protected me from knowledge of the past.

At what age, if any, they intended to tell me of the past, I do not know, but I was ten when I inadvertently learned the story by purchasing a tattered copy of Mr. Stoker's novel from a rare book dealer for a mere tuppence. I was fascinated then, like most young boys, by the idea of vampires, and I had already read many other wonderful tales of ghosts and witches, so the novel appeared to be exactly what would appeal to my taste.

In any case, I brought the novel home, curled up in my bed after school, and began to devour the wonderful story, wondering at the coincidence that the characters had names very similar to my own parents and their friends. I was discovered a couple of hours later by Uncle Abraham, who had been invited to have supper with us, and who had come to my room to fetch me to the table.

I remember when he entered the room, he asked me what I was reading. When I showed him the book, his face instantly turned pale. When I asked him whether he was ill, he quickly muttered, "No," and bid me hurry down before the food was cold. He then turned and left the room. Setting the book upon my bedside table, I went down to supper, not thinking again of the episode until I returned to my room a few hours later to discover the book was gone. At first, I thought I had misplaced it. When I questioned the housemaid, she said she had never seen it. Thinking I might have brought it downstairs with me and then absentmindedly set it aside somewhere, I began to retrace my steps. When this search proved fruitless, I went into the library and asked my father and Uncle Abraham whether they had seen my book.

"What was the name of it?" asked my father.

"*Dracula* by Bram Stoker," I replied. I waited for a response, wondering why, when my father was looking straight at me, he did not answer immediately.

"No, I haven't seen it," he said after a moment, "but I don't think you should be reading those types of stories. If you do find it, I want you to promise me that you will bring it to me, and then I will get rid of it."

"Why, Father?" I asked with surprise, for my father treasured books and had never censored my reading before.

"You will have nightmares from reading such stories," he said, suddenly looking as if he were ill, but I only assumed he was tired from a long day at the office. I knew my father's health was frail. He had the appearance of a man a score of years older than his age. He had been grey-haired as long as I knew him, and I had often wondered about this, for none of the other boys my age had such old-looking fathers, even those whose fathers I knew surpassed mine by a number of years. I had always hesitated to question my father about his health, not wishing to worry him, since he always appeared so careworn; once, however, I had asked Uncle Abraham about my father's health, and he had told me my father had suffered a great nervous strain to his system from an illness he had contracted prior to his marriage to my mother; that event was the reason for his ill health, although my uncle told me I was too young to understand the details of what had caused that strain. Uncle Abraham also explained that for a few years after this illness, my father's health had largely returned, but the death of my mother had brought back his previous complaints. Knowing his frailty, I usually obeyed my father on all points, but this restriction upon my reading so caught me off guard that I could not resist argument.

"But, Father," I reasoned, "I've never had nightmares, and I've read far scarier books than *Dracula*."

"We will not discuss it," my father repeated, turning his face away and then rising and walking to a nearby bookshelf, as if searching for a book, but I could tell he was merely seeking to avoid further argument.

"Father!" I persisted.

"Quincey," Uncle Abraham said, "your father is right. You are young and impressionable, and there is no telling what effect such foolish tales might have on your imagination. Be a good boy now."

I was stunned. I had always thought my uncle the wisest man I knew, and while I agreed with him that the stories were probably foolish, still he had always told me that knowledge was best acquired from reading widely in anything that interested me, for he firmly believed that by following one's inclinations, rather than a proscribed field of study, one would best discover his natural talents and then be able to apply them to his advantage.

I was too angry to argue further. I turned and left the library, slamming the door behind me, but not before shouting, "If Mother were here, she would let me read it."

I now wish I could have recalled those words, for to call my mother's memory to my aid was an unfair attack, and doubtless, she would have agreed with my father upon this issue more than any other, but children are cruel and selfish, especially toward those they most love.

I had another reason for invoking my mother's memory, however. My father had recently become engaged to Lord Godalming's cousin— once Miss Celia Holmwood—a kind but weak woman whose first husband had died from drink two years into their marriage, leaving her impoverished as a result of his gambling debts. Although penniless, she was of good family and good temperament, so my father and Lord Godalming had decided she was a suitable match for him. They were to be married the following week, and it had been explained to me that the reason for the marriage was because I needed a mother. I think more likely my father needed a helpmate in his old age, for he was already close to giving up the ghost, so to speak, and, as I would later realize, only holding on to life for my sake.

Here, let me explain that this woman, my father's second wife, gave birth to a daughter, my half-sister, and that daughter would in time marry the Earl of Delaney, making her Bram Delaney's mother and your grandmother, Adam. I can see you are all trying to wrap your brains around this—yes, it means Cedric and Bram were first cousins, and you, Adam and Anne, are second cousins, although Cedric and I kept our family histories secret from Bram so he never suspected anything—that Bram was of King Arthur's line had long been forgotten by his family, but let me cease this digression and return to my story.

You will understand, I am sure, why I did not like my new stepmother, for what boy wants his real mother replaced, or, after years of independence, desires a woman to tell him what to do?

What matters is less that my father remarried than that I never again saw that copy of *Dracula*, and I have no doubt that either my father or my Uncle Abraham had stolen it from me and destroyed it.

CHAPTER 2

NOT LONG AFTER the loss of my book, my father married and my stepmother moved in with us. She tried to befriend me, but I would have none of it. My rude behavior toward her upset my father a great deal until my Uncle Abraham suggested I be sent away to school to give us all a break from one another. I was sent to a private boys' school an hour from London, but with the understanding that I would come home most weekends.

Surprisingly—even to me—my anger over my father's remarriage and this new household situation knew no bounds. I became violent, biting Uncle Abraham when he tried to take me to the train to send me to the school. I then threw curses at my father until my stepmother was in tears and my father speechless with astonishment over the change in my behavior. Finally, by physical force, Uncle Abraham managed to get me out of the house, but he had quite a struggle of it, for at age ten, I was nearly a match for him since by then he was an old man.

But I calmed down once we were on the train and heading toward the school.

"Quincey," my uncle then told me, "you must understand that your father is ill. You should do all you can to be a good boy for him; your mother would wish that, as well."

"I am a good boy," I retorted. "Don't talk to me about good. I love my father. It's that woman he married who is the bad one by seeking to come between us."

My uncle tried to reason with me, but it was to no avail, for my anger would not be quenched. When we reached the town where the school was, it was all I could do to step off the train and follow Uncle Abraham to my new quarters. I met the headmaster and then coolly parted with my uncle, feeling relief to be free of him and my father since they were so easily willing to forsake me.

After a couple of days of sulking, I warmed up to my new companions at school and forgot about my home life.

Living among the other boys, I quickly discovered I was growing bigger and stronger than most of them at a fast pace, and within a year, I was entering puberty, a good year or two ahead of my classmates. With my increasing maturity came enhanced strength and agility so that I could soon outrun my classmates, and I found I could climb higher and more quickly up trees or buildings, and soon my physical strength surpassed that of everyone my age and even many a boy a year or two older than me.

I began to excel in sports, but I was lazy about my studies—perhaps because good grades did not lend themselves to the same public recognition one receives from winning a race, but I was certainly intelligent enough that I could pass my classes without studying. And I loved the admiration I slowly came to understand I was gaining from the other boys. Many of the boys my age, give or take a year or two, wanted to befriend me, so I suddenly enjoyed the wonderful feeling of being popular with my classmates.

I did not know how to explain the charisma I seemed to assert over my classmates, but I realized soon enough that most of them were willing to do whatever I wished, from small matters, such as allowing me to wear a favorite article of their clothing, to more serious ones, including stealing cigarettes for me from the druggist. Before I knew it, I was the other boys' ringleader, encouraging them in breaking the rules, yet I never broke the rules myself, finding no pleasure in rebellion so much as in asserting my power over the others so they would do for me what they would not have done on their own or for anyone else.

I realized these boys greatly esteemed and respected me, and perhaps some of them even worshipped me, but it was not until I was fourteen that I came to understand it was more than just my personal charisma that gave me such power over them. That year, I began to notice that when I walked down a hall, they would step out of my way, and sometimes, they would look at me with fear in their eyes, which surprised me greatly. At first, their behavior troubled me until I confessed my uneasiness to one of my closest friends, who said, "Quincey, of course they fear you. You're the strongest boy in our class, probably stronger than the boys in the class above us, and when you speak, your voice is so very commanding."

Astonished, I asked, "Are you afraid of me?"

When he hesitated to answer, I knew his answer, and I was tempted to say, "You don't need to fear me," but something held me back.

Nevertheless, I was curious to learn whether what he had said was true, so I felt the need to test the other boys to find out just how scared they were. I began with little things, bullying the boys a year or two younger than me through such antics as dropping my books in the hall and saying, "Charles, pick those up for me." When Charles obeyed, I decided to try it on a boy my own age, and he did the same. And before I knew it, I was telling the boys my age to give me things that belonged to them. I didn't ask—I told. "James," I would say, "I like your necktie. I think I'll wear it Saturday night," and, of course, James then gave it to me—and when I didn't return it, he clearly was afraid to ask for it back. This kind of situation soon evolved into "Peter, all my socks have holes in them. Give me three pairs of yours." Needless to say, Peter handed over his socks. Clearly, my classmates feared me—at least, most of them.

Philip, however, was my nemesis. He was the good boy in the school, two years older than me, with the face of an angel and the strength and athletic skill of a Greek god. He was my rival, for I quickly realized that while the boys admired and feared me, they admired and loved him. When we had the school races and he beat me by a split second, I could stand him no longer. I was determined to make him worship me.

Philip's birthday occurred about a week later, his eighteenth birthday, while I was but fifteen and a half. For his birthday, Philip received from his father a beautiful solid gold pocket watch. No other boy at the school had such a valuable watch. Of course, I had a fine pocket watch of my own and no real desire to possess a gold one, so what I did next was not out of greed—I merely desired to put Philip in his place.

One day after morning chapel, after the headmaster and most of the boys had left, I put myself in Philip's path as he was about to exit. He tried to step around me, but I would not let him.

"What do you want, Quincey?" he asked.

"Your pocket watch," I demanded. "Give it to me."

"Like bloody hell I will," he said, trying to push past me. I shoved him backward a couple of steps. He stood there, glaring at me.

"You're not getting my pocket watch," he said, smirking, half-laughing, as if wanting to make it out to be a joke, which I knew to be a sign of his fear.

"Give me the watch," I said, holding out my hand.

There was silence. About half-a-dozen boys had still been in the chapel and seen our exchange. By now, they were surrounding us, waiting to see what would happen.

"Philip, give him the watch," said Arnold. He was Philip's closest friend and a great athlete himself, but clearly a coward at heart.

"No, I won't," said Philip.

"I don't want to hurt you, Philip. I just want the watch," I said, although I felt the blood in me aching to hurt him, to smash his beautiful face.

"Get out of my way, Quincey," he said.

"Give me the watch," I repeated.

"I'm not afraid of you," he said, but his voice trembled as he spoke.

"Not afraid?" I said, clenching my fist. "You won't be saying that after I hit you."

"Quincey, leave him alone," Arnold begged.

"I want the damn watch," I said, "and I will have it." Suddenly, rage filled me and the fist I clenched swung out into the stained glass window just above my shoulder, shattering the glass while my companions dodged it.

"Are you afraid now?" I asked Philip as I pulled back my hand.

One of the younger boys rushed over to see whether I was bleeding, but not a scratch appeared on my skin.

I watched Philip's Adam's apple move as he swallowed, and then, almost unable to force the words out, he said, "Yes, now I'm afraid."

I put out my unwounded hand to receive the watch, and he handed it to me just as we heard the chaplain shout, "What was that noise?" and rush into the room.

I shoved the watch into my pocket, and then we all turned to face the chaplain.

The old man came to a stop when he saw the window. "Who did this? Who did this?" he screamed.

The boys all looked at one another with dread, while I simply smiled at the chaplain's hysterics over a stupid piece of glass. I knew none of the boys would dare to tattle on me.

"Philip," asked the chaplain, "who did this?"

Philip, as I said, was a good boy, the favorite among our teachers. He could not lie. Or could he? What if he did lie—what if he—?

"I did it, sir," said Philip, looking down in shame.

"You?" said the chaplain. "But why?"

"I—I don't know, sir. I guess because I'm not as good as I pretend to be, and I, well, I just wanted you to know the truth about me."

"Well, eighteen or not, you'll be getting the rod for this," said the chaplain. "You'll follow me to the headmaster's office this instant."

"Yes, sir," said Philip, looking at the ground.

The chaplain stomped off and Philip went to follow him, but Arnold clasped his sleeve and said, "Philip, why did you take the blame?"

"It's my fault," he said. "I should have given Quincey my watch when he asked. I'm the one who angered him, so I felt compelled to make it up to him by taking the blame."

At this speech, the boys all stared at one another in astonishment, but as I watched Philip follow the chaplain, I could not help smiling, my hand still clasping my new gold pocket watch.

As I thought over the incident later in Latin class, I realized that the moment before Philip had confessed, I had been forming the wish that Philip would take the blame; I had wished it because it was so outlandish a thought—because no one had ever heard Philip tell a lie. Now he had proven himself a true Christian, laying down his life for his friend, or rather, the man he knew was his better—his master if I so wished it.

A few weeks later, Philip graduated and left the school to go to Oxford. I regretted that I would have no further opportunity to torment him, but I had gained a pocket watch, and more importantly, the realization that when I exerted my mind and looked into my victim's eyes, I could often make him do my will. I then decided to try this newfound power on my teachers, although I was not as successful, for they were intelligent men with wills of their own while the boys were used to obeying their betters; nevertheless, I had no doubt my power would grow as I grew older and became more willful. I now began to read voraciously about telepathy and mesmerism in an effort to understand how I might have acquired such power, and more importantly, to nurture it to grow stronger.

Yet I admit that while my new power fascinated me, it almost equally scared me. It was one thing to make my schoolmates clean my room and give me their pocket watches, but what if I could use this power for true evil—to make a man rob a bank for me or to turn a gun on himself? What did it truly mean to have such power? And how might I use it wisely to obtain all I could desire? Answering those questions would become my very *raison d'être* in the years to come.

CHAPTER 3

I WAS TOO unnerved by my powers to try to assert them when I visited my family during the holidays. In fact, while I had no qualms about exerting my mysterious influence over my classmates, I found it somewhat exhausting and feared that my anger might someday get out of control before I had thoroughly mastered it. Therefore, I found it a relief to return home and pretend I was normal for a short while, and I found that my absence at school caused my family now to spoil me, so I did not have to worry about them again trying to thwart my will. I decided to be amiable and make up for how I had railed earlier against my father's marriage—after all, what did such a small thing matter to me if I could make other men do as I wished? In time, I would be able to have anything I desired. Possessing great power in the not-too-distant future seemed a likely possibility for me, and so I would wait and plan until I was a man, and then, even if I should not be master over others, I would at least be my own master.

My stepmother and I got along surprisingly well during the next few years whenever I visited home. She was a sweet and good-natured woman who tried to win me over by making me her confidant in her worries about the household and my poor father's health, which continued to decline. She also told me she expected me to set a good example for my little sister. That was not difficult, for I came to adore Celia, named for my stepmother. She clearly worshipped me of her own free will. She was the only one who could command me, and I only feared that my power and my occasional bursts of anger would make me lose control someday and hurt her or another family member.

So my visits home passed pleasantly until the Christmas holiday following my eighteenth birthday, the last Christmas before my completion of school. That Christmas, the question arose of my going to university.

Uncle Abraham was a frequent guest at our home, and I saw in him the only person intelligent enough for me to discuss my interests and my hopes and fears with, although never the strange powers I felt coursing through my veins. We often went out for walks together, and one day, just after Christmas, we happened to turn into a bookseller's shop not far from my home. There were few shops in London that sold any books in Dutch, but this was one of those rare shops, so Uncle Abraham would often frequent it and bring home whatever he could that was written by his countrymen, although he had been living in Britain for some twenty years by then.

That was a fatal day, for it was in that bookshop that I again saw a copy of Bram Stoker's *Dracula*. I had almost forgotten about the book since the day several years past when my uncle and father had forbidden me to read it. Not surprisingly, I had never seen any of my classmates with it, for it would not achieve true popularity until it was made into a film in the 1931 starring Bela Lugosi; as a result, I did not yet know the actual details of the story.

When I saw the novel there on the bookstore's shelf, I could not resist wanting to look at it again, but first I waited until Uncle Abraham was gone to another section of the store. Then I picked it up and began to read it, and I was stunned by what I read. I do not know why, but I had turned first to the last page where my father described all of his friends and the trip to Transylvania when I was a small boy, and then I read how I had sat on Uncle Abraham's knee and he had said, "We want no proofs. We ask none to believe us! This boy will some day know what a brave and gallant woman his mother is. Already he knows her sweetness and loving care. Later on he will understand how some men so loved her, that they did dare much for her sake."

Suddenly, I felt like I had been socked in the head. I knew those words, I recalled them, and I remembered sitting on my uncle's knee that day, and the name "Transylvania" came back to me as a word once very familiar to me. Doubtless, my parents had openly talked about their adventures before me, thinking me too young to remember or repeat what they said, and so now, it all felt very familiar to my memory. But why, since Uncle Abraham had said someday I would know their story, had I yet never heard it? Why had they kept it from me? What exactly had they kept from me? What could my family possibly have had to do with Count Dracula, the infamous vampire?

Gripped with desire to know these answers, I stuffed the book inside my coat as I used my willpower against my uncle and the shopkeeper to ensure that no one would look my way. My uncle seemed troubled when I rejoined him outside a few minutes later, he carrying a newly purchased copy of the Dutch classic *Max Havelaar*. He commented that he wasn't feeling well, as if the life had just been sucked out of him, an odd expression for him to use, I thought, in light of my just having purchased a book about a vampire.

It was all I could do to contain my curiosity when we got home.

It was almost time for dinner, so I hid the book in my room beneath my heavy dresser. My increased strength—I was the strongest boy at school now and did not doubt the reason was somehow connected to the enhanced powers of my mind—allowed me easily to lift up the dresser with one hand while I slid the book under with my other. No one else would have reason to look for the book there, and no one else would have the strength to move the dresser without help, so I figured the book would be safely hidden. Then I dressed for dinner and joined my family downstairs.

I found only my stepmother and Celia in the dining room.

"Your father is in bed with a sudden cold," my stepmother told me.

This news did not surprise me, for my father was sick more often than he was well these days, but I was surprised that my uncle had not come down to dinner.

"Abraham says he has a horrible headache," my stepmother replied when I asked.

I was even more surprised by this statement. It was almost as if he knew what I had done in the shop—willing him not to look my way—or at least, that he suspected it and was in dread of the consequences. I felt these were his thoughts—I did not guess—I literally felt if not his actual thoughts, the emotions behind them—that he dreaded what I was to learn from the book I was about to read. I could not understand why he dreaded it, for according to Mr. Stoker, Uncle Abraham had said that someday I was to know the truth, but perhaps the knowledge was so dreadful that now he wished I would not know. What could be so horrible that my father and Uncle Abraham felt they must keep it from me? How could it be that the tale of Dracula the vampire should be tied up with my family?

I tried my best to eat as if nothing were the matter, but Celia was being stubborn, refusing to eat her vegetables, and her whining irritated me until I snapped, "Do as you're told!"

This outburst surprised both her and my stepmother, who usually indulged my sister's fussing without reprimand.

"I'm sorry," I apologized. "I'm just not feeling well. I think I must have caught a bit of Father's cold or something."

"Just what I need," said my stepmother, "a houseful of sick men to care for."

"I'll be fine," I said. "But I think I should go to bed. I'm probably just tired. We've been so busy since I came home for holiday. A good long sleep is all I need. I'll see you all at breakfast."

Five minutes later, I was locked in my room. I retrieved the copy of *Dracula* from under the dresser, and after changing into my nightshirt, I lay in bed reading. But after a few minutes, I could not lie still. I was overcome by the story's feverish intensity. I spent the night pacing the room while reading the book, eagerly turning each page, but also stopping every so often to exclaim quietly to myself, "Can it be? Can this be true? Could my father have been a prisoner in Dracula's castle? Did Dracula really come to England? Did my mother's friend Lucy actually become a vampiress, and did her dearest friends really stab her through the heart? How could this all be true? And yet how could it not be when I knew so many of the people mentioned within the pages?

I could not stop reading. I read well past midnight. I read while the rest of the house was quiet. I read into the wee morning hours, astonished by every word written and spoken by Dr. Seward, Uncle Abraham, Lord Godalming, Quincey Morris, my parents, and even Dracula himself.

And then I came to the most revolting, most absolutely terrifying passage in the entire novel—novel?—but novels are fiction, and this story was true—the true story of my parents' battle against evil! How I was disgusted by that most disgusting episode when my mother...when Dracula...when...when my parents' friends broke into the room to find Dracula with my parents...when...I will let Dr. Seward describe it:

> What I saw appalled me. I felt my hair rise like bristles on the back of my neck, and my heart seemed to stand still.
>
> The moonlight was so bright that through the thick yellow blind the room was light enough to see. On the bed beside the window lay Jonathan Harker, his face flushed and breathing heavily as though in a stupor. Kneeling on the near edge of the bed facing outwards was the white-clad figure of his wife. By her side stood a tall, thin man, clad in black. His face was turned from us, but the instant we saw we all recognized the Count, in every way, even to the scar on his forehead. With his left hand he held both Mrs. Harker's hands, keeping them away with her arms at full tension. His right hand gripped her by the back of the neck, forcing her face down on his bosom. Her white nightdress was smeared with blood, and a thin stream trickled down the man's bare chest which was shown by his torn-open dress. The attitude of the two had a terrible resemblance to a child forcing a kitten's nose into a saucer of milk to compel it to drink. As we burst into the room, the Count turned his face, and the hellish look that I had heard described seemed to leap into it. His eyes flamed red with devilish passion. The great nostrils of the white aquiline nose opened wide and quivered at the edge, and the white sharp teeth, behind the full lips of the blood dripping mouth, clamped together like those of a wild beast. With a wrench, which threw his victim back upon the bed as though hurled from a height, he turned and sprang at us. But by this time the Professor had gained his feet, and was holding towards him the envelope which contained the Sacred Wafer. The Count suddenly

stopped, just as poor Lucy had done outside the tomb, and cowered back. Further and further back he cowered, as we, lifting our crucifixes, advanced. The moonlight suddenly failed, as a great black cloud sailed across the sky. And when the gaslight sprang up under Quincey's match, we saw nothing but a faint vapour. This, as we looked, trailed under the door, which with the recoil from its bursting open, had swung back to its old position. Van Helsing, Art, and I moved forward to Mrs. Harker, who by this time had drawn her breath and with it had given a scream so wild, so ear-piercing, so despairing that it seems to me now that it will ring in my ears till my dying day. For a few seconds she lay in her helpless attitude and disarray. Her face was ghastly, with a pallor which was accentuated by the blood which smeared her lips and cheeks and chin. From her throat trickled a thin stream of blood. Her eyes were mad with terror. Then she put before her face her poor crushed hands, which bore on their whiteness the red mark of the Count's terrible grip, and from behind them came a low desolate wail which made the terrible scream seem only the quick expression of an endless grief. Van Helsing stepped forward and drew the coverlet gently over her body, whilst Art, after looking at her face for an instant despairingly, ran out of the room.

My mother, my dear, poor mother, had been forced to drink the Monster's blood! It was disgusting, repulsive, but what was worse, as I read on, my mother developed a type of psychic power as a result—she was able to know Dracula's movements.

And...and...it was too terrible for me to believe, but it was the only explanation. I had found curious pleasure in exerting my will over my fellow classmates at school, although I had secretly feared my power, and I had often exerted it only to convince myself it worked, for I remained largely in disbelief that I could have such power. But now

I knew it was absolutely true, and I understood why. My mother had passed on to me the blood, or whatever mysterious power lay in the blood, of Dracula—the blood he had forced into her, causing it to soar through her veins and, in time, to pass into my own.

Dracula's blood flowed within me! That meant—if he were not quite my father, I was his son in some small way—but, no, it certainly wasn't a small way, for my own father could not have passed such power on to me.

When I finally finished reading, dawn was breaking. Though it was nearly eight in the morning, it was close to the winter solstice, so the darkest time of the year. I lay on my bed, my eyes exhausted from reading all night. I closed them, almost wishing to fall asleep and never to wake again. Surely, I had to be dreaming. I couldn't possibly have Dracula's blood pulsing through my veins. I couldn't possibly believe, could I, that the ridiculous story, the bizarre, impossible tale I had just read truly chronicled events that my parents and their friends had experienced?

After a few minutes, I drifted asleep and woke to a pounding on my door. I looked at my clock. I had slept only five minutes. As I sat up, the doorknob jiggled; whoever was on the other side was trying to enter my room.

"Just a minute," I said. "I'm not decent."

I sat up, and seeing the book on the bed beside me, I quickly shoved it under my blankets.

When I opened the door just a crack so I could stick out my head, I found my stepmother sobbing.

"Oh, Quincey," she cried. "Your father...he passed away in the night."

CHAPTER 4

For three days, I tried to push away all my thoughts and fears that the tale of Dracula might be true as I assisted my stepmother with the funeral. I was saddened that my father had died, although I admit my regret was mostly based in my now being unable to ask him the truth about the book. I had once loved him, but we had grown apart since I'd gone to boarding school, so I no longer felt the need of a father.

Uncle Abraham looked greatly troubled—weak and gaunt—in the days leading up to the funeral. As much as my questions about Dracula burned inside me, I felt I could not intrude upon his mourning at that time.

The day of the funeral, I was still pondering how I might question Uncle Abraham about Dracula and how soon after my father's funeral would be appropriate. We were preparing to leave for the churchyard that day when the doorbell rang and the housemaid announced Lord Godalming and Dr. Arthur Seward. They came into the parlor where I was seated, pretending to read a book, while my stepmother and sister sat gazing out the window, waiting for the carriage. Uncle Abraham was with us, sitting quietly, barely saying a word, a look of deep depression and perhaps dread on his face at the thought of burying his old friend.

But at the sight of Lord Godalming and Dr. Seward, his face lit up and he struggled to get up from his chair as I stood and stepped forward to shake the hands of my father's old friends.

"Thank you for coming," I said to them. Lord Godalming nodded and turned to give his sympathies to my stepmother, while Dr. Seward patted me on the shoulder and said, "Dear boy, we are so very sorry."

And then Uncle Abraham cleared his throat so they would notice him. "Help me from this chair, Arthur," he said, and Dr. Seward gave him an arm up.

"The carriage is here, my lady," said the housemaid, returning to the room, for we had stopped watching for it with the sudden appearance of our guests.

"I'll ride with my old friends here, if you don't mind," said Uncle Abraham to my stepmother. "I don't wish to be a trouble to the grieving family."

"You have never been a trouble," said my stepmother, but she did not argue and took my sister's hand as she walked out.

"Thank you for coming," I repeated to my parents' old friends, and then I followed my stepmother while our guests and Uncle Abraham brought up the rear.

I felt deeply troubled as we climbed into the carriage. Once seated, I turned around to watch Uncle Abraham being helped by Dr. Seward into Lord Godalming's automobile, complete with a chauffeur. I was surprised that my uncle would choose to ride in a modern contraption, but I sensed he had greater concerns troubling him. I do not know how to describe what happened next. I had sensed his grief over my father's death, but now, I also sensed a sort of fear in him—a fear he had been hiding in my presence, but one he was now allowing to show in the company of Lord Godalming and Dr. Seward. While I knew those two had been my parents' good friends in the past, during my lifetime, they had only been occasional visitors in our home, both busy with their own lives, so while I did not doubt their good nature or their friendship toward my father, I felt awkward approaching them. If I could speak to anyone, it was Uncle Abraham, and yet, I had felt almost afraid to do so, and now I began to sense why.

As we drove to the church, my stepmother and sister were so silent that I could hear every step of the horses' hooves on the pavement—and the noise of all the other traffic throughout London—I was surprised by this—everything felt so loud, but how could my ears have suddenly grown so sensitive?

And then, I know not how, I heard my uncle's voice. For a moment, I thought I must be dreaming, but it was his voice, though he was in the automobile following us and too far away for me to hear it under normal circumstances. And when I heard Dr. Seward respond to him, I knew I was not dreaming. Through some strange phenomenon, I was actually able to hear their conversation, to eavesdrop upon them through the power of my mind. I would find that I had this power in the future as well, although it usually took great concentration for me to use it, but today, my focus was so intent on wondering to whom I could turn to for help that my mind was providing me answers through this extrasensory power.

"I tell you," my uncle said, "that we have no time to lose. The boy concerns me greatly. I sent him away to school from fear he would learn the truth. Now I am certain he knows it, but I am less certain of how it affects him. I have felt his will pushing against mine very strongly. I felt it the day before his father's death when we went into the bookshop—he was willing me not to come near him. I could feel my limbs become paralyzed for a moment. I could not move, and when I was able to again, I felt as if all the life had been drained from me so that I was barely able to walk home. Once there, I went to my bed with a great headache that lasted until the morning hours."

"Are you sure?" asked Dr. Seward. "Perhaps you had a bit of a stroke?"

"No, it was no stroke. I am a doctor like you, my friend; I have seen many strokes. This was no stroke but a paralysis not of my own body's making. I questioned it a great deal that evening, but then yesterday morning, when Quincey went with his stepmother to visit the undertaker, I found the courage to go into his room, and there I found the book lying on a chair."

It was true. I had foolishly left the book out after rereading passages of it, trying to make myself believe it could be true. I had realized I had done so as soon as I left the house, and all the while I was out, I had felt panic-stricken about it, anxious to return, but unwilling to rush home and raise suspicion. Why had I been so careless? But how was I to know my uncle would sense my will, or that my will had created such a powerful influence upon him as he described?

"The boy should have been told a long time ago," said Dr. Seward.

"We always meant to tell him, but not until he was old enough," said my uncle. "He began exhibiting signs that frightened me years ago, and even now at eighteen, do you think him mature enough to use such knowledge wisely? I was a fool not to guess that the blood held such power that his mother would pass it on to her child."

"Van Helsing, my old friend," said Lord Godalming, "that book has been very popular, so it is only natural the boy would eventually read it. I see nothing to be alarmed about in this. I never read it myself, but I thought Stoker changed some of the names in it, so the boy is unlikely to realize it relates to his own family. Plus, you are not young any longer—perhaps your health is not what it should be; I think your temporary paralysis is more likely the result of your age. I think you are more in need of a doctor than the boy of a straitjacket."

A straitjacket! What part of the conversation had I missed?

"I warn you," said my uncle, "do not mock me. None of you believed me at first when we went through the great terror before; you did not believe me until we had to cut off the head of poor Miss Lucy, and then you saw that I was right. Do not doubt me now. I admit there is no known tale of such a thing happening before—a vampire's power being passed on through his blood—but that does not mean it is not true, any more than the existence of the vampire Dracula himself was not true."

"But to restrain the boy before we even know whether it is true!" said Lord Godalming.

"We need not restrain him," said Dr. Seward. "Just simply detain him, observe him to see whether Professor Van Helsing is right. I could simply do an examination of him. I could tell him I fear his father died of a hereditary illness of sorts and that we want to make sure he is not susceptible to it."

"Will he not suspect something?" asked Lord Godalming.

"I do not know," said Uncle Abraham. "Count Dracula was very clever. That we were able to defeat him was only because we had Miss Mina to help us determine his intentions. We do not have that luxury with young Quincey. We do not know what power he may have or how aware he is of that power. We can only hope that his power is far less powerful than that of his sire, but we must be careful nevertheless.

Even if his power is only a fraction of the vampire king's, if it is allowed to go unchecked, we do not know how he might use it."

My sire? Surely, they were not referring to Count Dracula as my sire, even if his blood did course through my veins. My mother could not have drank that much of his blood in that moment when he exerted his power over her. Surely, a few drops of blood could not—but had my uncle not said that I had nearly paralyzed him? Had I not forced Philip, the most morally upstanding and physically the strongest boy in the school, to do my will? And was I not still only experimenting with what I could do—and thinking how I could use my power solely for my own selfish purposes? Was I already to be branded a monster by the very men whom I had most thought to be counted among my friends? And were they correct in so defining me?

"How are we to do it?" asked Lord Godalming.

"We will ask the boy to go for a ride in the morning. We will take him to my hospital," said Dr. Seward, "and there I will exam him."

"Do we tell him what we suspect? Do we question him?" asked Lord Godalming.

"I think it best if we confront the problem head on," said Van Helsing. (At that point, I felt I could no longer call him my uncle for how he plotted against me.) "We will keep him restrained where he can do no harm to himself or anyone else, and then we will tell him what we believe he already knows, and we will question him as to his intentions—namely, does he know of his powers, and will he use them for evil?"

Lord Godalming laughed. "Use them for evil? So melodramatic, Professor. Surely that is not so necessary. You have been the boy's friend all your life. I'm certain we can engage in less extreme methods."

"You, sir," replied Van Helsing, "are his cousin by marriage, and his half-sister is of your blood. Do you feel that precious little girl, that tender young child, is safe in a house where also resides one whose sire was Count Dracula? Do you not recall what the evil one did to Miss Lucy and Miss Mina? Do you wish to leave that sweet young child helpless in his power? Do we know for certain that he has not yet reached a stage where he will exert his will upon her because she is young and innocent and helpless?"

My sister! Harm my sister! Why, were they suggesting that I might rape or kill her? How could they think I was capable of such horrid crimes?

"Quincey, what is the matter? You look ill," said my stepmother as I looked at my sweet sister whom I loved dearly and would never harm.

"I think the rattling of the carriage is just upsetting my stomach a little," I said, trying to repress a tear at the thought of my sister suffering any injury from me.

"We will be there in another minute," said my stepmother. "We are all bound to have upset stomachs on a day like this. I am so sorry, Quincey, that you have lost your father. You know you will be man of the house now. Your sister and I will rely upon you for protection."

Protection? Did they not know I was their worst enemy, or so my parents' dearest friends suspected me of being? How could I protect them when I had suddenly become the hunted? I was the one who needed protection.

My stepmother's interruption had broken my ability to listen into the conversation of my father's friends—friends? Hardly friends when they sought to hurt his son under the guise of protecting his daughter!

I had considered I might go to them for advice, for consolation, for understanding, but I could not do so if they thought of restraining me. Had their fear of Dracula led them to defy reason, to fail to realize that

I might be able to control my powers, even that I could use my powers for good?

But did I even truly believe that? I may not have used those powers for true evil yet, but I had used them for my own benefit, had used them in selfish ways, and had thought nothing of hurting others to fulfill my desires.

Was I capable of restraining my selfishness?

I struggled with these thoughts throughout the funeral, hearing not a word of the service. Then at the churchyard, I stood over my father's open grave beside where my mother rested, and I asked my parents what I, their son, was to do, now orphaned in the world when I most needed them. I was bereft, alone. My stepmother was not of my blood, my half-sister but a child, and my uncle willing to sacrifice my wellbeing for that of others.

And as we walked out of the churchyard, I saw Lord Godalming stop at the tomb of my mother's dear friend, Lucy Westenra—the woman he had loved, but whose heart he had pierced with a stake to protect the children she sought to prey upon once Dracula had transformed her into the living dead. I could not help but shudder and to fear that someday Lord Godalming might be called upon to do the same to me.

CHAPTER 5

PERHAPS YOU THINK that I was overreacting in my fears. After all, I was not an actual vampire. I was not about to go out and suck people's blood. I had no desire to perform such behaviors. Such thoughts were completely revolting to me.

It is true I was of an age to desire women, and I had toyed with the idea of using my will to acquire pleasure from one. That I had not yet done so was probably only because I had no access to female company, having been at a boys' school and not having any sisters close to my age who might introduce me to young women. I did have classmates who had sisters, and I considered that through them I might be introduced to young women, but it all felt so complicated, and should my will exert itself when I was with a young woman, such that I forced her to my service, what complications might then ensue? After all, I could not live in society if it were known I had robbed a young woman of her virtue—I would be forced to marry her, or to become a social outcast. I was not ready to be an outcast visibly, no matter how much I already felt like one internally. To commit a selfish crime against a woman would be far worse than to do so by imposing my will upon other boys and men, who would be too ashamed of their own weaknesses to admit I had harmed them, but I knew if I hurt a young woman of my class, the moral outcry would harm me for the rest of my life.

I considered I might do as I had heard Jack the Ripper did—have my way with young women no one else knew, prostitutes and street wanderers—but such pleasure did not appeal to me—and I certainly was not so morally depraved yet as to take anyone's life. Yes, I was bursting with desire, but I also had strong memories of the love that had existed between my parents as well as between my father and my stepmother. I did not wish to have a woman for but an hour; I'd prefer to find a true companion, someone to whom someday I might confess my dilemma, someone who would comfort me and help me learn to live with this curse.

Curse, indeed. I had thought it a game, a great advantage to have such power to control others' wills, but now it was forcing me to abandon my family and leave all those I loved and the only life I had ever known.

For leave I must. How otherwise would I avoid falling into the clutches of my enemies—Professor Van Helsing, Lord Godalming, and Dr. Seward? And I had no doubt that however well-intentioned they might be—they were clearly my enemies now.

And I had to leave right away—this very night, for tomorrow they planned to lay their trap for me. What other choice did I have? If I submitted to being locked up in a madhouse until they were convinced I was no threat to anyone, how long would that be? And how would they know that I was not still a threat and just acting otherwise to secure my freedom? No, I could not rely on their trusting me, nor I them.

I did feel guilt over abandoning my stepmother and little sister. I had no choice, but I thought perhaps I might leave them a note explaining my departure. But what could I say? If I told them I was leaving for their own good, my enemies would know I was on to them, or at least that I was aware of my powers. If I did not give a reason and left no message, perhaps they would think I was kidnapped or something ill had befallen me, and then the police would go searching for me. No doubt I would be searched for regardless, but my enemies could not as easily go to the police for help, not considering I was of age, a full-grown man. And they could not yet accuse me of any crime—nor could they go to the police and try to convince anyone I was a danger, for their theories of the vampire blood within me would only be laughed at.

I agonized over what I should say most of that day, all the while realizing how much in danger I was, for throughout the funeral luncheon and all that afternoon and evening as guests came to pay their respects, I saw my enemies now and then whispering among themselves, or I would catch one of them staring at me.

Finally, when Dr. Seward was departing, he said to me, "Quincey, I have some things your father gave to me that I would like to show you. Would it be convenient if I came for you about ten o'clock tomorrow morning and brought you back to my office to see them?"

"Certainly," I lied, fully aware that Lord Godalming and Professor Van Helsing stood behind him, their ears keenly listening for my reply. "It would make me very happy to spend some time with such an old friend of my parents."

"Good. I will see you then," he replied before passing out the door. But I knew better. I hoped never to see his face again. I would be long gone before ten o'clock tomorrow morning.

I went up to my room that night as early as I could. I thought to pack my valises, but I hesitated about what to bring with me, not wanting to be slowed down if I needed to make a quick flight. I also worried about being spotted wearing my own clothes, but I would simply have to change them at a pawn shop once I was far enough from danger. I had a fair amount of money on me—at least enough to feed me and keep a roof over my head for a few days if I needed it.

For a moment, I wondered how I would manage to survive when the money ran out—would I be able to find work in some distant place by the sweat of my brow, or would I starve? But then I remembered the power I had, and I realized that all my life I had obeyed my father and then my masters at school and followed a regimented life, but now I would never need to obey anyone again. No one need be my master once I escaped my enemies. I would be the only master of my fate, and when it became necessary, I would be master over others; whenever I needed a place to lay my head, or a meal to eat, or a few pounds to spend, I could use my will to gain all those things. I told myself I would not allow evil to control me—I would only use my powers over others when necessary—when needed to obtain my basic necessities—not to control, to torment, or to hurt. I told myself such, but even I feared I might be lying to myself—and that I would find ways to rationalize any behavior I chose. And in that fear lay all the more reason to escape, for being near my enemies would only make me continue to doubt and fear myself.

In the end, I simply penned a note that said:

> Dear Mother and Celia,
>   Now that Father is dead, I no longer feel the need to follow his wishes that I attend Cambridge. I wish to set

out on my own and have adventures. You may think that foolhardy of me, but I will only be young once. Do not worry about me. I know not where I am going or what I shall do, but I trust it shall all be well in the end.

Love,
Quincey

I felt this message vague enough not to raise any alarm, and my rebellious nature was well-enough known by my stepmother that it should not have surprised her too terribly that I would depart in such a manner.

My words were also for the most part true, for I did not know where I would go or what I would do, and I certainly didn't know whether it would turn out for the best or whether I would ever be able to see them again. I only knew I must leave immediately. As quietly as possible, I packed a small valise with a couple of changes of clothing, my razor, a comb, and my copy of *Dracula*. I hid the valise under the bed until I could safely make my escape. Then I lay on my bed, waiting for all the house to be silent, and then I lay there a bit longer to be certain I could leave without notice.

I pondered where I would go, but every place that came to mind, every person I thought might help me, I decided was a place or person my enemies might expect me to contact, and therefore, I might be caught. Finally, I decided my best option was to get out of England as quickly as possible. Where or how I did not know, and perhaps it would be best if I did not decide for myself, but I allowed Fate to guide me.

At about half-past one in the morning, when I knew everyone had gone to bed over an hour before, I quietly left my room with my few belongings and made my way out into the streets of London. In the dark, I intended to make my way down to the Thames, and there I would manage either to stow away, or if that were not possible, beg passage on some ship—but what was I thinking? I, Quincey Harker, the son of Dracula, beg? No, I would not beg for anything. And while it was imperative that I flee England, I would be no man's minion and fear no one going forward. I had been given a great gift, the ability to live life to its fullest, to have anything my heart desired so long as I did not endanger myself by letting other men realize the power I had over them. Why, I could easily become rich—set myself up as a king in some far off land, or better yet, use my powers to govern wisely some great nation, like the United States of America—a democracy where I could use my mental strength to influence people to vote for me as if it were their own will until I became their president, until I was able to influence them to—well, that was a good question—to do what? Could I justify having such power and being wealthy beyond anyone's wildest dreams if I used my power for good—even to end war and strife and poverty and hunger? But what did I know about how to govern people? Just because I might gain power over people did not mean I understood how to improve a nation's economy, relieve the impoverished masses, or increase commerce. Whom was I deceiving except myself to think such things?

No, all I must think of now was my escape from England.

When I had reached the street, quietly closing the door behind me, I stood before the house, looking at it for a moment in the glow of the streetlamps. I knew I needed to hurry; if someone in the house had heard me moving about, he or she might have woken, might have heard the door close, and so the whole household would be upon me in a minute; nevertheless, I stood at the front door, almost wishing someone would come out, preferably Van Helsing. He was my enemy now, and yet he had been my parents' best friend, so he could not wish me ill. I half-wished he would open the door and bid me come inside and promise me everything would turn out all right—promise me that somehow he could save my soul as he had that of my mother and even as he had helped to release Dracula's soul. How was it that I had Dracula's evil in me when the cross that had appeared on my mother's forehead, marking her as cursed, had vanished with Dracula's death? As I had read in Mr. Stoker's novel, Van Helsing had said that once Dracula died, his evil would cease for his victims and they would be free.

But he had been wrong! And that realization caused anger to rise up in me. Van Helsing and his cronies did not know all. Who were they to know such things or to decide for themselves how I was to be treated because of my heritage from my sire? Had not Dracula been centuries older and wiser than them? Had they not only succeeded in defeating him because it had been daytime so that he had been weak and trapped in his coffin? I obviously did not have such boundaries upon me. I could move about freely. And had I not already demonstrated that my powers worked during the daytime, worked upon whomever I projected them on to, both my schoolmates and even Uncle Abraham?

And then I walked away from the door of my house with scorn for their weak mentality, these humans who thought they were so terribly wise that they could defeat the ancient and powerful blood that soared through my veins. Blood that now drove me to desperation until I became conscious of the fury I was feeling and wondered whether I truly should despise my uncle and his friends—now my enemies—for their weaknesses and ignorance. That blood that made me wonder whether it was Dracula's evil itself that led me to think in such an arrogant manner myself.

These thoughts ran through my head as I walked through London, not knowing at first where I was going, not even thinking whether I was going toward the Thames where I might find a ship. I imagined the first one on which I could book passage and escape England would be good enough for me, whether it took me to America or the Ivory Coast or China, or I knew not where. I simply had to escape, and my escape would be successful, for there was no one I left behind who could read my mind and thus follow my movements.

Could I even afford passage on a ship? That I did not learn until I reached the harbor. After walking up and down for a few minutes on the docks, I spied an old man in a captain's uniform smiling upon me, looking upon me with admiration, and then I knew why he looked at me as he did—and consequently, what I would do.

As I approached him, he said, almost to the word, what I most desired him to say.

"Come aboard, young man. Are you looking for passage?"

"I am, sir," I said, "but I have no money."

"Money? Who said anything about money? A handsome fellow like you—why you'll bring us good luck, and you have the looks of a gentleman about you. I could use some company at night—good conversation I mean—I don't get any from these rough lowlifes I have under my employ, and I have an extra bunk in my cabin, so come aboard."

"Where are you headed?" I asked.

"Istanbul," he said. "Quite the city. Well worth seeing. Maybe the two of us could enjoy a nice Turkish bath there together. What do you say?"

"I bathed this morning," I said, intentionally acting clueless to what he was hinting at to give him hope.

"No, I mean, what do you say to going to Istanbul?" he asked. "A young lad like you should see the world, and I can show you all the best places there."

"Yes, Istanbul would be a sight to see," I agreed.

And so it was settled. I had no intention of letting the old lecher near me—I'd kill him first, but his will was weak because of his boyish lust, so I would use it to my advantage.

Within five minutes, I was in his chambers. He told me I could have his bunk—it turned out he did not have an extra, just one with room for two. He told his men I was his nephew; they said nothing in response, not to my face at least, although I listened in on their conversations when they were not about, so I knew they thought me the captain's special boy. But I never let it be proved true.

And what would I do in Istanbul? Use my powers to make myself the next sultan, or at least the vizier, of the Ottoman Empire? Not much of that empire was left by then, however. Still, I knew of no other place more likely to charm me, and so to Istanbul I sailed as soon as the sun rose that morn, leaving Van Helsing and my other enemies with no knowledge of my destination.

CHAPTER 6

THE RIVER THAMES was calm enough, and so was the English Channel as our ship proceeded through it. For the first few days, I spent most of my time in the captain's cabin. He appeared now and then to wait upon me; I wouldn't let him too near me, although I had to give in and let him sleep on the cabin's floor—once I woke and found him standing over the bed, stroking himself, but when I grabbed my shoe and hit him where Adam hung his fig leaf, the man knew better than to try again. I easily manipulated his will so that he desperately longed for me, yet he feared to come near me save to obey my orders. His own men clearly feared him, although they mocked him behind his back. Still, none of them dared to disobey him to his face, and so they did not disturb me, even when I would walk about the ship to get some fresh air; in fact, I believe they feared me as well, for they knew if I were the captain's boy, it would go ill for them if they displeased me. As for what they thought of me—well, I could not care less, for I knew I was master over each and every one of them, whether or not they knew it.

One day, out of boredom, I decided to be cruel. I went up on deck and found the roughest man on the ship. I purposely bumped into him, then shouted, "Watch where you're going, you scoundrel!"

He growled as he turned around, little suspecting who had assaulted him. When he saw me, he said, "You damned dandy—I'll show you."

But he had been swabbing the deck, and in his hurry to grab me, he leapt forward and slipped on the wet boards. In a second, he was lying before me on his back, and all the sailors were laughing at him as I had intended.

I reached down to help him up, and when he took my hand, he tried to pull me down with him. But I was ready for him, and despite his being nearly twice my size, I managed to pull him almost to his feet, then let go of his hand so he fell back again, amid more laughter from his fellow sailors, and not a few whispers of awe for my own strength.

I had long known my strength excelled that of any boy my age, yet it was good to see I had met the test against one twice my age who labored long and hard and so should have also been double in strength to me. After that incident, I knew none of the other men would trouble me, and the next time I made an appearance on deck, they all lowered their heads, stepping out of my way, and a few would even politely ask, "Sir, is there anything I can do for you?" Occasionally, I would let one of them fetch me a drink of water or polish my shoes so he would feel privileged to serve me.

And so our journey went along pleasantly as we sailed through the Strait of Gibraltar and into the Mediterranean. I had heard much of the Mediterranean's dark wine-colored waters and dazzling beauty, and I did not find myself disappointed, but I quickly grew weary of being at sea.

We had just passed the tip of Sicily one evening when a storm sprang up. I went down to the captain's cabin to stay out of the men's way while they fought to keep the ship afloat, but before long, I realized what dire circumstances we were in. Then I went up to the deck, intending for my phenomenal strength to serve a purpose in this desperate situation.

The ship was tossing and turning on the waves, and before long, try as they had, the men were forced to go from shouting and fighting the sea to praying out loud. Many an Irishman was aboard, so I heard prayers going up to the Virgin Mary as well as to God Himself, causing me to wonder what fools these men were to pray so. I had never seen any evidence that God existed—and if He did, how could He have let evil beings like Dracula into the world? Therefore, I had little hope for His assistance. In fact, I did not forget that in Mr. Stoker's novel, I had read of how my sire had traveled to England on a ship and killed all the crew in the process—where had God been when doubtless those poor sailors had also cried out for His help?

Not long after, I watched a giant wave sweep one of the sailors overboard. The shouts of horror from his comrades were only surpassed by their cries at the sight of a great two-masted ship, doubtless a century old or more. Even I could scarcely believe my eyes when I saw it. It miraculously floated just above the waves, and it gave off an ominous bright glow, as if it were aflame. At first, I thought the ship had caught fire, perhaps struck by lightning in the storm, but that did not explain how it floated above the sea. Then I heard my shipmates crying out, "It's *The Flying Dutchman!*"

I had heard of a ship by that name and that some mystery was associated with it, but I did not, in truth, know its full story.

Nor did I need to, save that it was an object of fear. The sailors screamed and pointed toward it, and they were all clearly terrified—indeed, they were so frightened that they went temporarily mad and rushed to the rowboat, trying to untangle it from the ropes that had blown it about; they intended to set the boat into the sea so they could flee before *The Flying Dutchman* pulled up alongside us. "It is death for sure if it reaches us!" cried one, and "Better take our chances in the sea!" shouted another. Several of them lost their lives in their mad attempt to climb into the rowboat, crowding into it, and those supposed to be lowering it instead let the ropes go so they could jump into it as well. Somehow, a few managed to stay in the boat once it hit the water. One of these survivors, looking back up at the ship's deck, cried out to me, "Sir, hurry! Save yourself!" and he beckoned me to join them, but before I could take a step forward, the waves had already separated the boat from the ship, and within a few more seconds, I found myself alone on the deck, mesmerized by the approaching ship whose ghostly glow had caused such fear. Although I could hear the wind rip away my own ship's masts and tear apart the very boards that held the hull together, I simply stared at the glowing ship and waited for its approach, inexplicably feeling that somehow my destiny was tied to it.

Just as I felt the ship begin to sink beneath me and the spray of the waves furiously come up on the deck, beating me so I could barely stand, the ghost ship swept up on a wave and flew above my own ship, crashing into it, landing on it, sinking it, but the collision also sent me flying up into the air, and before I could guess my fate, my face collided with the ghost ship's mast. Desperately clutching at its canvas to prevent my fall, I managed to grasp a rope from a sail, which left me hanging maybe ten feet from the ghost ship's deck.

I swung above the deck, swaying back and forth, fearing I would yet fly off into the sea, and almost equally fearing setting foot upon the legendary *Flying Dutchman*. Nevertheless, I lowered myself down the rope to the lesser of two evil fates until I felt my feet slipping onto the deck.

For a moment, I collapsed on the deck, not seeing anything to grab on to and knowing that lying flat was my best hope not to be swept overboard by the rollicking waves. I did not even look to see whether anyone was manning the ship until I heard behind me a deep, terrifying, bellowing voice.

"Quincey Harker, it is not your time yet!"

Turning around, I was stunned to see the ship's captain behind me, a great tall man with distinguished features, a pale face, a high forehead, and a red scar crisscrossing his forehead.

"I...who...what ship is this?" I managed to ask, fearing the answer.

"You know well where you are—upon *The Flying Dutchman*," said this terrifyingly gaunt and haunted-looking man. "Captain Vanderdecker at your service. Sit down, Quincey Harker."

"How...how do you know my name?" I asked, even as I sat up to perch upon my knees, suddenly noticing the sea behind the captain had become calm, white, almost glassy, the water clear. Surprised, I stood and stepped to the ship's edge, ignoring the captain and peering into the sea as the sun rose and caused the water to sparkle. I could swear I saw a mermaid swimming alongside the ship—she surfaced, waved, and laughed before returning into the ocean's depths.

"All gone. All gone, your shipmates; their work is done, but not yours," the captain was saying. He had been speaking while I stared at the sea, but I had not been listening.

"Where are your crew?" I asked, turning to look about the empty deck, afraid he would think me crazy to say I had seen a mermaid, and yet, I felt delighted to have done so. Had Captain Vanderdecker not been there, I might have jumped overboard to join her—especially now that I got a closer look at the captain. His clothes were like those of a pirate out of a fairy tale—centuries out of date. He wore a hat that would have made Sir Walter Raleigh green with envy, and a rich red silk coat that made his skin look all the more deathly pale in the light. His eyes were sunk back into his head and he had a cleft lip that suggested he may very well have now and then gnawed upon his own flesh.

"How...where is your crew?" I repeated.

"I bear my weird alone," he replied, sweeping his hand around the deck.

"What?" I asked, not understanding.

"I bear my weird alone!" he bellowed, still waving about his arm until he brought it back before me, just inches from my face so that I could see how his fingers were practically fleshless, like bones with pieces of meat run through a grinder dripping from them.

I dared not shriek at the sight, dared not ask him to explain himself, for I had no idea what might be "his weird"—nor did I wish to know.

But he must have seen the puzzlement upon my face, for he continued, "My life is that of a solitary wanderer upon the sea. To wander thus is my weird, my fate, but also my destiny. I have tried many a time to end this painful existence, to drown myself in this infernal sea, but the waters refuse me the kind gift of death. It is my punishment, my penance for the wrongs I committed, but it is also my great blessing, for I can stop others from committing the same transgressions I have done. Do you understand now, Quincey Harker?"

I looked at him closely. I found I could not tear my eyes from him. I had exercised my will upon other men by allowing my mesmerizing eyes to pierce their very souls. But it had been easy, for no one had ever challenged me, ever stared me down as this man—if man he were— now did with a power far greater than my own.

"Do you understand, Quincey Harker?" he repeated. "For three centuries I have wandered the seas, taking the lives of those who are evil, freeing those who have suffered by sending them to a watery grave, releasing them from the burdens of this life, but once in a century, I have a greater destiny. To save a soul—to save one who can become great and good—one who would become a demon among men if not for my intercession, allowed by the grace of a God who shows no grace to me. You, Quincey Harker, are one of those I have been sent to save because you show potential for greatness."

"What do you know of me?" I demanded. "How do you even know my name?"

"How do I know? You dare ask when I know you so well—as well as I know myself. I know what it is to have power and to have the choice to use it for good or ill. Do not use it for ill, Quincey Harker. I warn you. Your time to die has not yet come; you are being given a new gift of life, a second life, for you should be dead save for the grace of God, and so you must never surrender to the evil, Quincey. Do not surrender to the evils of this world, or to the evils of your heart, simply because you feel you have been unjustly wronged. Should you do so, you will never know happiness."

"Who are you to tell me what to do?" I demanded. "You are not my father. You are not my master. I am my own man, and I shall do as I please. You have no power over me. What right do you have to judge me?"

"Be not foolish, boy. I do not seek to control you. I seek to guide and help you. Do not spurn my kindness." His voice was ominous enough to make any man let loose his bladder, but I was not of the stuff from which mere mortal men are made. And whether I liked it or not, I was of a stubborn nature and could not resist being obstinate toward him.

"I know nothing of kindness," I spat back. "All whom I have trusted, have loved, they have betrayed me, become my enemies. Why should I trust you?"

I stepped forward and raised my fist in his face, and although his words sought to enter my heart, my heart was hardened against them.

"So be it! You also have chosen your weird to bear!" he shouted and then he cackled hideously, like a very banshee. For a second, I thought for sure I had destroyed myself. I had been rash and foolish when I knew not what power he had—the power perhaps to annihilate me. But the evil blood within me had refused to listen to him, to be ordered about. My blood had boiled up in anger and controlled me against my very will—I who could control others was quickly learning I could not control the hell within me.

Instantly, the sky grew black and the clouds opened. Rain poured down so hard that within seconds I could no longer see Captain Vanderdecker before me, and stepping forward, groping with my hand to touch him, hideous as he was, I found he had gone, gone before I even knew what had been his crime or what it was to bear one's "weird." And I began to weep because I had not listened to him, and now, perhaps, it was too late. And then the sea roiled beneath the ghost ship, tipping it, sending me flying over the deck until I plummeted into the sea, where water filled my lungs, and I lost all consciousness.

CHAPTER 7

"**SIR, SIR,**" **SAID** someone, slapping me on the face until I opened my eyes and revealed I was conscious.

"Bloody hell!" I shouted, swatting away the hand and quickly sitting up, finding the blinding sun left me unable to see my tormentor.

"He lives!" exclaimed the man.

He was not speaking English, yet I understood him, and I would have pondered this oddity a moment longer if his mouth were not running over with words.

"You live, sir; you live. We feared you dead. They say it is a bad omen that I pulled you from the sea, but see, I wear the evil eye," he said, pointing at a bluish type of medallion hanging around his neck, "so nothing can harm me, although I admit I have never seen the Fata Morgana before."

"Fata Morgana? What are you blabbering about?" I demanded.

"The Fata Morgana—the fairy ship—the sign of Morgan le Fay, yes. You, you are English—you must know the great sorceress King Arthur's sister. She appeared above the sea—we saw her ship—in the storm, we saw the ship floating in the air, and then it disappeared, and you were there in the sea as we fought to reach shore, so we pulled you aboard. We feared you were dead, but we had no time to try to wake you because we fought the storm, see, but we made it to shore, and now first thing, I slap you awake and here you are."

"Here I am?" I growled. "And just where is here? And who are you?" I wanted to hear no more about fairies or ghost ships. Surely, I had simply dreamt while unconscious in the sea—I could not possibly have seen a ghost ship or its weird master.

I felt waterlogged and wet and miserable, although I found myself wrapped in a blanket, but the fool who claimed to have rescued me had not removed my wet clothes. Thankfully, I was beside a fire built on the sand. As the man answered my questions, I struggled to remove the blanket so my wet clothes would benefit from the flames' heat.

"I am Bogdan, a fisherman. I pulled you from the sea."

"But where am I? Is this Greece?"

But I had learned a little Greek at school and I knew that was not the language he spoke, so it baffled me all the more that I could understand him when he certainly wasn't speaking English.

"No, no, not Greece—bah on the Greeks. This is Romania."

"Romania?"

I muttered it, but it registered no real reaction from me. It was too unexpected an answer because I knew Romania did not border the Mediterranean. I knew that much, but here was a sea, and—

"What sea is this?" I asked, geography not having been one of my strengths in school.

"The Black Sea," said Bogdan. "We pulled you from it, there in the waves, we saw you fall from the sky—from the fairy ship, we...it was a miracle...are you a fairy yourself, sir?"

"God, I hope not," I replied, sitting up and feeling my stomach growl. The noise was loud enough that Bogdan heard it and motioned to a woman nearby to bring me a bowl of some sort of gruel, which I gratefully accepted. It was spicy and full of vegetables and far from anything I had ever tasted back in England, but I ate it with fervor, then cast the bowl from me.

The woman ran to grab it while Bogdan looked at me with surprise.

"No need to be rude," he said. "We are trying to befriend you."

"How did I get to Romania?" I asked.

"You dropped from the sky, there into the sea, just about twenty feet from shore. We saw—"

"No, I couldn't drop from the sky. I—"

"I did not believe it either, but—"

"Be quiet!" I demanded, jumping to my feet. "Do not interrupt me again. Do you not know your betters? Now speak sensibly. How did I get to Romania?"

"I told you, sir, I—"

I stared into his eyes to see whether he lied to me, and when I did so, he cringed before me. I heard his wife muttering a prayer as I glared at him, and then I looked over and saw her making the Sign of the Cross as her husband knelt and then practically lay down in submission on the ground before me. The evil eye, still dangling on a string around his neck, was powerless against my mental powers.

"You fool," I said to him, feeling in my pockets and finding them empty. "Have you any money?"

"Just a few pennies. We are poor, sir. We—"

Great rage now soared up within me, for I would need money if I were to get anywhere, and I obviously had lost what I had in the storm. My anger suddenly turned so hot that I felt all the blood rush up into my face, and then I heard his wife scream.

"He is a vampyr!" she cried.

My eyes turned to her at these words. Losing all patience and without a second thought, I struck her dumb with my mind until she crumbled to the ground in fear beside her husband.

"Spare us, please, great lord," begged the husband. "We are poor humble folk. We only mean to serve you."

"Give me the money you have," I replied.

His wife scrambled closer to his side and reached in to pull the money from his pocket, for he was too paralyzed with fear to move. After a little struggling to wrench it free, she placed the coins on the ground, and then the two of them, on their knees, slowly moved backward to distance themselves from my wrath.

I reached down and pocketed the few coins, and then remembering my manners, I said, "Thank you for the food and for rescuing me from the sea. I am sorry to take what little you have, but I must look after my own needs first." And then, feeling great hatred for myself, I ran farther inland from the shore until I came to the forest. There I hid in a clump of bushes from all men—and wished I could equally hide from myself.

What had come over me? Why had I been so angry with that couple who had sought only to assist me? The woman had truly thought me a vampire! I was no vampire, but what astonishing power I had to make them cower before me—power that my sire, Dracula, had given me through his blood, drunk by my mother and passed on to me. Power so incredible that I now feared myself.

Then I heard voices—I did not wish to see anyone in my misery. Quickly, I stumbled from my hiding place and began to run away from the sound. I stumbled like a madman through the forest, not knowing where I would go, but dreading the thought of making contact with another human.

After about an hour, I noticed the sun was going down, so I thought I should find shelter for the night. I had been through quite the ordeal in the last several hours, and if I received a good night's sleep, then perhaps I could make sense of all this in the morning.

There was nowhere to take shelter save the forest trees, but since it was not raining, I saw no reason why I could not sleep in the open. I quickly climbed up a tree, amazed at my dexterity, for I had not climbed a tree since I was a young boy, but then I remembered how Dracula had been able to climb up and down his castle's walls without effort, so I should not be surprised by my agility.

I nestled into the bough of an immense tree and managed to make myself comfortable. I feared falling from the tree as I slept, so I ripped off my coat and tied my leg to the branch, not thinking it would hold me for long if I slipped, but perhaps long enough to wake me to stop my fall.

I never did sleep that night, but I lay in the tree, dozing now and then, but continually disturbed by the sounds of the forest coming to life so that I heard everything about me amplified. I had never been outside at night before, not alone at least, and I found I had amazing night vision. I could see the rabbits scurrying about, the bats flying within just a foot of my face, and at one point, an owl landed on my knee as if to investigate whether my eyes might serve for his supper. I quickly reached out and rung the bird's neck before it decided to attack me. Then I ravenously ate it—spitting out feathers and bones like a wild animal, amazed by my behavior but having no other avenue for satisfying my hunger.

In the morning, I swung down from the tree and began my trek through the forest again.

I was in Romania. Why I was alive and in this foreign land I did not know, but I felt it must be intended as some great test of my character, or perhaps in this land lay my very destiny—a destiny I feared to admit to myself, for I knew Romania was home to Dracula's castle, so my presence in this strange land could not be wholly by accident.

Yes, I was in my sire's native land. And so, no wonder I had understood the Romanian language instantly. And if it had happened as Bogdan had described, perhaps I had been dropped on Romania's shore for a purpose. I knew not what Morgan le Fay had to do with it— in fact, I knew little of her save what every English schoolboy learns— that she was King Arthur's sister. I had neglected to read Tennyson or Malory in school when they were assigned to us, and as far as I knew, King Arthur was a legend anyway, but then, most people would have said the same of Dracula. Still, I knew Dracula to have been real, and although I believed he was now dead, I felt his spirit, or rather his blood, had somehow drawn me to his land.

I will not prolong this tale with the details of my journey through Romania. It's sufficient to say that I walked far more than a hundred miles. At one point, I joined up with a band of gypsies long enough to sleep in a wagon on comfortable bedding, to eat their food and take some of their gold, and to make them subservient to me through fear.

During this time, I realized that not only did my mind have the power to control others' wills, but I also had a sort of photographic memory, for I could recall in detail everything my father had said in his journals, as reprinted in Mr. Stoker's book, about his own visit to the Carpathian Mountains and Dracula's castle. And so when I realized the gypsies were passing through the Carpathians, I exerted my will upon them to bring me to that very castle, for there, I had come to believe, might lie my destiny. They dared not oppose me, but I saw the fear in their faces when I made my demands, and not being without some shred of humanity, I allowed them to part from me when I was yet a few miles from the castle, and I traveled on alone.

CHAPTER 8

ONCE I PARTED from the gypsies, I did not think it would be too difficult to reach the castle. I had merely to follow Mr. Stoker's directions, although I suspected he had changed some details. Still, who would have thought anyone would seek to travel to Castle Dracula, so perhaps he had written down the actual route? And after all, had I not been there before? For I had read in the novel's final page my father's own words that my parents and their friends had, seven years after the horrific events, returned to see the place where they had slain Dracula; the castle had still stood there at that time, and I had accompanied them as just a small child, so perhaps I might now be guided there by instinct. I truly hoped the castle did still stand. I knew I had nothing to fear there, for both Dracula and his three female partners had been slain, but that was not to say I wouldn't find something of interest in its decaying ruins—perhaps some understanding of that creature who had once been human like myself—if indeed I were human. Somehow, I felt now that I was destined to come to my sire's castle—perhaps to take up residence there, to rule from it as he had once done.

I did not know what I actually expected to find there. Nor did I fear for my safety even if my sire had created others like himself who may have escaped the destruction by Van Helsing and his circle of crusaders, for was I not one of them, or nearly so?

Yet I shuddered to think that if I met those other creatures my sire had made, they might draw me to them, entice me to become evil like them, for while I was not above using my power over other men's wills for my own purposes, nevertheless, I had done no real harm to anyone, or at least very minor harm—petty theft and making people do what they did not wish—but I had not raped or killed anyone. I was not so very evil a person, now was I? But was I even a person, a human, considering my powers? That I ate normal food was a great comfort to me, for I did eat like a human—not like a monster—and thankfully, I felt no desire for blood. And I had often checked my teeth in the mirror to see whether they had turned into fangs, but to date, I had seen no such signs, despite the other changes that had occurred to my body in recent years, puberty coming early and causing me to grow taller and stronger than others my age. Yet, despite my fears, I felt compelled to reach the castle as if I had no other choice but to follow through with whatever Fate had preordained for me.

I will skip over the details of how I located the castle and simply say that I made my way to the Borgo Pass and there traveled until I came upon it, feeling that my very memory pulled me toward it.

Eventually, I saw Dracula's castle rising up on a great precipice. It looked so dark and desolate, perched a thousand feet up, that I was certain it had to be the one described in Mr. Stoker's book, the home of my sire for centuries. Its walls, even from a distance, were obviously cracked, parts of its battlements broken down, falling into ruin, for it had not been occupied for more than twenty years now, and even then, it had been largely in ruins when my father—I mean Jonathan Harker as opposed to my sire, Dracula—had first visited it.

In the distance, I could dimly make out that a road wound up to the castle, but when I approached the foot of the hill, I found the road blocked by several great boulders. In this mountainous area, such stones might have fallen and rolled there, yet the lay of the land made such an explanation feel very unlikely to me. It seemed more probable that someone had purposely moved these stones to prevent entrance to the castle, or perhaps to keep whatever beings were feared to reside inside it from returning back out—although such beings would not likely be deterred by boulders, no matter how large.

I knew I could not now be prevented from continuing my quest. I had great human strength, but not so great that I could lift the boulders. Perhaps my sire could have, for Van Helsing had said that Dracula had the strength of twenty men, but my own strength from experiments I had done was more likely that of three or four. That said, my agility was sufficient that I was able to find handholds in the rocks and pull myself up on to the boulders, and if need be, I knew I would have discovered a way to climb up the cliff itself, so intent was I now on reaching the castle.

Once I made it over the boulders, I found that the road had grown over with scruffy grass, and here and there, a tree had fallen over it. It was a steep climb up the path, and I imagined it would have been quite difficult for horses to pull a coach up it as they had apparently done when my father was brought here. Nevertheless, I kept on, and after about half an hour, I found myself before the gates, or what once had been the gates. Van Helsing had ripped off the doors so they could not be closed against him when he went in to slay the female vampires, and so I did not expect to find my entrance barred in any way. And from all signs, the castle remained deserted, unoccupied ever since Van Helsing's visit.

Once I arrived at the castle entrance, I told myself I had nothing to fear. I stepped into the doorway, yet I found myself hesitating to go farther. And I found myself asking, "Why are you hesitating? Don't you want to understand—to understand just who or what you are?" But what was here for me to understand? What did I think I would find? My sire had been a vampire, a horrible beast who had tried to create a race like himself and who had planned by all accounts to conquer England—perhaps eventually all the world—to become some horrible King Vampire who would rule all the earth—and in time, if he had succeeded, he might well have glutted himself with blood and exterminated the entire human race—for all I knew, such might have been his very goal.

And if he were such an evil being, why did I seek out his lair? Why did I feel a need to understand him? What could I possibly hope to gain? Would it not be better for me to forswear my dark powers—for dark they must be, and what possible good could come from them? They had to be evil, for I had used them to hurt others, perhaps not through serious injuries, but hurtful nevertheless, and I both feared and knew I would do the same again. But I could also use them for good, could I not? Perhaps I could manipulate the minds of people to make them do good—but would that be morally right? Could evil ever truly be used to bring about good?

"Why me?" I cried out loud, my anguish finally becoming too great for me to hold inside, for now I was ready to face my true nature, whatever it be, but I was terrified by the thought, nevertheless. I had not realized until now how great was the pain I had felt ever since I first had learned that vampire blood flowed through my veins. Why me?

My parents had been good people. They had saved the vampire from himself, for had not my mother begged her friends to see Dracula's destruction as an act of mercy, and had Dracula's face itself not settled into peace once he'd had the stake driven through his heart, so that he was free from his evil state? But when they had sought to accomplish such an act of merciful kindness, then why was their child cursed? Why had I been born to carry this cross, to be unholy, to be an outcast?

I had not chosen this state, and yet, here I was, helpless to change it. I could try to live like a normal man, but I would always have this secret, this power coursing through my blood, this desire to use my powers, be it for good or evil.

Finally, I told myself, "I don't know why this curse has been placed upon me, and I don't expect to find any answers here, but it cannot hurt for me at least to try to find answers. However horrible they might be, it is far worse not to know."

The day was growing dark now as a storm began to hover in the air. I felt almost like the elements themselves were intending to drive me into the castle, for when I heard the first clap of thunder and just seconds later the rain began to pour down, I knew I needed to seek shelter, and here I was in the castle's doorway, hesitating until the storm made the decision for me. I quickly stepped inside, my eyes adjusting to the dim, dusty chambers. In a moment, I found I had arrived inside a great hall.

I half-expected to find birds nesting inside, or that rats or other rodents had made their nests inside the walls, but the hall was actually quite clean other than some dirt on the floor and cobwebs hanging from the ceiling. A large stone staircase led up to a door, so I crossed the hall and stopped at the foot of the stairs. Another corridor led off the hall, but I thought if I were to find accommodations for the night, my best hope for a bed would be upstairs. Tonight only, I told myself, I would stay, for with the darkness falling, I would not risk being caught among the wolves and other creatures of the night. But I dreaded even one night in this castle. Still, I also wondered whether in the morning, in the daylight, I would feel otherwise and find it more habitable and to my liking. And deep down, I knew my fear to be outside in the dark was an excuse made by my curiosity, for I had slept outside now many a night, and I knew my strength and will were more than a match for any beast or man that might assault me.

At the top of the stairs was a heavy door that I nevertheless opened with little trouble, allowing it to slam behind me. I now found myself in a room fairly well-lit, due to a series of tall windows, which made me think I was in some sort of banquet hall even before I noticed the long table. Was it here that my father had eaten his first meal in Castle Dracula? Even in the dark, I could see the room clearly since my eyesight was almost as good at night as during the day. Not only did I have extraordinary extrasensory vision, but I also could hear the slightest movements, and by the time I had been in the banquet hall but a few seconds, I had sensed motion in an adjoining room, telling me I was not alone in the castle, and then the particular sound of a footstep told me I must be in the presence of another human.

I thought it best to be on alert without yet betraying my knowledge of this stranger's presence. For whoever it was clearly did not want me to know he, or she, was there—he must have heard me slam the door, but that he had not called out for me to identify myself was proof enough that he wished to remain hidden. I considered it might be another female vampire, one whom Van Helsing had not found and destroyed, but it was just as likely to be some poor gypsy or a peasant who had sought shelter in the castle before me.

But the main question was: Did this stranger wish me ill?

I moved to the windows to look out, but more to listen behind me for the person's approach.

The view was magnificent. The castle rose up on the very edge of a terrific precipice. A stone falling from the window would plummet a thousand feet without touching anything! As far as the eye could see was an ocean of green trees, with occasionally a break in them where the mountains fell away into a chasm. Here and there were silver threads where the rivers wound in deep gorges through the forests.

The windows were without curtains, and the occasional flashes of lightning enhanced the room's furniture when I looked about. I quickly noted that the chairs and table and even the candelabras in this room were not covered in dust like objects in the other rooms. In fact, a disturbance of dust was clear—the table was clean, as if someone had sat and eaten at it that very day, and the chairs only contained a little dust in hard to clean places. The walls had cobwebs in their corners where they met, but a fair attempt had been made to sweep away most of the dirt from the walls and floors. In short, someone had been living in this room. And since I could hear the person moving about in the neighboring room behind the wall, that person did not want me to know of his or her presence.

Should I remain or should I leave, despite the storm? If it were a vampire who spied upon me, whether with eyes or ears, it could doubtless overcome me, so it had no reason to fear my presence. Why then would it hide from me? No doubt, a vampire in this barren land would most likely be desperately thirsty and have attacked me already. If it were not a vampire, then perhaps whoever it was feared me enough to wait until it could kill me in my sleep. But it could also be a poor, weak human, who feared me. And whether or not the person knew it, there was good reason to fear me, beyond my appearance as simply a strong young man.

I pulled a chair close to the window and sat down to look out at the landscape. It was dark and I craved sleep, and I knew not where to go to find materials for lighting a fire, though I could see well enough without one. Nor did I wish to rummage about the castle looking for supplies or food, though my stomach was beginning to growl. Instead, I wished to wait until the stranger made himself known.

I sat and nodded off after a while. A few times in the night, I woke at the sound of movement, thinking perhaps someone was approaching me, but the sound was distant and would stop within a second, so in time, I realized my companion would not make his presence known that night.

I woke in the morning to the sun rising directly into my eyes, for I was facing east. I should note here that I experienced relief whenever I felt the sun upon my face, for it did not disturb me as it did vampires in tales I had heard, although in Mr. Stoker's book, it said that my sire had walked about London in the daylight without any such problems from the sun. Nor did I have any tendency toward being nocturnal, also a vampire misconception. My powers were great, I did not doubt— probably greater than I knew, for I had no means of cultivating them, of learning from anyone, save by my own accidental discovery of them, but they obviously did not include all the powers of the vampire, nor all the weaknesses such creatures were said to suffer.

When I opened my eyes, the sun was so bright that I instinctively went to raise my arm to block the light. Only, I could not lift my arm.

Within another second, I found I was bound by a strong rope around my body, and then a voice behind me said, "You are awake at last, I see."

I could not turn around to view my captor, and I would not wait to discover what ill he intended me. I instantly let my strength course through my body, lifting myself forward and snapping the rope as if it were paper, then leaping up from the chair and turning to face my capture.

For only a second, I saw his eyes open wide in disbelief and shock, and then I had him by the throat and was lifting him from the ground.

"Who—no, what are you?" he asked.

"Who are you?" I demanded.

"I asked first," he said, boldly, not showing fear but staring me bravely in the eye, "but if you must know, I am Zoltan, Son of Dracula, so you would do well not to interfere with me."

I was so stunned by this statement that at first I did not know how to answer.

"Who are you?" he demanded. "Tell me."

"I...I...." I stuttered, suddenly feeling fearful at the revelation of his identity, and yet I gathered my wits about me to protect myself. "I am also the Son of Dracula," I said. "I am Quincey Harker...and you have not even begun to see the full extent of my power."

He smirked at me, as if doubtful, and although I still had him firmly in my grasp, knowing that he was Dracula's son made me less confident in my ability to protect myself from him. Realizing that even if his power were greater than my own, I might still dominate him through intimidation, I focused my mind upon conquering his will, trying to force him to cry out in fear.

Instead, I was shocked to find his mind like a wall I could not penetrate. At the same time, I felt my own head begin to ache. I tried to ignore the pain, but he stared at me so fiercely that after an anguishing minute, I was forced to throw him down to break his intense stare.

"Who are you?" I repeated again as he rose to his feet. "I have never met one whose will is so strong. How is it that you are Dracula's son?"

"I ask you the same question," he replied.

He spoke in the Romany tongue, his voice revealing he was a native of this land. I answered him back in it, saying, "I am Quincey Harker. I come from London. Dracula tried to make my mother, Mina Harker, into his mistress."

"I see it must be true, what you speak," he said, "for I know Dracula went to the land of the English and that Englishmen came here later and killed him. And you have grey eyes like my own and the same jaw, and no one before has ever exhibited such strength or power in my presence."

"All you say is true," I replied, "but tell me your story and what you are doing here."

"It is a long story," he replied.

"I have time to hear it," I said.

"It is morning. Time for breakfast. You must be hungry. Come; we are brothers. Will you break bread with me? Then I will tell you all."

I was uncertain whether I should trust him, but I followed him from the room and down a flight of stairs to a kitchen where I saw he had already begun to prepare a meal for us.

"Sit down," he said, motioning toward a small table. "It will only take me a few minutes to make us some eggs."

To cook anything looked like a monumental task to me in the rude and ancient kitchen. But he had an open fire going in a minute and broke eggs into a frying pan; then he added some slabs of meat that resembled bacon of some sort. I knew not what they really were, but I was so hungry I would eat it regardless.

My head was full of questions, but I did not dare to ask them and disturb him as he cooked over an open flame. It was sufficient for me to see that he meant me no ill, at least for the moment, although I did wonder why he had bound me with rope the night before. He had not sought to bite me, to suck my blood, so even though he called himself the Son of Dracula, I did not think him a vampire. And when I had used those words to refer to myself, it had only been because I wished to make him fear me, for I did not know what power he did have, and I would not be bested by him if I could help it. I wondered whether his mother had been like my own—a mortal woman almost turned into Dracula's bride. He looked to be about my age, so it was likely. I also noticed he was dark and swarthy with black, curly hair, like those of the gypsies, which made me think his mother was probably a poor peasant woman who had lived near the castle.

But more importantly, I wanted to know how long he had known of his own powers, and from the way he had made my head ache, were those powers greater than my own, or at least, more fully developed? What could I learn from him? What could he teach me? And how could I come to make him love rather than hate me? For if he were Dracula's son, then he was my brother, was he not, and perhaps the only one in the world who might understand me. And he did not appear wholly evil to me—at least not yet. I had read in Mr. Stoker's book—indeed pondered over the words countless times—what my Uncle Abraham had said of Dracula's family—"There have been from the loins of this very one great men and good women, and their graves make sacred the earth where alone this foulness can dwell. For it is not the least of its terrors that this evil thing is rooted deep in all good, in soil barren of holy memories it cannot rest." I had repeatedly tried to believe in that statement, to believe there was good in me mingled with my evil, and yet I could not help but feel, whenever I grew angry and my temper made me show off my powers, that the balance inside me weighed more heavily toward evil.

But if there were another like me, as Zoltan purported to be, who understood my situation, shared my very strange existence, perhaps I could learn to control that evil, or use it to my benefit. I recalled from my days at school how we had been taught Milton's *Paradise Lost*, and how that great English poet had believed that good could come from evil, and how Adam and Eve's sin was ironically a *felix culpa*, a happy fault, because it allowed for good to come into the world in the form of Christ, who redeemed humans by forgiving their sins. Could my inherently evil nature undergo a similar transformation? Would Zoltan be able to guide me along the path to using my powers for good rather than evil?

I wished to know the answers to all these questions, but first, as Zoltan set plates of eggs on the table and seated himself across from me, I asked, "Why, when you are so powerful, did you bind me as I slept? You could not have known of my powers—did you truly fear me?"

"I fear anything in this castle," he replied. "I do not know what I might expect here."

"But you have been living here for some time; I can tell that," I said.

"Only a few weeks," he said, "but that has been enough to frighten me, and yet, I find myself enticed to stay. Enticed to seek for answers to who or what I truly am."

I nodded. "I have come for the same reason," I admitted.

"Eat then," he said. "Eat and I will tell you my tale, and when I have finished, you will tell me yours."

And so he began his story.

CHAPTER 9

ZOLTAN'S TALE

I WAS BORN to gypsy parents. They roamed with their band throughout the region of the Carpathian Mountains. I have no memory of my parents, however, for reasons that I will reveal. I knew only my grandmother, and when I grew old enough to realize other children had parents while I did not, I asked my grandmother the reason why and she simply said that my parents had died. When I asked how, she began to cry profusely, and after that, I so feared upsetting her that it would be many years before I would ask again.

But I soon realized there was a deeper mystery about who I was beyond that of questioning my parentage.

One day when I was about eight or nine, while I was playing with some of the other boys, an argument arose among us, and one boy, Mihai, who was a couple of years older than me, pushed me down. My pride was more wounded than my bottom when I found the other boys laughing at me.

I quickly regained my feet, ready to fight, only to have Mihai push me down again.

This time, in anger, I shouted, "Mihai, I wish you were dead!"

He only laughed and walked off.

I went back to my grandmother's wagon. She had a man named Boldo who helped her. I think he was her lover, for I would hear them making noise in the wagon at night when I was supposed to be sleeping, although I was too young then to realize what they must have been doing. This man saw my tunic had been ripped from when I had been pushed. Grandmother was out gathering berries in the woods, so he told me we would have to hide the tear from her or she would be angry. I only owned one other tunic, but he said he would sew the torn one for me. I suspected Grandmother would be able to tell anyway, but that fear was distracted when Boldo asked me how I had ripped it. I began crying then, for I felt ashamed to have been beaten, even if it had been by an older boy. But with a little coaxing, he got me to tell the story. When I told Boldo that I wished Mihai were dead, he warned me, "You must never say anything like that."

"Well, I do," I repeated.

"No, never say such things," he insisted, and then he made the sign of the evil eye.

I got over my anger soon enough. Boldo made me change out of my shirt, and then he gave me some stew, and soon after, my grandmother came home and we all ate together.

It was almost bedtime when we heard a startling cry. We were in the wagon, but Boldo opened the door and stepped out to see what was wrong, and in another minute, Grandmother and I also stepped outside as we heard angry voices mixed with wailing.

"Where is the boy?" demanded one of our fellow tribesmen.

"He is a demon. Bring him to us!" shouted another.

"There he is! There is the murderer!" bellowed yet another, and this time, I realized they were pointing at me.

Grandmother wrapped her arm around me while Boldo stepped forward to try to calm the crowd and understand what had happened.

"Mihai is dead," said one man. "He hung himself. His mother just found him hanging from a tree."

"But...but...." Boldo could not find words, so shocked was he.

"The boy said that he wished Mihai dead, and now he is."

"Zoltan has been here with me all evening," said Boldo. "He did nothing. Mihai knocked him down, and he came home in tears, and I patched his shirt. That is all that happened."

"You cannot blame my grandson because someone chose to commit suicide," added my grandmother, who had known nothing of the incident between Mihai and me until this moment, yet she was ready to defend me.

"He is evil!" screamed one man in the crowd.

"We know what he is!" shouted another.

"He is a boy," reasoned my grandmother. "How could he make someone commit suicide? It is ridiculous."

I do not know how long Boldo and my grandmother argued with the crowd. I could not believe the crowd's accusations against me— how could they think I had anything to do with Mihai's death? I admit I was somewhat glad he was dead, for he had always been a bully, but I never would have hurt him.

I don't remember what was finally said to appease the crowd, but eventually, they departed. My grandmother told me to go to bed. I was too frightened not to obey.

As I tried to fall asleep, I relived in my thoughts the incident with Mihai over and over. Why had he killed himself? I couldn't imagine why he would do such a thing. Later, I heard Boldo and Grandmother whispering among themselves; I could not hear their words, but I could sense the fear in their tones. Did they think the villagers would still seek to hurt me?

The next morning, I came to realize that Boldo and my grandmother had not feared harm coming to me from others; rather, I was the one they feared. For in the morning, Boldo was gone. He had been like a grandfather to me, yet he had left early that morning before I woke, and Grandmother would give me no explanation of where he had gone. When he did not return by nightfall, I knew he had left because of me, although I could not understand it.

I also soon learned that none of the other boys would bully me again—or play with me. They repeatedly avoided me, and I was too young to know how to ask them in a rational manner why they did not like me—and to ask them would have required being able to talk with them, but they would run whenever they saw me coming.

In the past when the caravan would travel, I had often walked alongside it with a group of the boys, but now, I found that their mothers kept them inside the wagons, not wanting them near me.

This situation went on throughout that summer, with my grandmother never mentioning it to me. She was simply quiet, but she looked unhappy, and I feared to ask her why—feared she would say that she was afraid of me also, and I continually had nightmares that she also was abandoning me.

Then one day, we came upon another gypsy caravan—the gypsy leader of this group was my grandmother's brother, Loiza. We had no family in our own caravan since my grandmother had married into our band and only had one daughter, my mother. When we met the other caravan, my grandmother told me to remain in our wagon and not let anyone inside it while she went to talk to Loiza.

An hour later, she returned and told me, "From now on, we will travel with my brother's caravan under his protection."

"Why grandmother?" I asked.

"Because I said," she snapped, and then I saw that she had been crying. After a moment, she added, "It is just that I wish to be with my family."

"I am your family, Grandmother," I told her.

But she ignored my remark and went back outside to gather firewood so she could cook us supper.

The next day, our old caravan departed, leaving us with the new one.

I was puzzled by this change, but after a few days, I found it was for the best, for the children of my new caravan did not fear or run from me, and for a time then, my life appeared to be normal again.

Life then went along peacefully for many years, and I almost forgot about the incident with Mihai. When I did think about it, I recalled how he had been a bully and a deeply disturbed boy and his father a cruel man, so I did not hold myself accountable for what had happened. However, because of the events that followed, to this day I still wonder whether my words triggered in him some desire to commit such a terrible crime against himself.

Only one other incident bears mentioning from this time of my life; somehow, through no efforts on the part of my people, I learned to read. Occasionally, we would pass a sign or some writing along the roadside. Once when my grandmother told me we were heading toward Bucharest, I saw signs along the road and began to distinguish among them until I could read "Bucharest." It happened quickly, so that I barely realized I could read—it was no more surprising for me to see a word and know what it said than it was to see a farm and know it was a farm—and so I made no fuss about it until one day I saw a sign that made me realize we were not going in the right direction. When I told my grandmother we were on the wrong road, she hushed me, thinking me only argumentative. Not for anything would she go to our leader to tell him I thought he had made a mistake, and yet, when we later turned around because the rest of the caravan also realized we were going in the wrong direction, she became curious how I had known of our mistake before anyone else. When I explained how I knew, she said, "Why, you can read!" and she was quite shocked. None of our people could read, so she knew no one could have taught me, and yet she could not account for my ability, but read I could. After that, on many occasions, I took advantage of it, practicing and puzzling over letters and words whenever the opportunity presented itself, which it rarely did other than for rare signs on buildings or along the road and the occasional poster that would contain not just words but actual sentences.

Yes, read I could, and soon, I discovered that I also had a great proclivity for languages, being able to understand the people in the villages, speaking in Romanian, even sometimes in other tongues, such as German or Polish. My grandmother was amazed, but she warned me to keep my ability to myself, for she did not think her people would like that I was so intelligent—reading, they thought, was one of the tricks of the devil and the *Gadze*—those not of the Romany race.

As I grew up, I began to realize I was quite handsome and that the girls of the caravan liked me. Even the girls several years older than me began to flirt with me, and many a boy acted toward me with a hint of envy. We were not a large caravan, so I only had perhaps a half-dozen young women to choose from for my future bride. We gypsies marry young among our people, and at only fifteen years of age, the young woman I had my eyes upon, Florica, was thirteen. I had waited two years for her to be old enough to be my wife, for she was a sweet girl and one who was kind to my grandmother, and so I knew she would make me a good wife, besides which she was even-tempered, intelligent, and beautiful—so beautiful already that I could only imagine how beautiful she would be at eighteen or twenty.

I was sure that she had similar feelings for me as I felt for her, although we had only exchanged a few words, but the glances we sent each other were enough for me to know she equally desired me. And so I went to her father and made my request.

"Zoltan," he politely replied, "it is not to be. She is promised to another."

I was devastated. I could not even form words to reply. My heart began to break within me until finally I managed to ask, "Who?"

"Gunari," he replied.

I knew Gunari. He was my chief rival among the ladies, my only competition in athletics among the boys, and he was our chief's grandson, my own second cousin in fact, and destined perhaps someday to be our leader.

"Then I will kill Gunari!" I shouted. The words escaped my lips before I had even thought them. Rage consumed me as I glared at Florica's father. Then I turned to go.

But before I had gone a half-dozen steps, Florica was clinging to me, begging me not to hurt Gunari, screaming to her father, "No, I love Zoltan!" And her father was trying to wrench her from my grasp.

Finally, I turned, grabbed her father by the throat, and told him,

"She will be mine!" And then, though he was a big, fat man who must have weighed twice my own weight, I lifted him up and threw him to the ground. When he landed, he struck his skull upon a rock and blood gushed forth from his mouth.

"Papa!" screamed Florica, running to his side. For a moment, she was frantic, but once it was clear he was dead, she stared at me with unbearable pain in her eyes.

I was just as astonished as she was. I had known I was strong, but the rage within me had caused me to behave as I had never done before. I did not know then what to do until Florica's mother came running out of their wagon and began screaming, "Murderer! Murderer!" and she began to assault me with her fists.

"No," I said. "No, I did not mean it; I—"

And then Florica screamed, "I hate you, Zoltan. I never want to see you again. You killed my father. I hate you!"

By now the women's screams were attracting the rest of the caravan's attention, so soon I found our people starting to circle us. Panicking, I turned, shouting behind me, "I'm sorry, Florica. I love you. Forgive me!" and then I ran, pushing aside those in my way before their shock would turn to rage and my own people would turn against me.

I ran into the forest and into the hills. I ran for what must have been an hour, seeking a hiding place. Finally, I found a rock outcropping up a hill where I could see below me whether my people—my enemies now—should try to follow me. I kept watch all that evening as darkness gathered for any sign that they would come after me. I waited for a mob of people with burning torches seeking to put me to death for my behavior. I have never been so terrified in my life, but what frightened me most of all was that they might not come and kill me, for upon reflection, I wondered how I could live with my guilt over what I had done. How was it even possible that I had exhibited such strength? And while I had loved Florica and would have been jealous had she married Gunari, I could find no explanation for how quickly the anger and rage had filled me, how quickly I had turned against her father, and most of all, I found it impossible to explain how I could have lifted a man who must have weighed over three hundred pounds, have grabbed him by the throat and raised him into the air with one arm and thrown him like I had, for I must have thrown him a good ten feet. How was that possible? I was terrified to know what it meant, and now all my fear and guilt over what had happened to Mihai—that I also might have been instrumental in his death—came back to me.

I did not sleep for many hours. Instead, I went mad. Once it was well past dark and I realized my enemies were unlikely to come searching for me so late, I stepped out from behind the rock outcropping and walked about on the hill. I was terrified by what I now contemplated doing, and yet I could not control my curiosity. I went up to a large rock that the strongest man would have found difficult to lift, and grasping it with both hands, I easily raised it over my head. And yet, I was not convinced that I could possess such incredible strength. Tossing the rock from me, I went up to the stone side of a cliff, and I inserted the fingers of one bare hand into an indentation in the rock; then with just the strength of my fingers, I tore away a sizeable chunk of stone.

My exclamations of shock at witnessing this deed can well be imagined.

Next, I went up to a large tree, a tree a good three feet in diameter, and wrapping my arms around it, I tore it up by its roots. I turned it easily in my arms and carried it about with me—it was not just a log, mind you, but a tree that must have weighed hundreds of pounds. I carried it up to the top of a cliff and then tossed it down.

And then in utter terror at whatever it was I had become, I returned to the rock outcropping and cried myself to sleep, hoping only to wake from the unreal nightmare that had become my life.

CHAPTER 10

I WOKE IN the morning to the sound of a fire crackling. Then opening my eyes, I saw first a small campfire and then a figure bent over it, tending it.

"Who is it?" I asked, struggling to get up.

But my eyes adjusted enough to recognize my grandmother before she answered.

"Get up and eat," she said.

"How did you find me?" I asked.

"You left footprints, broken branches along the way. My eyesight is not so bad yet, and when I saw the rocks and the tree destroyed, I knew where to look for you."

"Are they coming after me?" I asked.

"I think not. They are all afraid of you." She sighed and stirred something in a pot over the fire. "I tried to keep the truth about you quiet all these years. I had hoped by now everyone had forgotten about it, but almost the moment I heard of what you did to Florica's father, I also heard people talking about it—I did not know that anyone but my brother knew the truth among his people, but he apparently cannot keep a secret; he must have told his wife and daughter, who then told Gunari. Poor Gunari is hiding in his wagon, certain you will kill him next. And I understand you said you would. Does he have reason to fear you?"

By now, I had walked over to the fire. I took the bowl of gruel she handed me and sat down beside her on a small log.

"I don't know," I admitted. "I guess not since Florica won't want to marry me now. I don't know why I became so angry. I did not wish to hurt anyone. The rage just boiled up in me when Florica's father said she was to wed another. I loved her, Grandmother, but now she must hate me."

"Regardless, you can never come back to the tribe now. People fear you too much."

"I fear myself," I replied. "Grandmother, I don't understand it. What is wrong with me? I mean, how could any man have such strength as I have? I am hardly more than a boy, yet even a grown man could not do what I have done."

"No, he could not," she agreed, taking a bite of her food and staring into the fire.

"Grandmother, what have you not told me?" I asked. "What is this secret you have kept from me?"

She stared off into space for a moment, making me think she would refuse to answer me. Then she sighed and said, "I had hoped I'd never have to tell you. I had hoped it was just bad luck and coincidence that caused Mihai's death, but now I see it is what I always feared. The very thing that made even your father leave from fear of you."

"My father?"

"You know your mother died giving birth to you, but I have never told you that her death was also the reason why your father ran away.

Only, he left not because of grief but fear. I do not know whether he even still lives. We never saw him again once he left."

"But why did he run away? How could he abandon his son?"

"He was too scared, Zoltan. Too scared, too unwilling to accept that you could be his son, for you are also perhaps another's son."

"I don't understand. Was my mother unfaithful—?"

"No," she interrupted. "It was nothing like that. At least not of her own choosing. It is a long story."

"Tell me," I said. "I must understand what is wrong with me, or how else will I know what I should do?"

"I doubt you will know what to do even after I tell you," she stated. She took another bite as I waited for her to speak again. "I am an old woman. I don't know what I will do now. I won't be in this world much longer. I have tried to protect you, but now you are old enough to protect yourself. I hope you will only protect yourself and not harm others. I—I love you, Zoltan, but I am perhaps more scared of you than anyone else, for I know what that creature—that monster—was capable of, and—"

I could see her face change in the fire's glow. I could see the terror spread across it as she began to tell me the truth of my origins—a truth containing the most horrible words I have ever heard.

"Zoltan," began my grandmother, "you are not like other people. Indeed, I do not know if you are even human."

Such was the strange introduction to a tale that I would have found unbelievable if I had not just witnessed with my own eyes the rage and strength within me. I listened spellbound and paralyzed with fear as she continued.

THE GRANDMOTHER'S TALE

You know, Zoltan, that our people, the Romany, have long been treated as outcasts, and here in Romania, we were enslaved for many years. You are too young to remember, but when I was a girl, slavery was our natural state; it was what our people were used to, and while it was not a desirable state, we knew no other way to support ourselves than to toil on the land of our boyar. Then laws were passed, well-meaning laws, to free our people, and in time, those laws were good, but at first, they made life very difficult for us because we knew no other form of life than slavery.

I was a young girl when freedom came for us. My family and I traveled about with our people, wishing to leave our own boyar, who had always been cruel to us, but we could not find work anywhere. Our people might be free, but we were nevertheless outcasts. No one would hire us. We had no money to buy land. We were at the mercy of others. For years, we barely scraped by to make a living. Our people are often called thieves—if it is so, it is because we had no choice but to steal just to survive, until our children knew no other way. It was a sad turn of events, but it was the fault of those who had formerly enslaved us and now left us free but destitute.

In time, I married and gave birth to your mother, and I raised her as we continued to travel about year after year. Finally, when your mother was about to bloom into womanhood, our leader made an agreement with a great lord, one Count Dracula, who asked us to come and work for him. He was a strange man, a powerful noble, yet one who lived solitarily in a towering castle in the Carpathian Mountains with only a few servants to do his will. He had work he wished us to perform for him. We did not know his reasons for many of the tasks he gave us, but he paid us in gold coin, and so the men of our band did as he asked, while we women were happy that we could feed our families.

It was not long, however, before we came to realize that Count Dracula was no mere man, no regular lord, but that his power and his cruelty were greater than that of any boyar who had formerly enslaved us.

And when we came to know that, we also learned that we were completely in his power. The only access to his castle was through a mountain pass, and once we entered into his domain, we found the pass blocked off by an avalanche of rocks; in short, we were trapped within his estates. At first, we thought the avalanche a simple accident of nature, and the Count's headman assured us the stones would be removed within a few days. But while we waited, one of our children went missing in the night, and a couple of nights later, another child disappeared. When we reported these missing children to the Count's headman, he told us they must have been lost in the forest, but we did not see how that was possible when there were only a few square miles around the castle and we had searched thoroughly, nor could such small children—they were no more than three or four years of age— have gotten out of the pass on their own. And then a few mornings after the first child's disappearance, their bodies were both found just a few dozen feet from our camp, drained of blood, their skins drying and rotting upon them.

And then began the rumors...I wish they had only been rumors. People began to make the sign for the evil eye and the Sign of the Cross and to whisper of the vampyr. Within a couple of more days, a young woman disappeared and then panic set in.

When the Count's headman refused to listen to our demands to be let out of the pass, a group of our men went to the castle. They tried to break in. They threatened to burn it down. And then Count Dracula showed himself at the castle window, and I remember full well what he told us, for I was there and I heard his terrifying booming voice as he said, "You all belong to me now. I am your lord. I will do as I please while you will have no choice in the matter. I must slake my thirst."

When a man cried out in anger, calling the Count a "monster," the Count raised his hand and pointed toward the man, and a moment later, the man fell over dead.

Then we all gasped, shrank back; even some of the men began to cry with fear. What could we do against such a monster? What hope did we have?

"I will hold your people only for as long as necessary," said the Count. "You need not all die. It will only be for a couple of weeks. An Englishman is coming to arrange for my leaving this land. You will say nothing to him of my true plans. You will do my bidding, helping me to carry my belongings to the sea, and then when I am gone, you will be free. If any of you defy me, you will all die. In exchange for obeying me, I will take only a few more of your children and your wives. It is my right as the lord of the castle. You will obey."

His words were terrible, ghastly, horrifying, yet what else could we do? His power infiltrated into our very minds. He knew, being the monster that he was, that he could simply feed upon us and control us.

There was nothing we could do—we were utterly helpless, and our numbers dwindling. A few men tried to flee the camp, but later, their bodies were found in the forest, drained of life, killed by the vampire who held us hostage. I was relieved to know he planned to keep us as prisoners only for a few weeks, for he had a great plan to travel to

England, to scourge that land. The Englishman, who arrived at the Count's castle to help arrange for his journey, never suspected the Count's true purpose. After several days, the Count departed, leaving the Englishman behind as a prisoner in the castle. We heard the Englishman's shouts, the fear in his voice, but we dared not disobey the Count and aid the poor foreigner.

By some miracle, the people of England whom the Count attacked learned how to defeat him, for later, I heard that the Count tried to return to our land, but he was pursued by the English, and they managed to destroy him. But that was all after my greatest fear came true.

The Count, that horrible, damned creature, chose your mother, Zoltan, your dear beautiful mother, my beloved daughter, to be one of his final victims.

Your parents had fallen in love before we became the Count's servants, and it was on May Day, while we were the Count's slaves, that they were to be married. Of course, the night before, she was not to see her husband, but the Count himself sought her out. He summoned her to the castle, saying that he wished to give her a gift for her wedding. I was terribly frightened when the summons arrived. I begged her not to go because it was Walpurgis night, the night when the veil between the worlds is parted, so I thought the Count would be all the more powerful.

I could see in your mother's eyes that she was frightened, yet she told me not to fear. I begged and pleaded with her not to go while the Count's servant waited for her reply. Finally, she said, "Mother, I love you. I'll always love you, but if I don't go, it will anger the Count, and then he may seek to punish all of us. I love you and our people too much to let him turn his wrath against all of us."

I held on to her. I tried to force her to stay. I tried to think how I could hide her, but news had already spread through the village, and soon because of their fear, our own people came to force her to go as a sacrifice to save their own lives.

And so she went as a martyr to the castle, while our people pinned me down, not letting me follow her, and I wailed in agony, certain I would never see her again. Only her betrothed also tried to stop her, and equally, the other men held him back, while she walked with the Count's servant to the castle, never wavering in her step, doing what she thought best for the welfare of those she loved.

I cried myself to sleep that night, and I barely slept at all. Then as the dawn was just starting to creep into the sky, I nearly jumped through the roof of the wagon when the door opened, and there stood your mother, alive, before me.

"Jelena, I never thought I would see you again!" I exclaimed.

"Nor did I," she said. She was in a daze, so I led her to the bed and had her lie down. I fetched her water and some bread and fruit and begged her to tell me what had happened. She was so pale that I feared what the Count had done to her, but she was still alive. He had not killed her, perhaps only drained her a little.

She lay in her bed for three days after that. I feared the Count would summon her again, for I had heard how if he bit her two or three times—I was never sure how many—he could change her into a being like himself, but he must have left that next night, for we had no further word from him, and a day later, it was discovered that the road to the castle was no longer blocked. That's when we heard the Englishman begging us from the castle windows to help him, but we had no time, for we feared if we remained, the monster would return and enslave us again.

For three days your mother lay in her bed, pale and ill, as we traveled. Boldo drove the wagon while I sat and tended to her. We journeyed for days, until we must have been a hundred miles from the castle, and only then did we begin to feel safe, and it was still several more days before your mother regained her color and strength. Only then, for I had feared upsetting her too much before that, did I dare to ask what had happened when she had entered the Count's lair.

Yet when she spoke, it was as if she had found her mate for life. She told me Count Dracula was very gracious to her. His servant had led her into the castle and brought her to a room where she was told to bathe and change her clothes. A beautiful if old-fashioned gown was given her to wear, and then she was escorted to a great banquet hall where the Count awaited her. He immediately met her at the door, and though she drew back in fear, he only took her hand and raised it to his lips to kiss. He then fed her a sumptuous meal and filled her foolish young head with wine. He praised her for her beauty and for her choice of a husband, for he had observed that her betrothed was a good, strong man, and he told her what a good father and provider he would be. Then the Evil One presented her with a wedding present, a gigantic necklace of enormous diamonds set in gold—an ugly, gaudy piece of jewelry, but of great antiquity and value. She was stunned, overwhelmed with it. She realized the great security it would forever bring to her family. I have kept it all these years to pass it on to you someday. Many times I have thought of selling it when our people were starving, or I have considered destroying it because of the Evil One from whence it came, but it is rightfully yours, and you should view it as your payment, your inheritance in recompense for the crime that the Evil One has done to you.

[At this point, my grandmother broke off speaking to take from inside her robe the necklace of which she spoke. It was humongous. It must have weighed two or three pounds. Only a great queen, one who was tall and strong, could have borne its weight about her neck. The jewels—emeralds, diamonds, and sapphires—sparkled in the light of the small fire inside my grandmother's tent. I realized the great wealth and security that one could gain from such a necklace—enough wealth for a common member of our people to live comfortably the remainder of his days. I held it in my hand, feeling its eeriness despite its grotesque beauty as my grandmother continued her tale.]

Your mother felt a great debt to the Count for that gift, and with the wine that had gone to her head, and with the realization that the Count was by right her lord and, therefore, had ancient claims upon her as his servant, she gave herself to him that night, but not in the manner of a woman to a man. He bit her and he drank of her blood, and then he also forced her to drink of his blood from his very breast, as if he were her mother, feeding her as a babe. She told me all this in tears, not, she said, because it was painful—she admitted she had actually derived great pleasure from it—but because she feared she had done great evil and that I would despise her ever after and even cast her off. I assured her I could never do either, for she was my beloved daughter, my only child, and I would never let anything part us. Then she told me that for a moment, as she felt the Count's blood coursing through her veins, she had experienced such strength, such power in her limbs that she thought she must know what it was to be a man, even a god, of extraordinary strength.

And then the taste and power of the blood overwhelmed her body so that she fainted, and when she woke, the dawn was breaking and the Count was gone. Suddenly, fearful and not knowing what else to do, she had fled the castle, surprised to find the front door unlocked, and then she ran all the way back to our caravan, the Count never appearing or stopping her, for she had not known that he had departed the country that night.

I did not understand this strange turn of events—why had the Count chosen to spend a night of passion with her without killing her, without preventing her from telling others what had happened? I only knew my precious daughter was still alive, and I thanked God for it.

She then told me that she still wished to marry Marko, her betrothed, but he was now hesitant to carry through on his marital promise. He said, without giving explanation, that he thought it best to wait. Then your mother began to show that she was with child; she insisted that Marko had betrayed her, had taken her virginity some three nights before she went to visit the Count, yet he denied doing such, and soon after, he disappeared one night, having gone we knew not where. We never saw him again, and in truth, Zoltan, I honestly cannot tell you whether that man was your father, or whether you are Count Dracula's son. I have thought at times that you do look like Marko, and I never knew your mother to lie, but even if you are Marko's son, the Count's blood doubtless runs in your veins. She did say she blacked out from the loss of blood when he fed upon her, and who is to know what he might have done to her while she was unconscious?

Within nine months of her visiting the castle, you were born, above normal size, with a head already full of hair, and as you know, your mother died during your birth.

That, my dear grandson, is all I can tell you of your birth, save to remind you that regardless of whether or not you are the vampire's son, you are my grandson and I love you, and I have always tried to protect you. But I am an old woman now, and I cannot protect you from this situation in which you now find yourself. It breaks my heart to say it, for I have lost everything else I have ever had—my husband, my daughter, my brother's trust—and now I am to lose you, but I think it best that you go off on your own now to someplace where your past is not known. I wish I could continue to protect you, but it is safer for us both if we part. Hopefully, you can sell the necklace the Count gave your mother. You should be able to support yourself well on it, and if not, you are young and strong, so I have no doubt you will be able to make your way in this world, and I let you go with my blessing.

CHAPTER 11

ZOLTAN'S TALE CONTINUES

I NEED NOT describe the painful scene that followed after my grandmother finished her tale. I was heartbroken, disturbed, and felt like a death sentence had been placed upon me, but after a few moments of her reasoning with me, I saw she was right that we should part. She gave me her blessing again as well as the few coins she had on her—for she knew it would take me some time to find a buyer for such a valuable necklace—and then I kissed her goodbye.

Later, I wish I had convinced her to come with me. The necklace was worth enough that we could have sold it and used the money to find a place to live where she would have been comfortable the remainder of her days. She also would have ensured that I did not fall into the misfortunes that I soon after brought upon myself. But she was born a gypsy, and I think perhaps she was happier living out her days as one. She would have been very uncomfortable, I do not doubt, in the life that I then set about pursuing.

And so I parted from my grandmother, from my people, and from the only life I had ever known, and I set out to find my own way in the world. I did not know where I would go, or what I would do. I only knew that I must get as far away as possible from anyone who might recognize me. Part of me had died inside, and so I wandered about aimlessly for several days, not caring in what direction I went or what would become of me.

After a few days, I came to a village. I could tell by people's reactions there that my presence was undesirable. They moved away from me in the streets and eyed me suspiciously because I was of the Romany. I considered finding other clothes, although the thought of dressing like the *Gadze* was repulsive to me. I had run out of food the day before, but I had the few coins my grandmother had given me. I had the necklace the Count had given my mother, but I dared not part with it yet, for people would think I had stolen it until I could find clothes that did not proclaim me part of a race too often associated with thievery.

I proceeded to a couple of shops to buy provisions, but I quickly found myself turned away even when I showed my money and stated I was willing to pay. I was surprised that prejudice was so deep, for money usually soothes quarrels and prejudice due to most men's inclination toward greed.

I hated the thought of it, but if I were to survive in this world, I would need to change my appearance. I would have to buy new clothes and then find myself a place where I could wash up and don my new attire. I continued through the town, seeking a friendly shopkeeper who would sell me a change of clothing.

Finally, I came to a small shop where I heard from inside the language of my people being spoken. I entered and found a middle-aged husband and wife chattering away in my tongue. When I addressed them in my language, they seemed surprised but pleased to see me. I soon learned that they had long ago decided to live in the town and end a nomadic life. It had been a hard transition for them, but after many years, the townspeople had learned to accept and trust them. They even had a daughter who had married a *Gadze* a year ago and was now expecting her first child.

This kind couple took pity upon me. They not only sold me the clothes I needed, but they let me stay with them for several days, feeding me and telling me all they could about their experiences from their youth when they had been nomadic like myself until they had decided to leave their people and live in the city. I similarly shared my desire to live among the *Gadze*, explaining that I was tired of traveling from place to place, as well as begging and watching my people be mistreated. I told them my only close relative, my grandmother, had recently died, and so I had then decided to leave our people. I did not feel it was much of a lie, for my grandmother and all my people would be dead to me now.

My newfound friends understood my situation. They offered to help me further by finding me work in the village, but I felt it unsafe to stay in this town, for it was one that my people had visited in the past, and I feared them discovering me there. I also knew that if anything should happen to cause people to be aware of my great strength, my people might hear of it and seek me out to kill me. So I thanked my hosts for their kindness, but I told them I intended to journey farther on, perhaps to Vienna to seek my fortune. Why I chose Vienna, I cannot say, except that I had heard marvelous tales of it, and it being such a large city, I thought I would easily be able to acquire a new identity there. Vienna was a long journey by foot or rail, and I could only go by rail if I stowed away since I did not have enough money for a ticket. Nor did I dare to sell the necklace yet, although I was sure I could get a very good price for it in Vienna, and then perhaps, I could use the money to set myself up in a business of some sort to provide me with a livelihood, though I knew nothing of being a shopkeeper or a farmer or any other occupation common among the *Gadze* because my people had been so nomadic.

And so I continued my journey, thanking my hosts for their help, and setting off with my new clothes and an extra pair to spare, and still a few coins and the necklace, for my kind hosts had refused any money for food or lodging. I now went forth to seek my fortune, this time with a vague purpose in mind.

It was a long and tiresome journey to Vienna. Often along the way, I considered going somewhere closer like Budapest, but I still longed to journey on whenever I came to a sizeable city. Every few days, I would stop and work for a day or two, splitting firewood or helping on a farm to acquire money so I could have a meal, and a couple of times, the farmer repaid me by giving me a ride in his cart to the next town.

As I traveled through Hungary and finally to Austria, I discovered I was surprisingly gifted in languages, quickly picking up various foreign words and understanding their meanings. I even learned how to imitate dialects and accents quite well once I realized such skills would aid me in hiding my true identity and becoming one among the people of Vienna. And while a couple of times I was called "gypsy," based on my skin color or the shape of my face, by the time I reached Vienna, such occurrences were few, and in such a large and cosmopolitan city, my appearance caused little surprise or scrutiny.

I was convinced that once the transformation of my identity was successfully accomplished, my future would be very bright. By now, I had almost immediately forgotten the real reason I had left my people, for no more strange signs of my powers had revealed themselves, nor did I try to experiment with them since I feared the result.

When I arrived in Vienna, I found a lodging, paying my last few coins for a couple of nights' stay, and then I went in search of someone to whom I could sell the necklace. I was deeply concerned about being cheated, not knowing what the necklace was actually worth. I spent considerable time visiting various shops and observing the shopkeepers with their clients when they didn't realize I was watching. Finally, I approached one whom I believed would be honest but discreet, and when I was the only one in the shop, I drew forth the necklace to show it to him.

"*Sacrebleu!*" he exclaimed—he was a Frenchman. He was frankly astonished and asked where I had found such an ancient and valuable piece of jewelry. I had been considering how to reply to this question, for I had long expected it, so I told him it was an heirloom that had been passed down in my family for generations (which was not untrue since it had been in my mother and grandmother's possession). In truth, he said it dated to the fifteenth century and would have been prized by the Hapsburg dynasty itself. He was quite regretful that it was too valuable for him to deal with, but he bid me come back the next day, and in the meantime, he would find someone who could assist me.

I greatly appreciated his help, while at the same time spending the rest of that day and night in dread that he would contact the police, not thinking me capable of having honestly come by such a valuable piece of jewelry, but I must have had an honest face, and my mastery of the German language no doubt had helped to make my story plausible because the next day, he introduced me to a gentleman who dealt in valuable jewelry and even had members of the nobility among his customers.

"It is a beautiful piece, and an antique," this man confirmed, and in another minute, he named a price many times more than I had ever thought to receive for it. When I did not reply, my mouth hanging open, he assumed I was unwilling to sell, so he raised the price another 10 percent, apologizing that he could not offer me more.

"It may be worth more," he admitted, "but times are hard, so I do not think we will find a buyer if we ask too much."

I was pleased beyond words and readily accepted his offer. He wrote me a cheque for the amount that instant, and before the day was out, I had opened a bank account and deposited my fortune, as well as pocketing enough money to purchase clothes worthy of a gentleman.

The next day, I took up lodgings in a fashionable part of town, and while I did not try to pass myself off as a member of the nobility, I began to live the lifestyle of the wealthy, knowing in time that my money might run out, but if I were careful, it would sustain me in such a lifestyle for a couple of years, and during that time, I intended to make many contacts and set myself up in business, or better yet, find myself a beautiful wife with a wealthy father who had no sons and would, therefore, be agreeable to taking me into the family business.

Such were my goals until I began to develop friendships with the young men of Vienna. I quickly joined a club and became popular with the members there. They were at first curious about me since I was new to the city, but I led them to believe I was from a good Austrian family who resided in the country, and after I bought them a round of drinks, they were more than happy to call me their friend. We soon engaged in the kinds of sports and play young men do—horse racing, drinking late into the night, the occasional orgy (which I visually enjoyed but abstained from participating in fully from fear of hurting any young woman with my superhuman strength), and all manner of ribaldry and bawdiness.

And then one day, they introduced me to the gaming tables. I was reluctant to play at first. I did not know how, in fact, so I simply observed as my friends played and lost, grew frustrated, played again, and lost some more. Only one of us ever seemed to come away with a profit—a young man named Wolfram, who was quite the cardsharp. Nevertheless, I could see that he was not always honest, and this fact, in conjunction with how he had once mocked a new suit I had bought, made me feel he deserved to be taught a lesson. So one day I agreed to play with him and a few other friends, certain I would win.

While others hope for luck at cards, I knew my luck lay in my ever-increasing understanding of my true powers, which continually revealed themselves to me in surprising ways without my seeking to develop them. I had begun to notice that I had the telepathic ability to read people's minds—no, I did not hear every word they thought, but I could usually read their facial expressions and pick up clues, perhaps a certain aura they had about them brought on by their emotions; in any case, while watching my friends play, I had come to realize when a gambler was bluffing. Now, as I played against Wolfram, I discovered that I could actually see, as if with his own eyes, what cards he was holding, and while the luck of the draw still factored into any game, I had a distinct advantage over him in knowing what cards he held. Nevertheless, to make him confident, I let him win the first couple of hands.

Then I changed the game—we would now play by my rules, though neither my victim nor my friends realized it. I made certain my friends won back everything they had lost from this man, and then I convinced them, telepathically and without their awareness, to resign the game for the night until only my victim and I were left at play.

By then, Wolfram was furious at having lost to my friends, and he was determined not to lose to me, the new member of his set, whom he had hinted, when mocking my suit, was only posing as a gentleman. Even though he was correct in that assumption, I was just as certain that he was only posing as a true sportsman at the gaming table.

I need not go into all the details of that night's game. It is sufficient to say I won hand after hand, and each time I won, his ire rose until he gambled more and more of his money, unable to resist the temptation, until by dawn, I had completely impoverished him.

I then took my winnings and his IOU. Our companions had watched our play on the edge of their seats for hours. They now begged me to be merciful to this cheat, but instead, I denounced Wolfram as a liar and thief until even those who had called him friend were silent and simply hung their heads as he made his way from the room, a beaten and defeated man. The last words he heard from me were, "I will call upon your bank in the morning to demand my winnings."

Wolfram then went into the street, wondering from whence would come his next meal, for even the clothes on his back were now my own.

I felt heartless, but I did not care. I had been pushed around enough in my life by my own people, not to mention by a vampire I had never met but who had destroyed my people's lives and my own by his blood entering my veins, and so, I was no longer inclined to be kind to anyone who wronged me in any way, although I could still be generous to anyone with a kind heart. I was only heartless toward criminals—and anyone who cheated his friends was a criminal and, therefore, deserving of punishment. In this belief, I was not heartless, only just.

And yet that night, as I fell asleep, I realized I was now extremely rich. And not just because of my winnings. In truth, I had been spending money faster than I intended, and the interest on the money from the sale of the necklace was not enough to live on indefinitely. Nor, if I wished to continue living as a gentleman, could I go out and earn money. But now I had found the solution—I had discovered my talent for making money by mental manipulation.

Still, if I played to win, using my mental advantages over my opponents, was I not as immoral as Wolfram? Was such behavior any different from cheating? Perhaps, but it was not so wrong if I only played against cardsharps, against scoundrels who would have cheated me anyway—then I was playing in self-defense to protect myself and any others whom such scoundrels would cheat. I could find enough such thieves in the world to play against and thereby keep myself in cash, while remaining respectable in appearance, and if the scoundrels who lost to me did make a fuss and draw attention to me, I could always travel elsewhere.

The next morning, I went to collect my fortune from Wolfram, but upon being greeted at his door by his valet, I saw the man bore a long, mournful face. When I asked to see Herr Wolfram, he replied, "I'm sorry, sir, but my master is no longer of this world."

"What do you mean?" I asked.

"Dead," he replied, and then he stood aside as two morticians bore out a body beneath a sheet.

"Dead!" I exclaimed. "Why, what happened to him?"

Before the servant could answer, I felt a hand on my shoulder and a voice asking, "What have you to do with Herr Wolfram?"

"Do?" I asked, turning angrily to see who spoke to me, but I restrained my anger when I found a policeman confronting me.

"Herr Wolfram was shot," said the officer. "We believe by his own hand. We do not know why, however, and it could still be a case of murder. Therefore, I need you to identify yourself. How did you know Herr Wolfram?"

"I—we—we were friends," I muttered, deeply insulted to be confronted on the street in such a manner that everyone in Vienna could witness.

"Were you with him last night?" asked the officer.

"Yes," I said. "I and a few of our other friends."

"Could I have your name and address?" he requested.

I gave him the information he desired. Then he told me he would be contacting me later since he did not have time to interrogate me at the moment, having to speak now to the coroner and the young man's family, by which I assumed he meant Wolfram's married sister, for he'd had no living parents, nor a wife nor children.

"Do not leave Vienna," the policeman told me.

"Certainly not," I replied. "I'll be happy to help in any way I can."

I had lied through my teeth so as not to arouse suspicion. I had no desire to aid in the investigation. What was there to say except that I had gotten the better of Wolfram in a game of cards, and he had found it appropriate to react by blowing out his brains? Though, I did not learn the manner of his death until later. Still, I knew that with him dead, I could not acquire my winnings. To pursue the money would put me under too much suspicion, and I did not trust my other friends to keep my secret of having been the cause of Wolfram's despair, for we were friends in revelry, but our affection did not extend beyond the bottle and gaming table.

I resolved now that I would immediately leave Vienna, despite what I had told the policeman—who was he to tell me what I must or must not do? I was innocent of guilt. Wolfram was a criminal and had chosen his own fate. So I went to my banker, closed my account that morning, and by noon, I had packed my few belongings and was riding in a coach on the way to Salzburg.

The journey there was long enough to allow me to turn matters over in my mind until I decided to leave Austria altogether. I did not want the law pursuing me, for I would be thought guilty of murder now that I had fled. I did not fear the police—not much anyway—for if any of them tried to arrest me, I knew I could easily beat three of them at once with my bare hands—but if they had guns, well, that was another matter.

And so I journeyed on, over the Alps, through Switzerland, which struck me as a tediously dull country of cleanliness and upright people, and then into France. I was badly in need of increasing my income if I were to live comfortably, and if I were to make my living by winning at cards from cheats, I might as well go where the greatest amount of success was likely to be found, and where else could that be than Monte Carlo?

And so I was called to the Riviera, to the great casino, and to a great fortune. Nor did I think twice about this decision. Rather than feel regret over Wolfram's death, I would find other villains like him, and take from them what they had unjustly taken from others. Then when I had finished with them, if they wished to end their miserable existences, so be it; I would be doing mankind a favor to rid it of such vermin, and I would share half my earned wealth with the poor, keeping the rest as payment for my benevolent services.

And so I arrived in Monte Carlo, the very gem of the beautiful French Riviera, a veritable paradise, and just like the Garden of Eden, crawling with snakes, snakes I would cheat. But I had not expected that those snakes would also have beautiful rich wives—or that I would equally find myself without scruples when it came to seducing them.

Yes, seduce. Could I not punish these men best by taking everything from them—not just their wealth, but also their wives? Nor did I doubt that most of those women were just as foul and black of heart as their husbands. I would make love to them, taking care of my own needs— needs still not met since I had lost Florica—and then I would drop them so they could share with their husbands the poverty into which I intended to sink them.

It was a sublime plan—a way to serve as God's vengeance upon the immoral, and why not? Count Dracula had been pure evil, but I would use my power for good—my mind to defeat evil men, and my strength and charisma to destroy their evil wives. It was a glorious strategy so far as I was concerned.

CHAPTER 12

I KNEW IF I were to get away with my plan, I needed to be subtle about it. I showed my face in the casino only once or twice a week, and I lost the first few times I played; then I won only occasionally and modestly so as not to draw attention to myself. To win enough to support myself was all I needed at first, until I found my victims—those evil men I would punish for their sins, enriching myself in the process.

For the first time now since I had fled my own people, I began to feel relaxed and at leisure. In Vienna, I had been still adjusting to my new life, but here in Monaco, I took delight in my new identity, passing myself off now as a lesser Austrian noble, and being accepted into the very highest circles of society as a result. Furthermore, because Monte Carlo was a town where people came to play for a few weeks and then departed, no one came to know me well enough to question my identity, and while I was friendly with many, I made certain to become close friends with none, and I carefully avoided becoming involved in the court of Prince Albert of Monaco or befriending any of the city's locals.

But while my life was amusing enough at first, and I frequented the casino until I became well-known and welcomed there, after six months or so, I began to weary of this life. I had not yet amassed enough money to let me live permanently in the style I desired, and I did not know what else to do until I was set for life with my fortune. I dreamt of perhaps going to the United States where I knew so many immigrants were pouring into the country that I would easily be lost among them and no one would question whether I were a self-made man. I also liked the Americans' self-confidence and lack of pretension when I met some of them in Monte Carlo. Yet another part of me yearned to travel to exotic lands—the jungles of South America or Africa, where perhaps with my prodigious strength and powers, I could set myself up as a sort of king or even a god among a tribe of bushmen who would serve me the remainder of my days. My prolixity for languages had quickly led to my reading English, and I did not doubt I could quickly master any African language in a matter of days. I filled my spare time by reading novels by Joseph Conrad, Robert Louis Stevenson, and H. Rider Haggard and dreaming of what a life I might live, free of the restrictions of society, a veritable god in such a wild place where I would prove myself dominant over the natives.

But the desire for power, as delicious as it appeared, was not so powerful an influence upon me as the loneliness I was beginning to feel, a loneliness that included a longing for my own people, or for any companion who would be my friend, or better yet, my mate.

And so I began to look about me at the beautiful women who came to Monte Carlo. Far too many of them were married. Rarely did a single woman make an appearance. But, I told myself, what woman would be fool enough to stay with her namby-pamby husband when she could have such a man as myself? Nor was my confidence and pride unwarranted, for by now, in my twentieth year, I had grown into the perfect specimen of manhood, and many a married woman I had seen gaze upon me with lust in her eyes when her husband was not looking.

I toyed with the thought that I could have any woman I chose—a string of women even—and I soon intended to seduce any woman married to a wicked man so I might destroy him. I say I *intended*, for I considered such possibilities, and yet when such married couples came my way, I did not act, perhaps because some vestige of morality remained in me. Despite the vampire blood in my veins that made me believe myself invincible and free from the normal rules that restrained man, I was still a man, and if I allowed that blood to seek its satisfaction, I feared I would be unable to restrain it from doing evil that I might later regret.

Then one day when I was sitting at the bar in the casino by myself, a strikingly beautiful woman came up to me. I had never noticed her before; it must have been her first visit to the casino, for I could not have missed such a stunning creature—not one with such a bosom, such piercing green eyes, such raven-colored hair. I was so surprised that such a woman would enter the casino alone, and her fragrant perfume was so intoxicating, so overpowering, that I was at a loss for words until she spoke to me.

"Bonjour, Monsieur," she said, "or should I say, '*Latcho dives*'?"

I was so stunned by this greeting that I knew not what to reply. It took me a moment even to realize, so distracted was I by her beauty, that she had addressed me in the Romany tongue; how could she have recognized my ethnic origins so easily?

"Bonjour, Mademoiselle," I replied, speaking French with my feigned Austrian accent, not yet ready to give away my true identity.

She looked at me, her eyes piercing mine as if to verify her suspicion, and then her lip curled upward into a smirk and she let out a faint laugh before saying, "Do not fear. I will not give your secret away. In fact, I believe it can be a benefit to us both."

"I do not understand," I replied, but as I gazed upon her, I was completely willing to participate in anything she thought mutually beneficial, for she was indeed intoxicating. Her thick black hair was up, as was the fashion that year; her evening gown was cut lower than perhaps it should be, but it was made of sumptuous cloth, and a mink stole was wrapped around her shoulders, though her arms were bare. Around her neck was a priceless string of pearls, or so it appeared. I knew nothing of jewelry or women's fashion, but I was wise enough to know that this woman dressed to show she was wealthy...and available.

"Buy me a drink and I will explain," she replied, again in Romany.

I did as she requested, calling the bartender and not being too shocked when she ordered vodka.

"I do not know your name," I said to her once the bartender went to prepare our drinks, "but I am—"

"Zoltan of the Romany. I know," she said, "although you claim to be Baron von Hoffmann."

I looked at her in astonishment until I found my tongue and asked, "And what, Madam, is your name?"

"I am known as Baroness Berchtold, but to you, Zoltan, I am Dame Fortune."

"I am pleased to meet you, Baroness," I replied, kissing her hand, for I would have to ingratiate myself with her if I wished her to keep my secret.

"Do not fear," she said. "I can see the worry in your face, but there is no need for it."

Then she lifted her glass and drank the vodka straight down in one gulp.

Astonished, I said, "Baroness, does your husband approve of you drinking like that?"

"Fortunately for you," she replied, "I am a widow. A very wealthy widow. And you are an attractive young man, badly in need of a companion."

I did not know what to say. She was so bold, so blatantly throwing herself at me. Who was she? And while I knew what I wanted with her, what did she want with me?

"I have been watching you, Zoltan," she continued. "I have seen your skill at cards, and I suspect it is more than skill, and furthermore, I believe I have some similar skills that will please and amuse you. I think we could come to a mutual agreement to both our advantages."

I felt the heat rise in my face. How had she guessed my secret? I had never even seen her in the casino before. She could not have simply guessed at my purposes, could she? My sixth sense told me to excuse myself from her presence, but I found myself too fascinated by her to leave, nor did I want to show fear by running off.

"Come," she said. "Let us go back to my room where we can discuss this in private."

My feet moved against my will. I took her arm as she offered it. I walked her out of the casino and to a neighboring hotel where, fortunately, we saw no one as we went up to her room. What self-respecting woman would invite me to her room? None. And yet, I did not doubt she had great respect for herself while simply dismissing society's false morality.

I need not explain what next occurred between us. In truth, to do so would be tortuous for me. She introduced me to what I can only describe as the Garden of Eden—a veritable paradise. There I discovered the greatest pleasures that any man can possibly know, and I am proud to say that while my phenomenal strength was sorely tested, it proved itself far from wanting. Indeed, we were to spend many nights of passion together.

But each evening, I left her, despite her making it obvious she did not wish me to part from her. I went back to the casino or to a private party to play cards and gain my fortune. She argued with me, telling me she had millions and millions of francs put away that we could never spend in ten lifetimes, and yet, I did not wish to take her money. I did not wish to be ingratiated to her, not after how she had already made me her slave every night; for as strong and powerful as I was in other ways, each night when the casino began to empty, I became helpless to resist returning to experience her charms.

Still, after several nights, I began to feel overly exhausted. Lack of sleep and countless hours of early morning passion had sorely begun to sap my strength. I dared not complain, but I knew I could not continue such exertion night after night.

And then one evening, in her chambers, while we were in the throes of passion, our arms wrapped around each other, the baroness—for I knew her by no other name—declared, "Zoltan, I wish to have your child."

When I heard these words, I was so shocked that I tried to shrink back, but she would not let me. She had her legs wrapped about me, her hands on my hips, and I discovered now that her strength was greater than my own as she forced me into a position to pleasure her. I was unable to fight her, unable to stop myself, unable to do anything but succumb to her will—or at least, I would have, except that, frightened like a mouse in the grip of a serpent, I found myself unable to perform.

Then she angrily thrust me from her, mocking me. "I thought you were a man. I thought you alone would be able to satisfy me, to give me the child I crave!"

"A child!" I exclaimed. "A bastard? Is that what you want from me?"

"Do not speak like that," she said as I stood in amazement at the foot of the bed and she rose on her knees upon it. "I will not be dictated to by the false morality of mortals."

Instantly, I felt shocked and puzzled by the word "mortals," but I dared not ask what she meant.

"Yes, mortals, Zoltan," she spat at me, making me cringe in fear, for I felt she was reading my very thoughts now—I could literally feel her presence inside my head, causing me to feel more naked than my body already was.

I scrambled across the room for my clothes, desperately trying to put them on as she ranted.

"I am no mortal, Zoltan, and neither are you. You alone of all men may be capable of helping me to achieve my deepest desire, to wreak my revenge. I need you, Zoltan, and you need a companion."

"What kind of evil creature are you?" I demanded, quickly pulling on my pants, grateful that I had not released myself before I had escaped her, and taking all caution to protect my manhood from her.

"What kind of evil being are *you*?" she retorted. "You have the blood of Dracula in you. Did you think I would not know it?"

"But what are you?" I demanded. "Are you a lamia, one who sucks the life from men? Is that why you are attracted to me?"

And then a fire lit in her eyes. In horror, I saw her hair turn into a nest of snakes, and when she stood up, naked before me, I watched as her nether regions became encrusted with scales, and then as she spoke, a serpent's tongue flickered in her mouth.

"I am she who is called Lilith, Mother of the Earth, and I will have my revenge upon the sons and daughters of Eve!"

"Lilith?" I muttered, not understanding who or what that was.

"You are my own son, Zoltan, of my bloodline through the blood of Dracula. Come to me. Come to your mother. Be my lover!"

Her slithering tongue reached out, enticing me as she offered me her hands. Her breasts were bare and luscious and would have seduced any man, but there was death in her eyes and her nether regions—should I ever again enter there, I—I felt like vomiting—it was unthinkable!

My shirt barely in my hand, my shoes lost to me forever, I turned, flung open the door, and ran from the room.

I tore down the hall, down the stairs, out of the hotel door, into the street, and for three blocks I ran until I reached my own lodgings. I entered them and bolted the door behind me, only then asking myself whether I might be half mad.

I collapsed upon my bed, shaking, terrified, wondering how it was that I had escaped. I told myself how fortunate I was not to have finished the act that night, but how many nights had I finished it? Had I already given her the demonic child she sought? Had she gotten what she wanted from me? Who or what was she? Lilith...she had said that was her name, but I did not know it. I had no idea who or what she was. I had read enough of English literature to be familiar with Keats' "Lamia" and Coleridge's "Christabel," but I had thought them only fantasies...and yet, did not Bram Stoker's *Dracula* proclaim itself a novel, for I had by now read that book as well, and therefore, I knew that what masqueraded as fiction could be—and in my case, was—

reality, for here was I, the Son of Dracula. My existence and powers were certainly no fiction.

And if I were the Son of Dracula—after all, that dreadful, terrifying, Medusa-like creature had herself confirmed it—then was it the monstrous blood within me that had been the reason for her attraction? Was I evil myself? But how could I question it? I was so evil that I had convinced myself I was good, that I could be some sort of moral vehicle for performing God's will by punishing the evil. But what could be more evil than to pervert good by using evil to bring it about? Had I truly done any good in punishing evil men by cheating them at cards? And had that evil been how I had attracted this demon woman into my life and my bed until I had potentially destroyed myself?

I lay on my bed, all these thoughts running through my head, as I curled up under the covers. I cried, I wept for my mother and her tragic life, and I dearly longed for my grandmother, who, for all I knew, might be dead by now, but she had been the only person in my life whom I could trust or who had ever shown any vestige of kindness to me. How I longed to see her again. It had only been a couple of years since I had left her. Could she still be alive? Would I find any solace in visiting her, in asking for her advice, or would I only bring more misery to her and I both?

No, I loved my grandmother and she would understand me. I would go back to the casino; I would win the largest sum of money I could this night, and then I would return to Romania and find my grandmother, and together, we would travel to America where I would make sure she lived out the last of her days in comfort. And if I should instead find that she had already left this world, well...I dared not consider that. I only knew I needed money, and I needed to escape this wicked town where I had encountered what I was increasingly beginning to think could only be a demoness.

If only I had been wise enough to flee the city immediately, to realize that, of course, the demoness would be wise enough to follow me to the casino....

That day, I wasted no time. I went and bought a new pair of shoes, and then I went to the bank and withdrew every franc I had, over ten thousand, and that evening, I went to the casino one last time. Not wanting to remain in Monte Carlo any longer than necessary, certainly not long enough for several card games, I went to the roulette wheel. I had never played it before, but no matter, for I had used my mental powers several times to move about small inanimate objects such as pens and playing cards; I could even make my shoes slide across the floor to me when I wished to put them on, and so, at first betting a small amount a couple of times, I quickly found that I could manipulate the wheel and its small ball so it would land in my favor. It took more concentration than usual, for I had to time the wheel and the ball together, but after a few tries with small bets, I was sure I could do it with larger sums of money at stake and succeed.

What passed as luck in others' eyes took great mental manipulation on my part, and I found my energy quickly waning after half-a-dozen successful wins. Finally, I was prepared for my last effort, and because even I was a bit superstitious, I had decided to make my fortune in seven wins. And so I now risked everything I had; should I win, the payout would be close to two hundred thousand francs. And while my win would draw great attention at the casino, I would then make my escape in the early morning hours after the city's nightlife had come to an end and all were asleep.

And so I placed my bet, and the wheel was spun, and I let it circle about a few times. Then, as I had done before, I set my mind upon slowing the wheel while the ball remained in place until it would stop on the very slot I had chosen to win my fortune. But suddenly, despite all my concentration, I saw the ball slip; in horror, I tried to concentrate and force it to spin forward before the wheel stopped, but nevertheless, I could do nothing as the wheel slowed. And just as I was about to realize devastating loss and defeat, I heard hideous laughter.

I looked about as the wheel stopped, foretelling my financial doom, but no one stood by laughing. Dozens of gamblers were crowded about the wheel, and a great collective sigh rose up from them once my loss became known, but there was no sign of anyone who could have laughed. And then, slowly, the crowd of ladies and gentlemen shaking their heads in shared frustration for me began to disperse, and in their parting, I saw my enemy, the woman who had seduced me—raped me in truth—and had now impoverished me.

And though she spoke not a word, her eyes said it all.

And then I heard her voice intrude into my thoughts.

"When you play with Dame Fortune, you take a ride on her wheel. The wheel goes up, but it also comes down, and then you are crushed. You are on the downward turn now, Zoltan, and be assured, the crushing awaits you. I will find and destroy you completely in revenge for how you have spurned me. You had the opportunity to rule this world with me, but now it can never be; it is your loss, not mine, for there is one other with the power to serve my needs, and so I shall now seek his devotion and his seed."

In terror, unable to bear hearing more of her terrible words in my mind, I now dashed from the casino. I heard the gasps of surprise from my fellow gamblers as I brushed past them, but I did not care. I would not be the first person to lose every franc he had in that dreadful place and then race off in despair—let them think my gambling losses motivated my behavior. Instead, it was pure instinct, the unadulterated desire to survive, that made me flee from this woman who sought to destroy me.

I ran that night. I ran and I ran through the streets of Monte Carlo and clear through Monaco until I came to the French border. There a guard tried to stop me, but when I saw him in front of me, I picked up speed and leapt right over the barricade; then I continued running and running until I came to the Italian border where I also leapt over its barricade and tore through the countryside, making my way toward the Alps where I knew it would be impossible for anyone to pursue me. I ignored the cries of the Italian officials, as well as the gunshots fired at me. I simply ran, terrified that the demoness might yet be at my heels.

CHAPTER 13

ONCE I WAS in the mountains, I collapsed and slept to rejuvenate myself, completely oblivious to the cold. When I woke, I spent many days traveling through the Alps. My prodigious strength and dexterity aided me when I needed to climb over a great hill or make speed, for I wished only to return home to my grandmother. But I had no food or money, and so, at times, I had to stop and make do with asking for charity from a farmer's wife—I avoided men whenever I could, finding it easier to use my handsome face to win approval from a woman. I have no doubt many of the young ladies I met would have gladly helped me in other ways besides simply food and drink, but I remained too shaken by my experience with the demoness to act on their advances. Once I was attacked along the road by a highwayman, whom I quickly dispatched from this world with my bare hands, despite his weapon, and I found his purse contained enough money to get me to Romania in style. After I reached Austria, I bought myself a fresh pair of clothes—mine were filthy and torn after my many days of mountain climbing—and I bought train tickets for Bucharest.

Upon arriving in my native country, I began making inquiries about the Romany, not caring who knew my intentions. I feared no one or nothing now, save the demoness—for I knew I could control anyone by virtue of my mind and my strength. I continued to speak with an Austrian accent and my fine clothes kept everyone from spitting upon me or treating me with prejudice because of my gypsy origins—not that I would have tolerated their rudeness any longer. But I had little success in finding out information about my own particular band of people. I traveled a great deal across the country without gaining any news of my grandmother until one day I was walking down the street of a village near Bistriţa where I saw a young man who had once been my childhood friend.

Almost forgetting the very reason why I had fled my people, I called out his name. "Djordji!"

He turned to look, for a moment not recognizing me, but then his face grew pale and he made the sign of the evil eye before he bolted down the street.

In a second, I was after him, and within half-a-dozen seconds, I had grabbed him from behind, spun him around, thrown him up against the wall of a house, and keeping my hand at his throat, I said, "Hello, Djordji. Why do you run from your old friend, Zoltan, huh?"

"Zoltan, I—I did not recognize you. It's good to see you. How are you?" he said, feigning happiness as his forehead perspired from fear.

"I will not hurt you, Djordji," I said. "But I have been searching for you a long time—not you specifically, but our people. Are they nearby?"

"I—Zoltan, please, do not hurt us. Please. Leave us in peace."

"Are they nearby?" I demanded, beginning to lift him by the neck from the ground.

In a panic, he struggled with both his hands against my lone one.

"Answer me," I said, squeezing his throat.

"Please, I don't want you to hurt my family."

"Is my grandmother with you?"

His eyes grew wide and began to roll up into his head.

"My grandmother!" I demanded. "Is she still with your people?"

He did not answer. His face was turning purple.

"Answer me!" I demanded.

"Zoltan, she—she—"

I loosened my grip to let him catch his breath, and then I repeated my question.

"Where is my grandmother?"

"Zoltan, you've been gone over two years. She—she's dead, Zoltan. She died the winter after you left."

I dropped him to the ground. I turned, hearing him gasping and choking behind me. He would be fine in a few minutes. I would be tormented the rest of my life.

I left the village and walked out into the hills, alone—alone for the rest of my days. Why had I ever left her? Why had I not insisted she come with me? She had been old but far from frail when I last saw her. I could have cared for her, made certain she had the best doctors, or if nothing else, I could have spent her last few months with her, have given her comfort in her final days rather than leaving her to die alone and among a people who must have feared or despised her almost as much as they did me.

I was heartbroken, distrait. I did not know what to do. The only person in the world who had ever loved me was now dead. The only human being I had ever trusted. And now I was completely alone in the world, a cursed being, likely being hunted by a demoness, and if she did not destroy me, then, no doubt, I would face years of misery to come.

I slept outside that night, in an open field. I exposed myself to the elements, wishing I would catch cold, become ill, and die. I also exposed myself there to predators in hopes that a pack of wolves would come and tear out my throat while I slept. When neither source of death found me, in the morning I took greater risks. I climbed the Carpathians, and when I had reached a cliff, I allowed myself to plummet down, hoping to dash out my brains; instead, I landed in a tree, my hand instinctively betraying me by reaching out and grabbing a limb and preventing me from self-destruction. I even tried lying at the bottom of a pond and holding my breath, but I discovered that I could hold my breath for an extraordinarily long time, and so I eventually became bored and returned to the surface.

But I will not prolong my tale by going on about the weeks of misery I experienced. It is enough to say that one day I had the idea I could visit Dracula's Castle. I actually thought that, if nothing else, I could find some more ancient pieces of jewelry there, something else I could sell, and then I would go to America to become part of the teeming masses seeking a new life in that distant land. Hopefully, the demoness would not think to look for me there, and perhaps I might still find happiness, for as terrible as grief is, life continues on, and slowly, I began to consider that my grandmother would not want me to be miserable. She had risked her own life to help me escape, so I could honor her best by living.

And so to Dracula's Castle I made my way. I had never been there, yet I had read a copy of Mr. Stoker's *Dracula*, and I had what can be called a photographic memory such that I quickly recalled the directions from the book, and without much difficulty, I found my way here.

I need not go into more detail. I found the castle much as you see it. I have only been here for a month, and in that time, I have only but wiped away the cobwebs in the rooms where I have resided and used the kitchen to make my meals. I spend my days sitting in the great banquet hall where we made contact so I may look out at a world with which I have nothing in common. I sleep in one of the bedrooms, I believe the very one where Jonathan Harker once slept, for it is the only room in the castle with a bed, the others doubtless having rotted away centuries ago since Dracula and his women slept in their coffins. In the lower levels of the castle, I found the coffins of the female vampires that Van Helsing killed, but there was nothing at all in them.

I have explored every inch of the castle, finding nothing of value save the antique furniture and a couple of gold candlesticks and some old silver. I have thought to take off with these things to pay for my passage to America, and I trust you will not try to stop me if I still decide to do so, but for whatever reason, I have felt compelled to remain in the castle for the time being. There are many ancient books and manuscripts in the library I have been reading, although I have discovered none so far that explain to me how it is that I could have the supernatural powers I do as a result of the vampire's blood. But regardless, the castle's gloomy atmosphere appeals to me, and save for when I must step outside its walls to capture game for my meals, which I usually do by chasing it and killing it with my bare hands, I find no desire to leave this place any time soon.

I am young, and I think I would do well to consider carefully my future before I venture forth again into the world of men, and as long as the dreadful creature Lilith does not follow me here, I feel I am safe. I have taken precautions as well, sprinkling holy water upon the doors and placing crucifixes in the rooms, items that will keep out evil, and which, I am almost surprised to say, seem to have no effect upon me, which shows that unlike Dracula and that terrible demoness, I am not predominantly evil, regardless of the vampire blood that flows within my veins.

And so that is the tale of Zoltan, Son of Dracula, and now, if you would so please, I wish to hear your own.

QUINCEY'S TALE RESUMES

I was greatly stunned by Zoltan's story, for it identified so much with my own, only his was far worse, for it was a tale of complete alienation, whereas I had at least chosen my own exile, and I was not without the possibility of being able to return to my native land and social sphere, could I learn to control my evil urges. I longed to question Zoltan more fully upon his experiences, but my mind was so overwhelmed with thoughts and questions that words would not yet come in a coherent manner to ask what our futures might be. I stored his tale in my memory to review later when I had time for reflection.

I then proceeded to tell him my own story, and since Zoltan's tale had taken several hours and my tale was not much shorter, dawn was breaking by the time I had finished.

"It seems we have both suffered a great deal," he remarked when I had told him all, "and that our experiences have been largely similar, despite our growing up in two foreign lands. You have given me much to think upon."

"I find it remarkable," I replied, "not only that we have both been through such hell, but that we have survived it and should meet in this manner."

"Yes, it would seem almost to be a coincidence or just sheer luck," he agreed, "and yet I think there must be far more to it, for it strikes me still as odd that the creature Lilith should know my story without my telling her—I do not think she simply read my thoughts, but more likely, that she was on a quest to find me, and that concerns me even more, for if she also knows of your existence, she may well seek you out as her next victim."

"I have already considered this possibility," I admitted, "and it makes me think it unwise for us to remain in the castle."

"I also think," Zoltan continued, "that your encounter with this Captain Vanderdecker adds to the mystery, for he also knew you when you had not even told him your name. Both Lilith and he are obviously supernatural beings, which leads me to believe they must have knowledge beyond that of mortal ken, and considering the telepathic powers we both appear to have, our ability to control mortals' minds, and our superhuman strength, to think what powers these superior beings appear to have is truly difficult to comprehend, and I think it can only suggest a greater reason for all that we have experienced."

"I believe you are right," I said, trying to stifle a yawn.

"You are tired," Zoltan now said, "as am I. I have come to believe that reflection is the best method for my life now, so let us rest. As I said, there is only one bed, but I can curl up in a chair in the banquet hall before the fire while you sleep in my bed. If it is agreeable to you, I would like for us to remain companions for some time as we consider our experiences and what would be best for us now."

"I agree," I replied, "and the thought of going to America appeals to me so I would not be averse to joining you on your journey, provided there is money enough for us both to make the passage, for I have little money as well. I have no experience with gambling and it sounds like that is not the best solution for improving our financial situation according to your story, but if need be, we could use our minds to gain ourselves free passage or manipulate some wealthy person to give us the money. Still, we can think on all that in the morning."

My brother agreed, for as brothers we now thought of ourselves, and then he showed me to the bedchamber where I quickly collapsed into the deepest and most comforting sleep I had known in a long time because, for the first time in many years, I felt I was no longer alone in the world.

CHAPTER 14

WHEN I WOKE in the morning, I ventured from my room and back to the banquet hall, only to find Zoltan asleep in his chair. I set the logs ablaze in the fireplace so he would not wake up cold, and when he still did not stir from the noise I made, I decided to explore the castle on my own for a bit. I was pleased to have a brother, a friend, if he were indeed honest in his stated intentions toward me, but I remained a bit suspicious and thought perhaps there were details he had not told me, for a profession of friendship is not reason enough to trust another with all one's deepest secrets. And so I thought it best to see what I could of the castle before he woke.

In truth, there was little to see. The structure was largely barren, what furniture it contained had rotted long ago, and in many a cushioned chair, a rat or family of mice had made a home. I found nothing of interest until I came to the library, which was quite a prodigious room and lined with bookshelves containing many old and musty volumes. Some I dared not even touch from fear they would fall apart if they made contact with my fingers, but I did pull those from the shelf that looked to be in good condition.

Most of what I found were volumes of history, ancient treatises on war, religious works of both Christians and Muslims, and even Jews, and finally, some accounting ledgers that dated back centuries. But nothing I found gave me any knowledge of Dracula himself or provided any secrets or understanding of the castle and its former inhabitants. I found nothing that made it seem to have been worth Zoltan's time to remain here for as long as he had said he had stayed to read these musty old books.

Nevertheless, I took one down, a history of the Roman Empire. I found it quite dull and flipped through its pages until the very end where I found mention of how the last emperor of the Romans or Greeks had died at the Fall of Constantinople in 1453. This information stunned me, for I remembered having learned in school that Rome had fallen in 476 A.D., but I had not realized that the Eastern half of the empire had survived nearly one thousand years after Rome was conquered by the barbarians. What a tragic moment it must have been to see the last vestige of an empire fall like that, but then, the Romans did not have the advantages that the great British Empire had, upon which the sun never set, nor ever would—or so I believed at that time. But then I never thought I would live so long as to see another empire fall. But I am getting ahead of myself.

When Zoltan came seeking me, he found me marveling over an illustration of the former Hippodrome in what was now Istanbul.

"Are you hungry?" he asked.

"Starving," I replied.

"Come; we will go hunting."

We had no weapons save for a few knives, although later I would discover some old spears and bows and arrows about the castle that we would repair for our benefit. Surprisingly, neither of us sought to obtain a firearm of any sort—perhaps because shooting an animal was far too easy, whereas the vampire blood in our veins delighted in the savage instinct of the kill. We were not above using our human cunning to build traps, but usually we simply went out on the hunt for our prey, chasing it, most times outrunning it, then seizing it with our bare hands to wring its neck.

While I did find such hunting a thrill, I admit I never got used to Zoltan's zeal for such behavior. I was content with killing my prey, then carrying it home to cook, but Zoltan would often open a vein in the creature and drink its warm blood or even rip out its heart and eat it, saying, "Is that not what a vampire is to do?"

"No," I said. "I mean, I do not know what vampires do, for we are not vampires. And I have never tasted blood myself until I began to hunt this way. We do not need another creature's blood to survive."

"There is strength in the blood," Zoltan insisted. "We will become stronger and more powerful this way."

It was hard to argue with him, for just within the first few months of our living together, he had become significantly larger and stronger. He was a few years older than me, approaching the prime of his manhood now and a veritable Tarzan of Romania—Tarzan being a popular story serialized in the newspapers at this time that we both took delight in—for we did not divorce ourselves completely from the world.

We made Castle Dracula our home base, but we did make journeys together to Bucharest, Vienna, and other smaller cities in Eastern Europe to buy ourselves the things we needed, including the occasional book or magazine in English, which is how we first became familiar with Tarzan.

Our friendship grew and deepened until we were more than

brothers—we were inseparable comrades who lived together, thought together, and acted together—indeed, we almost believed the very same things, considering ourselves supermen, setting ourselves up as forest gods—a term frequently applied to Tarzan by his creator—and suiting us perfectly in the forests and Carpathian Mountains of our surroundings.

The only difference between ourselves and Tarzan was that, while we were equally disgusted by "civilized" man's society with its snobbery and falsehoods, we did not feel any need to protect the innocent or punish the wicked—perhaps because in our usual isolation, we did not encounter any such people—and perhaps, although I cannot speak for Zoltan, because he had already so punished the wicked when cheating scoundrels at cards, only to have it result in his terrifying meeting with the demoness. Indeed, as fearless as Zoltan appeared, whenever our conversation turned to the demoness, a topic I soon learned to avoid, I could still see the terror in his eyes.

I do not consider this time in our lives as immoral, but simply amoral, and it remained that way until one day in the spring of 1914 when, after having been together for three years, and having explored every inch of the castle as well as having perused between us every book in the library, an unexpected discovery was made, wholly by accident.

While by this time we knew well all the main floors and living quarters of the castle, beneath us was a maze of filthy old vaults and subterranean chambers that we had barely ventured to explore, repulsed by their dirt, the cobwebs, and the insects and rodents that lived in them. However, one day Zoltan suggested that we would do well to explore these areas, for doubtless, there must be a secret passage through which to escape if the castle fell under attack, for what man would build a castle, only to let himself become a prisoner within it?

I saw the logic behind this argument, and I also knew that if ever anyone came to Dracula's Castle who was not friendly to us, and we were, for whatever reason, unable to defeat and kill him—then it would serve us well to have an escape plan. We especially thought such an escape route desirable for rumors of possible war were spreading in Europe at the time and no one could know what the future might hold. We liked to think ourselves invincible, but cannons and modern weapons left us doubtful we could take on an army; better to have a backup plan if we ever did find ourselves under attack.

So one day, armed with brooms to fight cobwebs and knives to fight anything more dangerous, and torches to light our way, we went exploring. It was a long expedition that led us to many musty chambers and dead-ends, and not a few appeared to have been dungeon cells, perhaps even torture chambers from the remnants of chains and other strange and unfamiliar devices that we found. We did discover an exit that came out in a mountain cave with a stone door that would have tricked the eye of anyone who tried to enter from the other side and was a good hour's walk from the castle.

But our most remarkable find occurred as we returned through the cave and up the final staircase to the main floor. Upon descending these stairs, we had not looked behind us, but now approaching the stairs, we found a doorway built into the side of them—actually a short tunnel not more than four feet tall. Ducking our heads, we made our way through this tunnel for about twenty feet before emerging into a room filled with frayed and decayed remains of rich tapestries, giant wooden chests equally falling to pieces from the dampness, and countless gold and silver coins leaking from them.

"A treasure room!" exclaimed Zoltan while I stood speechless in awe. "No more casinos for me." Then he let out a shout of joy and dove at a chest filled with gold, picking up handfuls and letting them seep through his fingers.

Not only were they gold coins, but they were ancient ones, dating back to the fifteenth century and showing the names and faces of various Wallachian princes, Byzantine emperors, and even Hungarian kings and Ottoman sultans.

Not all was coin—other chests contained necklaces and headdresses of jewels. There were goblets and even church chalices and plates. Ancient and priceless illuminated manuscripts had survived the dampness within bejeweled metal covers, and while most of these were Bibles or old romances, we found in a small gold casket a scroll, the greatest prize of all—or perhaps the greatest curse—for it was written in the hand of Dracula himself, or rather Vlad Tepes, Prince of Wallachia, which he had been at that time, as we now learned.

We spent much time exploring all these items, but to spare you suspense, I will translate what the manuscript said so you will understand the shock it was to us. It began:

> I, Vlad Tepes, Prince of Wallachia, knowing I may well fall in battle, do here present that information I once received in the Scholomance, the ancient school of knowledge, for the benefit of my successors.
> It has been said by many that I am no friend of the Holy Mother Church. Here let it be set forth the reason why, or at least partially why. Shall I live through the battle tomorrow, I will later write down all of my tale, but it is sufficient here to explain why I fight only for myself and the people of Wallachia against the Turks, and not for the Church itself,

save when it serves my purpose, for the Church is as much my enemy as the Turks, having long been the instrument of my family's enemies for generations.

In the Scholomance, I was made aware of ancient knowledge, ancient traditions, which the Church has long tried to suppress, and which mankind itself has largely forgotten. It is not a tale of good and evil, but rather one of a great wrong enacted against one who was pure of heart and soul, and undeserving of the treatment against her and her children made by the children of Eve.

Let it be known that I am descended from that good and holy woman who was so greatly wronged, whose gift was refused and turned into something evil. My lineage is thus:

No further explanation was given. Perhaps Vlad Tepes felt his words were clear, or at least the chart that followed was clear to explain who was that good and holy woman he claimed for his ancestor. The chart began with his name at the top and below him was that of his mother, and below her was the name of her mother before her. And as we unrolled the scroll further, more names in this family history emerged. It was a strange chart, for there were no fathers listed for many a generation until we came to a Geoffrey of Lusignan, son of Geoffrey, Count of Lusignan and Gudrun. Rather than follow the male line of Lusignan, however, the chart followed the line of Gudrun to her parents, a Duke and Duchess of Mayence, and then followed a female line until it came to Constantine and Gwenhwyvach, King and Queen of Britain. This line in turn continued back for many more generations, some names standing out as having been of noble or royal lines, some just obscure first names. None of these names or titles meant anything to Zoltan or me until we came to the very last name on the scroll: Lilith, 1st wife of Adam.

"Lilith!" exclaimed Zoltan.

I looked at him, surprised by his exclamation until I saw the horror in his eyes, and then I remembered her name and why horror accompanied it.

"She told me," he reminded me, quoting her, "'I am Lilith, mother of the earth, and I will have my revenge upon the sons and daughters of Eve! You are my own son, Zoltan, of my bloodline through the blood of Dracula.'"

"But...surely...she...she couldn't mean it...." I said, stumbling, trying to understand what seemed incomprehensible.

"I am her descendant," said Zoltan, the horror on his face being replaced by a dawning realization, the logic of which I feared to follow.

"But I don't understand," I said. "Adam and Eve are in the Bible, but I never heard of anyone named Lilith."

"Adam and Eve, yes," said Zoltan. "I know these biblical stories, and yet I never heard of one named Lilith either. Who was she, and how if Adam and Eve were the first people, could she be the mother of Adam's children and Dracula be descended from her?"

"Or us," I added, for if this Lilith demoness had told Zoltan she was his ancestor through Dracula's blood, then was that not the case for me as well?

It was a question that greatly perplexed us, for we were Dracula's sons in blood, but while I had been led to believe Dracula was evil, if he had acted to revenge an ancient wrong, then perhaps I had been wrong to think ill of him—yet what he had done had been ghastly. Still, I remembered in Mr. Stoker's novel how Professor Van Helsing had said that great and good men had come from Dracula's loins. Might I then be one of them? But what had I ever done that was good in any way? It was all confusing and enough to make my head hurt, and yet neither Zoltan nor I could rest until we knew the truth of it.

We did not know where to find the answers, but we needed to find out whom this Lilith might be and also what was the Scholomance where Dracula had acquired his information. Had it been some sort of school where he had gone—a university of some sort?

The only person likely to have answers to these questions would be a historian, a scholar, perhaps a university professor of some sort. After some discussion, we agreed that I would go to the University of Bucharest to find an explanation while Zoltan would remain and look through the rest of the castle for more treasure rooms or other valuable relics and manuscripts that we might have overlooked and that could help to illuminate this mystery for us.

I did not relish a journey, and yet I felt I could not bear the anxiety of not having answers, for it was clear now that Zoltan's encounter with the demoness had been no accident, but rather, Lilith was somehow deeply tied to Dracula and to our own destinies.

Yet I was not eager to draw attention to us. Zoltan wanted me to take the manuscript and show it to a university professor who might give us answers, but I decided to take a more cautious route, leaving the manuscript behind and simply copying out the family tree for myself.

A couple of days later, by foot and then by train, I arrived in Bucharest, but as soon as I reached its university, I feared for the security of myself and Zoltan and of Castle Dracula should I begin to ask questions about an ancient demoness. People would wonder who I was and why I asked, and a catastrophe for Zoltan and I could potentially result.

So I walked about the university grounds, pondering what to do, until I saw the library, and then I thought perhaps I could find the information I wanted inside it. I was of age to pass for one of the students, so I entered and spent hours digging through books until I found one about Jewish traditions and history that included an explanation of Lilith as having been Adam's first wife. While I, like Zoltan, had an excellent memory, I thought it best that Zoltan read about Lilith for himself, so I stole the book by tucking it into my coat. No one confronted me as I left the library, and had anyone done so, I would have manipulated his mind to let me go.

I then took the train from Bucharest to the town nearest to Dracula's Castle from which I could easily walk or run home, the castle being only a half-dozen miles away from the train station. While on the train, I was impatient to read the book further, but I dared not draw attention to myself, and the train was so filled with loud, angry, and upset voices that I knew I would not be able to concentrate enough to read. After a minute, when I asked my companion in the seat beside me why everyone was so upset, he handed me a newspaper. Its headline announced:

ARCHDUKE FRANZ FERDINAND ASSASSINATED IN SARAJEVO

Until then, I had only had some vague idea that relations between Serbia and Austria were strained, and I knew that in the recent Balkan wars, Romania had become involved, siding with Serbia and Greece against Bulgaria, but I had paid little attention to the details of these conflicts. Now, reading the news story and listening to the people arguing around me, I became aware of just how explosive the political situation in Eastern Europe had become.

"It's war for certain," said my companion. "Austria has been looking for an excuse to attack Serbia, and if it does, Russia will come to Serbia's aid, and that could lead to Germany entering the war on Austria's side."

"What of Romania?" I asked.

"It will side with Russia and Serbia. We want back Transylvania, which has too long been under Austrian rule."

I knew this fact, for Dracula's Castle was not far from the Austrian-controlled border. If war were declared, the castle might become a strategic battleground.

But the information I had found about Lilith still filled my mind too much to focus upon thoughts of war. When I disembarked from the train that evening, I quickly disappeared into the darkness, making sure no one followed me out of town since I did not want people to know I resided at Castle Dracula.

As I hurried home, my brain whirled with wanting to tell Zoltan all I had learned.

Little did I know another war had begun in the castle during my absence.

CHAPTER 15

I HAD NO doubt Zoltan could sense I was approaching when I was still a mile off, so I was surprised to find the castle dark and quiet with no welcome prepared for me. I did not expect Zoltan to run to greet me, but I had imagined he would at least be anxious to know what I had learned.

Instead, I found the castle silently looming over the mountain upon which it stood with its usual ominous air—there was no happy homecoming for me, and while I thought of Zoltan as my brother, my only family, still I felt a pang at the memory of my father, Jonathan Harker, and even my stepmother and sister and how they used to greet me when I came home from school. But I soon shook such nostalgia from me, for I knew I could not have a happy family, despite how I might now and then long for such. Once I was inside the castle, the longing feeling diminished and I succeeded to keep it at bay for many more days, months, and years to come.

Zoltan and I never used the front door since Professor Van Helsing had ripped it from its hinges so many years before; ever since, it had lain rotting and irreparable nearby. Instead, we had simply blocked the entrance with stones so no intruders could enter. We always made our way inside through a window that would have been inaccessible to any mortal man. So I scrambled up the castle's outer wall to an open window on the third floor, and from there, I made my way through the house, looking for any sign of my companion. Finally, I found him in the dining room, staring out the large window that overlooked the valley. He was more content than I to sit quietly in the dark, enjoying a sort of peaceful communion with the night, which to some degree I envied, for I was of a more restless nature than Zoltan.

"I have returned, brother," I said when he did not turn around in his chair.

"What? Oh, I'm sorry," he said, seeming disoriented, perhaps half-napping, but he quickly rose at the sound of my voice.

Despite the chamber's darkness, my enhanced vision noted how pale he looked.

Startled by his appearance, I began to say, "You look..." but then I stopped to laugh.

"What?" he asked.

"I was going to say, 'You look like you've seen a ghost,'" and I laughed again, although his expression told me there was nothing funny about my words.

"Not a ghost," he replied. "Lilith."

"The demoness!" I exclaimed, suddenly finding my hand shaking as I reached into my coat to pull out the book I had stolen and brought home for him to read.

"She is no demoness," he said, vehemently. "Do not call her that. I regret ever having used those words."

"Did she come here to the castle?" A flood of questions rushed to my tongue. "What did she want? Did she seduce you? Is she still here?"

"Come; I am hungry," he said, turning to go downstairs to the kitchen. I followed behind, demanding, "Tell me what happened!"

"I will, but it will be a long story," he said. "The main point is that she is not what I first thought her."

"Not what you thought her?" I repeated as we reached the kitchen and I collapsed into a chair at the table. "Why, she's evil, is she not? Did she not rape you, and then cause you to lose at the gaming tables? What kind of a creature—"

"She is not evil," he replied as he dug about in the cupboards, searching for plates and bread and whatever it was he intended to fix for us to eat. I know not what it was he eventually gave me—I ate it, but I barely saw or tasted it as I listened to him.

"She is not evil," he repeated. "And she is not a demoness. She never said she was—I simply jumped to the wrong conclusions about her."

"With good reason!" I replied.

"Quincey, shut up and listen to me. She is not a demoness."

"Then what is she?" I demanded.

"She is the Great Mother, or at least she should be," he replied, speaking slowly, carefully selecting each word. "She is a greatly wronged woman, an immortal, although mankind has continually misunderstood and tried to destroy her."

"Destroy her? She tried to destroy you, Zoltan!"

"I spurned her. You know how women are when their hearts are broken," he said, sitting down at the table with our plates.

I said nothing, not knowing, in truth, how women behaved, for I had never yet been in love.

"She wanted me to have her child, to make her fruitful, and in a sense, she is our sire Dracula's ancestress. She has existed since the beginning of time. She was Adam's first wife in the Garden of

Eden, where she was greatly wronged."

"Greatly wronged!" I was shocked by his words. "Why, she was an outcast from Eden. She betrayed her husband. She—"

"How dare you speak of her like this?" snapped Zoltan, throwing his plate at my head, but I caught it and placed it on the table. Then I slid it back to him so he could finish eating the sandwich still upon it.

"I dare," I replied, "because I have read all about her and I brought you a book to read."

I here drew the stolen book from my coat, opened it, and began to read it to him.

For a moment, he sat down and allowed me to read.

"Lilith," I began, "was created by God to be Adam's helpmate. However, she refused to lie beneath Adam when they engaged in sexual intercourse, and in her unreason, she fled the Garden of Eden, taking for her lover the Angel of Death, Samael, which resulted in her giving birth to a hundred demon children a day—"

"Lies! All lies! Lies of the Jews and Christians!" Zoltan exclaimed, his anger so hot that he used his mind to tear the book from my hands, and before I could stop him, he sent it flying across the room and into the fireplace. Then he used his eyes like a laser beam to light it on fire. I was shocked, for I did not have such a power, nor had I ever seen him display it before; I now realized he had greater control over the powers of his mind than I did, perhaps because he was older than I. And for the first time, I began to fear him.

"Zoltan," I said, trying to calm him, "you told me to find out information about Lilith. That is why I brought home that book."

"I told you to find out information, yes, but not lies—I want the truth," he replied. "But no matter. I learned the truth while you were away."

"And what is the truth?" I asked.

"Quincey, she came to me; she just appeared before my eyes in the library while I was poring over Dracula's manuscript and wondering what it could mean. When she appeared, before I could say a word, she told me, 'Zoltan, my love, you knew you would see me again, and now you understand why I sought you out. I love you and need you to be my true dark knight, my hero. I need you to set right how I have been wronged since the beginning of time. You are of my line, the hope of my people, the savior of our lineage. You are called upon for this quest to stop the evil, vermin race that has usurped the place of our family. The children of Eve seek to destroy the earth that I came to give life to. You are my only hope.'"

What could I to say to these words? More importantly, what had my brother said to them?

As if reading my mind, Zoltan said, "She convinced me, Quincey. Don't you see? We are the chosen ones."

"But isn't she a demoness?" I asked, trying to understand.

"No, there are no such things as demons—they are old wives' tales—tales to make children behave, and tales told because man fears to take responsibility for himself and instead wants to blame the devil for his ill behaviors."

"But if there are no demons, then what was Dracula? Is not a vampire like a demon?"

"Don't trouble me with technicalities!" Zoltan shouted, his eyes flaming so red that I was beginning to suspect he had gone mad.

"I'm just trying to understand, Zoltan," I said. "Please don't be angry with me."

For a moment, I thought he was going to come across the room and pummel me, but then I saw the anger leave his eyes and he said, "You are right; I am overreacting." He paused and sipped his wine while I waited, not knowing what more I dared say. Finally, he continued, "We are brothers, allies now in bringing about Lilith's blessings to this earth. The children of Eve are about to destroy this world, but we will aid them in their own destruction so good can prevail again."

"I don't understand," I said. "If through Dracula's blood, we are the children of Lilith, aren't we also the children of Eve? Isn't all of humanity descended from Eve, including my parents and yours?"

"We are not pure children of Lilith, it is true," said Zoltan, mulling it over slowly. "But we must right the wrong Lilith has suffered. Even if Eve caused us all to be born in sin, we can still fight against our sinful natures and seek to return the earth to Lilith, its true mother."

I could not argue with him, but I knew the earth did not belong to Lilith. She was not its mother. She was not its creator. But my head was dizzy with exhaustion from my long journey and from trying to make sense of this sudden change in my brother's mental processes.

"I am exhausted, brother," I finally said, "and you have given me much to think over. I need some sleep."

"Yes, you need to sleep so we can begin soon upon our quest to rid the earth of humanity. The time is coming. Lilith told me the humans are about to engage in the greatest war in history."

And then I remembered the headline of the Archduke's assassination and the predictions of war I had heard, and I began to think how Zoltan could not know of these things, nor could Lilith if she had visited him, unless she had powers to foresee the future, for the news had just broken but hours ago.

"Will Lilith return?" I asked, half-fearing Zoltan's answer, yet still adding, "I would like to speak to her myself."

I hoped to remain doubtful until I had seen her for myself; after all, everything I knew of her I had heard from his lips. Perhaps he was insane and she was but a figment of his imagination—although I doubted that, also.

"I do not know," he replied. "It is not for me to question her comings and goings. I hope you sleep well."

And then as I prepared to leave the room, I noticed the gold ring upon his finger, a ring I had never seen before.

"Where did you find that?" I asked, motioning toward the ring. "Is it part of the castle treasure we found?"

"No, Lilith gave it to me. It is to seal our love."

And then he made a disgusting smile, like that of an old lecher who had finally gotten lucky. It was all I could do to smile back and say, "Goodnight" and not retch.

I retired to my bedchamber, but I did not sleep that night. The early morning dawn was already approaching when I crawled into bed. I lay there for many hours, watching the sun make its way through the daytime sky, pondering over everything Zoltan had said and wondering what to do next.

Could he be insane? Could he be imagining things? Could the finding of the manuscript that said we were descended from Lilith have jarred loose something in his brain? But he had told me of Lilith before we had ever found the manuscript, so I realized it could not be simply a coincidence. And while I wanted to believe his talk of Lilith was all craziness, I realized such a supernatural being truly could exist. After all, I had no doubts about Dracula's existence—my and Zoltan's gifts were the very evidence that he had lived, and nor could I forget my strange meeting with Captain Vanderdecker. I had refused to listen to that cursed wanderer of the seas, and yet he had warned me not to turn to the evil side. Now my brother was telling me Lilith was of the good and we were to aid her in the destruction of Eve's children, literally of the human race; was I was not to view such madness as evil? How could I ally myself with such a mission? Yes, I had made mistakes—I had used my powers for selfish gains, but only small, piddly ones. Never had I taken a life or even tried to do so.

When I finally stirred from my bed and went to find my brother, he said little to me. We hardly spoke all that day; we sat reading, and later, we went out hunting for a deer. It was a quiet day, but when bedtime came and I rose to return to my room, he said, "Quincey, we must be patient, but the destruction of Eve's children will occur, by their own hands in this war to come, although we will greatly aid them in their destruction. Have faith in it happening. And be proud of the role we will play in it. Why, the very thought of it thrills the vampire blood within me."

CHAPTER 16

NOT LONG AFTER, my brother made a trip into the neighboring village to buy some supplies. He returned to the castle ecstatic with the news that war had broken out—Austria had declared war on Serbia, and Russia was coming to Serbia's aid.

In the weeks and months that followed, we heard plenty of news of the war—all Europe seemed involved in it, yet Romania would not join in it until 1916, and even then, the armies stayed far from our castle.

Yet, as I feared would happen, Zoltan was impatient to be involved. "We will fight alongside the Germans!" he declared, even though I told him Romania was likely to side with Russia and Serbia, not Germany.

"Brother, we are not on any country's side. We are on Lilith's side," he replied. "The Germans are likely to cause the most destruction, and we wish to see the human race destroy itself as much as possible. Do you not see they are all our enemies—Russian, Serb, Austrian, German, even Romanian? They are all the children of Adam and Eve and, therefore, antagonists of truth and goodness and purity. We must wipe them from the earth, or better yet, help them wipe themselves from it so the world is safe for Lilith's children to reclaim their birthright."

"Should we not then wait for Lilith to return to tell us what to do?" I asked, for months had now passed since I had gone to Bucharest and still I had not seen her, and so, my doubts persisted regarding her existence; fortunately, until now, I had skillfully managed to shield these thoughts from Zoltan's penetrating mind.

"She does not need to return to us—we know our mission. I am sure she is busy elsewhere helping to manipulate the war to our advantage."

"But, brother," I said, "who is there among her children besides us?"

"There are others I am sure," he said, "and it matters not. She will come when the time is right for us to plant our seeds in her so we can be her new Adams and father her pure children when the world is safe again for our kind."

I knew better than to ask him more. The last thing I wanted to hear again was that I had to plant my seed into a demoness. I should have known better than to ask Zoltan anything to begin with. He was clearly no longer sane—Lilith had somehow managed to brainwash him. Furthermore, when I did ask him questions, his answers only made me fear him more. His eyes now ignited when he spoke, and whenever I questioned him so I could try to get a logical response, he would explode into rage, telling me, "Do not question our mistress!" and "Who are you, my younger brother, to know what is right or wrong? Do you not know that any of these humans you express concern for would kill you in a second, would put a stake through your heart as they did to our sire, if they knew your secret? Did not your own parents' closest friends plot against you, leading you to seek sanctuary here with me? But our sanctuary can never be safe until our enemies are driven from this earth."

"Yes, Zoltan, you are right," I would then submit to quell his anger. "Forgive me, brother. I only wish to be certain I understand what we must do so our mistress is properly and fully avenged."

Then, still glaring at me as if I were a fool, he would return to studying his maps of Europe. He had taken to traveling to the village every day to buy the newspapers so he could follow the war, and soon he had giant maps displayed in the dining room where he kept track of the various armies and their movements.

"The Germans are at a standstill on the Western Front," he finally said one day. "We will go there. We will help them. We will lead them in the taking of Paris, and then on to the sea, to London—we will conquer Britain and destroy the dogs who drove you from your native land."

"Romania is my land now," I said. "We have no need to leave it."

"All the earth is our home," he replied. "All the earth is the Eden that God intended for us. Is it not clear to you that God loves us? Did he not destroy all mankind in the Flood because of its evil ways?"

"What of Noah and his children?" I asked. "He made certain they were saved."

"Yes, well, they did not die, but their claim to have been honored by God—that is just a story they have made up—only liars claim God saves them as a way to justify their evil behavior."

I need not go into further detail; anyone could see the lack of logic in all my brother said. But neither did I dare to oppose him. I had no desire to fight anyone, but I thought if I went with him to the Western front, to partake in the trench warfare, that perhaps Lilith would come looking for him, and then I could speak to her myself and determine whether she truly was some evil demoness or whether Zoltan was simply deranged.

And so to the Western Front we went. We enlisted in the German army, or rather, we found a couple of dead Germans on the battlefield who had been gassed, and we donned their clothes and took our place among the Germans.

I will spare you the details of that war's horrors—of the good men on both sides I saw shot down by the dozens, even hundreds. I experienced shells flying through the air, cannon gunfire, cavalry men riding their horses into swords and pikes, blood and death everywhere, and the more horrifying it became, the more gloriously exciting Zoltan found it.

And the men celebrated him for it. The German soldiers quickly fell under his spell until he was made a major and would lead charges on the battlefield, attacks on the enemy, and then came that strange and disturbing day.

We were at Verdun during the long and horrifying battle that composed most of 1916. The historians now say that nearly a million men died there that year, and I am not surprised, for Zoltan and I helped to add to that number, shooting at the French, whom we, the Germans, outnumbered easily two to one.

It was then that Zoltan and I learned that besides having superhuman strength, speed, and agility, we also had superhuman regenerative abilities. We wore our gas masks like everyone else so as not to reveal our full powers, but one day when our trench was gassed unexpectedly and we were all caught without our masks on, we discovered that while many of our comrades died around us, the gas in no way affected Zoltan or me. We were also both shot in the arms, but after recovering from the initial shock, we pulled out the bullets and our bodies healed within the hour. As a result, we became fearless, often charging out at the opposing army, shooting at soldiers as they retreated or even charged us. And when we came close to colliding with the enemy, we would run and leap over a group of soldiers until the men looked up at us in shock. I have heard stories that angels were sighted at the Battle of Mons—but the French who saw Zoltan and me probably thought us demons, for once they overcame the shock of seeing us leaping through the air, they would turn and flee back to their trenches.

The gunfire, the shells blasting, the cannons' roar, the gas killing men left and right, the bullets flying like raindrops—these became our daily life, and Zoltan often spent many a night laughing about it, while I fought out of respect and comradeship with my fellow soldiers, all the while wondering why I was fighting at all.

And then, one day, we advanced on the enemy; we went running across the field and down into their trench. Most of our men were shot dead before we reached the enemy's base. The others largely went down in hand-to-hand combat with the French, save for Zoltan and me and a handful of others. No Frenchman, or any man for that matter, was a match for us when it came to hand-to-hand combat. A man would raise the butt of his rifle to strike, but Zoltan would grab it, tear it from his hands, block a fist, then reach for the man's neck and snap it within a second. My brother's bloodlust was astounding. Our own soldiers should have cheered him, but instead, they stepped back in shock and fear at the sight, and yet, they thought of him as being almost their secret weapon. I equally would kill many a Frenchman, but usually by beating him with my rifle—I could not bring myself to murder with my bare hands, and I only did it in self-defense, not aggressively as Zoltan did.

On one particular day when we entered the enemy's trench, the French soldiers tried to scramble out and retreat. In the mêlée that followed, Zoltan and I became separated, both of us so intent on chasing the enemy that we never worried about one another, knowing we would reconvene after the battle.

I was racing through the trench, pursuing a Frenchman who was all but screaming for his mother in his fright, having lost his rifle and knowing his feet could not save him from me, but he did not know the rifle I carried was out of bullets, and so I could only pursue him on foot. If it were not for the twists and turns of the trench, I would have caught him quickly, but it was several minutes before I cornered him, as he struggled to climb up out of the trench, stepping on the bodies of his dead comrades to do so.

In a second, I had grabbed him, twisted him around, clutched him by the throat, and I was just about to look into his eyes and choke him to death when I heard a sudden, terrible and deafening sound like a million women weeping.

"What is that?" I asked, slightly loosening my grip on my victim.

It sounded like a siren, but it also sounded human. It burned my ears. I will admit it was the most horrible sound I have ever heard.

"What is it?" I asked, fearing it was some new weapon the French had created to deafen the enemy. I wanted to cry, it was so piercing and upsetting to my nervous system.

"What is it?" I demanded, looking into my victim's eyes.

And then I saw a tear run down his cheek, as he said, "It is Melusine."

"Melusine? Who is Melusine?" I demanded.

"She is France, the very Mother of France. What you hear is Melusine weeping for her children; she was once the great and ancient lady of Lusignan, and legend says that she appears whenever a member of her family dies, but so many centuries have now passed that all of we

French are descended from her, and so she weeps for all her children, and she will not be comforted until you leave our land. Indeed, her vengeance will be great once she overcomes her grief."

"Nonsense!" I cried. "It is a fairy tale. It isn't true!"

And yet, the cry continued; it was like a spear into my heart, a needle through my eardrums.

"It is nonsense!" I repeated, but the cry did not stop, and unable to bear it any longer, I let go of my victim. I thrust him from me so that I might cover my ears and block the deafening wail.

But even then I could still hear it. I had to get away from it. I ran back down the trench, not knowing which way to go, seeking only to distance myself from it. I leapt over the dead who lay in the trench, the children for whom this fairy-tale Melusine wept. I ran and ran, not knowing where I was to go. I raced through the maze-like trenches until, finally, I turned a corner and suddenly found myself in a wintery scene.

It had been autumn a moment before, but now it was winter—deep winter. Inexplicably, here was snow all around me, several inches on the ground and more coming down so fiercely that I could not see more than a few feet before me.

Then, stepping forth from the falling snow, a beautiful woman approached me. A woman with long dark hair, a blue robe, and a black cloak drawn about her.

"Winter is coming, Quincey Harker," she said, arresting me with her words.

Who was she? What was she doing in a trench? Why was she dressed like some woman from the Middle Ages?

"Are you Lilith?" I asked her, although I felt surprise that if she were, I felt no fear.

"No, Quincey," she replied. "It is almost winter now. How many more seasons will you follow evil? Were you not warned by Captain Vanderdecker?"

And, suddenly, my heart sunk within me. I did not know who she was, but I was astonished by the instant sorrow her words caused me.

"Your mother, Mina," she said, "fought and nearly gave her life to stop evil. Your father, Jonathan Harker, lost years of his life in the fight. Would you so dishonor their sacrifice? Do you really consider yourself more Dracula's son than theirs?"

"Lady, who are you?" I asked, astonished by her words, astonished that she knew so much about me, but most astonished of all by how the pain in my heart rose up at the mention of my parents. I had never grieved them because I barely remembered my mother—and I had never had the opportunity to grieve my father, for I had fled from home the night after his funeral. In truth, I had been on the run ever since.

"What do you fear, Quincey?" she asked rather than answering my question. "What do you have to fear except the Hell within you? Yet you can control it. Do not continue this evil life, Quincey. Leave the battlefield. Seek peace. Seek good."

I bowed my head as I felt tears spring to my eyes. I did not know why I cried, except that the snow was cold and the world silent. The gunfire had ceased and so had the wail of Melusine, and there was just me and this beautiful lady standing in the newly fallen snow, and I found myself wishing the snow could cleanse my heart the way it cleansed the earth.

"My lady, I don't know how you know so much of me. You do not answer my question of who you are, but you do not look sad enough to be Melusine, and I feel you cannot be Lilith, although I thought she was the lady who watched me."

"Lilith reached your brother before I had the chance," said the lady. "No, I am not she. And Melusine has other work to do than look to your care. Instead, I, the Lady of Avalon, known as Morgan le Fay, watch over you, for I am among the ancestors of your mother Mina. It was because she was of the bloodline of Avalon, of the bloodline of myself and King Arthur, that Dracula sought her out, seeking to destroy all of Arthur's descendants, just as Lilith now seeks to do, as well as destroy all the lineage of Adam and Eve. But you must not let her, Quincey. You must seek what is right and good."

I knew not what to say. I found myself kneeling in the snow as my only means of expressing the deep sorrow that I now felt consuming me. I knelt to show I understood and accepted what she told me of Avalon—of my mother—of King Arthur—accepted it because it meant I was not solely of Dracula's line—I was of a line of light and goodness. Was it possible I had been wrong all this time?

And then my thoughts turned to one even more wrong.

"What of Zoltan, my lady? Is he not my brother?"

"Every man is your brother, Quincey," she replied, "but while I know you love Zoltan, there are some we cannot save—we cannot make anyone be good—each of us must individually choose so to be. Zoltan is not of the line of Avalon, but he is as surely Eve's descendant as he is Lilith's. You can love him. You can pray for him. But you cannot save him, and it would be best if you would separate yourself from him now. Do you understand?"

I felt like crying, but all I could do was nod and accept what I knew to be the truth.

"You did the best you could for him," Morgana told me. "Now do your best to live a good life, and when the time is right, one will come who will guide you to fulfill your purpose."

CHAPTER 17

IN ANOTHER SECOND, Lady Morgana was gone and the snow had stopped. I was back in a dirty, stinking trench full of death and destruction. I was back in the thick of the madness of war. The sky was red with cannon fire. I could hear bullets zipping by my ears, and the smell of gas was heavy in the air as I saw a few men running about. Turning to my left, rather than going forward or back, so I would travel between the opposing armies, I continued to walk until the smoke cleared, the gunfire ceased, and I saw nothing but darkness. For many hours, I then walked in the dark, coming upon no one, until finally the morning sun found me walking far from the battlefield.

Soon, I came to a village where a poor old frightened Frenchwoman quickly obeyed my request for a change of clothes—a pair of trousers and a shirt that had belonged to her late husband. And then I continued my journey, trekking across France, ever westward, wondering what my brother Zoltan would think when he did not find me. Would he fear me dead? Would I ever see him again? I did not know. I only knew I must make my way far from the battlefield and from him, as Morgan le Fay had told me to do, until I had more time to reflect.

I walked many a day until I reached the English Channel, and there I paid for passage to England, and then to Ireland, and finally, to America.

By the time I reached the great metropolis of New York City—which required me to jump off the ship and swim to shore so as to avoid the authorities since I had no immigration papers—I found that the United States' entrance into the war was imminent, and while I felt sorrow over its involvement in the war, I also hoped its entrance would be the turning point to end the bloodshed.

So that I would not be forced to enlist, nor draw the American authorities' attention by not being enlisted, I claimed I had a war injury and had received an honorable discharge from the British army. Then I made my way westward, finally taking up employment in a mine in Colorado to hide myself away from the world I had known. I did not have to lie about my war injuries for long, for the war ended in late 1918, and by then, I had set about making a new life for myself.

I admit I thought of Zoltan constantly during this time. I missed my brother, but I dared not seek him out from fear he had grown even more delusional and maniacal since I had last seen him. I also wondered what had become of my stepmother and half-sister, but as the years went by, these thoughts lessened. I decided it was best to keep my distance from other people, and I soon realized I had good reason not to grow close to anyone. By the time the 1920s came to a close, I began to notice that I was not aging. A man can look like he is in his twenties for many years, but when I saw wrinkles slowly appearing on my coworkers' faces and people began to comment that I never seemed to age, I knew the time had come for me to move on before someone became suspicious of who I was.

When the stock market crashed in 1929 and the Great Depression began, I was laid off from the mine, so I saw it as my opportunity to move on. After that, I drifted from job to job, traveling across the country, wondering just what my purpose in life might be, what it was I waited for. Would Morgan le Fay again appear to me, or would Lilith come seeking me? I saw all of America in those years—I saw how the American people worked hard, did not give up, and held on to hope in a way I had never seen in Europe—I saw fear and want, but I also saw courage and the belief by these people that they could rise above their stations in life. I respected and pitied them; I helped them when I could, and I hoped for the best for them and for myself, for we were all just wanderers upon this difficult earth, wishing for guidance, for an understanding of our purpose and destiny, and just hoping for a small slice of happiness.

And then another war began in Europe.

I waited. I waited to know what I should do. Was I to be involved in this war? My heart told me, "No," for Morgan le Fay had told me to leave my evil ways, and war was evil, no matter what false justifications people used for it. Yet I longed to see my brother. I knew I could do nothing for him, but my heart ached somehow to save him from Lilith's clutches. Still, all I could do was wait. I waited through the invasion of Poland. I waited through the German occupation of France, and I waited through the bombing of Britain.

And then the Japanese bombed Pearl Harbor and the United States entered the war. I knew I would then have to spend the next several years until the war ended in hiding or else enlist, for although I was now nearly fifty years old, I appeared no older than twenty-five, and my lack of involvement would look suspicious.

And so I joined the army, even though Morgan le Fay had told me to stay away from evil, for I truly believed the Nazi party evil, and I thought I would be doing good this time by opposing them. I went through training and quickly rose up through the ranks until I was a captain. I was there when the beaches of Normandy were stormed, and I was there as the American army moved across France and into Germany. I saw bloodshed, horror, men without limbs, women and children murdered, villages destroyed, fields running with blood, death and destruction everywhere—even worse than what I had seen during the First World War. And I wondered how mankind could bring such destruction upon itself, especially hardly more than twenty years after the last war had ended. And I wondered what hand Lilith, and perhaps even my brother, might have in this destruction.

And then one day I was with the army when we marched into a concentration camp. I was sick to my stomach at the thought of what we would find there, but I also felt an incalculable dread like I had never known before and, consequently, could not understand.

It was not until we had broken through the concentration camp's gates—the few German soldiers who had not fled having to be shot by us so we could enter—that I realized the full reason for my dread.

While many of the soldiers accompanied our medical crew to assist the poor tortured souls who had been practically starved to death in the camp, I was among those who went to the officers' barracks, looking to capture any camp leaders who might be hiding from us. We had to make sure they did not act as snipers trying to kill us, but rather, be taken captive so we might have them tried for their war crimes.

It was while I was outside a large building, what looked like it might be some sort of laboratory, that I heard voices inside. I had tried to resist using my telepathic powers for many years now so I could live like a normal human being, but this day, I could not stop the voices from penetrating into my head. I listened in horror to words that were clear to me, though muffled to my fellow soldiers' ears as they tried to force open the door.

"Take the pill, Zoltan," I heard a female voice say. "You have failed me like the coward you are. I will not help you to live. It is time for me to depart this world myself, but I shall return in a new form to bring about my destruction of Eve's children. A little more time and I would have succeeded, but that I have failed, I blame you for."

"My lady, I beg you; save me," cried the man.

I knew the voice. It was my brother, reduced to tears, to a whining shrill voice of horror like nothing I had ever expected to hear from one who had always been so brave, so daring, bold, and confident, yet it was undoubtedly his voice.

In another minute, we heard a couple of gunshots just as the men burst through the door and rushed inside. Just seconds later, I found my brother lying slumped over a desk with a bullet through his head, and turning, behind him, slumped in a corner, still holding a gun, was a beautiful woman with long raven hair up in a bun and in a German uniform. She was also dead, the gun still smoking in her hand, having shot out her own brains after having done the same to my brother.

It was all I could do to contain my emotions, not to let my fellow soldiers see the agony I felt, for most of us by now had become hardened to such scenes; otherwise, we would only become overwhelmed by all of war's horrors. I walked over to my brother while the other men left to search the rest of the building.

Brother, can it be you are really gone? I thought to myself, for I knew that in the past when he had been shot, that his body had healed. But a bullet in the brain was different than one in the arm, and he had clearly taken a poisoned pill as well at Lilith's urging. Still, I put my hand on his forehead as if I could heal him, just wanting to touch him, to feel a connection to him one last time. But I felt only his cold damp blood. Then just as I was about to take away my hand, I heard his last thought: *Farewell, Quincey. Take the ring.*

I was so startled I could not conceive at first what the words meant. I waited, trying to communicate with him telepathically, hoping for more words. I told him through my thoughts that I loved him and I was sorry that he had come to such an end, but he did not reply—his spirit was gone and his thoughts silent.

And then I looked down at his hand and saw the gold ring on his finger. It was an ancient ring with a carving upon it of a snake swallowing its tail. It was the ring I had first seen upon his finger the night I had returned from Bucharest and he had told me that Lilith had visited him. Clearly, she had given it to him. I did not know the ring's significance, nor what I should do with it. I only knew it must have some power of its own. I slid it from his finger, vowing to keep it safe until Morgan le Fay or some other wise and great being should tell me its purpose.

CHAPTER 18

THERE IS LITTLE more to tell. After the war, I made my way to Dracula's Castle again, not knowing what called me there. I found it in greater disrepair than it had been before. There was evidence that people had sought shelter in it at various times, probably as refugees from the recent war, but it was now empty again. Most of the books in the library were gone, as was most of the furniture. There were signs of fires having been lit on the stone floors. Doubtless, nearly everything in the castle had been burnt to keep the vagrants and refugees warm.

I dug behind a bookshelf until I unhooked a latch to a secret panel I had known, and there I found the manuscript detailing Dracula's descent from Lilith. I knew my brother had hidden it away there for safekeeping, doubtless thinking someday he would return to the castle. I also found a few other documents in his own hand that he had written down, information that Lilith had apparently given to him, including mention of three golden wedding rings with the imprint of the snake swallowing its tale upon them. It was noted that these were the rings of Adam, Eve, and Lilith, and that the ring in Zoltan's possession was that of Lilith. Two other rings existed. One was known to be in the possession of the Earls of Delaney, but the other ring had been taken generations earlier by a Welsh family named Morgan to the American colonies. These rings needed to be found so the three could be made one and the balance of power upon the earth restored—or so Lilith had apparently told Zoltan. What exactly the balance of power being restored could mean I did not know, except perhaps that Lilith would have all power by having destroyed Eve's children.

Nor did I know why there were three rings if they were wedding rings—I would not know until years later when I finally got around to reading the Bible just how common polygamy had been in ancient times.

I believed Lilith had been the woman whom I had found dead beside Zoltan, but I wasn't taking any chances on her finding me or coming to look for the ring I had taken from my brother. I collected these documents from the castle and then left it to whatever its fate would be, although as you all must now realize, we are currently within it.

While in the United States, I had never made any close connections with anyone, but I had remained curious about what had become of my half-sister. By now it had been some thirty-five years since I had left England, so I assumed my stepmother and my father's friends had probably passed away—certainly Uncle Abraham had to be dead— and if Lord Godalming or Dr. Seward remained, they would be so old now, each past his seventieth year, that I did not imagine they would be much threat to me, who still appeared as hale and hearty as if I were twenty-five.

So I went back to England. I found my parents' former home empty, but after making some discreet inquiries, I learned that my sister had married the Earl of Delaney—yes, she had become Bram Delaney's mother. I found this surprising, though it was wonderful because my deepest interest was the mystery of the rings, one of which I knew was in the possession of the Earls of Delaney.

As I have mentioned before, I had a photographic memory and could easily retain any information I read, so I decided to become a solicitor like my father had been, and in this manner, I made connections until I came to the notice of Charles Delaney, Adam's grandfather, who was then the new earl. Eventually, I became his solicitor, paving the way for the friendship that would develop between our sons. I was also able to watch over my sister in this way; she never guessed I was her brother since I had matured to manhood after she had last seen me, although she now appeared many years older than me. Imagine my delight to learn I had a baby nephew, for my sister did not have children until quite late in life, and then only the one child, Bram.

As for children of my own, well, I had never thought about marrying—in fact, I feared the thought, for I did not wish to pass on Dracula's blood to my children, but after years of being alone, and being quite a handsome man, I gave in when a young waitress began to flirt with me. I was terribly alone. All those I had ever known or loved had disappeared from my life, and so it was not unusual for me to seek human companionship. However, I did not intend marriage, for I knew in a few years I would have to move on before people began to notice I was not aging.

Cedric's mother was named Roberta, and she was an innocent sweet girl whose parents had been killed in the war. She was alone in the world like myself, and once we became lovers, I began to think perhaps I could trust her with my secret, yet I held off day after day, thinking there was plenty of time. I would have to leave her eventually if I did not tell her my secret, and even if I did, I knew that in time, wherever we went, people would think her my mother and then grandmother rather than my wife—and I feared the time would come when I would be physically repulsed by her as she aged while I did not.

I finally decided to break it off with her and move on to another city. I went to York, not telling her why or where I was going, but I thought I could still stay in touch with the Earls of Delaney from there.

Two years later, Roberta managed to track me down to tell me she had given birth to my son, whom she had named Cedric Harker, and also that she had a rare bone marrow disease and was unlikely to live much longer.

Of course, I comforted her the best I could, caring for her in the last few weeks of her life and in time taking care of the burial arrangements. And then I was left to raise Cedric.

I had never had a desire for children. In fact, I feared what my son might turn out to be, but Cedric appeared to be a perfectly normal boy as he grew up, and I instantly desired to give him all the best in life. Through my connection with the Earl of Delaney, I managed to get him accepted into the same private school as the earl's son, Bram, and thus began their lifelong friendship, or rivalry, depending on how you look upon it.

I became adept during the 1950s and '60s at applying stage makeup, disguising myself each day to appear slightly older so no one would notice my failure to age. Nevertheless, I knew the day would come when Cedric would catch me in the act of hiding my true face, or simply, because he was an intelligent boy, he would realize the truth. He later told me he had guessed it a few years before I told him on his fourteenth birthday. At that time, knowing how he was intrigued by adventure and fantasy novels, I explained to him my story and how Dracula's blood flowed within me, but I added that I did not believe I had passed the evil on to him. I hesitated to tell him the whole truth, but after all those decades of living with the secret, I selfishly longed for a reprieve from it, and who better than my own son to tell? Plus, I wanted to warn him about Lilith—that she was likely to reincarnate and might seek him out because he was my son. And so I shared with him the manuscript of Dracula's family tree, as well as those papers Zoltan had written up about Lilith.

But after Cedric had studied these documents for some months, I was devastated when he told me that I must have been deluded not to understand what a special race I was from, that obviously some great wrong had been worked upon Lilith that left the human race brainwashed into believing she had been an evil wife to Adam. Cedric was quite fanatical about his interpretations of all I told him, and he would not see reason when I tried to suggest to him that there were two sides to the story.

And then, one day, my son murdered me, or so he thought, by messing with the brakes on my car. His motivation was solely his impatience to inherit the wealth I had accumulated and all the knowledge and secrets I had kept from him. And he did not believe me, I realized, when I said I could heal quickly from any wound, and so when his wickedness resulted in an accident that would have killed anyone but me, I decided I was finished with him. Or rather, it was decided for me. I had thought I would vanish then, so I played dead, knowing I could slow my heartbeat until it appeared that I had truly died, for as I had learned in the war when I had been gassed, I could live without oxygen for a considerable time. I allowed my body to be carried off to the funeral home, planning to let myself be placed in a coffin and then to use my great strength to dig myself out of the grave in the dead of night.

But once my body reached the funeral home, I heard the man I thought to be the mortician say in a very clear voice, "You can open your eyes now, Quincey Harker. Your secret is safe with me."

I was so stunned by these words that my eyes instantly flew open, and there, standing before me was Uncle Abraham—yes, Professor Van Helsing!

"It can't be," I said, sitting up in shock. "You have to be dead. You'd be well over a hundred years old by now."

"I am far older than that," he replied, "but I never did tell you my other names, did I?"

I was terrified by these words, and for a second, I feared he intended to kill me. After all, the last time I had seen him, he had wanted to lock me up in an insane asylum. And now that he knew my secret, what did he plan to do? Did he still believe I was evil, although all I had wished was to escape a son who had attempted to murder me?

"Have no fear," he said. His beard was longer and whiter than I remembered. Could he really be over a century old? "You are in good hands. You are safe. And the time has come for you to understand far more than you have been told to date. You will recall that Morgan le Fay, or Lady Morgana as I call her, told you the time would come when one would guide you to your purpose. I am that one."

"Lady Morgana...but...how...why would you...?"

"I have been known by many names," Uncle Abraham continued. "Some have called me the Wandering Jew, and some have called me Joseph of Arimathea, or Professor Van Helsing, the name you have known me by, but perhaps my best known name is that of Merlin, the Arch Enchanter, wizard to the court of King Arthur."

I believe I actually fainted at this point, for I had been holding my breath a considerable time until just a moment before, so perhaps the rush of oxygen to my lungs was a bit much for me, or perhaps it was the shock of seeing my adopted uncle and learning he was Merlin. In any case, I would wake to find myself not in a British funeral home, but rather, back in Dracula's Castle.

CHAPTER 19

I WOKE IN my old bed, but at first, I did not recognize the room. The walls had been whitewashed and hung with exquisite paintings. The bedclothes were made of velvets and satins; the furniture was the same antiques I remembered, but newly polished and sparkling in the morning sun, and if it were not for the view of the Carpathians from my window, I would not have believed myself in the same place I had once known so intimately.

I sat up in wonderment, almost in disbelief. I swung my feet to the floor and found Turkish carpets covering what had previously been cold stones, and then my eyes fell upon the wardrobe, formerly a rotting old piece of furniture, now a shining gilded antique filled with exquisite suits and dress shirts and pants, and all in the sizes I wore.

I bypassed dressing myself and instead grabbed a bathrobe, since I found myself only in my underwear with no sign of the torn clothes I had been wearing from the car accident. Then I opened my door, imagining at this early hour of the morning that if someone had brought me here, I would likely find that person in the kitchen. I remembered well the way and slowly headed in that direction, all the while marveling to see how nicely the castle had been restored.

I hoped to get a glimpse of whoever my host might be before he saw me, but as I descended to the kitchen, the stair creaked, so he turned my way just as we both came into full view of one another.

"Ah, you are up," he said. He was a man in his thirties with a short beard and dark features. He was dressed in a long red robe with elaborate golden-trimmed cuffs, long sleeves, and jewels sewed around his collar and down the front of his robe. I would have thought him a Chinese mandarin except that he was clearly of European and not Asian descent. But what surprised me most about his appearance was that over his elegant, if gaudy, clothing, he had a common housewife's apron tied around his waist.

"Pardon?" was all I could think to reply, so stunned was I by his appearance.

"Oh, excuse me," he said, following my eyes as I looked him up and down. "I don't usually dress like this around the castle since I have no court to impress anymore, but I wanted to make a good impression on you, and I feared that getting egg yolk on my robe would ruin that."

"Don't mention it," I said. "I'm Quincey." I reached out to shake his hand, not knowing what other response would be appropriate, and he seemed friendly, even if he had apparently made himself more than comfortable in the castle I still considered my own.

"I'm Constantine Palaiologos, former Emperor of the Greeks," he replied, accepting my hand and squeezing it warmly.

"I...I'm afraid I don't understand," I said. "You—I've seen pictures of the King of Greece—Constantine II—but you don't look like him."

"No, no relation," he replied, reaching behind himself to untie his apron. "Not a close one at least. I'm Constantine XI. Sit down and I'll have breakfast in a minute."

"I'm afraid I still don't understand," I said, sitting down at the table. "How can you be the eleventh Constantine if the current king is the second one?"

"He's the king of modern Greece. I'm the former emperor, although you might understand it better if I refer to it as the Byzantine Empire, rather than saying I'm Emperor of the Greeks. We liked to think of ourselves as Romans actually, but we were really Greeks."

"The Byzantine Empire," I said, astonished, trying to place it— history had not been my strong point in school. "But hasn't that been gone for hundreds of years?"

"Yes, of course, over five hundred now," he said, setting a plate of scrambled eggs before me.

"But how could you—"

"You're no spring chicken yourself, Quincey Harker; you look twenty-five, but you're over three times that, aren't you? So what makes my age so astonishing?"

I began to fiddle with my eggs on my plate, thinking upon this, and eventually admitting, "All right. Fair enough. At least, I know a long life and youth are possible, but it is still astonishing."

"Yes, it is, isn't it? But it's all well, regardless. Everything is all right, Quincey. Even when your son tried to murder you, it was all right. All is right with the world and always has been and far more so than you know."

"I—I've had many strange experiences," I said, setting down the fork and looking him straight in the face. "I've met some strange beings—long-lived ones, I mean. Captain Vanderdecker, Morgan le Fay, and the wizard Merlin, although I never thought any of them were real people until I met them—but I also know of Dracula and Lilith, who apparently are historical, and now you, I believe you must be historical too. Is that what you're trying to tell me?"

"Well, I'm still alive, not dead," said Constantine, laughing, "but I guess you could say I'm historical. More importantly, what do all these experiences lead you to believe, Quincey?"

"I don't know what to believe," I said, casting my eyes to the table and picking up my fork again.

"Oh, that's not true. You're just being shy. You can speak freely here."

"I don't understand," I said, pausing to take a bite of my eggs, "how I got back to Castle Dracula and what you're doing in it. I can only think all these strange experiences mean that there's some force in this universe guiding it all, and I can only hope that it's a benevolent one since despite all the turmoil I've experienced in my life, I'm still alive."

"Very good, and right you are," he said, although rather than elaborate for me, he dug into his own scrambled eggs.

We ate in silence for a minute before he said, "Oh, excuse me. I forgot that you might like some juice—orange juice—freshly squeezed from Greek oranges no less."

He got up and found a pitcher in the refrigerator—yes, there was a modern refrigerator—not something I would have expected at all. Castle Dracula had not even had an icebox when I had last been here.

In another minute, he had poured us each a glass of juice, and then he pulled out some elaborate kind of bread that he said he had made special for my visit.

"I thought you always made it just for me," a voice said, startling me. Turning toward the door, I saw Merlin standing before us, in a long blue robe, his beard white and flowing down to his waist and a walking stick in his hand.

"Merlin," said Constantine, smiling, "well, it doesn't hurt to make something that I think both my guests will like, now does it? Sit down and eat. You're late, and I'm sure Quincey is dying with curiosity to have answers to all the questions I can see written on his face that he's afraid to ask me."

"Very well," said Merlin, sitting down next to me. "How did you sleep, Quincey? Do you like that new mattress we got for your bed?"

"I slept like a baby," I replied, "but I'm really confused about what I'm doing here."

"Let me have a cup of coffee, and then Constantine and I will explain it all," he replied.

I nodded my willingness to wait a moment.

"No reason for you to wait while he drinks his coffee," said Constantine, filling a cup from a coffeepot I hadn't noticed on the counter before. "I can talk while I eat. My tale is of little matter anyway—it is simply one of failure, and—"

"Constantine," Merlin interrupted, "how many times have I told you not to talk about yourself that way? You had to fail to save Constantinople for a greater purpose."

"When I think of all who died at the fall of my great city. When I—"

"Hardly anyone died at all compared to all the deaths in the wars just in the last century."

"Still, I failed to protect my people, and then to have failed with Dracula—"

"You're getting ahead of yourself," Merlin interrupted again. "Start at the beginning."

Constantine nodded and sat down at the table. He took a sip of his juice and then began to speak.

CONSTANTINE'S TALE

The beginning is really an end, but in the end, there was also a beginning.

I was, as I have said, the last Emperor of the Greeks, the ruler of Constantinople. I will not go into all the details. Although it makes me feel like a failure, regardless, I know that, logically, there was little I or anyone could have done to save the city from the Turks, especially when all the rest of Christendom refused to help us, the Pope not even coming to our aid because he wanted us all to convert back to Catholicism and my Eastern Orthodox people refused. There were plenty of signs in the skies that made us believe even God Himself and the Holy Virgin had abandoned us. And so, on May 29, 1453, the city fell to the Turks. I was dressed in armor that morning and fought in the streets with my men, assuming I would fall in battle, preferring such a death to being captured, taken alive, and made to pay homage to Mehmet II, Sultan of the Ottoman Empire, who would soon make my city his capital.

I did fall in the battle—I felt the battle blow that was struck against me, but at the same moment, and thinking I had died suddenly, I saw an angel descend and lift me up into the sky. Doubtless, some of my people saw the angel as well, for since then, tales of the marble emperor have arisen. Legend says the angel turned me into a marble statue and buried me under the city gate until the day when the city shall be Christian again and then I will return. But I daresay that day shall never come now. Upon its conquest, the city became Muslim and was renamed Istanbul, but then in 1920, the Republic of Turkey was declared and the country became a secular state, and who is to say that such is not for the best, for I think often that religion has led to more trouble than anything else in the history of mankind. Certainly, if it had not been for religious bickering between Eastern and Western Christendom, the city never would have fallen.

Anyway, you can imagine what a shock it was for me to find myself being carried by an angel up above the city. As I watched Constantinople fade into the distance, I was completely in awe and terrified at the same time—for men did not fly in those days; we had no airplanes as in your modern world. Eventually, my astonishment was surpassed by my exhaustion and battle wounds, and I lost consciousness as I was conveyed through the sky.

When I woke, I found myself in a bed in what I would later learn was Snagov Monastery, and—oh, I have forgotten perhaps the most important part. The day before the city's fall, in the palace gardens, I had encountered the Wandering Jew—I had heard rumors that he had been seen in the city, which everyone took as an ill omen, for he was reputed to appear at great historical moments. I only saw him for a second that day in the garden, so imagine my surprise when I opened my eyes in a monastery hundreds of miles north of Constantinople and found the Wandering Jew there, staring at me.

And then he told me his name. And you have already guessed it— the Wandering Jew and Merlin are one and the same.

I learned then that most of what I believed true about the world and God's rule over it was, if not completely false, a jumble of confusion, for not even the angel I thought had saved me had been an angel, although Merlin assured me angels exist. Rather it was Melusine, the ancient and immortal flying serpent daughter of Avalon, who had borne me through the air and brought me to Snagov Monastery where I was met by Merlin. Later that day, I was to learn that several others—priests from Hagia Sophia—had also been borne away. They had been saying the Holy Service just as the Turks broke into the church, and suddenly, a passage appeared in the wall behind the altar that had not been there before, a passage whose opening they did not question as the Turks advanced toward the altar. Rather, they grabbed the holy vessels and disappeared into the passage, which sealed itself behind them. This passage was actually a portal created through Merlin's magic, and by taking just a few steps rather than traveling hundreds of miles, the priests of Hagia Sophia found themselves emerging into the sanctuary of Snagov Monastery.

There, they and I have resided all these years, and I have found it a pleasant enough life, for I was better fit to be a monk than an emperor. In time, my companions from Constantinople passed away, but I have remained as a sort of guardian of the monastery's treasures, which include the Holy Lance and other sacred items, as well as the Thirteen Treasures of Britain. Merlin has moved these treasures about the world over the centuries, but finally, they have been stored here in Dracula's Castle, awaiting the hour of King Arthur's return and the human race's salvation.

I know that sounds remarkable, and perhaps it is, for that salvation has not yet happened, and it sounds like it is in contradiction to the sacrifice made by the Christ, but this is a different kind of salvation.

In any case, I have resided near Dracula's Castle at Snagov Monastery these past five centuries waiting for you, Quincey Harker, and now the time has come for you to reside here and also to wait, although I promise that your wait shall not be a tenth so long as my own. And there will be much for you to do in the years of waiting.

But you wonder why you will reside here and what you will wait for. Before I explain that, first I must enlighten you about a key part of your past that remains unknown to you and in which I played a significant part. You know the story of Dracula as told in Mr. Stoker's novel, but what Mr. Stoker did not include was the history of Dracula prior to his encounter with your parents. He hinted at it, but he did not tell the full story; since his time, many historians have come to understand that the legendary Dracula was based upon the Wallachian prince Vlad Tepes, sometimes called Vlad the Impaler for how he punished his enemies by impaling them on great stakes. Vlad's behavior was horrible and reprehensible, and yet, you might call him the St. Paul of our mission, for it was my and Merlin's mission to convert him to fight for the good—not to be confused with the Church, nor Constantinople, nor even to be the enemy of the Turks, but rather to enlist him in a much greater battle for the good of mankind. But despite all our efforts, we failed in that mission, and so this drama has continued on five centuries longer than we had planned, although that is not surprising since it has been in motion since the beginning of the world.

I see the question on your lips: What does any of this have to do with Lilith? For, surely, you realize that she is tied up in all of this since she is the only being on this earth who has existed since the Creation, although not in the same form, for she has reincarnated herself time and time again, and now, just as we speak, her latest earthly mother is about to give birth to her at any moment, and when she does, we have it planned that she will be imprisoned so she can do no further ill to mankind, but such caution is not sufficient, for her evil can never end by our imprisoning her or even destroying her. A much greater source is required, and that is where you and your family—yes, your family, including your murderous-hearted son—come into the story.

But before I explain the role you will play, you must understand Dracula's full story. I have struggled for centuries to understand it myself, although I confess I do not fully because I did not witness most of the events that factor into the story. Fortunately, Dracula left behind him a manuscript; it is incomplete, and I do not know how truthful it is, but it provides some understanding of his ill-fated decisions.

Let me read it out loud to you, so in the process, Merlin and I may refresh our memories of it as well. It will enlighten you about the man you have long considered your sire—for despite his supernatural powers, he began as a man, and one who did have his merits, but who also had very poor judgment, in my opinion, and I say that with great sadness.

[Here, the Emperor Constantine drew forth from the sleeve of his robe a sort of small tube, like one used to contain a poster. From it, he pulled out a scroll filled with writing that I could not quite read, both because of the script it was written in as well as its older style of phrasing. The emperor then began to read from it.]

CHAPTER 20

DRACULA'S MANUSCRIPT

I, DRACULA, PRINCE of Wallachia, hereby write down the story of my life, so those who come after me shall know and understand what I have done and so it be not forgotten why I so hated the Turks and brought terror and vindictive punishment upon all those who opposed me. Foremost of all, I have hated Mehmet II, who styles himself Sultan of the Turks, and who, through his evil nature, has murdered or had his minions slaughter good Christians, as well as engage in all manner of other despicable, unjust, and wicked behavior. He has committed crimes against my own family, he has destroyed the most holy city of Constantinople, and he has wreaked all manner of other terrible horrors upon Christians everywhere. I hate and denounce him to my dying day, which I suspect may not be far off, but if it be in my power, I will continue to seek to cause him pain and even destroy him in any way I might.

It is a strange tale I have to tell, but one nevertheless important. Not all will agree with my actions or my reasons for them, but I state them here nevertheless, and it matter not if even God Himself does not understand my reasoning, for God did nothing to prevent the slaughters I denounce or the crimes committed against my own family by that evil sultan, as well as by countless other princes who call themselves Christians, yet equally have engaged in unholy, sacrilegious, and disloyal behavior, seeking their own power and interests rather than those of God.

My detractors will say that neither did I ever seek to do God's will. In truth, I know not whether there is a God who watches me. I know only that He has never interceded for my benefit during the years when I most needed Him to assist me and my family, yet I have fought for the Holy Church and my country time and time again against the pagan Turks and those who would do evil within my own borders. If God is watching me, it is for Him and Him alone to judge me, and He must take into account His silence and inaction when I most needed Him to aid me in fighting His and His Holy Church's enemies. Such matters are between Him and me only, and yet, an explanation of my own deeds will hopefully justify me to my fellow men, who are otherwise ill-prepared and unworthy to judge me in any way.

I was born in 1431 A.D. to noble parents. I will pass over my earliest years, for I was then but a child who understood little of the political maneuvers of those days. I had a mother, who is of little importance to my story. I daresay she loved me as much as she was able, given that she would have known that my life would always be fraught with danger.

As for my father, he is of more importance to my tale, for as ruler of Wallachia, he raised me in the ways of manhood and statesmanship. His father had been Mircea, often called "The Old" or "The Great," both titles of which he was worthy, for he ruled our land for over thirty years, constantly fighting off threats to his throne. He died some fifteen years before my birth, but I heard tales of him in my boyhood that made me aspire to the same greatness he had achieved. And my father raised me with the understanding that someday I might be a ruler, for life was unstable and it was not unlikely that my older brother, also named Mircea, and my father's heir at the time, should die before he ever became king or had children of his own, which could then propel me to a throne I did not seek but knew I must be prepared to take if Fate should so decree. My other brother, Radu, who was to become known as "The Handsome," was four years younger than me. While I admired and respected my father and older brother, it was Radu whom I would be closest to, as I will explain shortly.

My father made certain that my brothers and I were well-educated by great scholars, and he had us participate in athletic activities even in the rain and other elements so we would grow strong and be prepared to be warriors. Never did I fear rain, nor thunder, nor lightning, nor snow, nor hail; nor did I let them stop me from succeeding at anything. In swordplay and athletic pursuits, I learned to rely on my own strength and courage, rather than trusting in other men to aid me.

In time, I would obtain the name Dracula because the year I was born, my father, as ruler of Wallachia, was initiated into the Order of the Dragon, a secret fraternal organization made up of many kings, princes, and other noble men. As a result, my father became known as Dracul. My title Dracula means "Son of Dracul," or "Son of the Dragon." While I am Vlad Tepes in name, I have adopted Dracula as my title out of respect for my father. The Order of the Dragon was founded to fight the enemies of the Holy Catholic Church, all those who were heretics to true Christianity, and most especially, to fight our great enemy—the Turks. For many years, I would devote myself to this cause.

My father did not directly succeed my grandfather, but in time, he made his way to the throne as Prince of Wallachia. In those days, there were many wars and conflicts among the rulers of Hungary, Germany, the principalities of Wallachia, and many other Christian lands, but most especially between these Christian lands and the Turks, who had staked their claim to land in Europe, surrounding and almost cutting off Constantinople, the last remnant of the great Empire the Romans had founded. In 1365, the Turks had conquered Adrianople, a city well into the Balkans and north of Constantinople, and they had made it their new capital. From there, they had gradually encroached upon the last remnants of the Roman Empire until only Constantinople remained; that the imperial city had survived for so long was a miracle in itself. The Turks had become the greatest threat to Christendom, yet because Constantinople and its people were members of the Orthodox Church, the Pope and the European kings who obeyed him would scarcely lift a finger to save the city and hold back the heathen Turkish tide.

My father was constantly caught up in all these wars and political intrigues. While the Order of the Dragon sided with the Catholic Church, survival often required switching loyalties, and so my father—and later, I, myself—would change religions, being Catholic or Orthodox as it suited us, for were not both branches still Christian and preferable to the Islam of the Turks? My father despised the Turks, but he also knew that in order to protect his own throne, he needed to be wise in alliances, so when the balance of power shifted in the Balkans to Sultan Murad II with the realization that Constantinople was destined soon to fall, my father had no choice but to sign an alliance with the

Turks and pay tribute to them, rather than let them ravish his own country. Then because of his alliance, when the great Christian leader Hunyadi launched a crusade against the Turks, my father tried to remain neutral, allowing Hunyadi's army to pass through Wallachia, yet refusing to take up arms against the Turks. Nevertheless, Sultan Murad grew very doubtful about my father's loyalty toward him, and rightly so.

Times were complicated then, as were the politics. I will not discuss all the wars and intrigues of those times, although I know them all like the hairs on the back of my hand and recall them repeatedly to my memory. It is sufficient to say that, in time, the sultan became very displeased with my father. He took my father hostage, treating him as a guest at the Ottoman court, although he was a prisoner nonetheless. My brother Radu and I were forced to join our father at the Ottoman court, while my older brother, Mircea, was left to rule Wallachia.

After a year, my father was allowed to return to the throne of Wallachia, but Radu and I were left behind as hostages, as surety for our father's good behavior in the future toward the infidel Turks. That year, I was but barely turned twelve, on the verge of manhood, so I was highly impressionable and sensitive to what was happening to me, and I knew full well that I was a prisoner at the Ottoman court. My brother, Radu, however, was only seven years old, so he did not fully understand why he could not remain with my father and our family. In time, he would grow to understand our dire situation, though he would never hate the Turks as deeply as I. Ironically, it is largely because of Radu that my hatred for the Turks grew in my soul until it finally ripened into the violence for which I have become famous.

CHAPTER 21

MY BROTHER RADU and I truly were prisoners. Sultan Murad II did not treat us unkindly, but being a prisoner is an unkindness in itself, and I wholeheartedly detested my Turkish enemies and wished to return to my father's side. I was old enough not to be beguiled by my captors' manipulations, their attempts to raise me as if I were a Turk to ensure my future loyalty to the Ottomans; in truth, they hoped someday I might rule in my father's place as their ally, thus making my country into a buffer against their Christian enemies. I, however, was determined to thwart them in these schemes.

At that time, I was a gangly and gaunt young man, perhaps not handsome at all; certainly, my looks in no way compensated for my temper tantrums and insolence toward my Turkish captors. I was allowed to move about freely through the palace, and I was educated by the finest of tutors, not only with the other valuable, young, and noble Christian hostages at the Ottoman court, but even with the sultan's own children. But I was not one to listen, and my stubbornness often got me into trouble. Then my captors found their kindness challenged until they deemed it necessary to whip, starve, and imprison me, sometimes for days. Such punishment was intended to break my spirit, but in truth, all it did was make me more stubborn and determined to endure, to survive, and, someday, to return to Wallachia as its prince. Then I planned to lead a crusade against the Turks and kill every single one of them.

My brother, due partly to his innocence and compliance, and even more so to his pleasing looks, did not receive anywhere near the brutal treatment I received. In our first months as prisoners after our father left the court, Radu, in his childish fear, would beg me to be humble, to be subservient, not to give in to my anger. He told me how he needed me, so I must do nothing that would cause our captors to punish or torture me, for if anything happened to me, he would be unable to bear it. While I loved my younger brother and wished to protect him, I found it impossible to control my temper. And so, before long, my brother realized that rather than seek my protection, he would be safer from punishment by creating a distance between us. In time, the bond between us probably would have been broken anyway, but now, a terrible, godless event occurred that permanently severed our affections.

I was old enough by then to be attracted to the opposite sex, although no opportunities arose for me to satisfy my desires. The sultan had his harem, but we boys were not permitted any indiscretions with the women who belonged solely to him. Nevertheless, I and my fellow students talked and joked, as boys will, about young women.

Among the boys who were tutored with Radu and me was the sultan's son, Mehmet. I will never forget one day when we boys were discussing the various beauties of women. Radu, who was no more than ten years old at the time, was present when Mehmet remarked, "Radu has skin as soft and beautiful as that of any woman." It was true my brother was very handsome, and I had noticed that many of the girls at court whom I secretly lusted over had made eyes at my brother and commented upon what a fine man he would soon be, although he was completely unaware of their interests, being still so young.

A few months later, Mehmet had managed to get some wine from the kitchens—the Muslims are not to take strong drink, for it is against their religion, but just as with most Christians, they could be hypocritical, and Mehmet certainly had a fondness for wine. Although he was a year younger than me, at thirteen, Mehmet was already my size and stronger, and because he was the sultan—for believe it or not, his father temporarily abdicated the throne to this mere boy for about two years at this time—I knew I must be polite to him, so my brother and I agreed to join him in drinking the wine. I only sipped it, though, refusing to lose self-control before my enemy.

Mehmet, however, had sufficient drink to make him lose his inhibitions, and that night, before my very eyes, he suddenly pounced upon Radu, pinning him to the ground and demanding a kiss from him.

I was in such shock at this behavior that I knew not what to do. At first, Radu tried to laugh off the request, but such a response only made Mehmet angry, causing him to declare, "I am your prince and you will do as I say." When Radu again refused, Mehmet slapped him across the face, then tried to force a kiss upon his lips.

"Mehmet, let him be!" I shouted, fearful of what would happen next. If I assaulted this boy sultan, I might be put to death, and then who would protect Radu? But doing nothing was equally no protection for my brother.

I watched in horror as Mehmet pinned my brother down, then lowered himself upon him, saying, "Radu, you are so beautiful. I just want to kiss you and show you how much I love you. You can be my prince if you will only kiss me."

And then he slowly began to rub himself against my brother. When Radu began to scream in fear and agony, I, laying all reason aside, jumped upon Mehmet, trying to wrestle him off my brother.

As strong as Mehmet was, he could not fight us both, and seeing me as the greater threat, he turned and wrestled me to the floor, hitting me in the face until I fell to the ground with a nosebleed. Then he stood over me, threatening to kill me if I should ever touch him again. I did not care, however, for my action had given my brother the chance to escape. But my brother stupidly stood there and watched. Once Mehmet had thrown me to the floor, he grabbed a sword lying nearby; then going up to Radu, he poked him in the leg with it, just sharp enough to make blood flow. Then he said, "Next time, I will put something other than my sword inside you, and I know you will enjoy it."

Terrified, Radu bolted out of the palace and into the gardens, finally climbing up a tree to hide. Mehmet followed after him, and a couple of minutes later, I did the same. I found Mehmet kneeling on the ground, now almost in tears, begging Radu to come down from the tree and to forgive him. When Radu repeatedly refused, I, through many pleadings, managed to get Mehmet to calm down before he woke the entire harem outside of whose walls we were. Then I convinced him to return with me into the palace where I managed to put the drunken sultan to bed.

I then made my own way to bed. I found Radu there in our bedchamber, having come down from the tree once he thought it safe.

When he saw me enter our room, my brother said, "Vlad, you could have been killed for attacking Mehmet like that. Let us hope he was too drunk to remember what happened, or in the morning, he may have you thrown into prison."

"What did you expect me to do?" I replied. "I cannot let that beast attack you like that."

"I don't know," said Radu, "but we must not make him angry if we value our lives."

"Would you rather have submitted to his disgusting animal lusts?" I asked. "Go to bed now. Do not expect me to defend you again if you are only going to be ungrateful."

"Vlad, I am not—"

"Go to bed now," I replied, and then I lay down and turned my back to him, ending our conversation.

How do I describe the horrors of what followed? My own brother had become a coward; he was ready to be the plaything of the sultan rather than act like a true Son of Dracul. After that, Mehmet did not need drink to be brave enough to make advances upon my brother, and after a short while, I soon came to think my brother enjoyed the prince's attentions. I then swore to myself that if my brother were to be the prince's lover, he would most certainly be my enemy. And I was left without a single friend in this world.

CHAPTER 22

At the end of 1447, news came to Adrianople of my father's death. I was in my room, quietly studying, which I had begun to do more often, seeking solitude from my brother and Prince Mehmet, and all the court, when I was summoned to a private audience with Sultan Murad II. He, not surprisingly, had taken back his throne until his son should grow to be more mature.

"Vlad," he said once I was in his presence, "I wish to inform you that your father and your older brother are dead."

So did the sultan speak to me. He gave me no expression of sorrow or sympathy and he minced not his words. I stood in his presence, not daring to sit down and not being offered a chair as I was told of my father and brother's fates, and then of my own.

"How did they die?" were the only words I could find, all my anger and stubbornness brought to a standstill by the shock.

Murad II explained that Hunyadi, the Hungarian general with whom my father had often been at odds while playing a dangerous game of trying to appease both Hunyadi and the sultan, had turned against my father, deciding he wanted a true ally in Wallachia. He had decided to set upon Wallachia's throne a pretender, one Vladislav II—my own family's distant kin and a longtime rival for Wallachia's throne.

Hunyadi and Vladislav II had crossed the Carpathians, heading toward Târgovişte, where my father held his court.

"Your father," the sultan told me, "had the city gates locked to prevent their entry, but the city's boyars revolted against him and let in the enemy. Your brother was captured by the citizens of his own city who tortured and killed him."

"How did he die?" I repeated.

"He was blinded and then buried alive," replied the sultan, still with no show of sympathy.

I swallowed, struggling to accept such a horrible death, envisioning my brother's face with earth being thrown upon it as he screamed for his life. But I quickly wiped the image from my mind and asked:

"And my father?"

"Your father survived the attack," Murad replied. "He escaped from the city and fled toward our troops on the Danube, but before he could reach my army, he was attacked and killed in the marshes in a village near Bucharest. His followers took his body and buried it in a small wooden chapel. That is all I know."

My father and my brother, both dead, turned against by their own people, and why? Because they had allied themselves with the Turks to maintain the balance of power, to save the lives of themselves and their people, to try to stop the Turkish tide of horror from advancing farther, and to save the rest of Christendom. And yet, they had been betrayed by those they sought to protect by making such concessions to our enemies.

I was disgusted, enraged. If I'd had a knife, I would have stabbed the sultan as he sat there before me on his pompous throne. If it had been in my power, I would that very moment have slaughtered the entire Turkish army, then gone to Wallachia and slain all the boyars who had turned against my father, and I would have put to a torturous death Hunyadi and Vladislav II and all their supporters.

But by now, I had learned better how to control my temper. An outburst would lead only to my own death. Instead, I knew I must maintain self-control.

"You take the news very well, young Vlad," said the sultan, observing my stony face with admiration. "You have grown strong. You are now sixteen, I believe. The awkwardness of your youth is slipping away. You have not Radu's charm, but he has proven himself weak compared to you. I think someday you will be ready to rule your people, but first, you have much more to learn. I think the time has come to give you a commission within my army. You will learn the skills of warfare, for which I am sure you have a great aptitude. And then, when I feel the circumstances allow for it, I will help you regain your father's throne. Then you will sit upon it as my ally and puppet."

I bowed in acknowledgment of his calculated generosity and replied, "As it pleases you, my lord."

CHAPTER 23

TOMORROW, I FACE a great battle, yet another one for my throne. I have begun this record for the sake of my son, so he may have some understanding of the man his father became and why, but I have spent more time writing than I intended, so I will not finish this history before the morning. Should I survive the battle—which I have every intention of doing, having countless times in the past fought my enemies, driven them to their knees, and impaled them on pikes, and also having also lost and regained my throne three times now—I will complete this history.

The details of the battles I have fought, the laws I have passed, and how I have punished my enemies are all recorded by my enemies, who now call me Vlad the Impaler. They spread lies about me as one who drinks the blood of his enemies, as if I were the very Antichrist himself.

There is much I could write of my life, but there is one secret I have withheld all these years; without it, my story can never be fully understood. It is a secret I have not dared to share with anyone until now, for it explains all my behaviors to a degree that makes me feel both ashamed and yet justified in all I have done.

All my life I was raised among my enemies. I have known nothing but bloodshed, treachery, imprisonment, and betrayal. Many a less determined man would weaken and break amid such horrors and miseries. But I never have. I have taken delight in it all, enjoying punishing my enemies and coming to realize that all are my enemies, be they Muslim or Christian, Turk or Wallachian, Hungarian or Greek, Catholic or Orthodox. All are my enemies, for all are the Children of Adam and Eve, while I am not. I do not deny that the forebears of mankind's tainted blood may flow in my veins, but so also does the blood of the Great Mother Lilith, and it is that blood, Dragon blood, Serpent blood, the blood of righteousness, that, ultimately, has been my salvation. Each man must work out his own salvation. The Church cannot provide salvation for us— priests promise it, but they only try to withhold it in their attempts to control us, when in truth, they do not even have the power to give it. Salvation is free for all of us when we take it and do not let evil control us.

I have been called evil, a very devil by many, but it is not so. I have striven to follow the truth, the noble way of being true to myself, and that is because I was honored to learn the secret of the Great Mother Lilith, and since that day, all my life has been a sacrifice to please her and win salvation in doing so.

I swear by the Grace of God who never showed grace to me that every word I have put down in this manuscript is true, for I am:

CONSTANTINE'S TALE CONTINUES

There ends the manuscript. Vlad was apparently called away before he could even put a date or seal to it, but we do know that he wrote it on the night of December 28, 1476, as he prepared for his final battle against the Turks. The events that followed have been lost to history, save that his headless body was found several days later near Snagov Monastery, and there he was buried.

QUINCEY'S TALE CONTINUES

"But," I said as Constantine finished speaking, "it is such a coherent story until the end when he starts to talk of Lilith. It's almost like a madman's rantings at that point."

"No, not that of a madman," said Constantine, "but the words of a believer, one of the faithful, one who believed himself educated in the very truth, although what he believed true was clearly distorted. That said, you can understand why we confiscated the manuscript when we found it, so it would not be passed down to posterity, for people would think he was crazy, and despite how Lilith has operated all these centuries, we have tried to keep the human race ignorant of her existence and intentions, for we wish to relieve mankind from the terror such knowledge would cause."

"I really don't understand," I replied. "I have for decades tried to comprehend just who and what Lilith is, how she is connected to Dracula, and how she is by extension connected to myself and to my late brother Zoltan. Please, don't you know more that you can tell me?"

I saw how my pleas caused Merlin's stern brow to soften. I was actually surprised by the perplexed look on his face—was he not the great wizard, highly knowledgeable on all things? Could he have nearly as many questions as I did? Or was he simply trying to decide how to answer my perplexing questions?

"We have answers," Merlin said after a moment, "or at least, we can fill in the missing events of Dracula's story that he does not include in his manuscript. I think you can understand from what he says why he was filled with anger and felt justified in the many heinous acts he committed throughout his lifetime. The stories of his impaling people are all true, and they were a horrible sight, for I saw them with my own eyes, but we need not dwell on those horrors. You are no stranger to the evils that men wreak upon one another, having yourself seen the misery of the German concentration camps, which were as much the work of Lilith as were Dracula's many impalements."

"Is she truly the evil behind all this then?" I asked. "And if so, can Dracula and...and my brother...can they in some way be forgiven or redeemed for their behavior because of the power she held over them?"

"That is a question I cannot answer," said Merlin. "Only God has the power to bind and loosen souls, but I can tell you, having once had the privilege to be uncle to the Christ and to have walked and spoken with Him as He grew up in His human form, that evil as it exists is buried deep within the heart of man and is based solely in his fear. Once that fear is removed, love and wisdom remain and rule. When both Dracula and your brother died, the fear that too often controls this world was released from them, and so I am sure they exist in a better place now, and who is to say that like Lilith herself, they might not reincarnate themselves or have already done so, but this time so that they might do good and make reparation for their pasts."

"I hope it is so," I said sadly, and then I excused myself, promising to return in a moment. I made my way through the castle and back to my bedchamber to use the chamber pot, only to discover I could not find it where it used to be, and looking in my closet, I found instead a completely modern bathroom in its place, and I found this change so wonderful that it became a pleasant momentary distraction for me before I was to hear the rest of Dracula's tale.

CHAPTER 24

"A T FIRST," BEGAN Merlin, after I had returned from my room and found him and Constantine now seated in the drawing room, on comfortable modern furniture with coffee poured for sustenance as we continued our discussion, "we had the highest hopes for Dracula."

"He was really quite a remarkable leader from the very beginning," Constantine agreed. "I never did meet him while I was yet emperor, but of course, I kept a very close eye on everything that happened in the Balkans. His first reign lasted only two months in 1448—he led a coup and regained his father's throne only to have Vladislav II reacquire it. The years that followed were not easy for him, and he sought sanctuary at various courts until the accession of his enemy Mehmet II as Sultan of the Ottoman Turks. That led to Vlad's opportunity, and I might add, the end of my glorious city, or at least, what remained of its glory.

"By that time, Constantinople was more a symbol than a treasure to be gained. Little of the empire remained and the Turks had us surrounded in both Asia and Europe. Many times the city had withstood attacks from our enemies, but Mehmet II was determined to become the conqueror, and for whatever reason, God allowed it to happen in the spring of 1453.

"It was following the fall of Constantinople that Vlad had his chance. Here in Snagov Monastery, while Merlin educated me upon the world's true history and how Lilith had long battled against the Children of Eve, I heard the news that Hunyadi, longtime enemy to Vlad and his father, had made peace with Vlad, for he believed that because Vlad had grown up with Mehmet II, he would have a special understanding of the young emperor's mind and, therefore, would make a good ally in the war against him. Finally, Hunyadi and Vlad—who was now beginning to style himself Dracula, and so I will refer to him as such henceforth—made an agreement. Dracula obtained a position at Hunyadi's court and accompanied him to the coronation of the new King of Hungary, to whom he swore his allegiance. Soon after, the Turks attacked Belgrade and were defeated, causing the people of Christendom to take heart in fighting against their longtime enemies. Hunyadi then died of the plague, and Dracula regained his throne from Vladislav II.

"Dracula was now Prince of Wallachia, and consequently, Merlin and I hoped for the best. We had been watching Dracula long enough to decide that he was the one who could defeat evil—yes, defeat Lilith—for he seemed more fearless than any other man. Still, he knew he must be careful, so while he agreed to send tribute to the Turks, he refused to go to Constantinople to pay homage to Mehmet II. During this time, he also slew in single combat the man who had killed his father, a sign he was able to right wrongs, at least in his own mind.

"So, at this time, Merlin and I approached Dracula by luring him to Snagov Monastery. He was then trying to ingratiate himself with the Church in Romania by founding several monasteries and churches and making up for his past sins by seeking to gain God's favor. And so, it was natural that he would, in time, come to Snagov, and Merlin and I made certain when he did that he felt compelled to endow it with gifts, and more importantly, to make it his favorite monastery.

"'Why Snagov?' you may ask. It was on an island in the middle of a lake, and Merlin had a weakness for islands since he had spent so many years in Avalon. And I had agreed to live at Snagov until the time came when we might act, when we might be prepared for the future."

"But I don't understand," I broke in. "Prepare for what?"

"Prepare to defeat Lilith," Merlin said. "God, of course, does not involve Himself in the wars of mankind—He does not care whether the Turk or the Wallachian wins, nor even the Christian or the Muslim. He is the source of Love and above the pettiness that mankind has made of its lives and even its religions, but Lilith—now she is another story."

"But," I objected, "Zoltan told me that all the cruel things that have been said and written about Lilith are lies. Is that not true?"

"Lilith's story is very complicated," Merlin replied, "and it is not necessary for you to understand it all now. It's sufficient to say that she feels she was betrayed by Adam in his love for Eve, and for that reason, she desires revenge upon all mankind, for all humans are Eve's descendants. Lilith has herself been mother to a few children now and then, notably the son of Constantine of Cornwall, whom she helped to usurp King Arthur's throne, and whenever she does generate a line of descendants, she will reincarnate herself as one of them. For example, Constantine's descendants included Gudrun, who became Queen of Denmark and later married Geoffrey of Lusignan. Gudrun was a reincarnation of Lilith, and in that life, she gave birth to the line of the Counts of Lusignan, among whom is numbered one of Dracula's ancestors through his mother's line. It should be noted that while Lilith reincarnates herself into her own line, she always seeks to couple with one of the line of Avalon, and in turn, of myself, for I am the ancestor of Arthur and Morgana, having been born as Joseph of Arimathea, and fortunately, granted long life through my nephew the Christ's good grace."

"But then," I said, my head spinning with all the names Merlin had just mentioned, "if Dracula were one of Lilith's descendants, wouldn't that have naturally inclined him toward evil, in which case, why did you think he was special and someone who would turn out to be good? Was it because you thought he could defeat the Turks?"

"No," said Constantine. "You are not listening. This is not a battle between Muslim and Christian. God cares not for such things. We chose Dracula because we thought he could stem the tide against Lilith."

"But he did not?" I asked.

"Lilith is very wise and cunning," said Merlin. "Nor is she fully evil. She is full of knowledge that she could use for good, and at times, she has done so, for example, when she once instructed women in the land of Prester John about how to be true sisters to one another, how to be good wives and mothers, and how to spread love in the world without submitting to the cruelties of men. For, at times, she realizes it would be impossible for her to reclaim the world for herself and her descendants without the descendants of Eve since her own descendants must couple with those of her enemies, as she terms them. At the heart of her agony is her betrayal by Adam and the wound it caused to her heart; if only she could find the love that Adam failed to give her, then there would be hope that she might also be redeemed and be freed from her pain and anger. For that reason, she has sought out only the greatest men, the only men she deems worthy of herself, considering her great knowledge and power—men such as King Arthur, who rejected her, causing her to turn to Constantine of Cornwall. But also men she won over like Geoffrey of Lusignan. And finally, she sought out Dracula. When we realized Dracula was the one she would next persuade to become her mate, we hoped he might actually be the one to heal the wound in her heart."

"I still don't understand," I said.

"Let me then explain," said Constantine, "the events surrounding Dracula's death...."

CHAPTER 25

CONSTANTINE'S TALE OF DRACULA CONTINUES

I WAS NOT the head of the monastery at Snagov at that time, but the monks there knew my identity, several of them having been transported by Merlin from Constantinople, so they often deferred to me as if I were still an emperor. We were all sworn to secrecy, and aware of Merlin's actions, and in his service really, so when he requested that we invite Dracula to the monastery, everyone was in agreement. Dracula had just regained his throne for the second time and begun to strengthen his country's defense so we all had great hopes he would create stability now in Wallachia. The other monks believed that we sought to win Dracula's favor because he was our hope against the Turks, and in time, he might help us to retake Constantinople; some even thought I wished Dracula to place me back on my throne, but by then, three years had passed since the Fall of Constantinople, and I had no desire to return to my former life. What I wished, after Merlin had told me the entire story of Lilith's battle against humanity, was for Dracula to help bring about the end of Lilith's misery, for despite all her evil, Merlin and I felt sympathy for her. Nevertheless, I did not share her story with those at the monastery.

And so, at Merlin's request and while he was off seeing about other important matters, I invited Dracula to visit Snagov. He was doubtless surprised when he was first summoned and told he would have a private meeting with a great prince. Perhaps he feared treachery of some sort, and he must have speculated who this prince might be, but his nerves were as strong as a steel blade, so he showed not the slightest sign of anxiety when he arrived at the monastery and was shown into my presence. Nor did he twinge when, before knowing who I was, the door closed behind him, leaving us in private.

"Welcome, Prince of Wallachia," I greeted him, arrayed in splendor befitting my previous station. Somehow, Merlin had whisked away several of my finest robes from Constantinople, and I had kept them in a trunk, never wearing them at the monastery, but this day I had made an exception. I was dressed in the finest gold-colored silk with embroidered jewels and my crown upon my head.

Dracula nodded, too proud to bow, but I saw the glint of surprise in his eyes, despite how he tried to conceal it.

"May I have the honor of knowing whom I am addressing?" he asked.

"You may," I said. "Be seated," and I gestured toward a chair beside me.

Although Dracula was a prince accustomed to others standing in his presence, he must have gathered from my manner that I was born to a higher station in life than he. After a moment, he sat down, his eyes never leaving me.

"Prepare yourself to be surprised," I said, "and I will not take it amiss if you show disbelief at first. You see, save for the monks here at

Snagov, most believe me dead—dead at the Fall of Constantinople. I am the former Emperor of the Greeks, Constantine XI."

Dracula did not blink an eye, and thus, he confirmed for me that Merlin had been right. He was the one to take on this mission.

"You have the face of a statue," I remarked. "I have no doubt you are surprised, but you do not show it."

"It is nothing to me who you are," he replied. "The Fall of Constantinople was a great tragedy, but I show no respect to any ruler unless it is in my best interest, and while it was not your fault that you inherited a decaying empire, you were one of the weaker rulers of our time. I will not bow the knee to weakness, regardless of how you came by it."

"You are sharp-tongued and bold," I replied, "or perhaps not bold, for you are right. I have no kingdom and no power now, but I do have a secret."

"You Greeks are known for your secrets, your espionage, your blackmail. It helped lead to your destruction."

"Not that kind of a secret," I said, unable not to smile at his accurate words. "But you are correct that I come from a long line of less than moral rulers. But I guess this secret could be considered a form of espionage in itself. Still, the intentions behind it are good."

"I am Prince of Wallachia," he replied, "and no emperor-turned-monk is going to make me do anything I do not choose to do. Yes, I pose as a friend to the Church, but only because it serves my own purposes. Speak out what you want and I will tell you whether it is to my benefit—if not, I will depart. But think well on what you say, for you are in my domains, and I could get good money from the Turks for turning you over to them; they are my enemies as much as yours, so I would hate to do so, but I would not hesitate to use you as my pawn if needed."

"I speak not of politics," I replied, ignoring his attempts to intimidate me, "nor of anything concerning the governments of mankind. I speak of evil. I speak of threats to our very existence, and I speak of a chance for you to be a hero."

He turned and spat on the floor before replying, "I am already a hero to the people of Wallachia and to all who are the enemies of the Turks, and I know of no evil on this earth save for that of the sultan and his minions."

"You know of good and evil, the battle between God and Satan, falsely described as it is," I replied. "It is not some Satan who haunts us; rather, the wrongs man has done to man and the fear we allow to control us are what have brought about all our ills; equally, it was not some apple plucked from a tree in Eden, but the fate of a woman scorned that has brought about this evil, and if that woman has her way, all of us in time will turn against one another. She stirs up the wars between Christians and Muslims, and before either existed, she set Jews and Egyptians against one another, and Greeks against Persians, and every man she could against his neighbor, even husband against wife and mother against child—she ignites many of the evil deeds men do—by cultivating the fear already in their hearts and making it manifest in greed, lust, and all manner of other destructive behaviors. For centuries, there have been those who have fought her in secret—those whose names are renowned, yet their stories are only half-told—heroes such as King Arthur and Roland and Ogier the Dane. And now you, Prince of Wallachia, have been chosen to join this list of heroes who have fought against her and her evil."

Dracula looked me straight in the eye, and for a moment, I thought he would tell me I was mad, but then I saw in his eye his true weakness—the desire for fame, the desire for honor, for who would not wish to be in the company of the great heroes I had named?

"Speak on," he said.

And so I told him the story of Lilith. Of what had happened in the Garden of Eden, of how she had threatened the Children of Eve for all time, and how the Children of Arthur had fought against her for nearly a thousand years now as she continued to reincarnate herself, always succeeding in bringing about more evil, and never fully being stopped.

"And yet, do not be fooled," I said, "for she is part of God's creation, and for that reason, she can never be fully evil. She has been deeply hurt and wounded, and now and then, she has moments of illumination when she tries to repair the wrongs she has committed. She has taught in the schools of Prester John, being allowed there because she is the oldest, wisest, and most cunning being on the earth, and some of her blood flows in the veins of very special men and women, and that is where you come in."

I could see he guessed what my next words would be before I even spoke them.

"You see, Prince Dracula," I said, "You and I are both of the line of Avalon, but back during the time of the Crusades, your line also married with that of the House of Lusignan, which, in turn, is descended from this Lilith in one of her previous incarnations. In the past, those of the line of Avalon have always fought against her, but when she mothered a child by Geoffrey, Count of Lusignan, she intertwined her evil line with that of Avalon, for Geoffrey's mother was Melusine of Avalon, and his father, Count Raimond, was descended from King Arthur; therefore, there is as much blood of Avalon as of Lilith in your family line. Nevertheless, you, Prince

Dracula, would be the first to fight against his own ancestress, and in the process, perhaps save mankind, as well as Lilith's own soul."

"Fight?" he replied. "Fight a witch, a sorceress? How am I to do that? I always fight against men, soldiers, warriors. I have never fought against magic. I would not know how to fight such a creature."

"The first thing you must do," I explained, "is to find her. For many years, she taught in the secret schools of Prester John, but now she has decided her efforts to educate women there have failed, for men continue to abuse and mistreat their wives, and women continue to allow it, and she has all but given up on the daughters of Eve ever civilizing the sons of Adam, for it is against Adam that her greatest grudge lies. In short, she has founded her own school, with the intent to teach mankind ways to destroy itself. She calls this school the Scholomance, and she has kept it closely hidden, but Merlin, the Arch Enchanter—yes, he lives and is as real as Lilith herself, and he sides with us—Merlin has recently discovered its location in the mountains near Hermanstadt in Transylvania."

Not blinking an eye at what any other mortal would have been astounded by, Dracula simply replied, "And so I am to travel to this school?"

"You are the Prince of Wallachia," I said, "while I am just a humble monk, whatever my previous position in this world may have been. I cannot make you do anything, but as Prince of Wallachia, I am sure you could travel into the Austrian Emperor's domains to find this school for yourself."

"And what am I to do when I find it?" Dracula asked.

"I suggest you become one of Lilith's students."

"And what will that prove?"

"You will be close to her, so you can learn how she thinks, although you must be careful not to think like her, for she is very wise and cunning, as I have said, and so she knows how to play with a man's mind—not by intellectual argument, but through her feminine wiles. She has used sex to destroy many a man, and she will do the same with you if you give in to her beauty and sensuousness. But we believe you strong-willed enough to resist her—in fact, we doubt any man currently on this earth is as strong-willed as yourself."

"I am not interested in coupling," Dracula replied. "I have had women killed for lying to me about being pregnant as a way to trap me. No woman has, nor ever will, get the best of me."

"For your sake and for the sake of us all, I hope that is true," I stated.

"I will think this matter over," he said, looking bored, but betraying his interest by biting his lower lip. "I have enough to do in ruling my country and protecting it from the Turks, and as I have already told you, a task must benefit me before I undertake it."

"Saving the human race from further pain and devastation should be gift enough, I would think," I replied.

"The human race has done nothing for my benefit. I owe it nothing."

"Perhaps," I said, "you need to be the one who gives first."

"Don't give me your piety," he sneered. "I will not hear it from you, a puppet emperor who could not stop the Turks by your diplomacy, much less your good intentions. Do you know how many of the defeated people of Constantinople have converted to Islam? They are wiser than you, for all their countless hours of prayers did them no good, and once the city fell, they came to their senses. The Christian God abandoned them, so why should they not become Muslims?"

"The God of the Christians and the Muslims is one and the same God," I replied.

"Yes," he agreed, "and either way, equally uncaring what becomes of mankind."

"We cannot understand the ways of God," I said. "He has a greater plan than we can fathom. A greater plan that resulted in my being saved and brought here, along with the priests from Hagia Sophia and the holy vessels that we brought with us, including the Holy Lance, among other items. God is biding His time and will yet make all right, and I have no doubt you are part of that plan, Prince of Wallachia."

"The Holy Lance, you say," said Dracula. "That cannot be true. Mehmet II, after conquering the city, had the Lance sent to the King of France as a peace token."

"That lance is a fake," I replied. "Merlin hid away the true lance centuries ago, and it is now here in our safekeeping. The fake one was displayed in Constantinople for centuries, and I do not care if the Turks believe it to be the true one."

"So you have the true Holy Lance here? That is good to know, and since you are in my domains, perhaps I will someday take it and use it to defeat my enemies, for I have heard of its powers. I warn you, do not try to hide it from me. As for your request, I will let you know what I have decided at my own pleasure."

"Your highness," I said, "it is not my request. It is humanity's request, and you are part of humanity, as were your brother and father, whose deaths cause the desire for revenge to boil in your breast. Such evil deeds might never have been acted against them had Lilith not stirred up anger and hate among the Children of Eve. You are the greatest, and perhaps the only, hope this world has left."

"Enough of this foolish talk," he snapped. "I told you I will consider it, but for now, I must go and punish my enemies for their misdeeds."

And with that, Dracula stormed out of the monastery. Before I could rise from my chair and cross the room, he was in his boat, being ferried back to the main shore.

"I have failed," I later told Merlin.

"Perhaps not," he replied. "We will wait and see."

CHAPTER 26

I DO NOT know when or why Dracula decided to seek out Lilith. I do know that he did not seek further counsel from Merlin or me upon how to go about fighting her. In later years, it was rumored that he had visited the Scholomance and studied under the Devil himself, but since Merlin has assured me there is no Devil, I took these rumors to mean he was taught by Lilith. Sadly, it eventually became apparent that Lilith had gotten the better of Dracula, for he did not manage to destroy or thwart her; perhaps he never even sought to, but only to gain power from her. In any case, after meeting with her, he became more cruel and violent than he had ever been before. Stories now spread of how he impaled his enemies and openly drank their blood, despite his claims otherwise in the manuscript I showed you. I do not believe, however, that anything he said from the time he went to the Scholomance can be trusted. Instead, Lilith sowed the seeds of lies in his heart and fanned the hatred he already held toward his enemies, both those who had killed his father and brother, and especially the Sultan of the Turks who had, as far as he was concerned, raped and subjugated his brother, Radu.

In the years that followed, Pope Pius II called for another crusade against the Turks, but Dracula was the only one who responded. His weapons were brilliant and brutal, including sending men with illnesses disguised as Turks among the enemy to sicken them—one of the earliest uses of biological warfare. Indeed, whenever he could torture or hurt the Turks in any way, he took full advantage of it.

Even Mehmet II, his lifelong enemy, finally admitted no one was as terrible as this Prince of Wallachia. After the sultan saw twenty thousand of his men impaled by Dracula, he admitted he could not defeat such a man, and with the resulting plague in his camp, he came to believe he truly was under Dracula's curse.

Nor were the horrors Dracula inflicted limited to the Turks. At one point, he invited all his boyars to dinner, then had them slaughtered as revenge for how they had treated his father.

I heard all these stories, and although I did not witness them, I knew Dracula's stubbornness from the one time I had spoken to him, and I knew if Lilith had gotten the better of him when he had visited the Scholomance, then indeed, he was a true warmonger, a true heathen, and a vile being. I had heard from Merlin how once, in her incarnation as Gwenhwyvach, Lilith had turned Constantine of Cornwall into a warrior and bringer of bloodshed to King Arthur's land, and now she was doing the same through Dracula.

I was almost relieved when news came that Dracula had been tricked and made a prisoner of King Matthias of Hungary. For fourteen years, he then resided at the Austrian emperor's court, a curiosity among all the visitors while his throne was held by several others, including his brother Radu, who obtained it with Mehmet II's help, although Radu would still continually have to fight for it until he finally died from syphilis in 1475.

Dracula could not be more delighted that his brother, in truth, his enemy, was dead, for now Matthias of Hungary decided it was in his best interest to place Dracula back on the throne, and he even married Dracula to his cousin, with the stipulation that Dracula become Catholic, a conversion Dracula agreed to since God and religion meant nothing to him.

Nearly twenty years had now passed since last I had seen Dracula. Now, once again Prince of Wallachia, he revisited Snagov monastery, purposely seeking me out.

"I want the Holy Lance," he told me. "The Turks are advancing once more, and I will not let them take my throne from me again."

"The lance is a holy relic," I replied. "It cannot be used as a weapon of war."

"I will have it, for it will drive back the Turks in fear when they see its power."

"What power?" I asked. "You do not know what you speak of."

"It will cause them to come to a standstill," he insisted, "just as the Virgin Mary's veil once did."

"You do not know what is true and what is a fairy tale," I replied.

"Do not argue with me, monk!" he snapped. "Do not forget this is my country and you are my subordinate in it."

"And do not you forget," I replied, "that once I fought as an emperor against the Turks. Do you not think that if the Holy Lance could defeat the Turks, I would have used it to save Constantinople?"

"You obviously were not wise enough to do so, and too much of a coward anyway, hiding behind your city walls."

And then he ordered his men to search the monastery until he did find the Holy Lance, and taking it with him, he was convinced that he would so completely defeat the Turks that by spring he would take back Constantinople. "And when I reconquer the city," he told me, holding the Holy Lance in his hands, stroking it as if it were his pet, his own greatest treasure, "I shall set myself up as its emperor." And then he spit at me in disdain and took his leave.

It was the last time I saw him alive.

CHAPTER 27

THE BATTLE BETWEEN Dracula and the Turks took place many miles from Snagov Monastery on the road to Bucharest. It was a catastrophe for Dracula. I do not know whether he and his men fought bravely or whether his faith in the Holy Lance's power gave him a false confidence that destroyed his chances. Later, Merlin would find the lance where it lay on the battlefield and return it to the monastery—as I had told Dracula, it was not to be used as a weapon. But Dracula would have had little chance anyway, for the Turks outnumbered his men, two to one.

We received news at the monastery of Dracula's failure the evening after the battle. The next morning, I ventured outside the monastery walls to go for a walk as I often did at dawn, relishing the quiet and the island's serene landscape. I was walking along a footpath near the shore when I heard voices. Turning in their direction, I saw a woman in a winter cloak bending over, and in another minute, I saw a man lying on the ground, the object of her attention. At first, I was surprised, for I saw no boat or any other sign of how they might have arrived on the island. From the woman's posture, I understood the man must be ill or hurt, so I stepped forward to give assistance.

But then she raised her head. Great piercing green eyes looked at me, and then her lip curled as she spit out her words, "Do you think you can have him now, priest? I brought him here only for safety, but you shall never have him. He is mine."

And then in terror, I watched as she sunk her teeth into his neck and appeared to be sucking his blood.

For a few seconds, I stood there in shock before I exclaimed, "Woman, stop!"

"He is mine, I tell you," she repeated, pulling away from him, her teeth dripping with blood. "He was to be my lover, my perfect mate. He was the most perfect man I have ever known, and now, because of you with your false lies about the Holy Lance, he has been killed. For this misdeed of yours, I will make him live forever so I may wreak havoc upon the human race like I have never done before. You know me, don't you priest—don't you, Constantine, the weakling emperor? Now you will know what a real king is as the Prince of Darkness begins his reign."

And then she rose, not to her feet as a normal human would, but rather she levitated into the air, and stretching out her arms, she declared, "I am Lilith, Queen of Eden, Queen of the Earth, and I will have my revenge!"

Then she darted up into the air like Greek fire launched from a catapult.

I watched her soar above me, craning my neck to follow her until she disappeared fully from view. Only then did I dare to approach Dracula's slain body.

A great scar ran across his neck where someone had apparently tried to hack off his head. He had several other cuts and scratches upon him, but the two holes in his neck were the only ones still freshly bleeding. He was clearly dead, there being no sign of life about him, no breathing, no pulse or heartbeat, although his body was still warm, as if he had died just minutes before.

I knelt down and collected him in my arms, holding him for a few minutes, hoping for a sign of life from him, for despite how he had scorned and mocked me, I did not forget that Merlin had thought him once our greatest weapon in the war against Lilith. But now he was dead, and all I could do was mourn him.

I was still sitting there on the ground, the snow beginning to swirl around me as the sun rose when two of my fellow monks found me. At my bidding, they helped me carry the fallen prince inside.

That day, Dracula was buried within the sanctuary of Snagov monastery. We held a proper Eastern Orthodox burial service for him, and we showed him all the honor befitting a Prince of Wallachia. Because of the evil he had wrought during his lifetime, as well as his noble lineage, we buried him before the altar, a place of honor, but also one where we hoped his closeness to the Eucharist would bring peace to his troubled soul.

We did not reveal to anyone his death or final resting place at this time, not wishing to dishearten the people who looked to him to save them from the Turks or to let the Turks think they had gained a victory. We did not know how Dracula had come to be separated from his army, whether by his own will, or by Lilith's doing, and we did not make inquiries to raise suspicion. In time, we heard that his body had been unaccounted for following the battle, and then we heard the false tale that he had been beheaded and his head displayed on a stake in Constantinople by Mehmet II as a sign of triumph. Of course, we knew this story was only the sultan's false propaganda to dishearten the people of Wallachia and those of the surrounding Christian nations.

Dracula's throne passed to Basarab Laiotă, who had often fought against and opposed him, and who during the years his brother Radu had reigned, had continually fought with and taken Radu's throne only to have it taken back. And so the old battles for power in Wallachia were resurrected and the wars against the Turks continued, and little changed for centuries as men continued about their petty quests for power, bringing bloodshed and misery to all involved. The pride and greed in their hearts was no doubt all fueled by Lilith whispering evil thoughts into their ears.

But while I had not understood Lilith's threats that morning when I found Dracula's body, she was as good as her word that she would wreak a greater havoc upon the earth than ever before through a new Prince of Darkness.

As I knew from Merlin's stories, Lilith had previously sought to bring about the birth of an Antichrist, and this time, in her Prince of Darkness, I believed she had finally succeeded.

I had almost forgotten her threat until Easter morning the following year when I rose early to go to the church to pray and celebrate the mystery of Christ's resurrection. Little did I suspect another and even more shocking resurrection had occurred.

There before the altar was the stone that had covered Dracula's body. It had been lifted out of the ground and lay beside his grave. I was too terrified to approach it, and yet even more terrified not to look down into the grave. Slowly, I approached the altar, stepping toward the grave, fearing that seeing Dracula's decaying remains might make me nauseous, while the fear that his grave might be empty sent my head spinning with a thousand questions.

I paused a few feet from the grave, barely daring to move forward. Slowly, I inched my way toward it, not seeing anything at first until finally I was close enough to see the very earth at its bottom, and then disbelief filled me. His coffin lay empty!

What thoughts I had then! How do I describe them? *Has Dracula indeed risen from the dead?* I wondered. No, that was impossible—I knew what Lilith had said, but she had not said anything about his resurrection, only that she would wreak havoc, but she had mentioned a Prince of Darkness, and who else could she have meant? And if the Christ had risen, would not the Antichrist as well? No, surely, someone—I knew not who—one of Dracula's loyal supporters, perhaps a Turkish spy in the night, had come to take the body away, to prove Dracula was dead for whatever political reasons. Surely, that had to be it. It was inconceivable that....

"Be not surprised, monk," a voice told me. Terrified, I spun around, wondering who had spoken. I recognized the voice, but it was deeper, darker, stronger than I had ever heard it before. "It is what you expected, is it not?" the voice asked.

I continued to look about, but I saw no one. I had only just thought to look up when from the ceiling above me came leaping down a flesh and blood, all-too-alive Dracula, his ruddy cheeks the very picture of health, his skin pale but without a sign of decay. Indeed, he had been forty-five years of age when he had died, but now he appeared closer to thirty—in the very prime of his manhood—and impossibly strong, as he soon displayed to me.

As I stared at Dracula in disbelief, he reached for my throat and wrapped his fingers about it. Then picking me up from the ground, he flung me against the wall above the altar, against the crucifix depicting our Lord. Before I could even catch my breath, he was there, beside me, though I was feet above the ground. Levitating as he held me by the throat, he pressed me against the cross, staring at me with eyes that looked gaunt, filled with blood, and were penetrating my own.

"I should crucify you now, monk, for how you betrayed me," he ranted. "Betrayed me by giving me a worthless piece of wood rather than the Holy Lance. I should destroy you, but in truth, you have allowed me to begin a new and greater life. I spare your life only so you might let all the world know that I, Dracula, formerly Prince of Wallachia, am alive and now beginning my reign as the Prince of Darkness. You and everyone will do well to fear me. I will haunt the night, making children fear to sleep, feasting upon them as I see fit, seducing maidens to become my minions, and drinking the blood of the strongest men so they become weaker than mice, their wills, their lives, even their souls my very own. You have no conception of how powerful I now am, but you will begin to believe and know and fear me in the days to come."

And then he flew backward across the room, barely giving me a second to realize he had released me before I plummeted to the ground behind the altar.

For the first time in my life, I knew true fear, for even in battle when Constantinople fell, I'd had a fair chance at fighting those who were mortal like myself, but what hope did I have against a supernatural being?

This monster continued to fly about the church—I know not how else to describe it. He cackled to himself in great merriment as he equally laid out curses upon me, upon the Church, upon the Turks, upon the people of his own nation, and upon anyone and everything else imaginable.

"Know that I shall never rest," he told me, "until I have punished all who have betrayed me, and all who have betrayed my mistress, the true mother of the Earth, the Queen of Eden. The human race has not known what fear truly is until now."

I cowered on the floor, afraid to say a word, afraid to look him in the eye, although I could not help watching him as he darted about, occasionally pausing long enough to knock over a candle, to smash the church window, to heap blasphemy upon blasphemy upon me and all of God's creation.

How has it come to this? I asked myself, fearing he might yet truly kill me, his maniacal behavior, his tantrum, his evil laughter having seemingly no end. At any moment, my fellow monks would arrive to celebrate the Easter service and doubtless also suffer his wrath.

But at that second, through the smashed window, came Merlin. He flew into the room, brandishing a sword. "By the power of Excalibur," he declared, "I will not let you live!"

But Dracula took one look at Merlin, and stretching forth his hand, he caused Merlin's arms to become paralyzed, rendering him helpless to swing King Arthur's sword. The great wizard remained frozen in mid-air as Dracula flew toward him. I feared for a moment the evil creature would attack Merlin, would perhaps bite the great wizard as Lilith had bit him, but instead, he merely hissed and said, "I will let you live only a little while so you may see the destruction of all those whom you have sought to protect." And then with lightning speed, he flew out the window.

I know not how Merlin regained his movement or step, but in another second, he was standing on the floor, and then he was beside me, reaching down to help me to my feet.

I stared at the sword in his hand, wondering whether it truly were the famous Excalibur.

"Fear not," he said, "though there will be much to fear later. But he will not return here at least for some time. It is not chaste monks he will seek for his victims, but those who continue to populate the earth with Adam and Eve's seed, and especially those descendants of King Arthur and Lady Morgana who are sworn to defeat him. You, Constantine, as you know by now, are among those descendants, and you will yet play a key role in his own defeat if you are so willing. But first, I see you are wounded; his nails have scratched your throat."

And then Merlin reached into his robe and pulled out a small vial. It contained some sort of golden liquid. He opened the vial and poured some of its contents onto his finger so that I could see it was honey. Then, before I could speak another word, he had thrust his finger into my mouth, saying, "Swallow it quickly. It will heal you, but it will also make it so you will live long enough to see the end of this evil, even if it be centuries from now."

I was amazed by his words—for I was now past my seventieth year and knew my life on this earth was almost over—but I was even more amazed by the sting of the honey upon my tongue and then the feeling of power surging within me as the honey traveled through my body. Once Merlin had removed his finger from my mouth, not only did I touch my neck and discover the scratches were gone, but I felt renewed strength and energy pulsing throughout my body, and later, when I looked into a mirror, I saw that I had lost all the years of gathered stress and wrinkles I had accumulated since the time when I so feared the Fall of Constantinople.

Had that been the end of the story, I would have been content, for I was so overjoyed with my rejuvenated body. But the return of youth could give me little happiness when such an evil had now been unleashed upon the earth.

You know, Quincey, from having read Mr. Stoker's book, what evil

Dracula was capable of. For the next many years, no man, woman, child, or even beast in the field was safe from the terror he inflicted upon the land. Tales of vampires became commonplace throughout Romania, not only because of his own bloodthirst, but because of the legions of vampires he created.

I do not know what caused the horror finally to lessen except that somehow we believe Gwenhwyvach either was destroyed or saw fit to leave the world again, to reincarnate herself later in a new place. Dracula then became quiet. She might have chosen him for her Prince of Darkness, but in time, we believe she abandoned him, for we know she appeared in Mexico in the late fifteenth century, encouraging the Aztecs to reach an unprecedented level of blood sacrifice; later, she was present in another incarnation to spread the madness that led to the worst terrors of the French Revolution; finally, she incarnated again in the late nineteenth century, the incarnation which your brother Zoltan knew so well until she ended her and your brother's lives at the end of World War II.

As for Dracula, he continued to go out and feast upon the blood of mankind as needed to keep his strength, but for roughly four hundred years, he was fairly quiet about it until he forged his plan to strike England and destroy the Children of Arthur specifically, including your family. Your own mother, Mina Harker, dared not admit it in her diaries, but she was an orphan who had been taken as an infant to Avalon, where she was raised by Morgan le Fay in ways to fight the vampire, preparing herself for the battle she knew would one day come and in which she and her friends so well succeeded.

That, Quincey, ends my tale. You know what became of Dracula and your mother, and now you know, as Dracula's son, at least in some respect, that you have both good and evil blood in your veins. You have learned from your brother Zoltan and even your son Cedric what happens to those who choose evil.

It is up to you now to choose whether you will be good or evil. This is the third and final time you will be given the choice. You did not listen to Captain Vanderdecker when he counseled you, and when Morgan le Fay appeared to you, you turned from evil, but you did not specifically choose good. Merlin and I made a mistake in selecting Dracula as the one to try to stop Lilith; do not make us guilty of another mistake in thinking you will side with us finally. Before you answer whether you will join our crusade, let it be understood by you that each time Lilith reincarnates, she grows in power, and we have reason to believe she is about to do so again with plans to cause massive destruction in just a few more decades. How say you? Will you join us?

CHAPTER 28

QUINCEY'S TALE RESUMES

THERE IS LITTLE of my tale left to tell. When Constantine had finished speaking, both he and Merlin looked at me with no lack of anticipation or anxiety. How could I refuse to side with them against Lilith? What father, after his very own son has sought to murder him, would not seek to remedy whatever was influencing such evil in the world?

In the forty-plus years since I joined Merlin and Constantine and the many others of Avalon who fight with them, we have orchestrated the events that led to Bram Delaney's visit to the United States, and we made sure that Bram and Mary would meet at the hotel as they did. Oh, yes, Cedric has already told you that he had a hand in all that, and it is true we knew he was seeking out the Morgan line, and Mary, the eldest daughter, specifically, with the intent to rape her, but I used my power to control others' wills to convince Bram to go on the journey with Cedric and also to convince Mary to leave the hotel that day to go to the Renaissance Faire before Cedric could do his intended damage.

Unfortunately, his lust could not be controlled so he still acted—only, he wronged Mary's sister, Martha, instead.

DEVIN INTERRUPTS

At this moment in the telling, Devin let out a great gasp. For a moment, Quincey looked at him, as if to say, "I'm almost finished" before he proceeded. But Devin was staring at Cedric, whose eyes turned to the table, as if he wished he could crawl under it. Then Adam also let out a gasp and muttered, "But Uncle George is Devin's—" But Quincey drowned out Adam's words so only Devin heard him, and Devin reached under the table and squeezed his cousin's hand to silence him. He needed another minute to accept the truth.

QUINCEY'S TALE CONCLUDES

Later, I kept tabs on Adam as he grew, and also on Anne, once I learned of Cedric's evil in taking advantage of Bram's wife. We were also busy in those years because not long after Adam was born, Lilith was again conceived, so her mother had to be captured and imprisoned before this latest incarnation of Lilith could be born and begin a new reign of terror. That was when we arranged for Mary to become the keeper of Lilith—and to keep her away from Adam for his own protection, and also to have Adam's grandparents move so Lilith could not trace them. In all these matters, we have always done the best we could, none of us able to foresee perfectly the future or what might happen, but we have always sought to sway matters so the events would turn out as preferable as possible.

The most surprising event in our opinions was Cedric's behavior after Anne was born. I kept watch over my son, my heart grieving for how he behaved during those years when he thought me dead, and later, I watched over my granddaughter as well. I was astonished to see how, as just a babe, Anne began to work upon Cedric's heart, causing it to soften until he felt guilt over how he had betrayed his friend, and I even once saw him look at a photo of me and shed a tear. He rarely displayed his remorse in his actions, but my enhanced senses and my biological connection to him as his father made me sense how he was feeling during such moments. At times, he fought against the softness and love trying to conquer him, even as recently as when he lied to you about the ring, but I knew after his confrontation with Lilith and Mary's death that he would not turn back to evil again, and so it was I who convinced Merlin that he should be the guardian of his grandchildren—I am sure they are especially shocked by this whole story, for Cedric has never been other than a perfect grandfather to them.

Now, I have completed my long tale, but I am sure you all have questions and points you wish to have clarified.

When Quincey's tale had concluded, everyone was silent for a moment, trying to absorb it all. Then Anne, after having sat patiently for hours, admitted, "I need a break. This is so much to take in, and as important and amazing as it is, what I really want is to spend some time alone with my sons."

"Of course," said Quincey. "I completely understand. It has been thoughtless of me to talk for so long when you have waited years to get to know them. Please, go spend time with them. It is already mid-afternoon. Let us take a break and reconvene at suppertime. Take the time to go for a walk. We have some beautiful gardens on the castle grounds. The boys themselves have tended them these past several years; they have become skilled in so many things, from learning swordplay to repairing the castle to studying mathematics and foreign languages. They are amazing young men, and you have been separated from them for so many years that you barely know them. Let them show you about the castle and grounds and tell you all about their lives here. I'll come get you when supper is ready."

"Thank you," said Anne. Adam was already on his feet, and he pulled out Anne's chair for her. Lance and Tristan now quickly jumped up, eager as little boys to show their parents all the treasures of their home. In another minute, they were leading Adam and Anne on a grand tour of the castle, including showing them the room where they would sleep that night, and then they all went outside where they continued to get reacquainted.

Once Adam and Anne and the boys had left, Cedric said, "I'll clean up the dishes," and he stood up and began stacking the plates together.

"Do you need help?" Devin politely asked him.

"No, we have a dishwasher," Cedric muttered, quickly disappearing into the kitchen with his hands full. Devin could see Cedric was nervous and trying to avoid him.

"Devin, don't you want to join the others in the gardens?" Quincey asked.

"No, I think I should let parents and children have their private moments together," he replied.

Quincey smiled. "I suspect it gets lonely for you at times, Devin Purcell."

Devin was surprised by the remark, but he did not deny it.

"You have never married, or even really dated," Quincey added.

"I am too much of a scholar," Devin admitted, "and a workaholic. I have spent my life trying to know everything I possibly could, hoping that in doing so, in some way I could then help Adam and Anne and their children."

"By seeking archaic knowledge and reading old legends?" asked Quincey.

Devin found he could not help but be honest with Quincey as this immortal being looked him straight in the eye.

"It is all I am good for," Devin admitted, "and perhaps it is a useless pursuit, but for whatever reason, my inclinations have always been those of a scholar, though sometimes I think I've filled my days with books to avoid participating in life."

"It is not you who have avoided life," said Quincey. "No one can avoid it. Life comes calling for people when the time is right."

Devin did not know how to take this remark. After a moment, he said, "I do have one question."

"Go ahead," said Quincey.

Devin hesitated, unsure how to speak the words.

"It is all right," said Quincey. "I am not the one to ask anyway. Why don't you go help Cedric, even if he claims he doesn't need help? He only retreated because he fears having the conversation with you just as much as you fear having it with him."

"You must be reading my mind," said Devin, smiling as he rose from his chair.

"Mind-reading does help me to prod people when they hesitate," Quincey admitted. "Go ahead. Remember, I have told you that there is a reason for everything."

Devin started to leave, but then he turned around, looked at Quincey, and said, "Thank you, Grandfather," before going to the kitchen.

PART III
LILITH

CHAPTER 1

ADAM AND ANNE spent hours exploring the gardens, touring the castle, and all the while listening to Tristan and Lance recall countless childhood stories. Anne found herself either in tears or speechless most of the afternoon, continually having to hug her boys while trying to make sure she gave them equal attention. Even Adam could not help but keep a hand on the shoulder of one or the other, finding it hard to believe that the sons he had once cradled in his arms were now big, strapping men taller than himself. *What use could they have for a mother and father after all these years?* he wondered, and yet they babbled like children about everything they had done in their lives from building forts to studying calculus, eager to share it all with their long-absent parents.

Finally, Devin came out to the gardens to call them in to supper.

"What have you been doing all this time?" Adam asked his cousin.

"Helping Cedric make supper," he replied.

"Are you okay?" Anne asked, reading on his face that something troubled him.

"I'm fine," said Devin. "I'm just finding it hard to take all this in."

"So are we," said Adam, "and thank you for letting Anne and me have time alone with our sons, but you know you are part of the family. Boys, Devin is my cousin, but more like a brother since we grew up together in the same house, so think of him as Uncle Devin."

Devin did not bother to clarify that he really was the boys' uncle based on what he had recently learned. Instead, he said, "We better hurry in to eat. Wait until you see the feast Cedric has prepared for us."

Everyone followed Devin back into the castle and then to the dining room. There they found Quincey assisting Cedric in placing everything on the table.

"Do you need help, Grandfather?" Tristan and Lance asked Cedric, practically in unison.

"No, no, sit and eat," said Cedric. "I've brought everything out now."

"I see you've trained our boys very well, Cedric," said Adam. "And I thank you for it. I don't think Anne and I could have done any better job of raising them. They are polite, intelligent, kindhearted, and, of course, they are handsome like their father, although you had no influence over that."

Adam chuckled as he finished, having had to make a joke because he felt uncomfortable praising his father-in-law, although Cedric nodded in acceptance of Adam's gratitude.

Quincey also chuckled, which made Anne turn to him and say, "I am grateful to you, too, for all you've done to help raise our boys."

"You're welcome," said Quincey. "After so many years of your being separated from them, it was the least we could do."

Anne frowned, and a tear now ran down her face as she said, "I do wish I had not lost all those years with them."

"No time has been lost. Time is eternal," a voice now said. They all knew immediately who had spoken and turned to see Merlin enter the room.

"Welcome to Dracula's Castle, Anne, Adam, and Devin," he said. "I bet you never would have guessed that your journey would take you here."

"I hope it's the end of our journey," said Adam. "I assume it is since you've let us be reunited with our sons."

"We are close to the end, I do not doubt," said Merlin, pulling back the long sleeves of his robe to avoid getting them in the food as he sat down at the table across from Adam. "But I do not know how that end will play out. Still, whatever may happen, even if Lilith should manage yet to destroy us all, know that you do not have to mourn the time lost with your sons. We fight for the good of humanity, for its survival upon the earth, but there is always a greater power watching this world that will ensure, no matter what becomes of this planet, that we will live on in another plane of existence—life is endless, only earthly time is linear, and our spirits are eternal, so you really have lost no time at all with your sons."

"In a sense I think I know what you mean," said Anne, "although I don't really understand how it is possible."

"You don't need to," Merlin replied, picking up a bowl of mashed potatoes and spooning some on his plate as a sign that everyone else should start eating. "You just have to trust that in the end it will all be well, no matter what might happen. And it will be, so fear not."

"How can all be well?" asked Adam, who did not trust as easily as the others. "For eighteen years, Anne and I have been on pins and needles, missing our sons and waiting for Lilith to attack us, and now you say all is well?"

"Shh, Adam. It's all in the past now," said Anne, patting his arm.

"It's not in the past. Lilith still lurks out there, waiting to strike," Adam replied, his nostrils flaring.

"Merlin," said Devin, thinking it best he take up the conversation to divert his cousin's anger, "first, thank you for all you've done. It's a privilege for me finally to meet you in person, and we are grateful to you for keeping Adam and Anne's children safe. However, I'm sure you can understand that we are all still very stressed and anxious about what could happen, so could you at least tell us what you think likely to happen next?"

"It was my plan for us to have what you humans would call a Council of War," said Merlin, shaking his head, "but *war* is just such a dreadful, nasty word, completely uncivilized. Instead, I wish us to hold a symposium—a much prettier word you must admit; it reminds me of posies, and who doesn't like posies—whether they be of the flower or poetry variety?"

The wizard turned to look at Adam as he asked this question. Then he threw back his head and laughed when he saw Adam's nostrils continue to flare.

"Yes, let us hold a symposium," Merlin continued. "A symposium upon how we might prevent Lilith from harming herself or any others in the future. I had thought to have that symposium tonight—the Greeks loved to include dinner and drinks with their symposiums—but I do not want to push you all too much. I know you have had a lot to take in and have just been reunited. Instead, tomorrow morning, I will transport us all to Avalon, and there we will meet with all those who have in the past had dealings with Lilith and her treachery over the years. I'm sure you'll all be happy to meet with King Arthur and Lady Morgana, and also Ogier, Roland, Constantine, Melusine, and many others. Then between us all, I am sure we will devise some sort of plan."

"Devise some sort of plan!" exclaimed Adam. "Don't you have a plan already? What have you been doing all these years if not coming up with a plan?"

"My boy, how can you plan for something when you don't know what will happen?" Merlin asked.

"Don't know what will happen?" repeated Adam with exasperation. "We know Lilith is evil, and we know she's likely to strike at any moment, and we know we must be prepared for it. What more do we need to know?"

"Well, since you know so much," said Merlin, leaning back in his chair and curling his mustache around his fingers, "why haven't you come up with your own plan?"

"You're the wizard," said Adam, leaning across the table toward Merlin.

"Oh, yes, that's right," said Merlin, rubbing his chin thoughtfully. "After two thousand years, sometimes I tend to forget these little details."

And then he wiggled about in his chair to make himself comfortable before he closed his eyes and proceeded to snore.

Adam was seething, but Anne took his hand and squeezed it. After a few seconds, Devin could not help but laugh awkwardly to break the silence.

"It's not funny," said Adam. "Our lives are at stake. That witch killed my mother. We can't take this lightly, and yet Merlin acts like this is no big deal. I'm sick of waiting for him to give us answers."

"You need wait no longer!" screeched a voice. Immediately, they all turned in its direction, just in time to see the great window of the dining room shatter. As they dived for cover from the shattering glass, into the room flew the creature whom they all dreaded most to see.

Lilith had made her dramatic entrance. She was dressed in a rich green gown with what looked like leopard spots on it, perhaps to match the scales of a snake or dragon. Her eyes flamed with fury. Her long hair was a mess of curls and knots, as if to reflect her past life as Medusa. And when she held up her hands, in the pose of casting a spell, no one missed that Adam and Eve's wedding rings graced her fingers. In a second, she had set her feet upon the floor, and as she stepped toward the table, they all slowly slinked back into their chairs and sat there cowering.

All save Merlin, who had not moved at all. He continued, with his head thrown back, to snore until the noise made them all turn to stare at him.

And then the great wizard opened his eyes.

"My dear, you're early," he said, looking a tad surprised. "I really didn't expect you to show up until tomorrow, and I think it quite rude of you to make your entrance by breaking a window. Whom do you think you are—Liberace, flying in here in that getup? If you had just knocked politely at the door, I'm sure we would have gladly let you in, if only to get all this nonsense over with."

"I've had enough of your tongue, Wizard!" Lilith screeched. "You have spent your life trying to thwart me, but you have only grown weak and foolish while I have grown stronger. I will not suffer your existence much longer, but you shall be the last to die because nothing would delight me more than for you to see all that you have worked for all these years come to an end."

"Even should you kill us all here and now," Merlin replied, "do not forget that Arthur, Morgana, Melusine, Roland, and Ogier, and all the other inhabitants of Avalon will continue to fight you."

"Maybe so, but they will be heartbroken to have lost their leader, their very own ancestor, he who claims to be kin to the Savior. Well, I'd like to see Him try to save you now."

"Oh, I wouldn't worry about that. I'm sure everyone at Avalon will get over my loss quickly. We old men just tend to get in the way, you know," said Merlin, gently pushing back his chair to stand up.

Enraged, Lilith shot her hand forward, sending a ray of electricity at Merlin that threw him and the chair behind him against the wall, and then he crumpled to the floor, his beard smoking from where the heat had sparked it. His eyelids were closed, as if to open no more.

Adam and Anne watched in astonishment as Merlin fell. Devin did not dare to move. All felt their helpless mortality when they saw Merlin so easily vanquished.

"Just a minute ago, Adam," Lilith taunted, "you were asking the old fool about a plan. Now you see how weak and incapable he is of doing anything to stop me. I have been in control of this situation all along. I have just been toying with all of you, and I always have been because I have all the time in the world to accomplish my ends."

She now walked up behind Adam. He found himself frozen, either from fear or her spell, as she put her hands on his shoulders.

"And you, apparently, are not the hero you seem to think you are, just sitting here, waiting for me. Big, strong, middle-aged college football players with the start of a paunch are such a cliché; you do not even dare to oppose me...or perhaps...perhaps, Adam, you want this to happen. Is that it?" she asked as her hands slowly moved from his shoulders down onto his chest. "Is it that you really like me, Adam? Do you secretly desire me?" She bent down now so that her cheek brushed against his. "You secretly fantasize about being with me, don't you, Adam? You red-blooded American boys are known for liking badass girls? Is that what you want, Adam? For me to be your bad girl?"

For a second, Lilith cackled, and then a long, serpent-like tongue shot forth from her mouth to caress Adam's ear. The sight of it caused Anne to jump out of her chair and exclaim, "Leave him alone!"

Lilith quickly pulled back and turned to Anne. "Oh, is the little wifey jealous of Lilith?" she asked. Then she sneered and added, "But what else should I expect from a goody two-shoes bitch like you?"

She stuck her face just inches from Anne's as she continued, "You're a bitch just like your ancestor, Eve. That bitch stole my husband. But it was probably good riddance. Look at your husband; he has the same name as mine, and it fits him well because he's just as weak and cowardly and demanding. Look at all the bullshit lies that have been spread about me over the centuries, claims I wouldn't be subservient to Adam during intercourse, claims I wanted to fornicate with demons. And the fools who spread those lies didn't even know there are no such things as demons—they believed it because Adam had started the lies. I never refused to be subservient to him; he never even asked me to be. We were man and wife, equal in all ways, both created by the Goddess-God at the same time so we would perfectly complement one another. The Goddess-God never even conceived of the possibility that one of us might be better in any way than the other. That bitch Eve was the one stupid enough to be subservient and thus spark enmity and war between women who should have been sisters."

While Lilith spoke, she had her back to Adam and Quincey. Quincey now quietly stood up and tried to move toward the door, but Lilith must have had impeccable hearing, for she spun around, and in a flash, she was in the doorway, blocking his retreat.

"Don't even think of escaping, Son of Dracula. We have never met personally, but I have kept watch over you. You are the foulest of traitors. You betrayed your own brother, Zoltan. You abandoned him. I think you would have killed him if you had known how. And then you stole the ring from his corpse. Had things been different, I might have made you my mate, but you know nothing of loyalty; no wonder your son turned out to be a traitor. I despise you both. Sit down!"

And then she pushed Quincey as only a supernatural woman could have done, sending him flying back several feet into his chair.

"Why do you have to hurt him?" Adam asked. "He did nothing to you. None of us ever did."

"No, but your ancestors did, didn't they?"

"We are not responsible for our ancestors' actions," Anne replied.

"Not actions," Lilith replied. "*Crimes.* Crimes of mistreating me, crimes of lying about me, even of attempting to kill me. Even if you are not guilty, you have the DNA of your ancestors. If only that bitch Eve had not existed, had not stolen my husband from me, you might be my children, not hers, and everything could have been different, but no, instead you all chose to turn against me, treat me as a pariah, and never extend any milk of human kindness to me. The first seeds of hatred in this world were born in Eve's breast and fed like milk to all her foul children. I have borne that hatred long enough."

"But we don't even know what really happened in the Garden of Eden," Devin said, his scholarly curiosity overtaking his fear. "Will you please tell us? No one has really explained it to us yet. Please do not kill us before we understand why."

Lilith looked surprised by the request.

After a few seconds, she said, "How could you understand? I am the only one living who was there. Everything you have been told is based on distorted tales passed down by the descendants of hate-mongering liars."

"Then please," Devin insisted, "tell us what is the truth. Do not blame us for our ancestors' crimes until we are at least given a chance to understand."

"Why do you even care?" she asked, looking exasperated as she walked around the table toward Devin.

"I do care. I want to understand," said Devin. "If you were not at fault, how did Eve come into the picture to cause such trouble?"

"You wouldn't believe me if I told you," Lilith replied.

"Please, I want to know too," said Lance.

"Ah, fresh meat," said Lilith, stepping up to Lance to sniff him. "And I'm not talking about the sliced ham on your plate."

She put her finger under his chin until her fingernail pierced his skin. As he cried out from the unexpected pain, she pulled out her fingernail and licked the blood on it. "Fresh indeed. Young men are my favorite dish. They are so easily swayed because they are so sexually weak. No doubt you have heard tales that I steal young male babies, but they are usually babies who are eighteen or twenty, the age when men's hormones make them most stupid. I have had my eyes on you two—Lance and Tristan—you who think you will become knights in shining armor. Do you think you've been safe in this castle all these years? In the castle of my lover, Dracula? Perhaps I will make you my young lovers now."

"Leave the boys alone," Cedric demanded.

"Oh," said Lilith, now walking toward the boy's grandfather, "I see you've found your courage. What, no cringing and pleading like during that lovely night we had together at the Space Needle? I know you remember that night I sent your would-be lover to her death. Oh, yes, I know the carnal desires you had for that whore. I only wish I'd made her suffer longer while you watched. I took such pleasure in killing her."

"You goddamned witch!" screamed Adam, suddenly jumping up and running at her, unable to bear his mother being insulted. And before Lilith could turn around, he had grabbed the wine bottle off the table, preparing to strike her over the head with it, but as if she had eyes in the back of her head, Lilith stepped from his path, then turned around and sent forth a bolt of lightning that caused the bottle to shatter in Adam's hand.

"You pathetic fool," she laughed.

Then they all stood amazed as she sent another bolt of lightning across the room, this one picking up Adam and carrying him across the room until he fell in the doorway and tumbled down the stairs to the kitchen.

Anne shrieked and tried to run to her husband's rescue, but Lilith now sent a bolt of lightning against Anne, shoving her up against a wall until she fell and crumpled much like Merlin had done, rendering her, if not unconscious, too weak to regain her feet.

Everyone was now too afraid to utter a word. They all stared at Lilith, realizing how helpless they were against her power, almost wishing she would kill them all quickly and get it over with.

Instead, she stepped back toward Devin and said, "Now that we're done being interrupted, you were asking me to tell you what really happened between that bitch Eve, that fool Adam, and myself."

"Ye-ye-yes," said Devin, straining every nerve in his body to remain calm. "We understand Adam and Eve wronged you, but we don't know how. Would you at least tell us what happened in the Garden of Eden before you kill us all? Please? I really do want to know."

Lilith raised her eyebrows and stared into Devin's eyes, as if searching to see whether his request was honest or just a ruse to distract her. As she stared, she inhaled deeply, then exhaled. Finally, she said, "You know, no one has ever asked me before to tell my side of the story. Very well."

And so Lilith began her tale, and as she spoke, they were all mesmerized by the words falling from her serpent tongue, and more importantly, deep in their very beings, they felt that every word she spoke was true.

CHAPTER 2

LILITH'S TALE

WHEN THE GODDESS-GOD created us, man and woman, Adam and Lilith, He-She created us at the same time, from the same clay, and in His-Her own image.

And Adam and I were happy in Eden. Despite the lies that have been spread, we were not forbidden anything in the garden. Yes, there was a Tree of Life in Eden, and we ate of its fruit freely, and it kept us in perfect health and strength and beauty. And there was also a Tree of Knowledge—sometimes, it has been called the Tree of Knowledge of Good and Evil, but you see, there was no evil at that time. Evil arises from fear; everything wrong with this world has arisen from fear— anger, jealousy, greed, revenge, all those behaviors are the results of fear, fear that we are not worthy. But the Goddess-God made us worthy from the very beginning, and He-She created a magnificent world in which we could enjoy everything imaginable if we would only be open to all the joy that He-She had created for us and for all His- Her creatures in this world.

Wisdom had planted these two trees in the garden. Wisdom was a manifestation of the Goddess-God, a sort of guiding force for the universe, the Holy Spirit I think you Christians call It, although in those days, Wisdom would often manifest Itself in physical form so that It could visit us in the garden and teach us various and interesting lessons about the world and all the things in it, for we were new creatures and had much to learn. Wisdom would take various shapes, depending on the lesson for the day. Sometimes It would manifest Itself to us as a giant bird so we might fly through the air on Its back. Other times, It was a giant fish whose fins we might clasp hold of so we could go swimming through the deepest depths of the ocean with It. But you humans have forgotten all of that—you only remember when It manifested itself as a snake, and you have forgotten that the snake was Wisdom. Instead, you have chosen to name It Satan. Such is typical of Adam's children since Adam was himself the first to spread such lies.

Wisdom was not only all wise, but It was the very embodiment of goodness, for true wisdom seeks peace, love, and joy. Wisdom not only gave us fruit from the Trees of Knowledge and Life, but it also gave Adam and me each a golden ring with the sign of a snake swallowing its tale—a sign, It told us, of our own eternal souls and also of the eternal bond that was to exist between us. Of those rings, you know full well, although you do not understand their power.

I deeply loved Wisdom. I loved to spend time with Wisdom, and I learned everything from It that I could. Adam, however, soon became jealous of Wisdom. He felt that I was made to be his mate, so we should always be alone together rather than spending our time with Wisdom. It was this jealousy that was the first manifestation of fear into our world; Adam's fear that he was not worthy if I, his mate, should occasionally prefer to learn from Wisdom as opposed to spending all my time admiring him. For Adam wanted my attention all to himself, but I wanted to be wise and understand all I could about the Goddess-God's magnificent Creation. Adam was only interested in his own creation and took great pride in his physical beauty and abilities—as if he were responsible for them. He wanted to spend all his time outrunning ostriches, doing manly feats of strength to make the gorillas admire him, swinging on vines faster than the monkeys, and out-swimming crocodiles in the river, and because I wasn't there to tell him what a *god* he was—which would have been so very wrong, and yet there are women to this day who act like men are gods—he got mad and took it out on poor Wisdom, accusing me of—well, insinuating that I was doing unspeakable things with Wisdom—insinuations that were ridiculous and completely untrue, not to mention biologically impossible.

Adam was so narcissistic. I can't begin to tell you how filled with self-pride he was, as if he himself had painted his beautiful lips and eyes upon his face, or built his bulging muscles, or somehow created his impressive dexterity. We had been made equally, but Adam began to tell me he was superior because he was stronger and taller and larger than me. When I pointed out to him that my breasts were bigger than his biceps, he laughed and said they were also *mushier*—yes, that's the actual word he used—mushier—so they didn't count. Just imagine! He'd never had an issue with their mushiness before. Then he told me that because he was stronger, I should do what he told me and spend my time with him and not with Wisdom. I tried to explain to him that because the world was filled with so much to learn, I wanted to understand my place in it, but Adam was not interested in the secrets of the Creation; he much preferred to climb a tree or go wrestle a baboon.

Finally, one day he told me that because I was his mate, and all the other creatures' mates were constantly at their sides, I had to do the same, and if I would not, he would find another mate. I couldn't imagine how he would do that—after all, every other creature already had a mate, so none of them would want to mate with him.

I did not understand then that Adam, who already thought himself a god, had decided to play Goddess-God. He had decided he would fashion a woman in his own image. And he actually tried. He tried to build a woman out of sticks, but she fell apart. He tried to carve one out of a tree—but since he didn't wear any clothes for protection, the only result was he got a splinter in his penis—oh, he was grouchy that night, even after I made a balm and rubbed it on for him.

Finally, he succeeded in creating a mate out of clay, thinking since the Goddess-God had formed us of the same substance, in this way he would have success. But once the heat of the sun dried his muddy maiden, she began to crack, and after a day or two, she became just a pile of sand, slowly starting to blow away.

We were standing together, observing this pile of sand, when Adam told me, "In order to succeed, I need the stuff you and I are made out of—flesh and blood." Before I could even suspect what he was going to do, he then literally ripped out one of his own ribs. You should have seen the blood gushing out in every direction from his side, and he cried like a baby for about ten minutes after because the pain must have been excruciating. But his tears only lasted ten minutes, for we were in Eden and being nourished by the fruit from the Tree of Life, so his body healed very quickly.

Regardless, I thought he had gone completely insane—until that moment, I didn't even know that such a thing as insanity existed—but Adam apparently knew what he was doing—or more likely, he got lucky—because he thrust his rib into his clay maiden, and suddenly, the sand began to stick and then form around it until it transformed into flesh and blood, skin and bones, and teeth and eyes, and internal organs, and lush hair, and even more luscious breasts.

"What—what have you—how?" I tried to say as I watched this amazing transformation.

And then it—I should say she—spoke.

"Good morning," said this beautiful woman, turning to look at me. "My name is Eve. What's yours?"

It took me a moment to know how to reply.

"Lilith," I finally said, "and this is Adam."

"I am your husband," Adam told her as he stepped between us.

Eve looked at me, and then she looked at Adam, and then she looked down at her bulging breasts. Then she looked at my breasts. Then she looked at her nether region, and then she looked at my nether region. Then she looked at Adam's penis, and then she walked around him so she could stand in front of me, and she placed her hands on my breasts, and she said, "We are alike, so you must be my mate."

Before I could utter a word, Adam grabbed her arm and yanked her to his side. "No," he stated. "I am your husband; I created you from my own rib, and you must obey me, give me all your attention, and be constantly at my side."

And then he walked off, dragging her behind him. Eve looked back over her shoulder at me, and she gave me a wave as she tried to keep up with Adam.

Of course, now I've come to see how funny it all was, and after repeating it in my head thousands of times, I may have misremembered it a little, but at the time, being young and innocent myself, I felt confused and perhaps a little angry—and sadly, that anger would grow as the years went by, and with good reason.

Rather than follow them, I went off to my daily class with Wisdom, who was in Its snake form that day. I distinctly remember that the lesson was particularly fascinating that morning because it was about the miracle of how earthworms could regenerate if they were torn in half; that lesson stuck with me, considering how I had just witnessed Adam pull out his rib and make a person from it, and, therefore, it was natural that I told Wisdom what Adam had done.

At first, Wisdom seemed troubled by this occurrence, but then It asked me how I felt about it.

"I think Eve is beautiful," I replied, "and I think I would like to be friends with her if Adam will let me."

"Then be friends with her," Wisdom said.

"How?" I asked.

"Teach her what you know. Teach her how to be happy, how to live with Adam and love him. And love her yourself."

I pondered these words for a minute, and as I did so, I looked down and my eyes fell upon the ring on my finger.

"Could I give her a gift?" I asked.

"You certainly may," replied Wisdom.

"Only, what I want to give her I do not possess," I said. "Can you help me?"

"I can if it is truly your desire to show kindness to her," said Wisdom.

"Adam and I," I replied, "both have these beautiful golden rings that you gave us when we were created to show we belong to one another. I wish to have a similar ring to give to Eve so she feels like our equal and knows she is accepted and loved by us both."

"Certainly," said Wisdom.

I was about to ask where Wisdom would acquire another ring, but before I could formulate the words, It rose up on its feet—for after all, It was Wisdom so It had taken on a more advanced snake form—and then I saw a bulge form in its belly, and this bulge slowly progressed upward through its body until Wisdom opened Its mouth, and there on the tip of Its serpent tongue was a ring exactly matching those that Adam and I possessed.

"How—how—?" I tried to ask.

"Fire in the belly," Wisdom replied. "I melted and formed it inside of me. It is to be Eve's ring, a sign that she is one of those I will love and seek to aid. Go now and give her this ring, Lilith, and may the three of you know happiness together."

"Thank you. Thank you," I said, kissing Wisdom on the top of Its head, and then, delighted, I went back to my and Adam's—and now Eve's—dwelling.

When I arrived, I found Adam and Eve coupling. I did not wish to disturb them, for I knew how pleasurable such behavior was, so I sat outside and waited for them to finish so I could speak to them. I knew nothing of jealousy then, for I did not realize yet that I had reason to be jealous. I did feel some strange inkling that perhaps I should mind their behavior, considering how Adam had accused me of coupling with Wisdom, but I had not yet fully realized that his intention was to replace me with Eve.

Finally, Eve emerged from the dwelling because she had to pee. She came out the door and walked down to the river and tinkled in it. I followed her, and when she was done tinkling, I told her how I should like us to get to know one another and how beautiful I thought her hair was, and how happy I was that she had given Adam so much pleasure—for they had been quite loud about their coupling—and I told her that it had always pleased me to please Adam, so I was glad now that he had someone else to give him pleasure, since as pleasurable as coupling was, my inclination ran more toward the intellectual than sensual pleasures. *Now,* I thought, *I will be able to spend time learning from Wisdom while Adam and Eve couple, and that could only make us all happier than we already are.*

"Do you couple with Adam too?" Eve asked, seeming surprised.

"Yes, indeed," I said, "but he likes it more than I do, so I am glad you can please him while I study with Wisdom."

"Who is Wisdom?" she asked.

"The guiding force of the Creation," I replied, "created by the Goddess-God so that there might be harmony in all things."

"And what does Wisdom teach you?" she asked.

"It teaches me right and wrong. It teaches me why all things are as they are, and It teaches me how to love all of the Goddess-God's creation, and—I almost forgot—It told me to give you this ring. It is a sign of our eternal existence and also the eternal love that should exist between Adam and you and me."

I then placed the ring on her finger. She held up her hand, admiring it in the sparkling evening sunlight. And then I told her how Wisdom's favorite form was that of a snake, and how the snake swallowing its tail, as depicted on the ring, was a symbol of our own eternal life.

Eve now asked me many questions about Wisdom and what It had most recently taught me, so I told her all about my lesson that day concerning earthworms, which she said was fascinating, although she didn't quite understand how it could be possible—she was, after all, only a few hours old, so she did not comprehend many things yet. To try to understand, she broke a daisy from its stem along the riverbank and then watched it intently. After a minute, she asked me why the part she had broken off did not grow back.

I told her that daisies didn't regenerate that way, but they did look lovely in one's hair, and so I made her a daisy chain to wear on her head, and I told her that, as far as I knew—although I knew far from everything—earthworms were the only animals that could regenerate, except for Adam and me because we ate of the Tree of Life, which was why Adam had been able to heal after he ripped his rib from his side to create her.

We were deep into our conversation when Adam came down to the river, looking for Eve and wondering what was taking her so long to return. When he saw us getting along so well, he demanded of me, "Lilith, are you going to take Eve from me now, just like you made yourself Wisdom's favorite?"

"No," I said, "but we can all be friends."

"Eve cannot be your friend," he told me. "She belongs to me."

"She is like me, Adam," I said. "I want her to be my friend also."

"She is not like you," said Adam. "I don't know what you are—I don't know what creature made you, but I made Eve and she belongs to me."

"Adam," I said in dismay, "you know the Goddess-God made both of us at the same time."

"That is what Wisdom told us," he replied, "but how do we know it is true? We woke from sleep with our bodies fully formed. How do I know you and I were not made by two different creatures? How do I even know you were not made from me?"

"We know because Wisdom told us what happened."

"Wisdom cannot be trusted," said Adam. "It says that we were made to be mates, yet It prefers to keep you from me. Nor is Wisdom the Creator. Only the Goddess-God knows what you are."

"Then the Goddess-God must have made me if He-She is the

Creator and also made you."

"I don't know," Adam replied, too obstinate to admit the logic of my words. "I suspect Wisdom made you, which is why you wish to couple with It, just as I wish to couple with Eve."

"Let us go to sleep," I replied. "We are all tired, and I don't want to quarrel."

I rose to my feet and tried to walk toward the dwelling, but Adam grabbed my arm and said, "I will lead the way. Come, Eve."

He put out his hand to her and she took it, following behind him a step. I took up the rear. When we got inside the cottage, Adam told me, "Eve will sleep in my bed."

"I thought it was our bed," I said.

"I will let you sleep in my bed when and if I see fit," he replied.

Well, this situation went on for several nights, with him and Eve coupling most of the night while I lay awake on the floor, wondering whether maybe I should pull a rib out of my own side to make a new mate for myself, but considering how Adam was behaving, I was afraid I'd just end up with another creature like him.

I had thought, also, that Eve and I were off to a good start in our friendship, but as the days went by, she started to treat me like her servant, telling me our dwelling was her husband's house and she was his favorite wife, so I had better do what she said or she would tattle on me and then Adam would not be pleased. I kept my mouth shut, for I knew nothing yet of fighting, much less of self-defense and assertiveness.

But then came the final blow. One morning, I woke and found two little babies—a boy and a girl—in Adam and Eve's bed.

I was so amazed by the sight that I had to hold one of them. I reached down and picked up the little boy to cuddle it, but immediately,

Eve snatched it away from me.

"They're mine and Adam's," she told me. "You didn't have anything to do with them."

I didn't understand and was puzzled, but after I thought about what I had learned from Wisdom, I realized these children were the result of Adam and Eve's coupling. And then I wondered why my coupling with Adam had not had a similar result. And then I felt tears rise up in me. Not knowing what to do, or why I was crying, for I had never done so before, I ran from the house and went to Wisdom and told It what had happened.

"What will you do now?" Wisdom asked me when I had finished my story.

"What do you mean what will I do? What is there to do?" I asked.

"Will you continue to love Adam and Eve despite how they have treated you?"

"Love them?" I said. "Love them when they want nothing to do with me?"

"You can still love their children," said Wisdom, "for they are innocent."

"I will try," I agreed, "for they are sweet and beautiful little creatures."

At least, so I believed when they were yet new to the world.

In the days that followed, I tried to love them, but Eve would not let me near Cain nor Luluwa, the names Adam had chosen for their son and daughter. He let Eve have no say in naming them. "After all, I created them," he told her, and when she replied, "but they came out of me," he said, "only because I gave you my seed, and do not forget, I created you, so anything you create is my creation."

How I longed to hold those two adorable, giggling babies, and as

Adam and Eve began to teach them about the world and they began to cry more and more, I just wanted to cuddle and comfort them.

"Please let me hold them," I begged of Adam.

"They are mine and Eve's," Adam replied. "You have no right to hold them. You did not create them. I did."

"I want a baby to hold," I said.

"You will never have one," he replied. "I will not give you my seed."

"Then I will make one for myself," I said, although I did not know how.

"You can't," Adam replied. "You need a penis to make a baby, and I am the only one with a penis, and I won't let you use it. In fact, I don't think I'll even let you live in my house any longer."

"What?" I said. "This is our house. The Goddess-God made it for both of us. In fact, I have more right to live here than Eve does."

"It is my house," said Adam. "You claim we are both like the Goddess-God, but I am a creator—I created Eve and I created Cain and Luluwa. You have created nothing, so how can you be made in the Goddess-God's image? You would do better to go live with one of the beasts in the fields, for that is what you are: a beast. Perhaps you could find a zebra or a dingo to go live with, but you are not welcome here any longer."

I was devastated, beside myself, and I cried so deeply and intensely that I stumbled about, not even able to see where I was going as I left the dwelling. I walked several paces until grief overwhelmed me, and then I collapsed and cried until I could cry no more. I was close enough to the dwelling that Adam and Eve must have heard me, but they did not come out to comfort me, and that hurt me even more.

And then when my tears were spent, they were replaced with anger. If Adam and Eve did not want me, then I wanted nothing further to do with them. I decided I would leave Eden. So I stood up and spat toward the house, and then I walked out of Eden and the only life I had ever known.

I walked for miles, far beyond anywhere I had ever walked before. Finally, I came to the Euphrates River, where I found a hippopotamus willing to give me a ride upon its back, and in that way, I crossed the river, and then I began to walk again until I came into the wilderness and the desert.

The next day, as I lay on the desert sand, my heart broken, my skin burning, feeling that I would like to cease to exist, Wisdom found me and tried to console me, but I would not be comforted. "What good is all the wisdom in the world," I asked, "if there is no one to share it with, and what good is it to love others if you cannot make them love you?"

Wisdom stayed with me for many days and nights, trying to console me, but I refused to be comforted. Finally, I asked It to leave me alone, for as loving as It was, I knew It could not be my mate, only my mentor.

I do not know how much time went by after that. The pain in my heart never healed, but I did manage to find myself a mountain cave for shelter and to find food and water to give me sustenance. At that time, my only reason for continuing to live was because I did not yet know what death was so I could not seek it.

And so some twenty or so years must have gone by until one day when I was walking through the mountains and I thought I saw Adam. I later learned it was Abel I saw—the second son born to Adam and Eve. But he was so tall and handsome, and he greatly resembled his father, whom I missed despite how he had mistreated me, so I could not stop myself from excitedly rushing toward him, all the past forgotten.

"Stand back, foul creature!" Abel replied the moment he saw me, and before I could reply, he grabbed a stone from the earth and threw it at me.

The stone struck me in the temple, knocked me to the earth, and while it did not kill me, for as I would later realize, I had eaten of the fruit of the Tree of Life and so I was not able to be killed so easily, I felt hate burn in my breast over this violent attempt to hurt me. I had never experienced a blow before, and I did not like it.

From that moment on, hatred began to grow in my breast for Adam and Eve and all their children. Yet, I was lonely regardless. I soon discovered where they were dwelling, just a few miles from where I lived, and I began to spy on them—Adam and Eve and Cain and Abel and their respective twin sisters, Luluwa and Aklia, and their little brother Seth. I thought how wonderful it must be to have so many children and to see them now grown, save for Seth, who was probably just on the verge of puberty at this time. They were full-grown, strong, handsome boys and beautiful, youthful women.

I thought if I were one of them, I would then be happy, for I had always been happy until Adam had forced me from my home. They, however, clearly wanted nothing to do with me. I would sit outside their tent at night, concealed where they could not see me, and listen to their conversations. They rarely mentioned me, but when they did, Adam would get very angry and say that it was forbidden by the Goddess-God for my name to be mentioned—yet another of Adam's many lies, for I knew the Goddess-God had no reason to be angry with me. I soon realized none of Adam's family were happy, even though they were not lonely like myself. And as I spied upon them and listened in on their conversations, I eventually pieced together why they were now living among these desert mountains rather than in the beautiful

Garden of Eden where all their needs would have been met.

By the time Seth had been born, Eve had felt overcome by motherhood. Her children were not perfect little angels, but demanding and dirty, and needing her constant attention. Adam had forbidden her to go anywhere near Wisdom, telling her that It was not a friend to mankind or a manifestation of the Goddess-God, but an evil creature that had created deception and pride in my heart—indeed, he blamed Wisdom for turning me against him. Had I not feared that Adam or his children would throw stones at me again, I would have broken into their tent right then to speak in Wisdom's defense, but I did not. Instead, I continued to lurk and listen outside their tent and wonder what had become of Wisdom, for I had never seen It again after I had rejected Its consolation, and now I dearly missed talking to It. Occasionally, in desperation, I would speak to the birds or animals, for I knew all their tongues, but they were simple creatures, so other than pleasantries exchanged, we had little to say to one another. Only Wisdom's conversation had ever been edifying for me. And lonely as I was, I could not stomach the lies I heard coming from Adam's mouth, lies that by now Eve had long ago grown to believe out of fear of her husband, and lies that his children believed because they had no one to tell them the truth.

In time, I realized that not only had Adam forbidden Eve to associate with Wisdom, but he had also told her that they had been forbidden by the Goddess-God to eat of the fruit of the Tree of Knowledge and the Tree of Life. I do not know why he decided to tell such lies, but I suspect it was because since Wisdom had placed the trees in the garden, Adam was stubbornly refusing to accept Wisdom's gifts, even though the Tree of Life had kept us healthy and strong when first we were created.

But Eve became desperate. She was unhappy as a mother and wife. Her children were not loving but obstinate, and they would not obey her; instead, they constantly whined and demanded her attention, taking after their father, until she could not bear it any longer. So one day, Eve stole away and found Wisdom and asked It what she should do so her children would not be so troublesome and frustrating.

Wisdom told her that the problem lay in her and her children's ignorance—they were lacking in knowledge and common sense. However, if they would eat of the fruit of the Tree of Knowledge, they could be more like Itself and the Goddess-God in understanding goodness, peace, harmony, and, most importantly, the wisdom that comes from loving one another. Eve knew Adam had forbidden her to eat of the Tree of Knowledge's fruit, but she was so unhappy and Wisdom's words had given her such hope that she ate of it anyway. Instantly, she felt her senses awakening to the beauty of the garden and the joy that life can be. Then, eager to share her new understanding, she brought the fruit home to Adam.

As soon as Adam learned of what Eve had done, he began to berate her, calling her names and telling her that Wisdom had tricked her. "Wisdom is the Father of Lies!" he declared. "He only wants to make you unhappy so you will start to think crazy thoughts and then abandon me like Lilith did." Of course, he would not take any responsibility in my desire to leave him. He had conveniently forgotten how he had thrown me out of our home.

Eve bravely pled with Adam to eat the fruit, but he continued to refuse until finally he stormed out of the house.

Adam did not return for hours, and only after he had concocted the worst of lies. He told Eve that the Goddess-God had appeared to him and told him that they would have to leave Eden because they had disobeyed the edict not to eat of the fruit of the Tree of Knowledge. I knew this was a lie, for the Goddess-God had never forbidden that Adam or I not eat of the fruit. But, sadly, Eve had obviously not eaten enough of the fruit to be wise enough to realize that Adam was lying to her. After all, she was still innocent, and why should she doubt her husband's word? He not only told her they must leave the garden, but he told her that they must wear clothes; in fact, because she had disobeyed him and the Goddess-God, she would no longer have access to his penis. Later, she decided to cover her own body, for she decided that if Adam would not give her what she wanted, she would not give him what he wanted either. Of course, Adam liked coupling too much to withhold his penis for long, but when he did give it to her, he made it very clear what a great gift it was, one for which she should be very grateful, for he was doing it at the risk of the Goddess-God's displeasure.

It was all an elaborate and misguided deception brought about through Adam's own insecurity, his jealousy, and his desire to get as far away from Wisdom as possible. The result was that Adam and Eve's children were brought up to be ignorant and without the gift of immortality that I had received. Neither did Eve have immortality, for Adam had never let her eat of the Tree of Life. Only Adam and I had eaten of it, and Adam would in time discover that he was still subject to earthly dangers.

Once I understood what had happened to Adam and Eve's family, I felt great sorrow for them all, sorrow that they were so miserable. I decided I would return to the garden, to find the Tree of Knowledge and the Tree of Life, and to bring back their fruits for Eve and the children to eat sometime when Adam was absent.

So I went on a long journey, trying to find my way back to Eden, but I never was able to find it again. I can only think that Wisdom and the Goddess-God were so disappointed in all of us that They decided to flood the garden and wipe it from the face of the earth.

After I gave up on my quest to find the garden, I returned to where my fellow humans were residing. I had rarely ventured out in daylight to prevent them from seeing me, but I had been away from them for so long now that I was completely lonely and craving their company, even if they should not know that I was there, so I slowly approached their tents and found them all sitting together outside, watching Cain and Abel in a wrestling contest.

I was overjoyed to watch their sport, for they were having great fun. The boys were each taking delight in his brother's skill and agility, glorying in one another's strength, and finding delight in the pleasure that comes with tickling and tossing one another about, of picking one another up and throwing each other in the air as a father spins about his child, for they were both tall, powerful boys, beautiful to look upon and finding such joy in one another's company when they engaged in such play.

At one point, Abel had Cain in a headlock, but through agile twisting and turning, Cain managed to get out of it, bending over and picking Abel up on his back. But then Abel lost his grip, and as he did so, Cain grabbed him by the arms, and in an acrobatic move, flipped him up in the air and then caught him so that he held his brother over his head, putting Abel completely at Cain's mercy.

I was so stunned by the way Cain had flipped his brother into the air that I let out a gasp, a gasp I had not intended, and one far too loud because Cain heard the sound, and turning, he made eye contact with me. He was so startled to see me that he lost his concentration, and with it, he lost his hold on Abel.

In another second, Abel had fallen to the ground, smashing his head against a large rock. Later, I wondered whether perhaps Abel got what he deserved after the way he had thrown a stone at me, but at that moment, I was absolutely horrified. Adam and Eve and their daughters all rushed to Abel's side, trying to revive him, shocked and in horror over the first sight of human bloodshed. Then, when it became clear that Abel was dead—and also became clear just what death was—for it was new to all of us, I saw Cain's face first turn pale, and then I saw him look my way again. As he looked, his face changed from white to red as rage burned within him—so much rage that a blood vessel must have popped in his forehead, causing blood to flow from it; later, it left a perpetual scar upon his brow.

"Lilith!" roared Cain, pointing at me. "See how she causes us more pain!"

I did not wait to see his feet begin to move. I heard them pounding upon the earth as I fled in terror, more frightened by what I had just witnessed than that Cain was in pursuit of me. Until that moment, I'd had no real understanding of what death could be, although Wisdom had once tried to explain it to me as a reason to eat of the Tree of Life. As I now fled the scene of horror that I had unintentionally caused, my mind raced, trying to understand why Abel had not instantly healed— trying to understand what it meant that the children of Eve could die.

I ran and ran for what must have been an hour, trying to find anywhere I might hide, but eventually, Cain caught up with me.

And then...and then....

CHAPTER 3

LILITH GREW SILENT and her face turned pale as painful memories overcame her.

"Please, what happened next?" asked Devin.

She stared at him, searching for words she found too hard to utter.

"I know," said Anne slowly. "Cain raped you."

"Yes," said Lilith, tears springing into her eyes. "He raped me over and over, all that night beating me, calling me names, saying I was a devil, saying I had brought all the agony upon his family, saying I was to blame for everything wrong that had happened to them, and therefore, I must be punished.

"Not until morning did he let up. And then he left me beaten and bruised so badly that it would be days before I healed, even despite my having eaten the fruit of the Tree of Life.

"But worst of all, he had planted his seed inside of me—in me, his father's former wife—and his anger and hatred had done something to his physiognomy so awful that I don't think any modern scientist could explain it. But a similar change was now happening to me; the horror of Abel's death and my hate for Cain burned inside of me until my body began to do strange things; my tongue turned into that of a serpent, which I took to mean I had now acquired wisdom, wisdom that evil could exist in this world, but that it came not from some devil but rather from the human heart's restrictions when hate born of fear was allowed to rule over logic and love. I found it revolting that humanity could behave in such ways, and the horror of it all—not just the horror of what these humans would do to me, but what they might do to each other in time—made me feel sick, and while my outer beauty remained, inside, loathing and despair consumed me.

"Finally, I gave birth to not one or even two but four giant children, two boys and two girls—all from the seed of Cain and all giants who later were known as the Anakim. I did not train them up to be evil, but neither was I capable of nurturing them after I had received no nurturing, and so, by nature, they were always hateful and greedy children, so they became a scourge upon the human race from that time until well into the period you call the Middle Ages when the last of them was finally killed by Geoffrey of Lusignan, Melusine's son. My other children—such as those fathered by Constantine of Cornwall, Godfrey of Denmark, and Geoffrey of Lusignan—would not be such monsters, despite whatever evil streaks would be in them."

"But how is it," asked Devin, "that you ate of the fruit of the Tree of Life, yet you have died several times?"

"Ah," said Lilith. "One day, Adam found himself trapped in a cave, an avalanche of rock closing the entrance, and before any of his family could find him or dig him out, he suffocated. Once I knew that I needed oxygen to live, I knew how I could die, and also how to prevent my death. I then continued to regenerate whenever I would cut or wound myself, but I also began to explore all the mysteries of life. I lived for centuries and centuries, learning everything I could until finally I believed that I understood the secret of life, and then, weary in my loneliness, I decided I would make the great experiment—I would kill myself and bring myself back from the dead; if I failed, my lonely exile from the rest of my kind would end, but if I succeeded, then I would never need to fear anything, for I could return to life whenever I wished. Obviously, I succeeded, and I have enjoyed many incarnations since, allowing myself to be born of mortal women, making me a sort of daughter of Eve myself in my various incarnations, but by then, hatred had blackened my heart. I was horrified and disgusted by my Anakim children, who were even more rude and ignorant than Cain himself, though I attributed that to their sire's black heart being full of hate. Apparently, I was the only wise and sane human being in existence.

"Not long after, Eve's grandchildren began to be born—Seth and Cain's children by their sisters, and their daughters were remarkably beautiful, so beautiful that the Angels, the Sons of God, came down from Heaven and mated with them, creating the race of the Nephilim, giants like my own Anakim children, but benevolent giants who became protectors of mankind, and when I saw how beautiful these children were compared to my own, I allowed the jealousy that Adam had first felt to be nurtured in my own heart until I encouraged my own children in waging war against mankind.

"The battle between the Anakim and mankind, aided by the Nephilim, taught the human race to be aggressive and violent, and ultimately, to turn against one another, and I have taken never-ending delight in watching them destroy each other. If I were not to be loved, if I were to be treated as nothing, to be abused by Adam and his sons and to know no happiness, then I would not let Adam and Eve's children know any better life. In time, only the last of the Nephilim—Avallach—

had children capable of coming close to fighting me, children who intermarried with those of Joseph of Arimathea, whom you know as the fool Merlin, and from whom the Children of Arthur spring. You, the Children of Arthur, have been my greatest opponents throughout the centuries, and yet, it has been as if I were battling against an army of ants. You have no power over me; occasionally, you may get in a bite, but I could easily stamp you all to death whenever I choose. Only then, the game would end and I would be bored, and so I continue to wreak my vengeance for the wrongs inflicted on me by Adam and Eve and their children as it suits me, and I will do so for all eternity if it so pleases me. There now, you have heard my tale; are you satisfied?"

Lilith glared as she finished speaking, daring anyone to argue with her over a shred of its truth.

After a moment, Devin said, "You have been greatly wronged. I feel great sympathy for all your suffering, but if you hurt us now, it will not make anything better for anyone."

"I do not want your pity," Lilith snapped. "You are just like all the other sons of Adam, a man who would use your penis as a weapon to hurt and control women, a man who would make women subservient to you."

"Devin would never—" Anne began, but rather than let her speak, Lilith redirected her wrath against her.

"And you are like all of Eve's daughters—ignorant, stupid, allowing men to rule over you. If Eve had only stood up for herself, none of this would have happened, and if Adam hadn't been a coward and afraid of the wisdom that might have benefitted him, we might still be happy within the Garden of Eden."

"It is not pity that I feel," Devin said calmly, regaining Lilith's attention. "It's compassion for you."

"I don't need compassion from any of you weak and useless mortals!" Lilith screamed.

"Maybe not," said Devin, "but you could choose to be compassionate."

"Why? Why?" Lilith demanded, pacing back and forth in the room like a caged tiger about to break loose. "So I can be mocked and rejected again and again?"

"So, instead, you have chosen evil," said Merlin. No one had noticed when he opened his eyes, but he now struggled to his feet as he spoke. "Wisdom told you to love Adam and Eve despite their faults, but you chose instead to run and hide from them."

"Did you not hear a word I said, Wizard?" Lilith replied. "Adam threw me out of my home. Abel threw a stone at me, trying to kill me. And Cain raped me, his horrid act resulting in a race of giants that even I found repulsive. How does a mother love her children when they are monsters and born of rape? How does a woman love those who persecute her?"

"I think," said Devin, steeling his nerves against the rage he saw on Lilith's face, and slowly rising from his chair to step toward her, "that sometimes people only persecute one another because they are hurting deep within themselves. When people hurt us, we need to realize they are hurting even more, and so we must be compassionate toward them."

"Shut up!" Lilith shrieked. "What do you think you are, some bloody therapist? I don't need any of your trick child psychology. Why, your brain is mere mush beside my millennia of memories and my all-encompassing knowledge. You, you little college professor, you fool around with your medieval studies and archeology and theories about the past. Do you not realize that I am the past? I have lived since the very first day of the human race's existence. If you could see inside my mind, you would gasp with astonishment. I know the secret of life, the way to achieve immortality; I know how to turn lead into gold. I know the cures for cancer, leukemia, AIDS, and every other disease that plagues mankind, and I know how to mutate viruses and cause disease—I have created plenty of the diseases that I have afflicted upon mankind in a hope to put an end to your human misery, for all you humans do is inflict terror upon the world and all its creatures. You should thank me for such mercy killings, yet you think me evil—me, the wisest being on this earth in human form! Why, I know how earthworms regenerate, and why ducks do not have ears, and why bats are blind. I know the secret of the Loch Ness Monster and what the Sasquatch likes to eat. I know the exact population of China at this very second and precisely what it will be in thirty-six years, six months, three days, fourteen hours, nine minutes, and forty-seven seconds from this moment. I know, Devin. I know everything, and there is nothing you can say or do to change that. I know especially that I will never stop tormenting you humans. I may not ever destroy you all, for then my life would be dull, but I love to watch you mourn and cry and despair because I find it laughable since you bring all this misery upon yourselves, and for that reason, I will now take pleasure and comfort in destroying you all, and I think I shall begin with one of my oldest adversaries."

Lilith now stepped toward Devin, and after pushing him aside with her superior strength, so that he stumbled against the table and almost fell, she stopped just a couple of feet from Merlin.

"The time has come," she hissed, her serpent tongue escaping from her mouth. "The time has come, Wizard, Wandering Jew, Professor Van Helsing, Uncle of the Christ, or whatever name you choose to call yourself. Now you will know what real power is!"

Lilith raised her hands and began to chant in an ancient and forgotten tongue. Merlin instantly froze before her, not only physically froze, but slowly his body began to turn as white as ice while everyone watched wide-eyed at his complete inability to protect himself.

But just when everyone thought Merlin's end had arrived, a shout of "Stop, witch!" deafened the room.

Adam came running up the stairs from the kitchen, the Holy Lance firmly gripped in his hands like a javelin. He had found it in the kitchen when he recovered from his fall, and he had assumed it was placed there by Merlin, for Adam believed he had always been intended to be the hero of this story, a veritable St. George destined to slay a dragon.

But as Adam launched the spear into the air, Devin yelled out, "No! Be merciful!"

And before anyone could stop him or even suspect what he was about to do, Devin jumped in front of Lilith.

The Holy Lance soared straight into Devin's heart and then broke through his back and pierced into Lilith's own heart.

For a second, everyone stood in horror at the sight, and then the Holy Lance seemed to glow with such a blinding light that no one could see anything for a moment.

When the light faded, they were all astonished to find Devin and Lilith and the spear floating up toward the top of the room, and then Devin grasped the spear in his hands, and as if it were a mere piece of floss between his teeth, he gently slid it out of both Lilith and himself. Next, dropping the spear to the ground, he turned and caught Lilith in his arms as they slowly descended back to the floor. Devin then gently sat Lilith in a chair.

"Look at her face!" gasped Anne.

Lilith's black hair had turned to white, her cheeks had become paler, but a look of relaxation, of freedom from fear and stress, spread across her face and her entire body relaxed.

"Just like Dracula," muttered Quincey. "She's glad to be free from the evil that has possessed her."

It was on the tip of Anne's tongue to ask whether Lilith was dead when their adversary's eyes slowly opened. Then looking up at Devin, who was bent over her, Lilith said, "Thank you. Thank you. But why? I don't understand why you tried to save me."

"Devin, you're—aren't you hurt?" asked Adam.

Surprised by the question, Devin felt his chest. No hole existed in his body, not even a scar or a drop of blood where the spear had pierced him. Not even the slightest rip could be found in his shirt.

"No, I'm fine. I—why, I feel as good as I did when I was a kid. I—I haven't felt this strong and healthy in my entire life. The pain and anxiety I always feel in my stomach is gone. The—my God, you're beautiful!" he exclaimed, looking at Lilith. "You're all beautiful, every one of you—more than I ever realized—and look at the moonlight streaming into the room, and—"

"I feel wonderful, too," said Lilith, quickly standing up. "I haven't felt this good in thousands of years. I just want to sing and dance and celebrate the glory of life! I feel like a giddy child; I...I don't understand it. I don't even know how to express how exuberant I feel."

"I feel the same way," said Devin. "I feel joy and happiness, and love for all mankind!"

"I love everyone. I love you all!" exclaimed Lilith, taking Devin's hand and then hugging him tightly as everyone burst out in uncontrollable laughter, a laughter of relief mixed with unbelievable joy.

"What—how can this be? What has happened, Merlin?" Adam finally asked.

"It's the Holy Lance," said Merlin, who bore not a trace of the spell that Lilith had begun to work on him before being interrupted. "The Lance has the blood of our Savior upon it, blood that heals and cures all ills—greater than any royal jelly or water from Avalon's well—greater even than the fruit of the Tree of Life."

"Is that all that was needed—for Lilith to be pierced with the Lance?" asked Anne.

"No," said Lilith, releasing Devin from the hug but still squeezing his hand. "No. It...I don't even know how to say it. It's...."

"It's that for the first time you have felt loved," said Merlin, smiling. "Someone understood you enough simply to listen to you and then to stand up for you."

"Yes," said Lilith, nodding.

"But if Devin hadn't stepped in the way, Lilith would have been pierced with the spear regardless," Adam objected.

"Yes," said Merlin, "but she would have died. The spear would have killed her and the Savior's blood would have redeemed her in death, but it is Devin's sacrifice that has given her the freedom to continue to live."

Lilith now kissed Devin on the cheek, and while he remained stunned by all that had happened, he found he could not help but kiss her back, and on the lips.

Everyone watched in awe until Lilith's lips parted from those of her love—for apparently lovers they now were, and then Lilith said, "Only you, Devin, in all these centuries, has sought to do something for me without thought for yourself. All the other men—Adam with his jealousy, Constantine of Cornwall who wanted his lusts satisfied,

Dracula who wanted my help to drive the Turks from his land—all of them had selfish motives. Only you have tried to understand me for who I am and not what I could do for you."

Devin did not know how to respond. He felt humbled to be so acknowledged.

"You are the true hero of this tale," Lilith told him, clasping his hands in her own.

"I am honored," he replied, "in your saying so, and I am sorry it has taken so long for your suffering to be relieved, although I can't understand how I could be the hero. All of these years, I've expected that Adam would be the hero, or Tristan or Lance."

"Adam thought he would be the hero too," said Merlin, smiling, "but salvation cannot be worked out through violence."

Adam looked embarrassed and ashamed by this statement, but Devin, wishing to ease his cousin's pain, quickly added, "Yes, I did not want Adam to hurt Lilith, but at the same time, I did not want murder on my cousin's conscience because it would have been murder, even if in self-defense."

"And that, Devin," said Merlin, "is why you are the hero. You understand that. You humans in all your stories and movies always have to have the bad guy killed in the end—a justifiable murder, you tell yourselves, but it's all a bunch of bloodthirsty poppycock and balderdash that is detrimental to the welfare of your souls. Killing those you perceive as evil only brings about more pain and horror. You, Devin, realized that. You sought another way. You didn't know how that other way might be achieved, but that you desired it and tried to prevent a wicked end, that is what has counted."

"It has counted for everything," said Lilith. "For me to feel loved—why, it wipes away centuries of pain."

"But I don't understand how this is possible," said Anne. "We all hated Lilith; how could you have felt anything different, Devin?"

Devin felt embarrassed now. He did not like to admit his weaknesses, but after a moment, looking Adam in the eye, he confessed, "Because I have always felt alone. All my life, Adam was my best friend, but he always outshone me and was more popular, and then when he met Anne, I became second, and then after the twins were born, I felt like I counted for very little. I longed for love, but I never knew my parents. My grandparents were kind and loving, but Adam was clearly their favorite. So I know what it feels like to be alone. I know what it is like to have the ones you most love instead love someone else more. I understood that Lilith's quest, all her anger and rage, has always been the result of the deeper pain she felt, and so in the end, I could not let her suffer. I wanted her to know that at least one person understood her, could even love her if given the chance. And because...."

They all waited for him to finish, except Cedric, who walked over and put his hand on Devin's shoulder, and said:

"And because Devin is my son."

For a moment, they were all surprised, and then they instantly understood.

"You are then a descendant of Lilith," said Anne, "like myself... and...you are my brother!"

"Yes," said Lilith, "and he can be my mate, if he so chooses."

Devin was now speechless as he looked at this amazing woman in wonder, but his face expressed the thoughts churning in his mind until he eventually said, "Yes. Yes, for you are wise, and all my life I have sought wisdom, and you understand what it is to feel second like I do."

"And," said Lilith, as if completing his thoughts, "for the rest of our lives, we will each put the other first."

"Well said," said Merlin. "You know that the Holy Lance has also been called the Spear of Destiny. Now by your deeds, you have changed each other's destiny."

Devin and Lilith did not reply, but they kissed again, and then they held each other, clinging to one another for the longest time as everyone in the room felt his or her heart beat with joy at this unexpected outcome.

Finally, when Devin and Lilith released their embrace, Merlin stepped forward, and pulling the ring from his finger, he handed it to Lilith and said, "Here, my dear. I believe this ring is yours."

As Lilith took the ring and held it up, everyone again saw the other two rings on her fingers. She now possessed all three rings, but rather than try to destroy the world with them, she slipped the ring from Merlin into her pocket, and then she pulled the other two rings from her fingers and stepped toward Adam and Anne.

"Give me your hands," she told them.

They held open their palms, and Lilith placed a ring in each one.

"These rings," she said, "have been held in the highest esteem since the beginning of time, and many a person has valued them. I will keep my own, but you must have those of Adam and Eve, for their power is greater than any other on this earth, and someday, it will serve you well. But it is best that I not tell you the details of that power now; it is sufficient to say that there is no greater power on this earth than love. Place them on each other's fingers now and wear them as a sign of your commitment to one another."

Adam and Anne did as they were told, and then Lilith took their hands into her own and said, "Just as I should have wished for Adam and Eve so many millennia ago, I now wish you both all happiness possible until the end of your lives, and after that, happiness in the life beyond."

And then, before anyone could ask her what she would do with the third ring, she walked up to Devin. Retrieving the ring from her pocket, she held it up before him and said, "Devin Purcell, by virtue of this ring, I claim your love and wisdom as my own and give my own back to you unconditionally."

Devin could not take his eyes off her, for her beauty was beyond that of any other woman who had ever lived now that her heart was wholly pure, but his face expressed that he was uncertain how to answer.

"What will become of us now, my lady? What place in this world will you and I have? What will our future be?"

Lilith did not know how to answer. She understood, however, that Devin's question was truly whether she could now live in peace among the Children of Adam and Eve.

But Merlin answered for her.

"You, Lilith and Devin, will be the Adam and Eve of a new world. There are many dimensions and many worlds beyond our own, and the two of you shall populate one with your own children. You shall start anew. Tomorrow, you will start your new lives in a new world."

"Will you seek a new world with me, Devin?" Lilith asked. "Will you take up this adventure?"

Before Devin could speak, Adam burst out, "Devin, going to another world—are you sure—"

"Yes, I will go," Devin cut him off. "I love you, Adam and Anne, but it is time for me to live my own life."

Adam did not reply, but Anne whispered, "Be happy, Devin and Lilith."

"We will be happy," Devin replied. "For the rest of our lives, we will be all to one another and support one another in all our pursuits, including the quest for true wisdom, and we will raise our own children and populate a new world."

"That's a wonderful goal," Merlin affirmed, "but it's too much to do on an empty stomach. I'm starving!"

They all burst out laughing and then the twins confessed that they were also hungry.

"We should have eaten a long time ago," said Lilith. "I'm sorry that I interrupted your meal."

"No trouble at all," said Cedric. "It will only take a few minutes to reheat things. Tristan and Lance will help me."

The conversation that followed during dinner was filled with more questions and comments, most of them repeating and reconfirming what they already knew but were simply still trying to believe. Most of all, they were so full of energy, so relieved from all the strain and anxiety they had all felt for so long that they just rejoiced to be together and to know that everything had turned out in the very best way imaginable.

But as the evening wore on, the strain of years of stress and fear caught up with their bodies, now badly in need of rest, and so they began to yawn and their eyes to droop.

"I think we've had enough excitement for one day," said Merlin. "I will need all my strength for the events that are to happen tomorrow. Let us go to bed."

"Devin, may I sleep in your room tonight?" asked Lilith, looking deeply into his eyes.

"We are husband and wife now," he replied, clasping her hand and looking forward to experiencing paradise with her.

"No, let us not use those archaic, gender-laden terms," said Lilith. "We are best friends and lovers and partners. That is enough."

Devin simply smiled and kissed her.

Everyone said good night and started to head toward their rooms, but Adam, holding Anne's hand so she could not leave yet, stepped into Merlin's path.

"I thought," Adam said, "that because my father and mother are both of Arthur and Morgana's line that I was the Chosen One, or at least my sons were. Why have you involved me in this matter so much, even more so than you ever involved Devin, if he was the Chosen One?"

"Adam, are you jealous?" Anne asked in surprise. "We have our children back, so what does it matter now?" Then laughing, she added, "Do you want to go off with Lilith instead?"

"No," said Adam. "I just don't understand. I want Merlin to explain why he manipulated everything so you and I would meet and have twin sons, only to hide them away from us, if, in the end, our role was to turn out to be less significant than Devin's? Devin never even had any of the dreams we had, so why all this buildup if, in the end, we were to play minor roles in stopping Lilith?"

"First of all," Merlin replied, "I am not completely omniscient. Sometimes, I've just had to do what I thought was best and make it up as I go along. Yes, I placed the Holy Lance where I thought you would grab it to destroy Lilith, but I didn't know any more than you did that Devin would commit such a sacrificial act of compassion. That was just as unexpected for me as it was for you, although the moment I saw it happen, I realized it was meant to be all along. We can't always expect things to go as they are planned, but in the end, everything always works out for the best, even if you don't end up being the hero of the story. That is because we tend to forget sometimes that, for all our efforts, it is not us, but the Goddess-God who guides all."

Anne, hearing a tinge of irritation in Merlin's voice, pulled on her husband's arm, saying, "Come, Adam. Let's go to bed."

"No, I just want to understand," said Adam. "Merlin always acted like my role was somehow important in all this, and now it feels like I really didn't have much of a role at all."

"What have you done," said Merlin, now letting his frustration show, "to make you deserving of a greater role? You have been quite rude to me throughout this ordeal. You have been demanding, and you have argued with what I've done, even though it's always been in your best interests, and when I've asked you to trust me, or I've tried to make you see the playfulness and joy of this adventure, you have refused to do so. It might hurt your feelings when I say this, but while I love you dearly, my boy, perhaps being the great hero isn't what was meant to happen for you; perhaps instead, what was meant to happen for you out of all these events was to learn a little humility for a change. Perhaps there is a bit more of your ancestor Adam in you than is good for you, and perhaps you should think upon that a bit harder than you have so far. You have seen what happened as a result of his jealousy. Don't make the same mistake."

And then Merlin stepped around Adam and went out of the room and to bed.

Anne put her arm around Adam and walked him to their room, neither one of them speaking a word. Anne did not need to speak, for she could read on Adam's face what he was feeling.

Inside him, Adam's heart had nearly broken, for he knew Merlin was right. He was blessed with a beautiful wife whom he adored and two intelligent, happy, healthy sons, so it was petty of him to begrudge his cousin any happiness or mark of distinction.

That night, Adam lay awake, thinking over all these things, and for the first time in his life, he truly experienced the dark night of his soul. He came out of it well aware of his human weaknesses, having made peace with himself through the promise that he would strive to do better in the time he had left.

EPILOGUE

IN THE MORNING, Adam, Anne, Tristan, and Lance went to the kitchen for breakfast, only to have Cedric tell them to go out to the garden where they would find both breakfast and Devin and Lilith, who were ready to make their departure.

"Are Quincey and Merlin still sleeping?" Anne asked.

"No," Cedric replied. "Quincey told me to say goodbye for him; he's gone to Avalon to let everyone there know what has happened, and Merlin, you never know where he might be."

"Will you be joining us, Grandpa?" asked Tristan.

"No, my role in this story is over I think," said Cedric. "I already said my goodbyes to Devin and Lilith before you were awake."

Anne went up to her father and kissed him on the cheek.

"You're not going anywhere, I hope," she said. "Not running away or anything?"

"No," Cedric replied. "I'm afraid you're stuck with me, if you want to be. I know I'm a coward and have betrayed you. I don't deserve your love or even a kind word from you, but I hope you'll let me be involved in at least a small way in your lives."

"Father, don't say such things," Anne objected. "It was Lilith's blood in you that made you behave the way you did. Now she is healed and so are you," said Anne.

"Grandpa, you have always been good to us," Lance added.

"Yes," said Tristan. "You cared for Lance and me all these years and kept us safe. We can't be wholly blamed for what we do in our moments of fear. We just have to recognize it's fear and not give in to it."

"Well, I must have done something right in my life since I have such wise grandsons," Cedric replied, mussing Tristan's hair. "Now, please, go have breakfast with Lilith and Devin. I need some time to myself to make sense of all this, and...and to decide how I can find some purpose for my life now, something to make up for all the mistakes I've made."

"So long as we're still in the picture, that will be fine," said Adam, who after struggling all night with his own conscience, was finally ready to bury the hatchet with his father-in-law.

Cedric felt so surprised by this remark that he looked at Adam earnestly, and in another second, they were giving each other a manly hug.

"Okay, we'll see you later, Grandpa," said Lance when Adam and Cedric had finished hugging. And then parents and sons headed out to the garden.

"Dad did say we'd have breakfast out here, didn't he?" asked Anne as they stepped outside, "because I'm starving."

"Me, too!" said Lance.

"You're always starving," Tristan replied.

They quickly spotted Lilith and Devin seated on a picnic cloth beneath a giant tree beside the rose gardens.

"Welcome, Delaney family!" called out Lilith with such enthusiasm that they were taken aback for a moment.

"Don't be shy," said Devin, beckoning them into the shade beneath the apple tree.

"All is well, I promise you," said Lilith as they sat down upon the grass.

"You sound like Merlin," said Adam, laughing, "only I think this is the first time I've ever heard someone say that and I've actually believed it was true."

"It truly is. It has not been this well since the Goddess-God created the great Creation," Lilith replied. "We have all been on a long and tiresome journey, but in the end, it has all been quite illuminating. As the biblical Joseph told his brothers after they had sold him into slavery in Egypt, only so later he could save their lives, 'You meant it for ill, but God meant it for good.'"

Lance's stomach growled loudly, causing them all to laugh.

"Too much information for an empty stomach," said Lilith, and she waved a hand so that suddenly before them appeared a bowl of fruit, goblets of juice, plates and napkins, French pastries, and all manner of exotic foods from pomegranates to date-filled cookies and Turkish delight. "I hope this is ample nourishment for you all," Lilith said.

"Plenty," said Adam.

"Well, we'll see," Lance replied.

They all passed the dishes around and had begun to dig into the food when Anne let out a shriek. First, they all looked at her and then to where she was staring at the tree behind Lilith.

An enormous golden-skinned snake had come down the tree and glided onto Lilith's shoulder, and it was now beginning to wind its way around her.

"Be not afraid," Lilith said. "You humans have always feared

Wisdom, for it is in your nature to lack the aspiration to better yourselves—not traits you gained from me, certainly, but we won't mention names. This is Wisdom. It doesn't care much for modern languages, though It can speak well enough, and we often talk in Aramaic, Sanskrit, and other prehistoric tongues you humans have forgotten. Its medieval French isn't bad, but anything more modern than that it seeks to avoid. Furthermore, It is afraid that your frail human hearts and minds could not bear it if It spoke Its wisdom; nevertheless, you can probably sense the great peace It is causing to vibrate all around It. Like me, It has waited a very long time for this moment."

"Is it—is he—it's not—" Anne stuttered.

"The snake from the Garden of Eden?" said Lilith, helping Anne along. "I guess you could say so. Wisdom is the keeper and giver of knowledge and wisdom, the embodiment of it all, for It has never meant for them to be kept as secrets, but you humans nevertheless have many times refused Its gifts, being ashamed of knowing too much, for with knowledge comes responsibility, and so you have branded knowledge and wisdom often as evil and denied them, calling them forbidden and cursing those who seek them. All these are misconceptions you have received from your ancestors. It is unfortunate. I have always wanted it to be different, right from the beginning, but well...it's all past now, though it has created plenty of difficulties for us all, but that's also why you are here, isn't it? So we can learn to do things differently going forward."

When they did not reply, Lilith said, "Eat! Eat! Try these figs soaked in honey. They're delicious."

And so they all returned to eating, although barely taking their eyes away from Lilith and Wisdom, which had now slithered from

Lilith's shoulder onto Devin's and then encircled his waist, while he calmly stroked It, experiencing peace like he had never known before from communing with It.

"You still have many questions," said Lilith to them all. "I can sense them."

"I'm used to asking Merlin my questions," said Adam, although he did not relish the thought of seeing the wizard again, at least not just yet, for he still felt ashamed over the words Merlin had said to him the night before.

"He'll be along shortly," Lilith replied, "but he cannot answer questions meant solely for me."

"I do have a question," Anne admitted.

Lilith nodded her head, affirming that Anne was free to ask her anything.

"Your voice is so kind," said Anne. "Am I right in assuming that all of the evil in you is now gone?"

"If you want to call it evil," said Lilith, "then yes, it is gone, thanks to Devin."

She clasped his hand and smiled at him, which caused him to stop stroking Wisdom, who now contentedly curled up in a ball in Devin's lap.

"What I really want to know," continued Anne, "is if you were evil, why did you sometimes do what seemed to be intended as good? At least, I don't understand what you were doing in the land of Prester John where you were teaching those women."

"You humans are obsessed with good and evil," said Lilith. "You just have to have your evil—you have to make up all kinds of stories about how sin entered the world and so many other things, such foolishness to scare yourselves. Do you really believe the Goddess-

God needs or can be limited to such a paradigm? Or let me put it another way: Do you truly believe the Goddess-God can be put into a box, chained inside prison walls, chained inside the prisons you create within your minds? Do you think you can even begin to understand the Goddess-God, who is eternal and absolute, and unchanging and perfect, and all-knowing and yet ever-loving, and forgiving and wanting nothing but for His-Her children to grow and evolve and to perfect themselves?"

"I—I don't really follow," said Anne. "Are you saying evil is an illusion, something we create in our brains?"

"If that's the case," said Adam, before Lilith could reply, "then why did you try to kill us? And why...." He was nearly in tears at the thought. "Why did you kill my mother?"

"I am deeply sorry for the pain I have caused you, Adam, but let me assure you that deep in her being your mother knew the sacrifice she was making—knew it before she ever even chose to enter this life—and she knew that you needed to experience greater fear, which came about by her death, so the fear inside you would be released and you could find the courage to grow wiser and stronger. In fact, even in your attempt to destroy me with the Holy Lance, you grew wiser because rather than be paralyzed by fear, you chose to act. It was not the right action exactly, but do see what it has led to? After Devin's sacrifice, your own actions have been the most significant, but those actions never would have come about if your mother had not made her sacrifice out of love for all of you. And I tell you this—that you will see her again someday, and when that happens, it will be as if all the pain of her loss never existed.

"As for my teaching in the land of Prester John, a few of you humans have truly loved Wisdom, and when that has been the case,

I have done all I could to bring Wisdom to you. My love has been great for you then—all of you—in such times, and I have sought to help you as if you were my own children. King Solomon was one such, and in my incarnation as the Queen of Sheba, I visited him and imparted great knowledge to him, but as wise as he was, he was also human, and in time, he could not bear the burden of such wisdom, so he fell into greed, seeking wealth and pleasure, taking hundreds of wives from among the neighboring kings' daughters, and worse, denying the truths deep in his soul in favor of mankind's lies. After that experience, I was careful with what I taught to humans. In the land of Prester John, I taught only women, and I taught them simply to believe themselves worthy and deserving so that they could love their children and husbands better, for in those days, women's roles were limited, and so I only imparted what I thought could help them and make their world better, and I imparted it in small, digestible amounts, waiting over the centuries for the human race to advance. I have wrought war and disease across the world, but there are times when I have done the opposite. In my more optimistic and visionary moments, I whispered in the ears of abolitionists and young maidens who strove for women's rights, and sometimes, I truly thought the human race would advance and I became hopeful, but then one of you would do something horrible like assassinate a great leader—a Lincoln or a Gandhi—and then I would become so angry that I would incite wars among you, thinking you would never change and it would be better if you would only all destroy yourselves.

"You see, I am human myself, and so I have had my mood swings, but now...now all that anger has gone. There was love first, love in the Garden of Eden, and that love never left me, even if the anger repressed it more often than not. But now I am freed from all of that anger, and

I also realize I cannot force happiness or wisdom on others, and so I will not interfere in the affairs of men any longer."

"At least not on this planet," said Devin, kissing her hand.

"But will wars and hatred continue now that you are leaving the world?" Anne asked.

"Oh, yes, it is the human condition, I'm afraid. But just remember that all that hate and aggression comes from you humans believing you are not worthy and from fearing there is a God keeping score every second. No, no, it is not so. The Goddess-God is Love and only wants for you to know wellbeing and happiness. You have been given Free Will to choose to move forward or backward or stay where you are, and it is only from the choices that you make when you exercise that Free Will that you can learn, but never has He-She or Wisdom tried to impede you, trick you, or condemn you. He-She gave you life to enjoy yourselves and Wisdom gave you a beautiful tree full of fruit to help you to grow strong and wise, but you have twisted it all until you decided that the fruit of the Tree of Life causes death and you have chosen unconsciously to let your anger and hatred create disease in your bodies. But the Goddess-God does not work like that. He-She is all good, and His-Her wisdom leads to goodness, and so there are no limits, no boundaries, no conditions, no exclusions, no pass or fail tests, no walls to climb, no hoops to leap through, no crazy quests and no redemption required, not even any sacrifices that need to be made—no, none of it. Because you don't have to fix yourselves. You are not broken, nor are you damned sinners. You are the Goddess-God's children, and you always have been. You are alive, you are here, you are part of His-Her great Creation, and you are perfect as your Heavenly Mother-Father is perfect, save only for your own choice to live in fear, your own unwillingness to believe in your own goodness and worthiness."

"But aren't we, as humans, full of sin?" Anne asked. "Isn't that why Jesus came? To free us from sin?"

"Do you truly think," replied Lilith, "that a loving Goddess-God would wait thousands of years to save His-Her children from sin?" asked Lilith. "The concept of Original Sin wasn't even devised until four hundred years after Christ's birth, by St. Augustine, a sex-addict himself, who from his own self-loathing had to damn the whole human race with his concepts of Original Sin. He would have done better to learn compassion for himself, but even he allowed himself to be bound by the conditions of his time and fellow men. Yes, Jesus told you that sins were forgiven, not because you were born of sin, but because you believed in sin, and He sought to relieve your fears. Sin is not damnation, but it is what keeps you from living life to its fullest—sin is the outlet of fear. Christ came to conquer death, to show you that eternal life and happiness have always been available to you, yet you choose to continue to die, to rant about sin, and to commit what you think are acts of sin so you can seek a forgiveness you can't accept when you are given it, and so on and so on, in a vicious and insane circle. Frankly, it's all been quite tiring to watch you mortals all these millennia. No matter how I or Merlin or Jesus or anyone tries, you mortals keep refusing to accept Love and Life and Joy as your purpose, as your reason for living. Just simply relax and love and enjoy one another. That's all you need to do. Isn't that the greatest commandment that Christ gave you: 'Love one another'? If you can achieve that, nothing else will matter, and all the ills of this world will fall away."

Adam and Anne were silent, not knowing how to respond. They looked inside their hearts and realized the truth of Lilith's words. They had always doubted their own worthiness—lived in dread and fear every day that ill would come to them when it did not, yet they had gone on living in dread and fear the next day and the next, regardless.

While they all pondered these matters, Wisdom slithered across the picnic cloth, making Its way to Anne's lap. She found herself fearful, but she did not pull away, and after a minute, when she felt Its warmth against her body, she let her hand fall and she began to pet It, and suddenly, a great sense of peace fell over her, and then Adam felt the urge to reach over and pet Wisdom as well, and Wisdom curled Its body into Anne's lap, but It set Its head to rest upon Adam's knee, hissing contentedly. Adam found himself filled with uncontrollable laughter, and soon, Anne joined him, and then Lilith and Devin also joined in, and Lance and Tristan also pet Wisdom's head and laughed, and the apple tree's boughs danced in the breeze in time with the music of their laughter, and then it was as if all of Nature laughed with them as sun broke through the trees and the breeze made the sunlight appear to dance about the lawn, and for just a moment, they almost thought they heard celestial laughter coming forth from the skies.

After a little while, Lilith said, "It is now almost time for Devin and me to depart," and she rose to her feet.

Wisdom slithered off Adam and Anne's laps and back to the tree, where It paused, looked back, and seemed to wink at them all, and then It disappeared into a hole beneath the tree's trunk.

"We must say goodbye, Devin," Lilith told her husband.

Hugs and blessings were now given by all and to all, and not a few tears were shed at the knowledge that they would not see each other again, at least not in this lifetime, but they also felt so at peace that none of them truly mourned the parting but felt it the beginning of wonderful and exciting times to come.

Finally, when all the goodbyes had been exchanged, Lilith said,

"May the Goddess-God bless you all, and may you not forget what you have learned here, but instead, spread the message to the rest of humanity that only fear stands between each one of you and happiness. Fear is a powerful foe, but it is the only one—not demons, not damnation—just simply fear, a small thing if you choose to see it as small, and it can be defeated if you choose to be brave and fight it."

"It is time," said Merlin. He stepped from behind the tree, and because it was time, none were surprised by his appearance.

"Goodbye, everyone," said Devin, taking Lilith's hand.

"Goodbye," replied the Delaney family.

"Goodbye," said Lilith. "I love you all. I would have been proud to have had you as my children, and in truth, you are all part of my blood. I will always be with you in spirit."

And then Lilith nodded her head that she was ready to leave. And so Merlin chanted a spell under his breath, and within a second, Devin and Lilith, clasping hands, went soaring into the air like rockets on Independence Day, for they were now free to begin their lives anew.

After the Delaneys had all stared upward for a few moments, Merlin said, "My children, why do you stand here looking up at the sky?"

"Devin was my best friend," said Adam, turning to him, "and now I will never see him again."

"You do not know that," Merlin replied.

Anne put her arm around Adam, and then Tristan and Lance did the same, and they all stared at Merlin, lost in wonder and also feeling that they now had more questions than answers.

"What is next for us?" asked Anne.

"Yes, what?" asked Lance and Tristan in unison.

"I thought—" said Adam.

"You thought what?" asked Merlin.

"I thought—well, I know now I was wrong that I would be the hero of this story, but I thought when we first met that you told me that my children and I would somehow bring about King Arthur's return."

"I did not mean literally," Merlin replied. "I meant you and your family would be key in bringing about his return by leading people back to the ideals of King Arthur. For King Arthur has had his life in this world, and he is quite content now to be in Avalon and work behind the scenes for humanity's good. And besides, he was human you know, human and, therefore, flawed just like you. Why would you look to him to be your savior? And even if he were a savior, if his blood runs through your veins, are you not just as capable of greatness yourselves? Are you not King Arthur's Blood, and is that not the same as being King Arthur yourselves? Why do you need to be taught this again and again? You do not need a hero to save you. You need to be your own heroes. Live your lives like you are heroes until you truly become such. Live free of fear. Shake it from you. Do good. Love one another. Spend your time being kind to one another. Laugh more because life is fun when you let it be, so seek Joy in all you do. Then you will save yourselves from the pain that makes your lives so hard."

When Merlin finished speaking, he was met by four pairs of staring eyes that did not seem satisfied with his words.

"Very well," said Merlin. "You do not need King Arthur to return, and yet, you are human, and so you want it so, and even though your expectations are what cause your disappointments, I know you will not be satisfied otherwise.... Not until the day you finally all go to Arthur's Bosom...and so the story is not over yet."

AUTHOR INTERVIEW

TYLER, *LILITH'S LOVE* is a surprising mix of Arthurian legend, biblical story, late medieval history, and a sequel to Dracula. How did you come up with the idea to make all these connections and blend them into one novel?

It is quite a mix, isn't it? I began with writing the first novel in the series, *Arthur's Legacy*, and reintroducing Gwenhwyvach into the Arthurian storyline. Then as I worked on the successive novels in the series and realized what a major player Gwenhwyvach would be, I knew I needed to explain the source of her power and ability to live for centuries and, eventually, I had the revelation that she was really the reincarnation of Lilith. What better villainess to have than the very first villainess in history?

As for Dracula, what struck me about his story is that his historical source, Vlad Tepes, like King Arthur, is buried on an island, but then he disappears from his grave—giving the promise that he is still alive. Similarly, like King Arthur, the Emperor Constantine XI was prophesied to return again, and so I wanted to play on these similarities to the Arthurian legend and introduce them into the story—since Dracula and Constantine were really contemporaries and both adversaries of Mehmet II, I thought it perfect to include both of them.

Also, years ago, back in the late 1990s, after I finished writing the first version of *Arthur's Legacy* and long before I published it or thought to write sequels to it, I became deeply interested in Quincey Harker and began writing a novel about him. I only got a few chapters of that novel written and then set it aside. Now I think I didn't get farther because I hadn't yet noticed the similarities between the Vlad Tepes story and that of King Arthur, both being buried on islands, both destined to return. Once I made those connections, instead of two separate novels, I combined them into a series, and then I thought, why not have Lilith be the one Dracula learns evil from in the Scholomance where Stoker says Dracula learned the black arts? By putting together these pieces, I was having great fun creating a new history allegedly forgotten by mankind.

What kind of research did you do in writing this book?

I've spent years studying Gothic literature, as reflected in my book on the subject *The Gothic Wanderer: From Transgression to Redemption* and my blog at www.GothicWanderer.com, so I was very familiar with the narrative techniques of the Gothic. As for the scenes set in Istanbul, I visited that amazing city in 2012 as research for this book and many of my experiences there are reflected in those chapters.

Of course, I read everything I could about Lilith, Vlad Tepes, Dracula, the Fall of Constantinople and its key players, and the Arthurian legend. That said, it is impossible to read everything, and since I was writing a novel, while I wanted to provide a historical atmosphere, in the end I let my imagination take over, especially where facts were not easily determinable or known.

Will you tell us more about your interest in Lilith? What about her fascinated you so much?

Once I knew Lilith was my primary villain, I knew that since I had so many other viewpoints in the series, I had to let her tell her own story as well—how else can you be fair to your villainess or redeem her except by making her sympathetic to your reader? Of course, that meant addressing how she became evil in the first place, and that meant going back to the Garden of Eden story to give it a new spin. Surprisingly, few people even know who Lilith was since she's not in the Bible, but the Jewish tradition is that she refused to let Adam be in the dominant position (on top of her) when they had sex—which symbolizes that she refused to let women be submissive to men, and consequently, she was kicked out of the Garden and replaced by Eve. That the Jewish people even have such a tradition shows the subversive element of the story—men might hold Lilith up as an example of evil and a warning that women will be punished for not obeying their husbands, but I suspect Jewish women, even way back then, embraced her secretly for her refusal to be submissive. And certainly, the feminist movement adopted and celebrated her in the latter half of the twentieth century. I don't think we should forget her, especially since she seems to have roots that pre-date even the Jewish religion. Surprisingly, there aren't very many books written on her, but for readers who want to know more, I highly recommend *The Case for Lilith* by Mark Wayne Biggs.

Many conservative Christians might not agree with your rewriting the Bible stories in this series. Have you received any negative responses as a result?

First, let me say that I feel a writer should take the advice of the great poet Alexander Pope in his *An Essay on Criticism*, where he says that a true writer "Glows while he reads, but trembles as he writes." All of this legendary material is sacred to me, whether it is biblical or Arthurian or from another culture's myths. But I also feel that the goal of a good writer is not simply to tell a story but to create literature. The true definition of literature is that it makes people think and see the world in new ways, and that's what I want my readers to do—see the world in new ways. If they do not wish to do that, I believe it is fear that is holding them back, which is the primary fault of mankind— not some strangely imagined Original Sin that I don't believe does or ever did exist. That we've allowed this concept of Original Sin, created by St. Augustine, to exist for so long is amazing—anyone who reads Augustine's *Confessions* or *The City of God* can see that the man's thinking and logic were deeply flawed and the results of a fifth century mindset. Can't the human race progress past what its thoughts were sixteen centuries ago? Why are we still letting St. Augustine, who was a sex addict and self-loathing once he became a Christian, make us all self-loathing? I hope my readers will come to think for themselves and realize that sin and guilt are not concepts we need. As the English poet William Blake said, they are "mind-forged manacles," and they only retard the human race's growth. We cannot continue to allow belief systems from ancient times to keep our minds in prison. That isn't to say that the Bible is not full of valuable and life-giving passages worth preserving, but there is also much there we can do without. I know some readers will say I cannot pick and choose from a sacred scripture, but I'd like to know how many of those people obey all the rules in Leviticus. If they're eating pork or wearing blue jeans, they are doing no differently. If we can discard those rules, why can't we discard a concept like sin? Christ himself said that he came that men might have life and have it more abundantly, so I think it's time we learn how to do that. I don't believe Christ's message was that he conquered sin, but that he came to show us that we have immortal life and death has no power over us. It's time then for us to start living abundantly, not doubting our own self-worth.

Anyone who disagrees with me is entitled to his or her own opinion, but I think more and more people are coming to understand this viewpoint. Attendance at churches is dropping rapidly, and that is not a bad thing—it doesn't mean society will fall apart, and it doesn't mean people are becoming immoral. It means that we are seeking new ways to be spiritual, and, therefore, good and life-affirming people. As Tennyson said:

> The old order changeth yielding place to new
> And God fulfills himself in many ways
> Lest one good custom should corrupt the world.

The custom is changing. We should embrace it and look forward to a new stage in human evolution.

Adam Delaney has been the main character throughout the series, but then Devin seems to swoop in at the end and get all the glory. Why is that?

My intention was originally to have Adam and Devin be equal, but Adam kept getting into the limelight. Nevertheless, I knew all along that Devin would be the primary hero in the end. Adam is too stereotypical of a hero for me, being good-looking and athletic and all that, and besides, I don't think we really need heroes—not the stereotypical type anyway. What we need are people who can think for themselves. Devin has learned how to do that, and he also shows compassion—something he probably learned from being in Adam's shadow and feeling compassion for himself, but also from reading a lot of good novels, I imagine. Because Devin is a bookworm, he's learned how to control his temper and not act recklessly without thought. Adam never stood a chance next to him. I wish more people were like Devin and willing to ask questions and think rather than take things at face value. Devin wants to understand Lilith—he doesn't just start asking her questions as a way to stall her until Adam can kill her— he sincerely wants to understand her, and at the pivotal moment, he shows her compassion, and that's what makes the difference. When we seek to understand one another and set aside our irrational fears, we'll find we really don't have any enemies.

At the end of the novel, Merlin says the characters will not be satisfied until the day they go to Arthur's Bosom. That's a strange expression. What do you mean by it?

It is a strange expression, and it's also the title of the final book in the series, a title some early readers told me I should change, but I felt it the most appropriate term possible. It is derived from a line in Shakespeare's play *King John*, in which the young Prince Arthur,

King John's nephew and the rightful heir to the throne of England, is murdered by his uncle's thugs, and is said to go to Arthur's bosom. Shakespeare was creating a wordplay on the phrase "Abraham's bosom," a biblical description for heaven—perhaps more specifically, the heaven of the Jewish people descended from Abraham. I've never understood why heaven has to be the same for everyone, so for those of us who love King Arthur and the ideals of Camelot, why might we not go to Arthur's Bosom? What it is like to go to Arthur's Bosom will be revealed in the fifth and final book of the series.

In conclusion, if you had to sum up what the main theme of the Children of Arthur series is, how would you describe it?

I can sum it up in one sentence: Imagination is the salvation of mankind. It's a line that for a long time I thought I had read somewhere in Percy Shelley's poems, but I could never find it when I looked for it later, so I think I must have created it myself. I first wrote it years ago in my novel *Superior Heritage*. It's a shocking statement, I think, because it goes against the Christian idea that Jesus is the Savior, but I don't think it's a completely contradictory statement to that idea. I say that because while I believe there was a historical Jesus, just like there was a historical King Arthur, most biblical scholars will agree that plenty of stories and other elements were added to the Gospel depictions of Jesus so that in the Bible, He is largely a very literary and imaginative version of the real man, and so, given the imagination required to create such a figure, isn't it fair to say that if this figure brings us salvation, then imagination is the salvation of mankind? Furthermore, the whole message of Jesus is about imagination—people might call it faith, but I think it is largely the same thing, or at least imagination and faith are very similar. Christ said we could move mountains if we had the faith of a mustard seed. To me, we can move mountains if we can imagine it first and then have faith as we take action to make it happen.

The whole intention of this series is to ask readers to imagine a better world, and in doing so, also to imagine a better past. That doesn't mean that we have to deny reality and all the terrible things that have happened in the past like genocides of whole peoples, but it means that we can rewrite our myths and our history—not whitewashing them but learning to see the positive aspects in them. Even something as terrible as the holocaust has a positive side in that it has made so many of us commit to making certain it does not happen again. And in terms of our religious beliefs, if Jesus died for our sins, why do we keep harping on them? Because we're afraid of living up to our full potential, I think.

As Lilith says in the novel, it's fear that is holding us back. Rather than being fearful, let's strive to be brave and imagine a better world and then take action to make that dream a reality. When we do that, then truly, imagination will be the salvation of mankind. Not only is that the theme of this series, but it is a theme I invite my readers to make their own.

ACKNOWLEDGMENTS

IT IS IMPOSSIBLE to write a novel without owing a debt to a great many people, many of whom I have never met—authors who have influenced my writing—as well as close friends who have allowed me to bounce ideas off of them.

The authors I am indebted to are:

- The Bible writers.
- Bram Stoker for his Gothic masterpiece, *Dracula*.
- Lew Wallace, whose novel *The Prince of India* (1893) first depicted the Wandering Jew at the Fall of Constantinople.
- Countless writers of Arthuriana whom I cannot possibly list in full, but most deserving of mention are Sir Thomas Malory, Geoffrey of Monmouth, Mark Twain, and Marion Zimmer Bradley.
- Countless classic Gothic novelists, including Ann Radcliffe, Matthew Lewis, and William Godwin.

The people in my personal life I owe a debt to, with my apologies if I forget anyone, are:

- Diana Deluca who stuck with me until I got male-female

relations right when it came to depicting Lilith's final scene.

- Roslyn Hurley, who read the first drafts of this novel and gave positive encouragement.
- The Writers Ink group who gave their support in listening to me read chapters and providing feedback.
- Jenifer Brady, who assisted with proofreading and final comments, but more importantly, was enthusiastic about the series.
- Larry Alexander, who like a valiant knight took up the quest of turning my manuscript into a beautifully designed book.

Finally, I thank my readers for giving my words meaning by reading them and for all of their positive and encouraging comments.

THE CHILDREN OF ARTHUR SERIES

concludes in

ARTHUR'S BOSOM

THE CHILDREN OF ARTHUR, BOOK FIVE

BY
TYLER R. TICHELAAR

SEVERAL YEARS AFTER the showdown with Lilith, the Delaney twins, Lance and Tristan, are young men intent on finding their place in the world while wondering whether their greatest adventures already lie behind them.

But when an earth-shattering cataclysmic event occurs, the twins find themselves having to piece back together a world that only slightly resembles the world they knew, a world that seems more fantasy than reality in its strangeness and yet its familiarity.

Will they be able to find their parents and home, and resurrect their very lives? Or will they find themselves forever trapped in a time-warp in an

Arthurian world that until now they have only read about.

With *Arthur's Bosom*, the Children of Arthur series comes to a stunning conclusion after offering a wholly new and different world-view of mythology, human history, and what is still possible for the future of the human race.

Don't miss any of The Children of Arthur series:

ARTHUR'S LEGACY: THE CHILDREN OF ARTHUR, BOOK ONE

MELUSINE'S GIFT: THE CHILDREN OF ARTHUR, BOOK TWO

OGIER'S PRAYER: THE CHILDREN OF ARTHUR, BOOK THREE

LILITH'S LOVE: THE CHILDREN OF ARTHUR, BOOK FOUR

ARTHUR'S BOSOM: THE CHILDREN OF ARTHUR, BOOK FIVE

You might also enjoy:

KING ARTHUR'S CHILDREN:
A STUDY IN FICTION AND TRADITION

Tyler Tichelaar's nonfiction study of all the treatments of King Arthur's children from early Welsh references through the Middle Ages and in recent modern fiction.

and

THE GOTHIC WANDERER:
FROM TRANSGRESSION TO REDEMPTION

An exploration of Gothic literature from 1794 to the present, including the figures of the Wandering Jew and Dracula, which inspired The Children of Arthur series.

For the latest information, release dates, and to purchase books, visit:

www.ChildrenofArthur.com

A Sneak Peek at *Arthur's Bosom: The Children of Arthur, Book Five*
the final volume in
The Children of Arthur series:

ARTHUR'S BOSOM

PROLOGUE

THE NOT-TOO-DISTANT FUTURE

CAPTAIN VANDERDECKER LOOKED up into the night sky and reflected upon what a lonely life it was to wander the earth alone on the *Flying Dutchman*; he knew those few to whom he had shown himself believed him cursed, but it was not so; rather, he roamed the seas in his phantom ship to put a little fear into them, a fear that might cause them to repent and turn to good. He had committed no great crime, no great sin, but rather he posed as a terrible sinner for the sake of his fellow men, for they were mostly a weak and a cowardly race, and so while fear caused them to do evil, at other times, fear could steer them back onto the right path, and so he had taken the path of fear so they might find their salvation.

Years before, he had agreed to this role, in time playing upon the tales told of how he had been led to this cursed life filled with isolation and misery so that those to whom he spoke would tremble before him and then repent and change their ways before it was too late. Captain Vanderdecker enjoyed his fear-inspiring performances immensely, and once he had released his captive victims from his presence, he spent a great deal of time chuckling to himself, and often, he would use his powerful spyglass to watch them later in life and be pleased by the change he had caused in them.

Yes, at times it had been a lonely life, but Captain Vanderdecker knew his mission was nearing completion, for since Lilith had passed from this world, fear had been slowly losing its grip over much of mankind. Soon it would seem as if all his time spent in this wandering state had never happened at all. And in the meantime, he occasionally met with those who shared his mission—Morgan le Fay and Merlin and several others, all believed to be only characters from legend, but who, in truth, served the Goddess-God by serving mankind to bring about good for all.

Most days, however, Captain Vanderdecker's only companions were the stars in the night sky. They were his true friends, for they guided him upon the sea, and they were loyal and ever-vigilant, never swaying in their trustworthiness. Oh, he knew man's faulty wisdom believed the stars merely to be great flaming balls of fire like the sun, but he also knew that the stars had loving energetic souls that contributed to the music of the spheres, playing a beautiful visual and auditory symphony for him every night as a reminder that he was alone only temporarily and would one day be reunited with the great Source of All Wellbeing that guided the Universe.

And so tonight, like most nights, Captain Vanderdecker lay upon the deck of the *Flying Dutchman*, looking up at the stars, listening to them, sometimes wishing upon them, his wishes actually being prayers for the happiness of the human race, of which he had once been a member before he had tasted of living water and taken up his mission.

The stars entertained him, often singing to him songs of kings and queens, heroes and villains, mermaids and magical beasts, and of a world far better than that he knew currently existed because it was based in the beauty of the imagination and the love that someday the human heart would know when it was free from the fear and strife that mankind itself caused. Only then would mankind have learned enough to evolve into the next stage of its existence.

Suddenly, in the midst of this beautiful symphony, like a jarring wrong note, from high up in the sky, Captain Vanderdecker heard the whooshing of what first appeared to be a falling star, creating a dissonance as it whirled through the heavens. Standing up to get a better look, he saw it blazon with a fiery light through the night sky. Unsure what he was seeing, he ran down into his cabin to find his spyglass.

Once back on deck, Captain Vanderdecker put the spyglass to his eye, and looking up, he saw a comet with a flaming tail soaring through the heavens. Then, almost in disbelief, he said aloud, "Despite waiting all these centuries, it seems to have come so suddenly."

Prester John never gave thought to the passing of time. In his sacred kingdom, time mattered little, for he knew that everything happened in the time best suited for it, and so there could be no rushing, no hurrying of it, and certainly never any indication that it was too late—that not enough time remained to achieve whatever wanted achieving, for time was infinite, and hence, no need for worry of any sort existed.

Those who came to Prester John's land to seek wisdom usually came believing time was their greatest enemy, for they had spent all their lives living by its dictates, and they had come to know it as a cruel taskmaster, even if only an illusory one, for humans were ever prone to creating unneeded worry and anxiety for themselves, especially in recent centuries as they invented clocks and timers with alarms and all manner of technological, digital, and electronic taskmasters to capture every second and turn it into profit, affixing a monetary value to it until they came to fear it in their mad rush to produce, produce, produce before it was too late—but too late for what?

When Prester John did think of such matters, he only chuckled, for he knew it was never too late. Still, he felt sorrow for the scurrying madness of the human race, so he rejoiced whenever someone came to his land; once arrived, his visitors would require several days before they were able to relax, to let time's worry leave them, and once they did relax, they felt the freedom from time's restraints to be a great relief and then even a joy.

On this particular day as he walked about his kingdom, Prester John was musing over time's fallacy and reminding himself of the words he had once heard the Savior speak, "Look at the lilies of the field, they neither toil nor do they spin." Was not all mankind's toiling and spinning an effort to fight time, to prepare to have enough before it was too late? The Savior had told them to look at the birds and the beasts of the field and see how at peace they were with the earth, never worrying about the hour or day, but simply walking, running, eating when they felt the need, and not an hour or a minute before or after they so desired.

Prester John gazed out across the fields where he was walking, enjoying the solitariness of the moment, for at times he needed to distance himself from those he nourished when they came to his land, for he could still sense their internal anxiety and questioning as if they were bees buzzing beside his ear, and if he did not distance himself from it until it lessened, it could badly upset his spirit. He much preferred the calming presence of animals over humans, although it was the humans whom he was called on to serve.

But now, as he sought out the peace of the beasts of the field, he was surprised to find the landscape before him very empty. Where was the lioness and her cubs that he had visited with for so many days past? And why were there no birds soaring through the air? And looking down to see whether the ants were at least about his feet—he often looked down to be sure not to harm anything—he saw the earth appeared to be bare of moving life. But then, unexpectedly, a field mouse scurried between his feet, and then another, and then two or three, and soon he found himself standing amid a stream of mice, many tumbling over his feet in their panic, but what had so frightened them?

Then like a bolt of lightning, the words that the Savior had once said about him to his friend Peter sprung to Prester John's mind: "If I want him to remain alive until I return, what is that to you?"

Every day since she had become Lady of Avalon some fifteen centuries before, Morgana had looked into the Holy Pool after eating one of the Nuts of Knowledge from the Ancient Hazel that gave the gift of the sight. Some days she saw nothing of concern. Some days she saw the sorrows of mankind. Some days she saw acts of kindness. And now and then, she saw something that required her to take action. It had been several years now since she had been called upon to interfere in the ways of men. The final chapter before the epilogue of mankind's history had been enacted when Lilith had departed the earth, and now there was only waiting to be done; Morgana knew not how many years she needed to wait, but she had learned patience after all this time.

And so Morgana had expected this day to be the same as any other—doubtless there was some minor squabble in the Middle East, but they were nothing like they had been years ago; not a bomb had gone off in years; there might be a fire in Montana or an earthquake in Japan, but those were not caused by humans, so they were of less concern to her; what did concern her had lessened in recent years, though she still found interest looking into the Holy Pool and viewing the increased acts of charity and kindness she saw being done since Lilith's departure, and Morgana felt finally that the fruits of all of her and Merlin and their many compatriots' works were ripening.

But when Morgana looked into the Holy Pool today, for the first time in many years, she found herself surprised. What she saw was something she had never seen before, and yet something she had always imagined someday seeing since first she had become Lady of Avalon. She watched, eyes wide, her senses more alert than ever before in her life, her whole being caught up in the drama about to be played out, and when she came out of the trance, she knew what she must do.

Through the air, on invisible and inaudible waves, save to the intended receiver, she sent the following message:

"Merlin, the time has come."

A SPECIAL REQUEST

IF YOU ENJOYED this book, please write a book review for it at Amazon, Barnes & Noble, Goodreads, or another bookseller's website. Authors rely on book reviews and word-of-mouth to sell their books and you can make the difference in helping this book to succeed. Readers also rely on reviews to help them make their decisions on which books to purchase and read. Even just a couple of sentences can have an impact. The author thanks you for your time.

ABOUT THE AUTHOR

TYLER R. TICHELAAR holds a Ph.D. in Literature from Western Michigan University, and Bachelor and Master's Degrees in English from Northern Michigan University. He is the owner of his own publishing company, Marquette Fiction, and of Superior Book Productions, a professional book review, editing, proofreading, book design, and web design service.

Besides The Children of Arthur series, Tyler is the author of numerous historical novels, including *The Marquette Trilogy* (composed of *Iron Pioneers, The Queen City,* and *Superior Heritage*), *Narrow Lives, The Only Thing That Lasts, Spirit of the North: a paranormal romance,* and *The Best Place.* He has also authored non-fiction titles that include *My Marquette: Explore the Queen City of*

The author in Merlin's Chair at the Pera Palace Hotel, Istanbul the North, Creating a Local Historical Book, *The Gothic Wanderer: From Transgression to Redemption,* and *King Arthur's Children: A Study in Fiction and Tradition,* and he has written the play *Willpower.* An avid genealogist, Tyler has been fascinated by the Arthurian legend and medieval history since childhood.

Visit Tyler at:

www.MarquetteFiction.com
www.GothicWanderer.com
www.ChildrenofArthur.com

www.ingramcontent.com/pod-product-compliance
Lightning Source LLC
Chambersburg PA
CBHW020634020726
47494CB00001B/179